Planet of the Orange-red Sun

Series Volume 5

Age of the Lords

Planet of the Orange-red Sun Series

Volume 5
Age of the Lords

by Vic Broquard

For Morgan and L. Ron Hubbard

Table of Contents

Part I Countermoves

Chapter 1 The First Council of the Lords

The last week of April 1205, and a mere seven days before the Spring Council with Emperor Carl Christopher and Empress Calandra, Carmen Valen received a request for a formal but private meeting with the two rulers. Carmen looked to be an extremely attractive if not downright gorgeous woman of thirty-five, though she was in fact now ninety-seven, having made extensive use of the Imperium Rejuvenation Machine. She owned Elegant Fashions Inc and was the sole supplier of the elegant fashions for the Imperial Court. She checked her makeup, perfect. She adjusted the fall of her thick raven tresses, which fell to just below her curvaceous hips. It too lay perfectly straight. Looking into her full-length mirror, she admired how tiny her waist looked, a mere fourteen inches around, held that way by her pipe corset. Her eyes followed down the great curves of her red satin gown, from her head-sized, full breasts which all women on Tierra had, down to her tiny waist, from which two of her ribs had been removed to help support the three inch tall band which fourteen inches around, out to her full hips, down her pencil style dress to her black nylons, ending at her black patent leather toe shoes. All looked perfect, as it must, since she was the top fashion setter for the entire world.

Of course, her feet had also been altered so she could wear these tiny toe shoes and toe boots in the winter. Essentially, via the medical machine, her foot bones had been broken, re-shaped, and then healed so only her toes lay flat on the floor. Her heels were arched high above them and the rear of her heel aligned with the back of her toes. The toe shoes were rounded with just enough space to hold her toes. The stiletto metal heel was built-in to the solid arch of the shoe and touched the ground just behind the toes. Toe shoes gave the wearer only a very tiny amount of sole actually touching the ground, making standing and walking exceedingly challenging and nearly impossible on uneven ground, on slopes, or on snow and ice.

Carmen didn't mind at all. She was extracting the long-sought revenge against ex-Emperor Jan and ex-Empress Amy who had stopped Valen's attempt to control the world and murdered her husband, the man who had launched the Nuclears that wiped out Bettingham. Had Amy not intervened, she knew they'd now be in total control of the whole world. Well, she'd worked behind the scenes for years, plotting her revenge and it had come to fruition.

Amy and Jan had wiped out all previous forms of government of the world, replacing it with the all-powerful emperor and empress, whose word was law throughout the world. With that much power in two people's hands, those who held the positions had to be physically prevented from abusing it. With a lot of nudging from Carmen and even her help in getting it established, Amy and Jan decreed whoever held these positions had to be severely hobbled. By law, the emperor, empress, and their top advisors not only had to wear the pipe corsets and toe shoes or toe boots, but also had their arms removed. Their domestique helpers, while also corseted and wearing the toe shoes, had their voices eliminated so they could not overly influence those who they assisted. Thus hobbled and constrained, these top leaders were not tempted to abuse the incredible powers placed on them. Seeing Jan and Amy similarly handicapped three years ago continued to bring a joyous smile to her bright red lips. Her victory was ever so sweet, especially since much of it could not be reversed.

It had been two years and some since Carmen had last seen Amy and Jan, back then at the swearing in ceremony for the new emperor and empress. Rumors suggested they'd moved into Brom, the city, but she had had no actual contact with them. She didn't need to, armless and so physically constrained, Carmen just knew they had to be utterly miserable wherever they were.

Instead, she turned her attention to their new leaders. None of them had the *mentales* gifts, and as far as she was concerned, all eight of them were anything but smart or bright. She hesitated to call them dim-witted, but perhaps if the shoe fit, she thought. Empress Calandra and her domestique Elnora along with her advisor Felisa and her husband and domestique Aldo were Easterlings. Emperor Carl and his domestique Dan along with his advisor Carver and his wife and domestique Ada were from the Midlands. For a long time, Carmen mused over this mis-match of cultures.

Easterlings women were bound women, wearing fetter skirts, which allowed them to take at most a two or three inch step at a time. Their arms were chained to their waists at the elbows, while at night their lower arms were bound together in a leather tube across the small of their backs. All Easterlings men and women wore their never cut, brown hair in braids, two for the women, one for the man. In their culture, men spent at least a quarter to a third of their daytime hours caring for their women, not counting the evenings. Carmen knew in the Midlands or Westerlings, her homeland, men seldom spent much time with their women during the daytime, if any, and she saw the benefits the Easterlings women gained from their physical bindings.

Slowly, Carmen made her way out of her main office on the fourth floor of the five story Imperium Office building in Exchange City and walked the few hundred feet to the Imperial Castle and Tower where the rulers dwelled, there on the southeastern corner of Plateau Grado where the alien spaceport lay. Again, she grimaced. Originally, it was her father who had bargained with the aliens to be leased this very land, and her kin had built the original tower, manor house, and castle here, only to be confiscated by Jan and Amy who turned it into the Imperial Court. Yet another score to settle one day, she mused. Of course, walking was terribly slow in her toe shoes, barely three inches a step, but Carmen had had years of practice and swayed her hips elegantly. Men who saw her were definitely sexually aroused, which was the whole point as far as Carmen was concerned. What did her rulers want of her?

"Ah, Carmen Valen! So good of you to come," Emperor Carl said from his throne. He was now twenty-three, with shoulder length brown hair and blue eyes. Neither attractive nor handsome, he rated perhaps a four on Carmen's handsome scale of one to ten. He did wear one of her finest pod-silk suits, brown tweed, with a white silk shirt and three-inch black belt, highlighting his fourteen-inch waistline. His belt matched his black patent, fine quality leather toe shoes. Sitting beside him was Empress Calandra, a year younger. She still insisted on wearing her fetter skirt. However, today she wore her long brown hair un-braided, brushed out nicely. Hers nearly reached her ankles when she stood. Currently it lay draped over her left shoulder and down over her lap. Standing just beside them were their domestique helpers, who could not speak; their vocal cords were tied off. Seated off to either side were their advisors, Carver and Felisa. She noted Felisa and Elnora also now wore their hairbrush ed out.

"You all look so utterly elegant this fine morning," Carmen said coyly, flashing them a big smile with her bright red lips. *A little praise goes a long way.* "How may I help you today?"

Empress Calandra spoke up. "As you can see, I and my Easterlings women are making some compromises with our traditions. We are going to wear our hair as do the women of the Midlands."

"I noticed that. All three of you look absolutely stunning with your hair down," Carmen validated them. She wasn't fibbing, for they did look far more attractive and seductive this way.

The empress smiled, evidently please with her compliment. "Thank you. In return, at the coming meeting I am going to be asking women who are wearing toe shoes or toe boots also to wear fetter skirts. You see, as we are, walking in these shoes, we can take only the tiniest of steps, much as we always have when we wear our fetter skirts. However, I know elegant women here always follow your fashions, and our traditional skirts are far too ordinary and plain. So I would like to ask you to come up with something along the lines of our fetter skirts, which elegant Midlands women would choose to wear."

Emperor Carl added, "And as soon as Calandra makes that decree, I am going to decree Midlands men, who have wives who are wearing outfits like ours, to spend more daytime hours with them, just as the Easterlings men do with their wives." He seemed very pleased with his proposed decree.

"I see. Well, we fashionable women like to show off our black nylons, which is why most of our gowns fall to just below our knees. Most women will still want to show off some of their very expensive black nylons. How about a curve fitting fetter gown that falls to maybe six inches below the knee? I can keep the designs very elegant as well," Carmen thought swiftly.

"Yes, that would be a good compromise. Ruling is all about compromise. In fetter skirts, we cannot go up stairs nor can we handle inclines, but then in the Easterlings, we have neither as a rule. So here, with the steps and inclined surfaces, perhaps six inches of ease would help. However, Carl will decree any man who sees a woman in need of assistance negotiating stairs or inclines or whatever must stop and help them, just as men do in the Easterlings." She seemed terribly proud of her new decrees.

"Oh that will be perfect then. In fact, I'll do even better, Empress Calandra. As you have seen, many of our elegantly dressed women like their dresses to flair out some. I will make a second style that has the same inner fetter skirt but overlain with the flairs other women so love. That way they will be fettered just as you desire, but will give the appearance of wearing their flairs."

"Oh my, yes, perfect, Carmen, absolutely perfect! Thank you. Could you possibly have some samples for us to wear by the big meeting?" she asked pleadingly.

Carmen smiled, *Oh how easily these two are manipulated.* My revenge just keeps mushrooming! "Yes my empress, I will certainly have them ready. In fact I will have the alternate flair style for Ada here to wear. That way the many women who come can see both styles." Again, she was bombarded with many thank you's and she left.

Already having the women's measurements on file, she took the sample fetter skirt that Calandra donated to her some time ago to be used as a model for their current skirts and called her design staff to work. "Drop everything. We have a rush new design and look to create for our empress and her staff."

The next day, Carmen herself donned the first dual design, which she called the fetter-gown. The inner fetter skirt portion fit her tightly, following her every curve, but it was hidden wholly by the flair of the outer gown. Now she experimented with walking. On the level floor of her office, she found little difference, save it felt tight against her legs. However, she soon saw that like the fetter skirt, she could not take even one step on the stairs. *Well, that's why we have elevators,* she mused. An incline would also be challenging if it were steep, but then all inclines were challenging while wearing the toe shoes. She accepted the design and ordered more to be made and delivered to the empress and her staff.

Back in her office, she once more set her mind to her current three problems she wanted to solve. First, she wanted men to also wear the pipe corsets and toe shoes. Second, she wanted to make women in particular even more restricted, hoping Amy and Jan would later be forced to join that movement. Third, she wanted her vast enterprise to continue to follow her hidden agenda as well as thrive and prosper once she herself finally passed away. She already had used the greatest amount of rejuvenation possible from the alien machine, but she could still take a few more years off, extending her life to about a hundred and fifty years, she estimated. That would not occur for another fifty-five years, if she retained her health, but still she was always planning for the future.

As she sat there in her office mulling over these three problems, something from her meeting with the empress triggered an idea. She talked to her wall, "The Easterlings women have their arms bound to their waists at their elbows with chains. Well here in the Midlands, there is not a chance in hell of women doing that. We find it revolting. However, what if I added sleeves that come down to one's elbows to the gown, but have them sewn to the sides of the dress? They would then be bound in a similar manner to the Easterlings chains! Brilliant, Carmen, you've outdone yourself this time!" She rose and teetered a little in her excitement and anxious desire to get to her design studio.

"One more modification, please. A third type," she called out long before she physically crossed the floor to where the women were working at their tables.

Later that day, she returned to the Imperial Throne to discuss her latest idea. "Yes, these upper sleeves will be physically part of the bodice and cannot be undone or ripped out. For all practical purposes, Empress Calandra, they will be the equivalent of the chains Elnora is wearing. When she wears this dress, she will not evoke such animosity. Here in the Midlands we frown upon chains."

"Oh this is beyond perfect, Carmen! If I still had my arms, I'd hug you!" a very elated and relieved empress exclaimed. Once more, Carmen had scored a significant point with her rulers. Accumulate enough points and then you can ask them for something you desire — that was her guideline. Already, she'd scored many key points with her monarchs. She grinned all the way back to her headquarters.

"Welcome lords and ladies, kings and queens, one and all," Emperor exclaimed proudly from his throne, welcoming the huge gathering at the Spring Council. "So good to see all you once again. This year, we, my lovely empress and I, have only a few new laws to offer." Standing off to one side and wearing her newly designed an arm-fetter gown, Carmen heard several men either sucking in their breaths or groaning quietly, but not enough to call the emperor's attention to their protests. She smiled knowing what was coming. Once more, she would be cashing in on this law, which pleased her in many ways.

"You see, we of the Midlands and of the Easterlings must reach some compromises. Each of us has our own traditions. Your emperor and empress embodies the blending of the two cultures. Each of us, Midlands and Easterlings, must make some sacrifices and some compromises so we can better meld into one united peoples." Carmen thought this sounded like a well-rehearsed speech. It was.

"First, as you can see, our Easterlings women have compromised and are now wearing their hair in the style of you Midlands women. I find this highly attractive and downright sexy. So our first new law is all Easterlings women who attend our court must unbraid their hair and brush it out in the Midlands style. Next, Empress Calandra will tell you of our next new law."

Calandra spoke with authority, Carmen noted. "Yes, we are compromising on our hair. As you all know, we Easterlings women have a long tradition of binding, from the wearing of our fetter skirts to the chaining of our arms. We know Midlands women and men find chains appalling. So we will not ask that of you. However, those of you who have chosen to wear these elegant pipe corsets and toe shoes know you can take tiny steps at most. What you probably do not know is this is how we Easterlings women are when we wear our fetter skirts. So while I know many of you think I and my fellow Easterlings women have been unduly harsh on ourselves by continuing to wear our traditional fetter skirts, please take a good look at Felisa and my new dresses, designed especially for us by Carmen Valen and her Elegant Fashions Inc."

She rose so all could see her new fetter-gown, while Felisa also stood up, balancing carefully and hoping Aldo would not need to use his arms to keep her from falling. "You see these new gowns truly emulate our ugly fetter skirts. So from this day forward, we want you women who are the height of fashion and wearing toe shoes to also wear one of these new designs with this one being called the fetter-gown. You will find very little difference in your walking ability. Still, I know some women do not want to flaunt the fact they are wearing basically an Easterlings fetter skirt. So there are two other styles that Carmen Valen has created."

"For those of you who really wish to impress us here at the Imperial Court with your strong desire to help blend our two cultures together, there is a second style gown, modeled here by my domestique Elnora. As you can see, it looks like any other gown you are wearing, but there is a fetter skirt inside the flair completely hidden from view. No one will be able to see you are wearing one. However, notice also her upper arms are held tight against her sides by the gown. Please, I am not asking you to wear chains. I have compromised with your traditions here in the Midlands. Yet wearing this style gown, you will be able to experience our traditions and please me with your desire to understand my Easterlings heritage. Carmen calls this one the hidden-arm-fetter-gown."

"However, for those who do not wish to go that far, there is a third style new gown that looks just like this one, with the inner fetter skirt wholly hidden just as with Elnora's here, but whose arms are free and not constrained. She calls it the hidden-fetter-gown. Thus my new law is any woman who wears toe shoes or boots should also wear one of these three new style gowns, the fetter-gown, the hidden fetter-gown, and the hidden-arm-fetter-gown. Carl," she ended.

He spoke up again, "One last new law. Any man who sees one of these women wearing toe shoes and fancy gowns and who is having trouble negotiating stairs, steep inclines, and such is required by law to stop everything and assist her. We Midlands men must learn to pay far more attention to our lovely, sexy women. That is all I have for you in the way of new laws. Oh yes, Carmen wishes me to tell you she too is wearing one of her new hidden-arm-fetter-gowns. If I do say so myself, she looks positively stunning in it."

"One last point. Note, this is not an order, not yet anyway. I would like to see far more of you men wearing pipe corsets and toe shoes like I am wearing. You see we top rulers of our lands must set a very good example for our subjects. If it is good enough for your emperor, it's good enough for you. At this fall's meeting, I expect to see more of you men wearing them as befitting our top ruling positions here on Tierra. If you do not, then I may be forced to make such a law at our September meeting. That is all. So let's let the formal ball begin."

As she expected, Carmen found herself surrounded by a flock of most curious women. "You can't see the tight skirt can you?" "Isn't it hard not being able to move your arms much?" "Isn't this going a bit too far?" "How can you walk in it?" "Is it much more difficult to manage? I'm having a hard time walking as it is." Pummeled with questions, Carmen graciously answered them one at a time. She pointed out the only real difficulty she had was going up stairs or inclines.

"Besides, inclines were almost impossible before, so it makes no real difference anyway, and it goes a long way with our empress, showing her we are willing to compromise on our traditional dress. As far as the arms go, so far I have not found that too much of a problem. Again, wearing this dress really does please Empress Calandra enormously. She feels more like she is home again," Carmen poured it on.

Even though she was surrounded by gabbing, curious women, she caught snatches of the men whispering something from man to man. Finally, she used her psi powers to overhear it. *First Council of the Lords will be tomorrow at ten at Mac's.* Now she had something else to ponder. This was something new, but what were they planning?

As the musicians began playing, the women joined their husbands or dates, leaving Carmen free for the moment. She surveyed the large crowd and spotted her grandson, Diego Valen. The eighteen year old lad was enjoying himself, but she knew he was part of the Valen delegation. Smiling mischievously, she slowly navigated her way over to him.

"Hello Diego. You look very handsome in your uniform. It's been way too long since I visited Valen. How are you doing? How's my granddaughter doing? Isn't she twelve now?" she asked demurely.

"Hi grandmother. Gosh, it's so strange, you look more like my mother," he commented.

"Do I look like your mother, really?" she batted her eyes and gave him a flirting grin.

He laughed. "Hell no. God, Carmen, you look ravishing still. I wish you did come visit us more often. Nita is fourteen now. You're behind the times, grandmother," he teased her, pleased he'd gotten one on her.

"Touché, dear. Say, I heard some men whispering about some meeting?"

"Oh yes, we're holding a First Council of the Lords tomorrow morning. At least this time they are including us from Valen. I'm going along with everyone else. As far as I know, all the leaders are going to be there, but don't worry, grandmother, they will be sending their women to your Elegant Fashions Inc to shop. You ought to get plenty of sales again. How rich are you now, anyway?"

"Rich enough. Say, are you short of funds? Your dad giving you enough spending money?" she asked, a plan formulating in her mind. Children always could use more money and she was right.

"Not really. I'm in Valen's Elite Guards now, but I'm flat broke and here I am in Exchange City," he answered using a pathetic expression. It worked as far as he was concerned.

"Oh dear. That will never do for a Valen. Please dear, drop by my place in the morning before you go to your meeting, and I'll have a big money pouch waiting for you. Just don't spend it all in one place. And stay away from the local hookers," she teased him.

"Wow! Thanks grandmother. I will be by around nine, is that okay?"

"Sure, see you at nine. I don't suppose you wish to dance with your grandmother, do you?" she teased him again. He flushed, "Just teasing son. Go find yourself someone your age."

Relieved, he replied, "Thanks! Cya at nine." He moved off before she could change her mind on either point. She made a mental note to visit Valen soon, this summer perhaps. An idea formed based on the data Nita was of age, fourteen. *How time flies,* she thought. *I wonder what she looks like?*

At nine the next morning, Diego arrived at her office. He looked impressive in his Elite Guards uniform, handsome, Carmen thought. Now if only Nita did. "Here you go. I hope five hundred silver will tide you over." She handed him a money pouch and, from the expression on his face, she knew he was very impressed with the sum. As she gave him a hug, she slipped a Rigel-3 spy bug into his pocket. "Have a good meeting. I hope they don't continue to lock Valen out like they have been doing."

"Thanks, grandmother. Me too. It's time we have a say too. Cya," he replied and bounded off with the large, masculine steps of a new soldier. Carmen then headed into her private quarters and turned on her receiver. She put up the "do not disturb sign" on her door and then sat down on her sofa chair. Although she was held rigid by her own steel reinforced, pipe corset and her new hidden-fetter skirt, she attempted to relax. It promised to be a long day.

"Fifty year old Tom Rusden rose and pounded a wooden hammer on a bar table. "This First Council of the Lords is now in session. I am Lord Tom Rusden. As most of you know, from now on we are dispensing with all the old titles that were in use across Tierra. We will use the titles Lord and Lady from now on as our official titles. *Jefe*, king, and such are out of date and too confusing with the past for the common man."

"Now then note we have included all the Westerlings Lords as well. All we rulers share much in common and that is the purpose of this first meeting — to get our common goals laid out, and I sincerely hope arrive at some strategies at least. I will bring up the first goal we all share. Now that Amy and Jan are out of the way, we must find some way to nullify their emperor-empress rule. I think we can all agree the true and rightful rulers of Tierra ought to be us, the lords of our lands, not some idiot emperor." The room broke into a loud round of applause.

"Many of us have put a great deal of thinking into this problem Amy and Jan have left us. Today, I believe we may have contrived a solution, based partially on what we all agreed to do when Jan made her announcement we were to elect our first emperor and empress." Carmen swore, if someone had dropped a toothpick, she could have heard it! She too sat on the edge of her chair in anticipation, though she was forced to sit that way anyhow.

"Although those of you from Valen might not, as most of you know we've handpicked the current rulers. First, none have the *mentales* gifts. Second, none are too bright. Third, they are all quite young. Why? We decided back then we wanted these two to rule for two consecutive terms. Why? We hope they outlive Amy and Jan. We can take no effective action until those two meddlers are dead and buried." Several Valen men called out, "Right on!" Applause resounded in the bar.

"Our thinking now is once it is safe for us to make a move, we will take two actions. First, we, the rightful lords, will rule by councils such as this one, bypassing the emperor and empress wholly."

Someone called out, "But they left us no way to bypass them!"

"Yes, they did. It took us a long time to discover the way. We make the positions hereditary. Second, since we are supposed to elect them, we will do so, but always choosing two of their heirs to succeed them." Many clapped and cheered as they suddenly grasped what that implied.

Lord Tom continued, "Next, the heirs we choose will be infants." Several "huh" noises could be heard from around the room. "Of course, an infant cannot rule until they are say twenty years old. Therefore, we, the rightful rulers, will choose a regent to act for them, one who will do precisely what we tell them to do. This bypasses the emperor completely."

Someone then yelled out, "And when they get to twenty, they can meet with an accident and we can choose another infant." The room erupted into roaring laughter.

Tom soon regained control. "Next, we are going to body modify the potential candidates for emperor and empress while they are children to further subdue them to our will. Perhaps when they take office, they will already be our puppets and not need to meet with an accident. Further, we will make sure inbreeding occurs and never let anyone with the *mentales* gift mate with them. In a century perhaps we will have totally useless candidates, effectively ending this crazy system. However, I cannot caution you enough on this point. Whatever you do, do not breathe a word of this to anyone connected to the various towers or even your wives. We could well be undone if Amy and Jan somehow learn of this. Lord knows what deviousness they could still concoct against us. So keep this plan to those in this room, if you value your lives." His threat sounded very real. Even Carmen thought so as she heard it over her spy device.

An hour later, the next significant discussion began, led by Lord John Haverhills. "It seems to me at this point in time, women have gained far, far too much power for their own good. Veneradas and Capas. These have been historically male positions of great power. I say it is time we find some ways to limit their powers over us all."

Someone asked, "Do we really need the towers any

longer?" Pros and cons bounced around for some time. Lord John then said, "Well, you know, hobbling them like our empress might really limit them. I know we can't order them to lose their arms, but could we request they emulate our empress and wear the pipe corsets and toe shoes? If so, that should begin to limit them pretty severely." Carmen listened eagerly to the discussion that followed, smiling all the while. *Revenge is so sweet!*

After a good deal of discussion, the lords agreed to adopt this policy at their towers. All would continue to apply enough pressure to get all the women in the tower to comply, but at least those in circles and the Venerada.

"But what about the emperor's latest veiled threat? That we get modified too?" someone asked. A discussion followed, rather heated. Another declared, "Hell, if some of us don't show up this fall looking like the emperor, he is going to make it a law! Amy and Jan will surely back him up if we all protest his law or don't follow it. What do we do? Are we screwed?" Many thought was just the case. A lengthy discussion followed, quite heated this time.

Lord Tom Rusden finally rose and sighed. "Look everyone. This fall some of us have to get altered or Carl will take drastic action. I am fifty and past my prime, really. I will volunteer to be modified. If enough of us older men do so, perhaps that will placate Carl sufficiently to back off making it a law which we all must then obey. If he doesn't back off, then I'm afraid Carl will have to accidently lose his balance and fall down a stairs, and we'll have to elect a new emperor."

This met with the overall approval and some time passed while they discussed who would volunteer to save all the many other lords. In the end, a dozen older rulers volunteered to sacrifice themselves for the good of the others.

This amazed Carmen, that these powerful men would so band together. Even her uncle Lord Hector Valen, who controlled Valen and the Westerlings as their top lord, volunteered. He was fifty-five, she guessed, and wrote down the names of the volunteers, figuring to obtain their measurements from her files, since nearly every lord wore one of her fine suits.

While other smaller issues were being discussed, Carmen paid attention to another one. Since the emperor had the Imperial Guards to protect him and supposedly enforce his laws, a way was needed to somewhat neutralize them. The lords decided to offer higher pay to their Elite Guards, higher than was currently being paid to the Imperial Guards. The idea being over time, fewer young men would enlist in the Imperial Guards, while others already in it would resign and take similar positions within the Lord's Elite Guards. This also met universal approval.

As the supper hour approached, another man called out. "Say, I've been thinking about ways to limit the power of women, particularly those who have the *mentales* gifts. Many of our wives have already undergone the modification process. What if we encouraged all the women in our courts who have the gift to undergo the process as well? What if we encouraged our daughters to undergo it at a younger age? I've heard if they start in on it early enough in life, they can have even smaller waists. That might be enough of a lure to get our wives and younger daughters to commit at a young age, limiting them. What do you think?"

Again, Carmen paid close attention to the arguments. A half hour later, she was very pleased to hear that idea was also adopted. all the lords promised to begin a campaign at their courts to get their relatives converted and to put pressure to on all *mentales* gifted women there to do so as well. That done, they adjourned until the fall session, promising to meet again the next day after their meeting with the emperor and at the same pub.

Carmen smiled. Now all she had to do was to plant a listening device in the pub where it would not be discovered, and she'd be all set to again listen in. She found all this quite fascinating and highly useful. *It's amazing; so much is going my way.*

Chapter 2 A Visit to Valen

In 1205, Sector ID Minister Emeryk Donat arrived on Ashford-5. He replaced his predecessor Lech, amid stories Lech had allowed a Nuclear to be shipped to Ashford-5 and detonated there, wiping out an entire city. After his promotion and appointment, Emeryk had not come directly to the planet. Rather, he'd spent some years elsewhere on the rim, handling what he considered far more important problems to the Imperium expansion. With everything handled, he at last came to this strange planet. Single, he was tall and thin, quite handsome by Rigel-3 standards, appearing as a thirty-three year old man. As yet, he'd not married, wanting nothing to interfere with his rapid advancement within the Intelligence Division.

As he reviewed the many field notes, he came across his first problem. It concerned Project Gemini. Never having heard of this one, he accessed his computer and discovered to access it, one had to have extremely high clearance. Well, he did and entered his password and read up on the project. He sat back and mused about the project and the reported problems. *Evidently, this planet has a fair number of telepaths on it. Well, telepaths are highly sought after and Gemini is a way to get them off of a closed world,* he justified.

He reviewed the field notes and saw the problem. all the last two years' attempts to abduct a young female telepath had met with disasters of one kind or another. A half dozen of their expensive shuttle craft had mysteriously crashed. Not one telepath had been taken off-world during the last twenty-four months. Now the higher ups wanted the problem rectified quickly, before the end of the summer in 1205. After reviewing all his field agent's notes, he found nothing in them that would explain all the abduction failures.

Rocking back and forth in his chair as he always did while pondering a problem, Emeryk reviewed what assets he had to bring to bear on the problem at hand. He discarded the field agents. If they had nothing in their reports, there would be little to gain from talking to them. Everyone knew field agents put everything they saw into their reports and then some.

He consulted records and discovered there had been a fair number of interracial marriages during the last two hundred plus years and some were still alive and on Ashford-5. Still, most all lived in Exchange City and these too he discounted. His field agents were all over that city. So if they found out nothing, the half-breeds would know even less.

It was at this point he discovered Ashford-5 aliens, who had Imperium citizenship by virtue of marriage to a Rigel-3 man or woman. This pricked his interest, wondering why and how any of his race could possibly be attracted to these primitive aliens of this backwater planet. He scrolled rapidly through the id card images of these women, children, and a few men. Suddenly, he stopped and stared at the image of a very elegantly dressed woman with enormous breasts. He glanced at her name and occupation, then instantly pulled up all the information on her, one Carmen Valen. She'd changed her name back to her maiden name after rumors surfaced her field agent husband Jarek might have been somehow connected to the Nuclear detonation.

"Holy crap! Not only is she hot, but she's incredibly wealthy, owns three entire floors of the Imperium Headquarters in Exchange City! Ah, Elegant Fashions Inc. I must pay this woman a visit!" He logged off his computer and headed down the elevator and out to the spaceport, where he grabbed an electric car. A few minutes later he parked it in the underground garage of the building and rode the elevator up to Carmen Valen's office.

A receptionist greeted him as he walked in. "Hello. Welcome to Elegant Fashions Inc. May I help you?" She was a local woman, but extremely well dressed. Impressive, he thought, she even spoke Imperium Standard to him.

"Sector ID Minister Emeryk Donat to see Carmen Valen. Urgent," he said cordially. No sense in getting her upset, he thought.

She rose and bid him follow her. He could not help noticing her black nylons, heels, and satin dress. He smiled, watching her hips wiggle as she walked slowly. He decided this would be a most enjoyable one!

That her id picture did not do her justice was his first thought upon meeting her. Carmen rose from her desk. She had long, lush, raven hair and the tiniest waist he'd ever seen. His eyes drifted slowly downward, pausing briefly at her bosom, then continued down her incredibly shapely form. At the floor, he saw the strangest and highest heels he'd ever seen. She extended her hand, fully aware of the impression she was making. For quite some time now, she'd been wondering when the new Sector ID Minister would want to make her acquaintance.

He cleared his throat. "Sector ID Minister Emeryk Donat."

"Pleased to meet you. Won't you have a seat? What can I do for you today? An elegant suit perhaps? That synthetic cat suit does not do you justice, if you don't mind my saying so," she said charmingly.

"Well, I don't know if you can help me or not. From your eyes, may I assume you are one of Ashford-5's telepaths?"

"Tierra, sir. That's the local's name for our world. You won't get far in your questioning of folks around here if you call it Ashford-5. Yes, anyone who has yellow eyes with brown spots has the gift. We call it the *mentales* gift."

"Excellent. Tierra it is. I'm rather new to this sector of the galaxy. Your company seems to be perhaps the largest on this world."

"As far as I know, sir, it is."

"Well, I assume then you either get around a lot or have employees who do."

"Certainly. Why?"

"Well I've heard rumors young telepaths may have been abducted in the past. Is there any truth to those rumors?"

"Sector ID Minister Emeryk, don't insult me! You know damn well all about Project Gemini as well as I do. My field agent husband told me about that secret project. What is it you want to know?"

"Damn, you are as sharp as you are good looking, Carmen. Okay, within the last two years, every one of the abductions has met with some form of failure. Regrettably, five shuttle craft have been destroyed. By any chance do you know what is going on?"

Carmen thought a moment. One of her jobs for Valen was to keep an eye on the aliens and their plots. Of course, she knew what was going on, but it was not her place to tell him. However, she knew how desperately the leaders in Valen wanted to re-establish good relations with the aliens here at the spaceport. Hence, she said, "I am not privy to that information, but I do know someone who is. My uncle is the leader of Valen and controls all the Westerlings, that is, all the lands west of these mountains. My deceased father used to have a working relationship with Minister Lech, though they kept it secret from everyone so there could be no hint of lease violations. My uncle would very much like to meet with you and re-establish communications with you. Not everyone on Tierra believes in the total isolation of our races. I myself am taking a trip there later this week. If you like, you could tag along with me, and I'll introduce you to him." Nothing she just said would be news to Emeryk, if he read any of Lech's notes, she thought, save her uncle who she didn't name explicitly, knowing full well he had no way of finding out his name.

"Well, this is indeed very interesting. Why yes, I should like to meet your uncle. However, I cannot travel overland on one of your horse creatures. That would be an overt violation of the Imperial Directive #5, which I am sure you are well aware of, miss."

Carmen gave a coy, flirting laugh. "Do you honestly think that I, dressed as elegantly as I am and in these heels, am going to go off riding a horse or even sit for days in a carriage to get to Valen? Don't be silly. We are a telepathic society with many skills. If you want to go with me, we go by teleportation. One second your body will be here in my office and the next, you'll be in Valen along with me, where you can ask all the questions you can think of. I'm sure my uncle will be more than happy to answer them, if he can."

"You're, you're kidding me?" he asked, very much shocked. "Teleportation? You primitives have that technology?"

"I am not familiar with your Imperium technology,

sorry. Still if you want answers, then come with me on Friday, say at ten. However, you certainly cannot go there dressed like you are. Lord, you will be laughed out of the castle as a *primitive*! Please, allow me to give you an elegant suit to wear, no charge. My present to you. Look elegant, feel elegant, be confident — that's our motto. Will you be coming with me then?"

"Yes, this I have got to see for myself! Thank you for the suit. I'm afraid I've never considered spending the fortune in credits it would take to purchase such a suit from the Imperium."

"Oh, our prices here are but a trifle of what the Imperium charges. They've no taste at all. Come on, follow me. I'll get you fixed up pronto. Let me see what color best suits you? I'm sorry we've never met, and I don't know much about you. Would you prefer a suit that suggests a great leader or one that suggests a great lover or. . ." She didn't get to finish making suggestions.

"Leader will be fine, miss. Again, thank you." She rose slowly and he noted she could only take the tiniest of steps. Only her toes were touching the floor, but her wiggling body greatly aroused him, though he fought to keep from showing it.

An hour later, a discrete package under his arm, Emeryk took the elevator down to the basement, where his electric car awaited him. Once out on the open spacious landing field, he finally exclaimed, "My god, what a woman that one is! I can see why Jarek married her!" After cooling down some, he then pondered what he'd learned. *Teleportation? These people have this technology? Incredible!*

Carmen quickly focused and made contact with Uncle Hector Valen. She relayed what had just happened and her offer. As she expected, he was ecstatic. *Carmen, thank you! Once more, you have proven to be the most useful woman in our whole country.*

Of course, uncle. Now then, if you will listen to me, I have a suggestion. He was quite smitten with me. Therefore, round up some unmarried woman who is about thirty-three, good looking, and who wears a pipe corset and toe shoes.

Have her become his escort. If I am not off my game, you may well get him interested enough to want to marry her.

Do you think that's possible?

Yes, he's not married and was highly aroused by me, highly, uncle. So if you can find a woman who emulates me, you may well have the connections you desperately need. We'll be expecting to be teleported to Valen on Friday at ten. Let one of your circles know. I need to make a visit to my grandchildren. I've been neglecting them for some time and I aim to rectify that. Thanks, uncle.

No, thank you, Carmen! You are the best. Bye. See you Friday then.

Emeryk arrived a few minutes ahead of time. He wore his fine quality grey suit, but Carmen made a few adjustments. He'd never worn one before, she correctly assumed. He also carried a blaster and other equipment, but she pretended not to notice this. It would not matter to her uncle. If he didn't want Emeryk to arrive with his blaster, the circle would not teleport it. The gun would simply fall harmlessly to the floor as he vanished from her office. She adjusted his tie, "There, now you look most presentable as a dignified leader of men. Of course," she began subtly to lay the groundwork for her uncle, "many of the women in Valen are going to be attracted to you. I'll warn you up front. You are rather handsome looking in your suit."

He seemed pleased by her comment and she knew she'd planted the right seed. Almost always men could be controlled by sex. That she knew well. Emeryk was no exception. "So how does this work?" he asked.

"Oh simple really. We just stand here and wait. It's almost ten now. I've scheduled our transport to occur at ten. They are usually quite punctual. Ah." She didn't get to finish her sentence; she felt the circle's capa touching her, and then she was standing on the arrival pad within Valen Castle proper. "Here we are. Ah, Uncle Hector. This is Sector ID Minister Emeryk Donat, old Lech's replacement. Emeryk, this is the leader of all the Westerlings and Valen Castle, where we now are, Lord Hector Valen."

"Welcome to Valen Castle, Minister Emeryk. Is that the way I should address you?" her uncle asked diplomatically, shaking hands with him.

Emeryk's eyes opened wide, but his field agent training kicked in. He stifled his shock, his surprise, and replied formally, "Yes, or perhaps it would be simpler to just call me Emeryk. We are officially not meeting, not legally," he hinted.

Hector winked. "Right. I understand fully. You may call me Hector. Now then, Carmen, I believe your grandchildren are expecting you. I don't want to keep you from them. Meantime, Emeryk, I've asked one of my nieces to accompany us and to act as your personal host. Here she comes now. Miss Adalina Valen, this is our guest from Rigel-3, Emeryk Donat. Emeryk, Miss Adalina." Hector stressed the Miss portion and sensed from Emeryk's mind that his intention was received, namely she was unmarried and available.

Hector was fifty-five with greying but still black hair and eyes. In his suit, he cut a handsome figure, though Carmen also knew in two days, he would voluntarily visit her to undergo the body modifications his wife, Miranda, had done to her body two years ago. She secretly approved of her uncle's choice for the ID Minister. Adalina was thirty, with raven hair as thick as her own, though even longer. Hers touched her ankles. She too had undergone the modifications last year and now cut almost as striking a figure as Carmen, though Carmen wasn't jealous of her in the slightest.

"So very pleased to meet you, Emeryk," Adalina said demurely, flirting subtly with her eyes and offering him her arm. "Uncle Hector has asked me to be your hostess. I do hope I meet with your approval. I enjoy wearing the very latest in fashions, as you can tell, but I do need to have you hold on to me for support. It's challenging to walk in these gorgeous heels. Do you like them?" she asked, knowing he could not take his eyes off of her bosom and legs. They darted from one to the other.

"Yes, you are a very attractive young woman, Adalina. I'm afraid I've never had the pleasure of escorting one so elegantly dressed. And yes, Hector, I would like a grand tour, but might I ask you later about how I got here? This teleportation technology?"

"Oh silly, I can show you how we do that. Come on. Uncle, I'm confiscating your guest for a couple of hours," Adalina replied. She had been well versed in what she ought to say and do with the minister.

Meanwhile, Carmen quietly but slowly walked off to find her grandchildren, specifically Nita. As she walked the long halls, many others greeted her, frequently saying "long time no see" or "come back more often." She acknowledged them all politely, saying she would try. She noted perhaps one in ten women were dressed as she, in pipe corset and toe shoes. *Well, I clearly need to promote more here in Valen!* She knew her way around the castle well, but also knew she had two sets of stairs to negotiate, always a tough challenge in these heels, and she took her time. A fall on these stone stairs would be disastrous.

Nearly out of breath, she finally arrived a half hour later outside her granddaughter's suite. As she slowly approached the door, it opened revealing an excited Nita. "Grandma, wow, you really did come. You look fabulous!" The two exchanged hugs and Nita ushered her inside and over to a most welcome sofa.

After sitting down carefully though stiffly upright, Carmen said enthusiastically, "Well, let's see how you look, dear. My, you are now an adult. It is hard to believe." Carmen had an experienced eye and quickly saw how Nita would be developing as she matured further. After all, she was ninety-seven.

"So what do you think? Will I be as gorgeous as you? I do hope so!"

"Nita, I can say with certainty you most definitely will be!" Her praise pleased the teen immensely, as she knew it would. All young women needed confidence boosting at her age. The two chatted a while, before Carmen asked, "Nita, have you had your *mentales* training yet?" This was the single deciding factor. If she had not had it yet, Carmen would have to wait until she did. An untrained telepath was a danger to themselves and everyone else around them. She was pleased with Nita's answer.

"Yes grandma, all done with it. I have mastered all the attack and defense modes. I've got moderate telepathy, they say, but I apparently have some mental block which prevents me from fully using my psi powers."

"Ah, that's too bad."

"I know, they say only a katalyein could help me, but as you know, there aren't any of those in the Westerlings. So I am kind of stuck, but that's all right," Nita replied, though Carmen detected hidden grief.

"Nita, I have an offer I'd like to make you. I want you to come and live with me in Exchange City. I would like to train you to one day take over my Elegant Fashions Inc company."

"What?" Nita asked totally taken by surprise and quite shocked.

"Yes, I am getting old and someday I have to leave my business to someone and I've chosen you, Nita, if you are interested."

"Grandma! Are you kidding me? I'd love too, but do you think I can?"

"Of course you can. You do as I say, learn everything I know, work real hard and when I finally pass away, you inherit my whole business and, I might, add a whole lot of money. Plus, I think I can get you to a katalyein and get your gifts fixed up. I know quite a few personally. What do you say?"

"Yes, oh, yes, yes, yes! Grandma, this is the greatest ever! And I thought you didn't really like me cause you haven't visited for so long."

"I've been a very busy woman and in our line of work, timing is everything. Well, I'm here now and I know you will do fine, Nita."

"Wow, okay, thanks. Can I let mom and dad know the news?" she asked bubbling over with excitement.

"Sure, come, let's go find them. How soon can you come to live with me?"

"Anytime! Come on! Oh, I forgot, you walk very slowly." She was jumping instead of walking. Carmen could sense how excited the fourteen year old girl actually was and she felt a bit of pride herself.

Her son was away at the moment, but her mother was

just as elated to hear this incredible news. "We've all been wondering what you would do with your fabulous business. It's more than we ever dreamed possible for Nita. You know her gift is blocked," her mother pointed out.

"Yes, I will get that handled soon. I know personally several katalyein who can do it. Can she leave with me soon?" Carmen asked.

"Yes, but you must stay for dinner, please. I know Diego will love to see you too." She stayed for two days, catching up on family gossip and allowing her son and his wife to express their sincere gratitude. Besides, she actually was waiting for Hector and Emeryk to finish their negotiations. That it took longer than a day impressed her, as that could only mean Hector was getting what he wanted out of the new alien. Whether or not it would allow Valen to regain its former glory Carmen refused to speculate.

At last, Emeryk was ready to return and Carmen, holding on to Nita, made her way slowly to the teleport pod. She was not surprised to see Adalina there too, holding on to Emeryk. "Hi Emeryk. My granddaughter, Nita. This is Sector ID Minister Emeryk. We need to see him to get you your Imperium ID card."

"Very pleased to meet you sir," Nita said with a smile.

"Pleased to meet you as well. You've a fine looking granddaughter, Carmen. Adalina has volunteered to return with me to Exchange City. We're going to get to know one another better, and she'll act as our new Liaison Officer," Emeryk felt obliged to explain, but Carmen already sensed there was far more going on between them, though only time would be needed. That much was obvious to her.

He added, "So what happens next? I didn't really see how we got here. One minute we were standing in your office and," he didn't finished. The circle's capa executed their action, setting all four carefully down in Carmen's office — carefully, because of the two women's heels.

"Ah, here we are back home. Will Adalina be staying here with us or will you be making other arrangements?" Carmen asked.

Adalina replied, "Emeryk is going to put me up in a

guest suite in the spaceport's headquarters. I'll come by to visit when I can, and I know he will be by to get several more of your fine suits. I've promised to help him pick out just the right styles and colors. Bye for now."

"Yes, thank you for everything, Carmen. You've been of immeasurable help to me," he added and then carefully led Adalina out of her office.

The night before they arrived at Valen, Hector and Adalina discussed the situation. "Look, Lech must have left him copious notes about our *mentales* gifts and our circles — everything, since Jarek was considered one of us back then. Assume he knows all but our more recent secrets. Show him around, explain things he asks about, but do try your feminine charms on him. Carmen believes he will be highly susceptible to them. If so, you may use your own discretion on just how far you want to go with this. I give you permission to marry him, if that is your wish. We need to re-establish a good working relationship with him, because he controls the entire spaceport and more," Hector told Adalina.

"Terrific uncle, this sure beats tower work. Besides, I've not found the right man yet. Look, if Carmen could charm her way into Jarek's pants, I ought to be able to do it too, and this Emeryk is even more powerful than Jarek ever was. I'll be your eyes on the inside, leave it to me," Adalina insisted, eager to finally be free of Valen Tower and her boring circle work there. When Carmen made her pipe corsets and toe shoes available for all women, Adalina jumped at the chance, knowing she would be attracting the gaze of even more men. Although that truly happened, she still didn't find herself attracted to anyone in particular. Now Hector was giving her a golden opportunity to really do something extremely worthwhile not only for herself but for Valen. She threw herself into the charm-Emeryk project.

As they began walking away from Hector just after he arrived, Emeryk asked her, "How come you wear such impossible heels? You must find them terribly difficult to wear."

"They are sexy, aren't they? You like them?"

"Well, of course, I can hardly keep my eyes off of your legs, Miss Adalina."

"That's why I wear them." She gave his arm a gentle flirting squeeze, bringing a grin to his face. As she began their lengthy tour, he wished he'd taken the time to read Lech's huge mountain of field notes on Tierra. Still, he swore to compare what Adalina was telling him to Lech's notes when he got back.

Over a banquet in his honor that night, she sat beside him and chatted, explaining about their spicy dishes. Westerlings relished their hot spices, a bit too hot for Emeryk though. Then over a dark ale, the two leaders chatted formally with Adalina still clinging to his arm.

Hector began, "You probably know your former leader and our former leader often met together in secret in Exchange City and sometimes here in Valen. They were constantly exchanging information and ideas on how to improve relations between our people. I know your people consider us to be primitives, that is, I believe is your term for us, and our people consider your people to be wholly uncivilized barbarians. Strange the notions people have when they truly do not meet and try to understand the other."

"Quite right, quite right. When I arrived here on Ash- er Tierra, I was expecting the standard Imperium primitives, by definition you know. Now that I have actually met you, I can hardly say that is true."

"Yes, I know. In your people's eyes, we must seem a primitive people. We do not have electricity, spaceships, giant machines that move earth and so on. Yet Emeryk, as you have seen we have no need for such things. While we would love to have shuttle craft to use to travel about, we still use horses for the most part, though we routinely use teleporting for smaller, quicker, more important travels. We enjoy the land about us as we ride along on our horses. Ours is not a fast paced society. We live to enjoy life around us. Yet I can see how in your race's eyes that makes us primitive."

"Well, I don't know how I could survive without my computer and our extensive network of computers. They contain all our combined knowledge, all available to anyone to read at any time. However, there is one small matter I was charged to discover. It seems some of our shuttle craft have met fatal accidents."

"Ah yes. I believe those you are referring to were on a mission to kidnap some of our young female telepaths — to be taken off-world and sold as slaves."

"Well, that's putting it rather bluntly, but true," Emeryk cringed. Just how much did this man know? Well, that project was hardly a secret from these people!

"What would you do if we kidnaped one of your field agents? Would you not try to prevent that from happening if you could?"

"Of course. Wait! Are you saying someone on Tierra found out about the kidnaping and caused the crashes?" Emeryk suddenly put the clues together.

Hector raised his eyebrows and winked. "You see, all the towers have long been aware of your abduction attempts. Many years ago our Emperor decided to put an end to that. Her orders were to stay alert for such attempts and to prevent them from occurring by any means available. I'm sorry some took that to mean to destroy your valuable craft. If you are wise, you would find a way to cancel that project. I doubt it very much if your agents will ever be successful again at kidnaping our young telepaths."

Emeryk frowned. This was not good. How could he possibly report this on up the lines. Hector grinned slyly. "Of course, if what you really wanted from this was telepaths who were willing to travel to other worlds and be highly compensated for their work, I am sure on the quiet here in Valen we could find some who would volunteer."

"You're kidding? Volunteers? Say, that would be superb. We would not have to be breaking the rules any longer and that would definitely remove a barrier between us. I agree, it is highly unethical for us to be stealing your telepaths and selling them into slavery. As I understand the project's needs, three or four a year would be ideal, young ones preferably. Let me work at this from my end and get back to you. Perhaps we can work out an agreement."

"Oh I am sure we can, Emeryk," Hector backed him up,

knowing again he'd scored a major point with the alien leader. This was all too easy.

Later, Hector invited him to spend the night and visit more the following day. He agreed and Adalina took the opportunity to work her wiles on him. She accompanied him to his guest room. "Do you ever mix pleasure with business? I mean the business hours are over now. I am here and I find you very attractive." She wiggled her curvaceous body up against his. He lasted two minutes before he was seduced. "Have you ever made love with a telepath?" she asked coyly. He hadn't and his will power evaporated.

Thus, when Hector asked if he'd like Adalina to return to Exchange City with him and serve as their liaison officer, he readily agreed. Further, he suggested she move into a guest suite within his administration building at the spaceport. At that point, both Hector and Adalina knew she'd hooked him well. Now all they needed was time. The old connections between the Rigel-3 aliens and Valen had been re-forged.

Carmen found her granddaughter highly impressionable. While she already wore some of Carmen's dresses and heels, as did many women at Valen, Nita was eager to help in any way. She had to slow the enthusiastic teen down a little. "First, we have to get your *mentales* gifts unblocked. That must take priority."

"But grandma, I feel fine and can defend myself if I need to. Surely learning everything here is more important," she countered.

"Dear, nothing is more important than unleashing your full potentials. Come on. It's time we paid a visit to the emperor and put in a teleport request to get us to Brom Tower the easy way. So here's your first lesson." Nita suddenly began paying close attention, her eyes watching Carmen intently.

"When you visit someone, it is always best to appear before them as they would *really* like you to *appear*. That way they start off liking you or feeling good about you or at least okay about you. If you appear different than they would like, then you are beginning on the wrong foot with a disagreement, making your job even harder," Carmen explained.

"So what do we need to appear like?" Nita asked innocently.

"Based on what the empress said at the spring meeting, she is making compromises in her traditions and has asked us to make similar compromises with ours."

"Oh, like Uncle Hector. He's supposed to get modified to be like Aunt Luisa soon. Is that what you mean?" she asked, biting her lip, trying to recall what the adults had talked about when they returned from the spring meeting.

"Precisely. In this case, she wants us Midlands women to wear either a fetter-gown — either the visible style or the hidden version — or even better the hidden-arm-fetter-gown. So I will go wearing the arm-fetter-gown which is what she wishes. However you've not been body modified yet, so we'll see if we can't fix you up something similar."

Nita looked pleased. "So when can I get modified to look like you, grandma? You look so fabulous, you know. Everyone says so."

"After we get your *mentales* block handled. Let's see what we can do for the right dress for you."

An hour later, Carmen had Nita in a modified version of her newest style, the arm-fetter-gown. "Gee, it does restrict my steps," she commented as she took her first steps in it. She was wearing her usual heels and thus was in fact restricted a great deal.

"It will be good practice for you, dear. Once you begin to wear toe shoes, you will find you have to take such tiny steps and the hidden fetter skirt will not seriously restrict you. Right now, we have to get used to having our upper arms pinned to our sides, like a chained Easterlings woman. I could use your arm for support though," she hinted.

Nita found having her arms so immobile was rather annoying. The two spent nearly an hour walking the short distance from her fourth floor office in the Alien Headquarters building across the street to the Imperial Court and into the throne room. Carmen was somewhat out of breath by the time she'd walked the whole distance in her toe shoes. However, she'd gauged it perfectly.

"Oh so good to see you once again, Carmen. My, you do

look very nice in your new fetter-gown. Oops, even better, arm-fetter-gown. And who is this charming young lady who looks fabulous as well?"

"My granddaughter, Nita Valen. This is Empress Calandra and her advisor Felisa."

"Very pleased to meet you, Empress Calandra. You look very good yourself," Nita curtsied, but had a little trouble moving her arms.

"I am very impressed, Nita, Carmen. You so honor me by having your arms bound. Very well done. How can I help you today?" Calandra praised them. It was obvious Calandra and Felisa were quite pleased to see them sharing their Easterlings traditions.

"I need to take Nita to Brom Tower to see one of their katalyein telepaths. Could I schedule a time for the Imperial Circle to teleport us there?" Carmen asked.

"Oh certainly, certainly. Felisa, will you take them to the scheduling book please?"

The equally hobbled advisor rose and carefully began to walk the two out of the throne room into the long hall. Carmen moved to Felisa's side and slipped the lower part of her left arm around the advisor. "While chained like this, Felisa, I'm afraid about all I can do for you is to help you keep your balance."

"Oh thank you. It helps me so much. We have to walk so exceedingly carefully you know."

"Yes, I know. Your predecessors also had to do just that as well." Once at the reception desk, Carmen wrote her request in the log book. Later on via telepathy, their capa would schedule a time for the teleport, but only after verifying Brom Tower would accept their arrival.

The next day around ten Carmen and Nita, now wearing their usual gowns, arrived at the teleport platform in Brom Manor a thousand miles to the north. Venerada Luisa met them personally, rather pleasing Carmen. "So what brings you to Brom and who is this lovely young girl?" she asked.

"My granddaughter, Nita. Nita, this is Venerada Luisa Wycombe. She has had her tower training, but she has a *mentales* blockage. I was hoping one of your katalyein might be able to help her."

"Ah business, then. Well, let's see. I think my daughter Ann is free right now. Come. I'll take you to her suite. As long as we're on the business side, I heard rumors our empress wishes all us women to get similar body modifications and wear some kind of new fetter-gown."

"Yes, that is what she is asking," Carmen replied, as Luisa had to slow way down for her.

"Well, that is going to cause women like myself enormous problems, Carmen. We katalyein use our feet where you use your hands, plus we must be highly flexible. That's one reason we've not begun wearing your elegant corsets and matching dresses. It's hard enough on us to wear the heels, but sexy, I'll admit that."

"I know, Venerada Luisa. I'll be honest with you, the empress and her staff who are like you have a very difficult time managing the pipe corsets and toe shoes. I think she doesn't realize you have real work to do. She sits on her throne mostly, but you are a very busy woman. Perhaps if you find yourselves being forced to wear something else, try the new fetter-gowns. They will be the least restrictive for you. I'll send you some samples when I get back and you can experiment with them. I'm sure even that small step may well be enough to please her."

"Oh thank you. You are a lifesaver. Ah, here we are. I've let her know to expect you. I'll leave you now. Urgent business elsewhere. Just have Ann take you back to the teleport pad when you are ready to leave. I do hope Ann can help you, Nita, and very pleased to meet you." She left them at Ann's door and Carmen knocked.

A bit later Ann, now twenty and in the full bloom of womanhood, sat on a chair across from Nita. She'd tossed her long black hair to one side before sitting and now chatted with Nita, getting familiar with the young teen, discovering just what training and analysis she'd had at Valen Tower. "Okay, let's do this. All you have to do is place your hands on my shoulders. Whatever happens, don't remove them until I tell you to do so. Okay Nita?"

"Okay, but will it hurt?" she asked worriedly.

"Yes it might. You are going to re-experience whatever that blockage contains. If it wasn't painful or quite sorrowful, then it wouldn't be a blockage now would it? So you have to be brave and confront whatever comes up. I will be with you all the way and I won't let any harm come to you. Okay?"

"Okay." Nita placed her hands on the armless shoulders of Ann, for an instant admiring her looks as well. Then she felt Ann's mind touching hers and she again saw the huge black mass that was blocking her full *mentales* gifts. Ann used her gift and bit by bit, images, emotions, pains, and feelings began forming from the blackness. At once, Ann recognized the nature of this blockage; she'd seen it a dozen times now. A half hour later her eyes wet with tears, Nita finally confronted the Nuclear explosion which had annihilated Bettingham. The combined fear, terror, pain, and loss of all those who had died had finally been confronted and the blockage blew off, no longer reactive on her. Now her full *mentales* gifts became available.

Prime among them was her ability to tell when someone was lying or simply not telling all, that is, withholding some key information. After Ann got Nita sorted out, both women thanked Ann repeatedly, and the smiling woman led them back to the teleport pad. She too asked Carmen about these new dresses and requests of their empress. Once more Carmen told her what she'd told Luisa about the alternate style, bringing great relief to Ann's face.

The next day Nita again begged her, "Please, grandma, can I get the modifications now so I can look just like you? My *mentales* block is gone. So can I, please?"

"Yes, dear, but you must learn all about it, how it is done, how to best cope with the restrictions they place on you. Just remember, they cannot be undone." She purposely didn't tell her she'd had all the medical machines modified so the operator no longer had any of the menu choices to undo what could be undone or partially so in the case of their feet.

They spent half a day going over the procedures until Carmen was certain Nita had them all down pat. Then with a twinkle in her eye, she said, "Okay then, Nita, before we do it on you, there is one other thing. Since you are so young, it might be possible for you to have a smaller waist than me."

Her eyes opened wide as she grasped the full implications behind that. "If I have one smaller than you do, grandma, doesn't that mean I would be setting a new fashion statement for others to follow?"

Carmen grinned broadly. Nita was catching on very swiftly. "Exactly, dear. Very good of you to spot that. Yes, you would be doing just that. Of course, older women and men cannot hope to do better than I have at fourteen inches, but you younger ones, well, let's just see how it works out, shall we? If yours does end up smaller, then you can begin to market it to many others your age."

"All right!" Nita declared, raising her fist in the air. "I'll be Elegant Fashions Inc's teen model! Let's do it now!"

"Just remember afterwards, Nita," Carmen once more cautioned her, "no pain means no gain."

"I know, I know, you've told me that ten times, grandma," she replied holding her hands on her hips in mock defiance.

A short while later, Carmen began the procedure. When at last the excited Nita was unconscious, she took a number of measurements. "I'll be damned. She's right. If I do this right, she'll have a twelve inch waist." She issued some orders to her staff and within a half hour, she was handed a new outfit for Nita, including one of the few twelve-inch pipe corsets she had in stock. Few women could ever reach such a small waist, but then she'd been modifying adult women thus far. Nita was the youngest she'd done. Carmen set to work, pressing the menu items, and then waited patiently.

The part she disliked the most was the rib removal process. As usual, she closed her eyes until she heard the change in sounds from the machine, which indicated it was on the healing cycle. When it finished, she pressed the menu item, which handled Nita's feet. This process took less than half the time and soon the medical machine finished. Carmen removed it from over Nita's unconscious body. Some of her assistants joined her and they began putting their tiniest pipe waist corset on her. That took a while, since they allowed Nita's body to adjust a little as they slowly tightened it fully, though it took their combined strength to tighten it. The key factor that Carmen didn't know: would they be able fully to tighten it? After an hour, they succeeded and tied off the long laces. After that, her assistants put on a new set of black nylons, and Carmen put on her new set of toe shoes, choosing a shiny black patent anticipating the gown Nita might choose once she woke and observed her new dynamite look.

Her assistants left her, returning to their own work, while Carmen sat beside Nita waiting for her to rouse. A half hour later Nita finally woke up. She was still lying on the recovery table. "Oh," she moaned a little as her eyes fluttered and opened. "Is it done yet? Oh! I can't breathe, grandma!"

Carmen grinned, "I told you about that. Take shallow breaths, dear. Yes, like that."

Nita tried to rise and discovered she could not bend any longer except at her hips for there was just too many steel stays in the corset, by design actually. That didn't stop her but for a moment. She used her arms and got herself into a sitting position, straight as an arrow. "How big is it? Did we make twelve inches?"

"You bet we did! Exactly. Now you have bested me and you most definitely will be setting a completely new trend in fashion, Nita. I am so proud of you. Now see if you can stand. Remember, tiny steps like I take."

"Wow. My ankles and feet go straight down now. Oh! Only my toes are flat on the floor. Duh, I get it now. Look at these toe shoes! They are so tiny. Oh!" She wobbled wildly as she tried to stand. Carmen reached out and took her hand, stabilizing her. "I know, takes practice. Let me try to stand by myself. Oh, it's hard, isn't it?"

A bit later, she added, "I didn't know it was going to be this hard, grandma. Don't worry, if you can do it, so can I," she added bravely, as she struggled to take her first steps in her new shoes. After that, Carmen helped her into a new red satin dress that really fit her new form quite tightly. Holding each other's hand, they moved over to the full-length mirror so Nita could see her new total look.

"Wow, grandma! I look fabulous now, just like you!"

"No dear, better than I do," Carmen corrected her.

"Your waist is two inches smaller than mine." That brought a big smile to Nita's face. "Now, we must practice walking and then doing our normal things."

"It's really tricky, isn't it?" Nita asked, still wiggling precariously.

"Yes, but with lots of practice, you will be walking very seductively like the rest of us."

"Okay, when do I get to wear one of your new arm-fetter-gowns?" Nita asked.

"After you can show me you can walk on your own and seductively, dear." She cleverly gave Nita a new goal to achieve, making her work hard at her current tasks.

"I am going to master it so I can wear one when Uncle Hector comes to get his modifications next week," Nita said very determined.

During the next week, Carmen began teaching Nita how she ran her company, sharing many of her secrets of success. "Always remember, you have to be at the cutting edge of fashion. You have to plant your ideas for new designs and modifications into other's minds so they believe they truly desire it. Just remember to be fully prepared to deliver the product once they demand it of you. Let your customers sell themselves."

"For example, notice how I handled Venerada Luisa. She was all worried about being unable to wear a pipe corset, toe shoes, and the relevant gowns. If I had tried to sell her on the idea she could wear them — and I well could have, citing ex-Emperor Jan and ex-Empress Amy managed them very well — then she would likely have been very upset about the styles. Rather, I suggested she could wear the fetter-gown. Soon, she will be demanding those from us, not only for herself but likely for the others like her at Brom Tower."

"But can't we get her to go all the way, too?" Nita asked.

"One step at a time. Get them used to the fetter-gown first. Then, let all the other women around them get competent with their pipe corsets and toe shoes and peer pressure will eventually have them asking for them as well. It's a matter of time. Now based on all this, what do we need to plan for right now?"

Nita knew she was being quizzed. "Oh! Me. We need to be ready to supply these smaller pipe corsets to other teens like myself. Once others see me, they are going to want them too, right?"

"Right! Well done, dear. Well done. Now let's get everything ready for Uncle Hector, shall we? He's going to be a tough case, because he doesn't want to have this done, but he's doing it so the younger lords can be spared for now."

"Okay. Say, why do you call him Uncle Hector? He's not really your uncle, is he?"

"Heavens no. He's in his fifties and I am in my nineties. No, I call him uncle because our relationship is easier to communicate this way. I don't look ninety. Long ago, we both agreed to this, same with Aunt Miranda and many others at Valen." Nita grinned, she got it.

The following week, Uncle Hector and Aunt Miranda arrived at Elegant Fashions Inc. Nita walked reasonably seductively now, impressing her uncle and aunt. "Well, my favorite niece, you look extremely attractive," Hector admired her new look.

"Thanks! It's really hard work learning to adjust, Uncle Hector, but I'm getting the hang of it. You will too, I'm sure. I'll help you," Nita promised him.

"I really don't want to do this, Carmen, but I have to go through with it. If not, Emperor Carl may well do something all we lords will deeply regret. We must be very careful about defying our emperor. We must be exceptionally careful to choose to fight those decisions of his that are critical. If we do not, well — remember Amy Blackwater may have given up the throne, but she's killed forty-three of our valuable people, far more than any other kingdom. We have to bide our time until she and Jan have died. Still I do have to admit I love Miranda's looks, but. . ." He didn't finish.

Carmen did for him, interrupting him, "I know. It's really hard for us to adapt, but we can. And we women do look really sexy in our outfits. You men also look very handsome, if I do say so myself. Besides, uncle, you no longer are expected to go off fighting battles or even go out into the field with your soldiers. You are our leader."

"Yes, quite true. That's one of the reasons I agreed to do this. I really don't need mobility any longer, not as I did when I was twenty. What I can't understand is why does the emperor want us lords to be as hobbled up as he is?" Hector admitted and asked.

Carmen theorized, "I think he feels miserable and wholly helpless, even though he wields the ultimate in power. No one really respects him, if the truth be said. So you have an emperor who is relegated to being a mere figurehead of a person. He can't do anything for himself, physically, not like the katalyein can or even Amy and Jan, uncle. So naturally, he wants some of you who elected him to this miserable job to share in his pain."

"You have a powerful point, Carmen. Indeed, we didn't think our choice through to its end. He and they are truly helpless cripples now and lack the *mentales* gifts even to help them out. We may well have made a major blunder in our choice. Still, it cannot be undone for now and we have to make the best of it," Hector replied. "Plan for the future, that's what I am doing. Yet everything must be done on the quiet until Amy and Jan are out of the picture. God, just one thought from either one of them and you're dead!"

"You don't need to remind me of that; I lost Jarek to them," Carmen said angrily. Even after all these years, her anger had not subsided, not even after the revenges she'd had. Somehow, those two simply continued on their merry way. Just now, she wondered where those two were at and what they were doing. After they left the throne two years ago, they more or less vanished. Still no one dared challenge them by defying their new emperor and empress.

"I understand, Carmen. Our future lies with the aliens from Rigel-3. I know the other leaders feel just the opposite, but they are blind. Even hobbled as I will be, I aim to keep this secret alliance with them active and productive. Then one day, Valen will once again become the power on Tierra."

"I am doing my part to make that happen too, uncle, as you well know. Right now, nearly half of all women, who are nobles or who are *mentales* gifted and working for the lords or the towers, are wearing my high heels and tight dresses. Soon,

Vic Broquard

they will be also wearing pipe corsets and toe shoes as well. I give them perhaps another couple of years before they all will do so. My guess is within ten years, all women of power will be wearing them. Even more interesting will be the impact of the new arm-fetter-gowns. I planted that notion into the empress' mind. It's so damn easy with the head-blind. I did it after I heard what Carl was planning to order you lords to do. Anyway, I expect it is too soon to know if they will take off as well, but with the threat of being ordered to wear them via the insistence of Empress Calandra, I anticipate they will at least adopt the pipe corsets and toe shoes. While they will definitely be sexy, they will be effectively immobilized, no offense, Aunt Miranda. You are not expected to fight battles, Aunt Miranda, but those in the towers are. When Uncle Hector makes his moves, the hobbled up circles will be severely limited in actions they can take against him," Carmen explained.

Aunt Miranda smiled, "I am well aware of that, dear. No offence taken. I enjoy being sexy for your uncle and I honestly am still able to perform the functions required of a lady. I would be furious though, if I were a circle member and hobbled up like this. You have my backing, Carmen. Keep on with it. I know our other ladies are also behind what you are doing, even if they really are not fully aware of the overall goal."

Hector smile and commented, "Hum, I didn't know you were behind Calandra's orders, Carmen. Brilliant move, but dangerous. See if you can keep Carl happy with the few of us who comply with his orders to undergo this mess."

"I will, uncle, as always," Carmen smiled, knowing she'd scored another point with Hector.

He then responded to his wife's comments. "Miranda's right, Carmen. One day all Valen will sing your praises when we make our move and find all the opposing towers are hobbled up and ineffective, as our armies march to victory. There is no possibility of our acquiring more Nuclears, and I certainly would never use one if I got one. Too hideous. Nor will we have to face those awful acid and fire and chemical bombs. At least in that one area, I have to thank Amy Blackwater. I'll give her that much. She's neutralized that

40

threat. Now you are doing her one better by further hobbling them. Women should never have been allowed total control over the towers and circles, as Amy dictated."

"I agree uncle, that's the wrong goal for women to have."

Aunt Miranda agreed with her fully. "We should be raising our children and making a good home for our men, backing them up, not playing around with such ultimate power. Part of that, of course, is enticing our husbands to bed us, so I don't mind being dressed like this, Carmen. Hector, here, has been acting like a young buck since I started wearing your latest fashions." Hector flushed and cleared his throat. Carmen gave him a coy grin.

Nita, who had been silent, finally began to see the larger picture. Elegant Fashions Inc was actually an integral part of Valen's overall plan to regain its dominance in the world. Knowing one day she would be taking over for Carmen made her feel even more important and more dedicated to learning to walk and deal with her new restraints.

"Oh one more thing Carmen, we've heard strange rumors that up in Brom, they've found or invented or discovered some new form of *mentales* gifts. When you get a chance, could you look into this for me?"

"Absolutely, uncle. Will do. I guess we'd best get started. I have a whole new wardrobe ready for you. Your shirts will be tapered sharply to fit your new shape well and accent it, as will the tops of your pants. I've picked out only the very best quality materials for you. I've got to have my uncle looking more handsome than all the other lords," she teased him. Then she got serious. "Just remember, we women have endured this and have adjusted well so you can too. It will not be easy; no one ever says it is easy. I told Nita the motto, no pain means no gain. You will have to learn to take shallow breaths and, from your point of view, the tiniest of steps. But then, just remember how Aunt Miranda walks and you should get the hang of it. Like I tell everyone, you must practice a good deal to master walking easily and gracefully."

"But there are a couple of choices I need you to make up front. First, you can have toe shoes or toe boots. While the shoes are easier to put on by yourself, personally, I think men look much better in the boots, since they emulate the style of boots you men normally wear. Second, do you want to wear nylons or socks? Women, of course, wear nylons and they are cooler in the summers. But maybe they will not be manly enough for you."

"Boots and socks please," Hector grumbled as the reality of his transformation drew closer.

Miranda asked, "May I get samples of your three new fetter styles which Empress Calandra suggested? I'd like to try them on and see how they are. Even better, I would like to take a few back with me to show the other women at Valen."

"Sure thing, Aunt Miranda. I half expected you would ask about them. I've got several in your size ready for you and in your favorite colors too. We'll try them out while Uncle Hector is recovering. Are you ready uncle?" she asked. He grumbled but consented.

An assistant took Miranda into another room to show her the rack of new dresses. That way she would not have to witness the operation. This time Carmen had Nita operate the medical machine, though she oversaw each move. "You're testing me, right?" Nita whispered after Hector went unconscious. Carmen nodded and Nita proceeded with the operation.

After the medical side was finished, several more assistants entered, and the group then struggled to get the heavy man re-dressed in his new clothing and boots. Finally, they lifted him onto the recovery table. As the assistants left, Miranda made her slow, careful way into the room. Nita saw she was now wearing one of the new red hidden-arm-fetter-gowns. Nita bubbled, "Aunt Miranda, you look really good in that one. How is it working?"

"Well, the hidden fetter skirt is very hard for me to manage putting on or taking off, but it certainly doesn't impair my walking, though I know I'd never be able to climb any stairs in it. It sure is tight though. I am most bothered by the inability to move my upper arms. This, I think, will take quite some getting used to, if I am to wear it frequently. Still, it's not bad, so far anyway. How is my husband doing?"

"Perfect, Aunt Miranda. Have a look."

"Oh my goodness! He's lost his huge ale belly! He looks as handsome now as when I first met him when we were in our late teens! Carmen, thank you! I am extremely pleased with his new look!" Miranda's huge smile told all. She chatted, "I've been on him to lose some weight for the last ten years. Instead, he just got heavier and heavier. Okay, fatter. I am being kind." She grinned coyly and the three chuckled.

In an hour, he woke up. As expected, he grumbled and complained he couldn't breathe, following that with the fact he couldn't bend to get his own socks or boots on. "Dear, look at your waist. You've lost that unsightly ale belly of yours!" Miranda pointed out.

"Er, so I have," he finally noticed. "I've shrunk somehow."

"Dear, you look like you did when we first met — a handsome, fit, young man," she countered. "It's like I have you back like you were when we married." She was so happy about this aspect that Hector stopped grumbling until he tried to stand up, that is.

When Miranda went to put her arms around him to support him, she found the bound arms to be a big nuisance. "Dear, what's wrong? Oh, I see you are wearing one of those new dresses Empress Calandra insisted you women start wearing. Can you manage it?"

"I will somehow, dear. Let's get you balanced. Remember how tiny my steps have been. Let's try walking, dear," Miranda suggested. To be on the safe side, Carmen took his other arm in hers.

"My god, you women can hardly walk at all. I had no idea it was this bad for you," Hector exclaimed, wobbling wildly.

Carmen declared, "Uncle Hector, you are doing just fine. Everyone has a hard time standing and walking their first time. It takes lots of practice. I'm not letting you out of here until I'm satisfied you can walk well on your own. Let's walk over to the door now where the tall mirror is at so you can see just how handsome you look now."

Minutes later, he stared at his image, less his new

jacket. "My god! I have lost thirty pounds or more. Well, if you like it, Miranda, then I will endure it for you, my buttercup." Carmen liked his reaction and response and finally relaxed. She knew in time her uncle would manage the big change.

As the four dined that evening, Hector complained, "Damn, I can eat hardly anything now! I feel like I am bursting and I've barely begun!"

"Dear," Miranda countered, "this way you will not put on all those extra pounds you just lost. That's a good thing." All four chuckled, but he grumbled.

Carmen kept him there for three more days before she felt confident he could manage on his own. Often during these days, he and his wife went for walks around Carmen's large office suites. From now on, he didn't have to focus on going slow enough for her. Miranda was very pleased with this minor detail she'd not anticipated.

Just before they left to return to Valen, Carmen asked her uncle, "Now, I need to ask a favor of you, Uncle Hector. When you get back to Valen, I want you to watch the reactions of not only the other *mentales* gifted and your men in the castle, but also your common workers. I am particularly interested in how the average citizens of Valen, not your soldiers, aides, and such, but your blacksmith, chefs, teamsters, and so on now look at you."

"Why? Do you think they'll all laugh at me, tell crude jokes about how foolish the old man is?" he asked growing rather worried.

"That's what I want to find out. We've only done a few of you men and I've not been able to get feedback yet from the others. Yes, they could react that way. If so, you might be able to use that as ammunition with Emperor Carl to have him rescind his new law. On the other hand, I suspect they might have a higher opinion of you for this. I just don't know which way the ordinary folk will see these changes Emperor Carl has ordered."

"Ah, excellent point. If they humiliate us, that will weaken our ability to lead them and Carl would have to cease this nonsense," Hector brightened up, seeing a possible way to protect all the other younger lords.

"Exactly, uncle. Keep me posted," Carmen replied and gave him a big hug. He kissed her forehead.

After they departed via a teleport, Nita said, "Well, that went well. I sure learned a whole lot from this, grandma. Plus, I can see I need to practice walking and doing things tons more, if I aim to be the role model of teen fashion on Tierra, which I aim to be."

Carmen grinned. "I'm certain you will be, Nita. No doubt of that. Come on. We both need more practice in the hidden-arm-fetter-gowns. We need to be real pros in them before the fall session comes."

"Plus, we need to be ready for all the new orders that will be coming too," Nita added with a smile. "When do I get to wear makeup?" Carmen grinned; her granddaughter was growing up fast.

Chapter 3 The Die Is Cast

In late August 1205, Venerada Luisa received a message from her Communications Network. It came directly from Emperor Carl. Her capa carefully wrote down his exact words and then brought it to her. She'd read it five times before she finally acted on it. She sat down in her sofa and focused. Her crystal glowed.

Amy. Venerada Luisa here. I'm sorry for interrupting you, but I've just received an official order from Emperor Carl over the comm network. I've debated whether to comply or not, but then I am worried it might be some kind of trap.

Go ahead and tell me, Luisa.

Okay. I'll read it to you.

"Venerada Luisa Wycombe, the last anyone heard of Empress Amy Blackwell was she had gone off to Brom Tower. The Imperial Circle told me they transported her there. I need to talk to her personally in my throne room. It is very important and very urgent we meet, face to face. If you know where she might be, I am ordering you to relay my request, no my order to her, that she come and visit me immediately. Yours truly, Emperor Carl Christopher."

What do you make of that? I fear he is somehow laying a trap for you. What should I send back by way of reply?

Give me a minute, Luisa. Amy sighed; the last thing she wanted now was to be pulled back into the political arena. She focused and found Carl, then looked over his surface thoughts, unwilling simply to rape his mind. With the head blind, this would be a simple matter. Satisfied, she broke the connection. *I do not sense any malice in him towards me. I think it's not a trap. He is worried about something. I'll go. Tell him I'll be there tomorrow around ten, if one of your circles can teleport me there and back again. I don't trust the Imperial Circle to return me here.*

You got it. I'll have them monitor you as well.

Promptly at ten, Amy's body materialized in Emperor Carl's throne room. Amy looked around and saw only the two leaders present. Even their advisors and domestique helpers were absent. She wore typical town clothing, having shunned all the fancy Elegant Fashions Inc gowns. Still she had little choice but to wear the normal tall heels.

"My, a peasant look?" Emperor Carl exclaimed rather surprised at her vastly different apparel from the last time he'd seen her.

"Comfortable apparel, emperor. I'm retired, if you remember and no longer active politically. Why have you sent for me?" Amy asked.

"Okay to the point. I don't know if you are aware of our new laws we passed at the Spring Council." She was but allowed him to explain anyway, which he and Empress Calandra did at length.

"I've been checking every week with Carmen who is in charge of making the modifications to the lords that I ordered. It is now less than a month before the Fall Council and thus far only a dozen lords have complied with my order. I am a little frustrated with them, more so when I figured out it is only the older lords who have followed my orders. A dozen out of hundreds! I had so hoped they would see reason and obey my orders."

"Likewise with my orders," Empress Calandra added. "I've made numerous compromises with my Easterlings bound traditions and I so hoped many of the ladies would show an equal compromise. But according to Carmen's figures, only a few dozen have purchased even one of the new three types of fetter-gowns as I asked."

"I see. What does this have to do with me?" Amy asked point blank. She had no idea where these two were going with this discussion or why it was so vitally urgent they see her in person.

"Okay. Here's what we are planning to do next. At the Fall Council I want to issue the law all lords have the proper modifications done before next spring's council and all ladies wear one of the fetter-gowns, as well as having the proper modifications done. And all the nobles and those in the towers too."

"Wow, that is pretty drastic," Amy answered.

"Yes, we know. But look at it this way. We have the

ultimate power and so to temper that power, we have to be like this, totally helpless. Now the lords and ladies and the tower folk — they too have great powers, though obviously nowhere near as much as Calandra and I do. We think they too should have their power balanced with some physical restraints as well. That's our reasoning."

"Yes," Empress Calandra added, "in the Easterlings we have a saying that goes: what is good for the female is good for the male. Often that is used in a sexual way, but in jest. If our powers are to be tempered this severely, then we feel theirs too should be tempered, but less than ours. Are we totally wrong in thinking this?"

"No, I set it up so with the tremendous powers you have, you cannot easily be tempted to abuse that power, as so many rulers in the past have," Amy replied.

"Damn, we can't even feed ourselves or dress or even go to the bathroom without the total assistance of our domestique. How could we possibly abuse our powers?" Carl griped.

"True. I'm sorry. I hope those who elected you warned you about what you were getting into by accepting your positions as our emperor and empress," Any replied, having the horrid thought perhaps the lords had not done so.

"Oh yes, yes they were quite clear about it. No fault there, Amy. The reason we asked you here today is to ask this. If we make these orders, did what you said when you were on the throne still apply? That is, you would ensure they follow our orders? If you don't, then we're both scared the lords and ladies will simply defy us both on this matter and undermine our authority," Carl pointed out.

Damn! I made that solemn pledge I would see to it their new emperor and empress's laws would be obeyed. I'm obligated to do so. Yet, this is a nasty thing to do to all them! "Look, think this thing through. If you make such a blanket order, while I am obligated to ensure your order is followed, think what the results will be. You both will instantly become the most *hated* two people on Tierra! That alone will undermine your rule. They might even be driven to assassination plots against you both. Besides, think of the special katalyein telepaths who were born without arms. They depend upon their flexibility and feet to be able to live reasonable normal lives. You would be dooming them utterly. Might I suggest an alternative?"

"Oh! Damn, you are right! We've not fully thought this through. Please, tell us," Carl replied, utterly shocked by what she'd just said.

Amy fought to keep her growing opinion he was an utter fool and an idiot from becoming visible to the two rulers. "My suggestion would be to order all the actual men, the lords, who rule a kingdom or territory, and their ladies to be modified. Perhaps you could add the venerada of the towers to the list as well, but make an exception for the katalyein gifted. If you must do something to them, suggest they wear the new fetter-gowns to formal meetings. Even going this far will make you enemies though," Amy answered.

Amy continued to manipulate them, "However, although I know this is your desire, there *is* a better way to go about it, though it will take more time to come to fruition, but there would be little or no animosity towards you over it,".

Carl took her bait. "Please, tell us this better way, please."

"One gets better results with honey than with a whip. At the fall meeting, heap tons of praise and validation on those men and women who have obeyed you. Make them feel like they have really succeeded in pleasing you and in benefitting their own people by showing they too support a tempering of power."

"But what will that do?" he asked.

"As long as you keep on praising them each time you see them, keep validating them, rewarding them for having done so, for having compromised as Calandra has asked, then others will very likely volunteer to go along with it themselves. Give those who do as you've asked a heaping bowl of honey and, seeing this, others will follow suit."

"Brilliant, Amy, positively brilliant. Calandra, we should've thought of this ourselves!" an enthusiastic Carl replied. "Thank you ever so much for coming to meet with us. You've saved us from making a bad mistake. I can see that clearly now. Thank you, thank you."

Amy smiled and then left the two rulers. Luisa's tower teleported her back to Brom Tower, where Luisa was waiting anxiously to hear what had happened. Amy told her all about it and was repeatedly thanked for having once again diverted a potential disaster.

Two weeks before the September Council meeting, Carmen and Nita again requested an audience with the Emperor. Carmen was ready to send out eight complete new Elegant Fashions Inc stores to the eight cities with towers. Her problem: one of security. Nita had asked her, "How are we going to get all these things and equipment delivered to the cities? We could be robbed. And isn't sending out the medical machines of the aliens violating the lease agreement?"

She's matured rapidly. Keen observer, Carmen thought. "Technically, yes. However, what the aliens don't know won't hurt them. It is legal for us to import them here; we both hold Imperium citizen ID cards. I've had dummy boxes built to look like the machines, so if the aliens come by to check on them, they will see the dummy machines still in their crates, while the real ones will be out there where they are needed. As for your first question, it's time we used up some of our credits with the emperor. After all, the lords don't have a monopoly on using him for their purposes. Come on, dear, we're off to see the emperor." Nita grinned at the deception Carmen was using, but was baffled over how the emperor would help them get their new stores delivered.

"Ah, so good of you both to come and visit us. Honestly, we do get terribly lonely; so few come to just visit," Emperor Carl admitted as the two were announced and moved slowly, but seductively into the room.

"Oh Carmen, Nita, you so do please me!" Empress Calandra exclaimed. "It is so good to see you both are wearing the finest compromise dresses. I do so like your new open outer skirt style. Very elegant and regal. Please, you must make one for me that I can wear to the council meeting. Please, you simply must!" Indeed, both wore bright red satin arm-fetter-gowns, but in a new style Carmen had just dreamed up. Instead of hiding the tight form-fitting satin fetter skirt portion of the dress, she'd used folds of satin for the outer skirt, but left them fall straight down from her broad hips. The center front of the outer folded skirt was open and cut so that as it reached floor length a gap of two feet allowed the inner fetter skirt, nylons, and heels to be elegantly visible. Of course, their sleeves were part of the bodice, effectively chaining their upper arms to their sides, as the empress so desired. "What a marvelous new gown! Stunning! Carmen, you and Nita have outdone yourselves this time." Clearly, the empress was pleased and Carmen mentally added another point to her score. Well, now it was time to use some of those points.

"Why thank you. I will see you and your women get them in time. We plan to introduce it at the coming meeting. I hate to do this to you, but we've come to ask a very big favor of you, Emperor Carl. We are now ready to ship out eight new storefronts fully equipped to perform the body modifications you've requested on men and women and to make and supply the necessary shoes, gowns, and suits for them. One store will be located in each of the tower cities, somewhat near the castles and towers proper. Now all those lords, ladies, nobles, and tower folk who want to follow your laws can do so without having to make the very long and tedious overland journey to us here in the Exchange City. I think you can see just how this will so greatly benefit your majesties."

"Carmen! This is the best news we've heard all year," Carl effused. "We cannot thank you enough for making this happen."

"Well, yes you can, actually. We have a slight problem in transport. You see, while we can crate everything up and transport via a small wagon train, we have no way to guard and protect the shipments. We could easily be robbed, perhaps even by those who do not wish to see other lords and ladies being modified. There is some resistance to following your orders, as you know."

"Yes, I can see that now. They could disguise themselves as bandits and rob the wagons. Then they can claim they could not get to Exchange City to have it done, using that as an excuse. How can we help, Carmen?"

"Could you send along a strong regiment of your Imperial Elite Guards to escort the eight shipments safely to their new locations?" Carmen asked.

"Absolutely! After all you have and are doing for us, that is the very least we can do for you. Carver, go fetch our general now. Tell him we have a vital project for his men," Emperor Carl ordered.

On their way home, Carmen pointed out to her protégée, "See how it's done? We cleverly supply and appear to back someone, and then after we build up enough points, they do precisely what we need them to do. Works every time, dear."

"I can see that clearly. By providing the means and clothing and shoes he needs to get his wishes brought into being, he feels obligated to assist us. Besides, you played right into what he wants done. Making our field offices right there in the capital cities, the lords and ladies no longer can use the extreme travel distances as an excuse to avoid complying with his wishes. Grandma, you are positively brilliant. I hope I can become half as good at this as you are," Nita praised her grandmother. There was just a hint of her doing the same thing to Carmen as Carmen had done to Carl, but both women knew it.

Carmen smiled, "I am certain you will, dear, perhaps even surpassing me." Nita grinned too. They had timed the eight trips to begin at the end of the council meeting. With luck, they'd reach the more northern cities before the heavier winter snows came. Already, Carmen had eight new women store managers there in the cities. They'd purchased the new store buildings, hired a dozen good seamstresses and tailors, and were now awaiting delivery of the medical machines, a good supply of finished products, a large supply of cloth bolts, threads, and leather, and of course the two trained women who would operate the medical machines.

Time-wise, Valen and Wyth would get theirs first, they being the two closest tower cities. Brom and Rusden would be next, about double the distance from Exchange City. Wye would follow. Much later, Welsham and Northend would get theirs, while Adelmira in the Easterlings would be last, some four thousand miles distant. Originally, Carmen had considered using circles to teleport the supplies, but decided against that because of the overall total weight and because the tower circle members might be opposed to Carl's laws and sabotage the shipments. While drastically slower, this way guaranteed a safe delivery.

Carmen and Nita both wore their newest open arm-fetter-gowns in red satin to the Fall Council meeting. Empress Calandra and her advisor Felisa wore similar modified gowns, emerald green, since they didn't have arms to fetter, but the domestique helpers Elnora and Ada wore light blue gowns which matched Carmen's. Carmen and Nita stood off to one side while the hundreds of lords, ladies, and other representatives entered, and witnessed a new policy of Carl's being implemented.

As Hector and Miranda reached the large entryway into the throne room, a loud bass voice announced, Lord Hector Valen, Lady Miranda Valen. A loud but regal fanfare followed as they moved slowly into the room. Behind them, a young lord and his wife entered next accompanied by silence. Then another modified lord and his wife arrived and again the bass voice announced them, and they were given an identical fanfare. Quickly, Carmen realized Carl was validating and honoring those lords who had complied with his request last spring and had gotten their body modifications done. She thought this was exceedingly clever of Carl, but began to wonder how the man had ever thought of this. He was far too dull to have dreamed this up all by himself.

A dozen older men and their wives received similar honors. By the time the last had entered, everyone knew the emperor was giving the men who had obeyed his request special treatment. That became even more evident as Emperor Carl opened the meeting. "Welcome lords, ladies, and representatives one and all to our Fall Council. I am especially pleased to see so many of you lords have gone ahead and are setting a fine example for the younger lords and so many of you elegantly dressed ladies as well. At our formal dinner, the lords, who are setting a good example for the rest of you, will sit at my table, along with your ladies. Also at that time, I will present you lords with a gold medal for your service to Tierra and the Imperial Court. It's my way of thanking you for making the sacrifice which will help lead our world into more prosperous times."

"For all the rest of you lords, ladies, nobles, and tower folk, please do not worry. Neither Empress Calandra nor I will be ordering you to have the modifications done. Rather, look to your peers and do what is best for our world. Now then, I would love to call your attention to the extremely beautiful new gown designs Carmen and Nita have created for us this fall. They and Empress Calandra, advisor Felisa, and our domestique helpers are modeling them for you. I'm told they will be ready for you ladies to purchase today. Never have I seen them looking so fabulous."

"Finally, we know what a hardship it is for many of you who live thousands of miles from Exchange City to get here to either purchase such elegant fashions or to avail yourselves of the body modifications. Hence, Carmen has asked me to announce to you all she is opening up branch offices of Elegant Fashions Inc in all eight tower cities, where you may not only more conveniently obtain the modifications, but also any and all their incredible apparel. She is doing her part to help us all. And as always, there is no charge at all for those modifications."

"Our world is at peace and I am pleased to announce to you all that this fall your empress and I have absolutely no new laws to decree. We are pleased so many of you are taking those positive steps to demonstrate to your subjects that you are tempering your *great* powers with physical restraints and you are doing your *part* to compromise on cultural traditions, blending east with west. So unless anyone has further business to bring forth, I declare the rest of the day to be a day of celebration and dance. I will personally dance with any lady who is wearing one of the new fetter gowns, while Empress Calandra will dance with you twelve lords who have followed our desires to temper our governing powers. Let the music begin."

"He's lost his ale belly, nearly thirty pounds! His physique reminds me of the Hector when I first met him, sleek and trim. Besides, he doesn't slouch anymore, perfect posture! The best part is he spends ten times as much time with me now than he used to," Miranda gabbed to several other ladies, who had quietly asked her about how the transformation had gone with Hector. Miranda had long ago resolved only to relay positive statements about her husband's situation. In her mind, there were enough other wrongs in the world than to add to them. Besides, she was a Valen and intended to set a good example herself.

Similarly, Hector was also quizzed by many of the other lords. "Oh, it does take an *enormous* amount of getting used to, but I've managed with my wife's constant help. I've lost so much weight — she's been hounding me for years to go on a diet. Well, that's handled. I can still ride my horse. It's just walking is pitifully slow and tricky, especially stairs, slopes, and on snow. My feet have so little surface area on the actual ground now. Yes, it's a huge bother, but it's not as bad as I had imagined it. Don't expect to do any fighting though," he added with a grin.

Hector also realized there was nothing to be gained by bitterly complaining about the modifications. Such would only polarize the other lords against the emperor, who could very well issue new laws they would have to follow, at least until Amy and Jan died. Besides, he was gaining valuable support among the Midlands lords and the Easterlings lords for Valen. Valen had been effectively blocked from active participation in the election of the emperor and empress. Now he took this opportunity to begin to mend fences, though he doubted much would come of it. His goal was to help further hobble all his future lords with whom he might have to battle when Valen could once again make its move to conquer Tierra.

Carmen, on the other hand, reveled at just how successful her long planned revenge now was. Her smile at the festivities was genuine, but not for the reasons others imagined.

Part II Beginnings of a New Era

Chapter 4 Turmoil Begins

"Is it really true?" Lord Rusden asked. It was mid-summer of 1243 and the fortieth Council of Lords, meeting this time in Rusden Castle to elect a new emperor for the third time. Emperor Carl and Empress Calandra served two terms, but were in their sixties and in failing health. They could not serve a third term. Lord Brom had just broken the news.

"Yes, it took some doing on my part, but I've confirmed it. Jan has died too. I saw her grave next to Amy's. Finally, we are done with their threat of meddling in our affairs," Lord Brom replied. Spontaneously, loud cheering from the one hundred men broke out. Finally, the lords were free to act without fear of a deadly reprisal from Amy or Jan. Their figurehead emperor was now really quite powerless. He didn't have the *mentales* gifts, and the Imperial Elite Guards had been systematically plundered of its key soldiers, who were offered far better paying jobs and promotions within the many other Elite Guards of the larger kingdoms. That plan from the First Council had worked to perfection.

Lord Rusden retook control of the meeting. "Okay, then our first order of business is to elect a new emperor and empress. We should follow the First Council's original plan, putting two children or babies on the throne and electing regents to oversee the throne for them."

They had insisted the two sons and one daughter of Carl and Calandra marry the children of their advisors: Carver and Ada, and Felisa and Aldo. Their domestique helpers, Dan and Elnora's children had been married to some of the children of their other advisors. That had happened around 1223. These young couples had then had children of their own, making Carl and Calandra proud grandparents. Of course, all their children had been appropriately body modified at an early age so there would be no doubt of their one day gaining the throne, or so Carl and Calandra were led to believe.

Last year the lords had ordered their grandchildren also marry and thus began the planned interbreeding of that whole line. all the lords knew full well what would eventually happen to that line in future generations, which was ultimately their aim, to end up with weak, sickly, morons.

"Lord Rusden, I believe the first action we must take is to make the emperor and empress line be hereditary in nature," Lord Wycombe interrupted him.

"Quite right, quite right! All in favor of that motion say aye," Lord Rusden called out, first apologetically and then in a commanding tone with the second sentence. The vote was unanimous. Following that, it didn't take them long to elect the new emperor and empress. They chose the two year old Leonard Christopher and the one year old Adelina Christopher to be their new emperor and empress. They also picked several other children to be their advisors and domestique helpers. They then issued orders to have the children body modified as appropriate. That is, the two advisors and the two new leaders would have their arms removed as prescribed by law. They all would undergo the remaining changes when they grew older.

Next, they voted to reduce the imperial taxes by fifty percent, retaining the other half for their own use. No one considered lowering the taxes on their own citizens. After all, starting now, they, the lords, would really be ruling Tierra, all except the Westerlings, which was still under the thumb of Lord Valen. Old wounds never die. None of the many Westerlings lords was present at these Lord Council meetings. For all his efforts, Lord Hector Valen had been unable to break through that long-standing barrier. Beyond these points, the many lords agreed upon nothing else. By dinnertime, the council had finished and Lord Rusden played host to a formal banquet and dance.

All of the many lords, ladies, advisors, and noblemen and women who attended now wore the pipe corsets and either toe shoes or toe boots. As Carmen had anticipated, peer pressure over a long time duration yielded results. In 1243, it was unthinkable for a lord or lady or one who held significant power or authority to not be so modified. While the men wore fitted tailored suits, the women all wore their arm-fetter-gowns made popular nearly forty years ago. Of note, their formal dances had also evolved, based upon the very small steps they could take. Interestingly enough, as a teen model,

Nita Valen had indeed set a new standard for the ladies, who now insisted they begin to wear the pipe corsets when they turned fourteen. As a result, more than half of the women present had the characteristic twelve-inch waistline that was all the rage at this time.

Carmen Valen turned fifty-eight this year, and it was widely known she now suffered from frail bones and the onset of dementia. In fact, she was really one hundred thirty-five years old and had already left her post as head of Elegant Fashions Inc, retiring to a suite in Valen Castle. Nita Valen now ran that entire enterprise from her office on the fourth floor of the Administration Building in Exchange City. Her company now had a field office in all towns with a population of five thousand or more, some twenty-five of them, though the actual body modifications were still limited to the dozen largest cities as well as at her office. She was now fifty-eight herself but like her mother, she'd begun using the alien rejuvenation machine and didn't look a day over twenty-five. Her figure was striking and she went to great pains to prominently display her twelve-inch waist.

Nita was as clever and bright as her grandmother had been. She realized early on if she formally married, then her husband would have a legitimate claim to her vast and wealthy company. Hence, she refused all offers of marriage and instead took lovers on the side. She now had a son and a daughter, the latter of which she was grooming to one day take over for herself. Her son had joined Valen's Elite Guards and was seldom around Exchange City or in her life. Her daughter, Inez, had just turned fourteen and underwent her own body modifications eagerly. She'd been waiting to have it done for several impatient years.

Noticeably absent were all the Valen lords of the Westerlings. They were holding their own private meeting around the same time in Valen Castle. Lord Paco Valen, thirty-five, and his wife, Adora, had taken over for Hector who had passed away some years back. "Yes, it is true. Emperor Jan has now passed away. Finally, we are free of Amy and Jan's constant meddling in our affairs. As you know, we are still not invited to join the councils of the Midlands and Easterlings. So be it. We can make a good guess at their current plans. They'll probably put one of the weakling children on the throne. Rumor has it they will then elect a regent to care for the throne until they come of age to rule at twenty. I bet they never make it to twenty-one, though." Many laughs and chuckles echoed around the Great Hall.

He went on, "Well, we can expect they will make new laws, but those laws will not be applied to us. They have no power over us. We are truly now independent once more!" Loud cheering resounded in the huge space.

"At this time, I will no longer pay any taxes to the Imperial Court. Instead, we will keep them for ourselves, using them to build up our armies." Again, his announcement met with broad approval from the many other local lords.

"Now then, to the real business at hand," Lord Valen spoke far more seriously. "Our spies tell us the former dead-zones around Oakham and Haverhills and even Bedwurth are now habitable once more. Our first order of business is to find a way to secure those foothill lands for ourselves. We once rightfully owned them before Amy kicked us out. It's time to reclaim our due!" The room exploded in wild cheering, for he had given them what they most wanted to hear.

Later he continued, "On the alien alliance front, I am pleased to report Adalina has succeeded in acquiring four alien engines we can modify to power our old air cars. Soon, we will have fast travel by air once more!" Again, the group of lords cheered. Amy had nullified their crystal networks used to power them when she took over control of Tierra over a half century ago. Now they would once more be able to take to the air.

Adalina had easily seduced Sector ID Minister Emeryk Donat and they had been married in 1206. Already they had a son and a daughter, who were thirty-five and thirty-three respectively and head blind. Antoni was now a field agent and on assignment somewhere in the Midlands. Dorita begged to emulate the gorgeous Nita and had undergone the modifications just as soon as she turned fourteen. She now worked at Elegant Fashions Inc and reported regularly to her father. Thus, far, Dorita had learned little of strategic importance, but she had high hopes she would one day learn something key from the many women who visited the huge store.

Both Adalina and Emeryk had used the rejuvenation machines and they both appeared still to be in their early thirties though they were in fact in their seventies. For the last forty years, Adalina had been quietly passing on information about the alien operations on Plateau Grado to first Hector and now Paco. She proved to be an effective lobbyist for Valen and had finally worked out a trade for the desperately needed engines. Valen paid for them by giving Emeryk an equal number of telepaths, who volunteered for the greater good of Valen. That Paco had also subtly implied their families might be harmed had also played a factor in their volunteering.

Lord Paco Valen then adjourned the meeting. Time for the fall feast, celebration, and dance. Like the other lords, here in Valen, the body modifications had also taken a strong hold on the men and women who held the real power. It was unseemly for a lady not to be so modified and not to wear the arm-fetter-gowns. Hector Valen and Miranda had indeed set a strong precedent in Valen. Like the Midlands, after some forty years their styles of dances had changed to accommodate the tiny steps the lords and ladies now took.

Two days after the Council of the Lords meeting, Lord Henry Bolivar of Brom summoned the Venerada of Brom Tower to his office suite inside Castle Brom. With the enforced separation of the ruling of the territory from the tower personnel, here at Brom, they handled it by designating the western manor house as the Territorial Administration building and the eastern manor house as the home of the tower personnel. The tower proper stood in the middle of the two huge buildings and had long corridors that connected them, making movement between them easy when the winter snow depth outside often reached twenty feet. Lord Henry was thirty with the family heritage black hair and eyes. His face was rectangular and his countenance was stern, he rarely smiled. He sat stiffly in his chair awaiting the arrival of the Venerada. Like nearly everyone here, he had undergone the body modifications when he was eighteen and was now comfortable with their restrictions on his movements.

Having just returned from the meeting, he knew he had to make a report to his venerada, but he also needed more information. Battles and wars were likely imminent. He needed to know the status of everything he could command. Already, he issued orders to his aides to report on the status of his Elite Guards, the Brom Army, and the Brom field *mentales* gifted he commanded. Now he needed to know the status of the Brom Tower personnel, who he could command, if war came to the Brom territories.

Ann Wycombe was now fifty-eight. She had taken over for her mother, Luisa Wycombe, some twenty years ago, but was now in the process of handing it over to her daughter Marisol Wycombe-Brom, twenty-eight. Both women had the katalyein gift and the physical deformity, which always accompanied it: they were born without arms. Because of their deformity, they alone of the lords and ladies and nobles were not expected to undergo the body modifications, but were expected to wear their fancy heels and their fetter-gowns to formal meetings. Since they could not put these on themselves, they had to have others dress them, which caused the long delay in their arrival at his office. Had they not had to dress formally, they'd have been they shortly after being summoned.

At last, Lord Henry heard their heel clicks on the stone floor and knew he had to open the door for them. In their gowns, they couldn't raise their feet high enough to slide the door latch. Slowly, he walked over to the door and opened it. "Welcome, please come on in and have a seat. You both look well today," he made a stab at pleasantries as he took nearly ten small steps back to get the door fully opened for them. They nodded and moved equally slowly over to the two chairs before his wide desk. Another ten steps and he got the door shut and began his long walk back to his seat. *With power must come restriction,* he repeated to himself.

"I've asked you here to brief you on what occurred at the Council of the Lords meeting." Quickly he outlined the relevant points emphasizing no longer would the emperor and empress wield any real power. The lords now took over ruling Tierra. "I fully expect there is going to be some minor skirmishes as the lords attempt to reclaim the dead-zones of Oakham, Haverhills, and Bedwurth. What we don't know is what Valen will now decide to do with their alien alliance. I am personally expecting trouble from them. Hence, I am taking stock of all our forces. I have my aides out now obtaining a full status report on our entire armed forces. Veneradas, what I need from you is a similar report on what tower forces I will have at my command should we be invaded or have to fight a battle. How soon can you provide me with a detailed report?"

Never having done such a report before, Marisol nodded to Ann to handle this one. Ann said calmly, "I think we can have that for you by tomorrow. Will that be soon enough?"

"Yes, excellent, excellent. Times have changed. Amy and Jan are no longer with us. I fear the long years of peace are swiftly coming to an end and we must be prepared once more," Lord Henry declared rather ominously.

"Surely you men won't start in fighting again? Lord help us if we're back to acid bombs, fire bombs, and chemical bombs," Venerada Ann replied growing rather annoyed. *Damn men anyway. Always having to fight.*

"Well, veneradas, as far north as we are, we are not likely to come under attack until most of the rest of the Midlands has fallen. Still, we need to be prepared for the worst and hope it doesn't happen. Well, that's all that I have, thank you for coming. Venerada, if I may have a private word with you before you leave?" Again, he rose carefully as he got his balance and began his slow walk to get the door for Venerada Ann. After Ann stepped outside, he shut the door, taking another ten small steps to do so. Venerada Marisol had followed Ann and was standing close to him.

"Venerada Marisol, as you probably know, my wife Isabel is pregnant again. I would dearly love to have you share my bed for a time; perhaps we could even have a fosterling. You know how I have long admired you," Lord Henry made his pitch. "Besides, Isabel would be grateful to you if you would satisfy my desires during this time when she cannot."

Damn, all he thinks about is sex. His own wife is pregnant and now he wants to impregnate me with his lust. She smiled and replied, "No, Henry. You know I have no love for you. Respect, yes. You are our lord, but I am not sexually attracted to you. Let's leave it at that. Please open the door for me, my lord."

Lord Henry hated to be turned down, especially by this beautiful, long black haired beauty. He knew he could just take her right her in his office, but the telepathic waves of rape would be picked up by all the *mentales* gifted in the whole castle and tower. He sighed, took another ten tiny steps to open the door for her, and watched her sexy form walk slowly through the door. Well, he tried, he justified to himself.

He wanted into my pants again, Marisol sent to a curious Ann. Both women chuckled to themselves as they made their long, slow walk back to their rooms to change. Sometime later, the two looked at their figures and their records. "We are down again," Marisol pointed out the rather obvious fact that during the last fifty years, the number of operational *Círculo de mentes* had dropped from five to three.

"The question is why and how. He's going to want to know that," Venerada Ann said with a sigh.

"As I see it, Lord Bolivar has been taking more and more of the *mentales* gifted into his services and not letting them join our tower. It's almost like he wants the tower to either fail or to be very weak, not like it used to be," Venerada Marisol declared. "Well, he did say wars or battles might be coming our way. I wonder how the other towers are holding out? Where are the figures for those?"

A bit of digging and the two found the latest figures, now several months old. To the northeast, Welsham Tower had one and a half circles. South of them, Northend Tower had two circles. East of them, Wye Tower had one and a half. Just south of Brom, Wyth Tower had two circles. Rusden Tower in the far south had two. Adelmira Tower in the Easterlings had one and a third, while Valen Tower in the Westerlings had one and a half. "Well, we are stronger than any other tower, but every tower has steadily been losing *mentales* gifted too. What is going on here? A systematic reduction in every tower?" Marisol asked.

Ann commented, "Imperial Circle still has just the one. No change there. Looks like all the lords have been systematically raiding their circles of qualified personnel."

"But can that account for such a drastic loss of us?" Marisol asked.

Ann rubbed her forehead with her toes, pondering another possibility. "You know, there is something else going on here. Many of our children are being born without our *mentales* gifts. Two of my own didn't have the gift. Fortunately, they were both boys and were happy joining the Elite Guards of our tower. I know others have had head blind children. Perhaps it is time we study this drop in the birth rate. I'll give this one to you, dear."

For the next week, Venerada Marisol visited all the women in Brom Tower who had given birth, asking how many had the gift and how many didn't. She soon modified her questions, adding a third. How many who had the gift but only marginally so, just enough to qualify as a *mentales* gifted? She then plotted the results versus ten-year intervals. Her graph covered nearly fifty years and the curve was shocking. Here in 1243, over half of the births in which the child should have a strong *mentales* gift had either none or a weak gift. They were rapidly losing their gifts! Shocking!

This time, she sent for Lord Henry, who had to make the long walk over to her office. Was there a bit of revenge in her request? Yes, he'd have to endure the many, many tiny steps this time, payback for his propositioning her. She grinned to herself as she waited, imagining the lord making his way towards her office, probably cursing her all the way. He knocked and she called out, "Come in Lord Bolivar." Panting heavily, he stepped inside, again taking ten steps just to close the door. He took the first available seat.

"This had better be good," he grumbled, still trying to catch his breath.

"It is." Marisol showed him all her findings.

"Well, on the positive side, we are in far better shape than the other towers."

"Yes, but on the down side, unless you have an alarming number of *mentales* gifted in your army special field units, we're in trouble. The birth rates are dropping at an alarming rate. If you extend the curve, there will be none in perhaps another fifty years, Lord Henry," Marisol pointed out what had shocked her the most.

"Now that you've called my attention to it, we are having more and more children who are head blind. I've got two of them myself," he said, rubbing his chin. Marisol saw he was indeed deeply concerned over this unexpected discovery. "Very well done and analyzed, Venerada Marisol. Very good work. Now it is up to me to see if this is holding true with the other lords and their towers. If so, we've got to figure out why and correct it!"

"I will look into it as well, my lord. We are both being affected by this. Anyway, there is your status report as you asked. Bit scary if you ask me," she stated what she felt. No sense trying to hide her fears from another telepath.

"Fine. Please, for now keep these findings to yourself and Ann. It will do no good to frighten the others," he requested. She agreed and he rose stiffly and began to make his slow exit. Marisol sensed that right now, he wished he had not gone along with all the other lords. These modifications were impeding his ability to react to serious situations. None had any idea that was the full intention of the retired Carmen Valen!

After Lord Bolivar left her office, Marisol had no idea how to proceed. All this graphing of statistics left her curious about another entirely different matter, one that involved herself. She was a katalyein and though she was only twenty-eight, she'd already worked her miracle on a dozen men and women whose *mentales* gifts were either wholly blocked or partially so. All but one had the same mental block: images that contained pain, unconsciousness, fear, terror, and horror of those who had died in Bettingham when Jarek dropped his Nuclear bomb on them and Amy Blackwell had made sure all *mentales* gifted felt the full experience of those who died there. Eleven times now, she'd had to help a person confront and re-experience this event.

However, that was not what bothered Marisol. Rather, in all eleven cases the person upon whom she was working her magic, her catalyst gift, had not even been born when that happened! "How can someone who wasn't even alive back then have that event blocking their *mentales* gifts?" Following her own methods once more, she interviewed all the surviving *katalyein* gifted women, tallying how many had this incident as the primary blockage and whether or not the person had even been alive when it happened.

When she looked at the final tallies, she was again shocked. Only a handful of others had different painful images, which comprised their blockage. The vast majority had this single event as the culprit. Further, only a very few were actually alive when it had happened! How then could someone who was not even born have a horrific incident like this blocking their *mentales* gifts? Or put another way, how could an awful incident which happened long before you were born or even conceived have a overwhelming effect on you? Marisol stared at her results dumbfounded. She had no explanation. Marisol now had two unsolvable problems with which to deal and few ideas of how actually to proceed with either one.

Lord Henry, on the other hand, had way too many problems to solve. After the long walk back to his office in the west wing of the manor house, based on what Venerada Marisol had told him, he knew he had to act immediately. Although he'd mentioned it in passing, neither Marisol nor Ann noticed its huge significance. *Well, that's why I am the Lord and not those in the tower! Who to send on this errand? Legally, I ought to send our Venerada, but hell, on this mission, she'd be a liability. They must be ones who I trust completely.*

Chapter 5 The Mission

"Okay, dad. You can count on me, I will not fail!" Major Howie Bolivar saluted Lord Henry, his father. Howie just turned forty. An above average soldier, he'd done everything he possibly could to make his father take note of him, to find him worthy. Yet, he always knew he wasn't; he was head blind, and that meant in this world he was a second-class citizen, hardly worthy of his father's respect. Often he'd cursed fate for making him the eldest son who could not inherit a damn thing because he lacked the precious *mentales* gifts of his parents. He'd worked harder than most trainees and later most soldiers, striving always to be the best, hoping somehow that would make his father accept him. Hostility and anger seethed within him, but he kept it buried, out of sight of the many telepaths around Brom Castle, at least he hoped so. He had the Westerlings black hair and eyes, just like his father and siblings, the former kept closely cropped, though in later years, he'd begun to grow an impressive moustache, feeling it added to his rapport with the many men under his command.

Now against all conceivable odds, his father, Lord Bolivar himself had just entrusted a vital mission to him and him alone. Perhaps all his laborious toil had not gone unnoticed after all. He strode tall out of his father's office, more confident than he'd ever been in his life. Now he would show Henry he was a force to be reckoned with.

As he strode quickly down the hall, his tall boot steps echoing from the walls, he considered his youngest brother, Andres, who he was told was coming along to do the actual work. *Andres, damn, why him and not me? Why does he get the mentales gift and not me?* he asked himself yet again. This was the unspoken sore spot that kept the two brothers so isolated from each other, not the nineteen years difference in their ages. There was no getting around the need to have *mentales* gifted along on this mission and he knew it. *Will he get all the honor, the acclaim, if we succeed?* He sighed, knowing the answer. This mission was really all about those mysterious crystals and powers, powers the gods had denied him. No, he was merely the soldier whose only real duty lay in getting Andres and his wife Rafaela there. They would do the real work and get the praised heaped upon them if they were successful. They, not he. He spat at an imaginary ant on the floor, an outlet for his inner anger.

It wasn't he hated his youngest brother. Andres was always kind to him, often going out of his way to attempt to make him comfortable at the family gatherings. No, it was only one thing, always that same damnable thing which kept him isolated from his own parents and many siblings. That cursed gift. Well, he'd show Henry he could be counted on, he wouldn't fail on his part. That would fall on Andres. *If perhaps he fails, then. . .* Quickly, he fought to squash that notion. *I can't hate Andres merely because of that quirk of fate. Hell, this mission is going to be a nightmare for him and for Rafaela. Well, it's their own damn fault. They had to go and look like dad and mom and all the leaders.* He discarded the immediate thought that one day Andres would be picked to become the next Lord of Brom. *Focus on what needs to be done.*

"Six men, winter mission, prepare for the worst," he said aloud. That action brought him out of his introversion. Action always did. Automatically, he began picking the best men in his command for this unique mission, along with the needed winter gear and supplies. Probably lots of rope and bags would be required and good mounts. *At least Andres and Rafaela can ride well enough. We'd not get far if we had to go by carriage.*

About this same time, Andres and Rafaela were in their suite changing and making preparations of their own. "My god, love, do you realize how critical this mission may well be?" the twenty-one year old asked his wife, as they were helping each other change out of their formal suit and gown. With her really long black hair, she did need his help getting into and out of the arm-fetter-gowns, which she was obligated to wear most of the time. Her hair fell to her rear, straight but thick, so typical of those in Brom who had the Westerlings heritage. Her face was round with bushy brows, thick lips, and high cheekbones. She was the eternal optimist. In a way hobbled as they were by the socially required body modifications they'd endured since turning fourteen, she had to be, he thought, as he lifted her hair up and helped her get one arm and then the other free of the dress' sleeves.

"Yes, super critical. After all, since Amy Blackwater outlawed all the giant crystal networks, everyone has forgotten even how to make them. Think of all the lost technology her decision has brought us? Now that it is finally safe to enter those three dead-zones, with some luck, you and I will be able to find some of those ancient crystals undamaged and bring them back with us. Think what that will mean? Dear, I've heard Venerada Marisol's dire predictions the *mentales* gifts might be dying out. If we get attacked again by Valen, these very crystals we are going to find could well save us all." Of course, she spoke as if they had already recovered them, bringing a smile to Andres' face.

His face was rectangular and pronounced, just as his father's, but with a vastly kinder countenance. His lips were such that he always seemed to be smiling, something Rafaela had fallen in love with. At last, down to their inner wear, their steeled pipe corsets were plainly visible as were their pronounced waists. Hers was twelve inches, but his two inches larger due to the fact his body had become more muscular than anticipated. Neither could bend except at their hips, which was one reason they always helped each other.

While she sat stiffly on the edge of their bed, Andres carefully bent his knees until they reached the floor. Efficiently, he removed her black patent toe shoes and then unfastened her pod-silk, black nylons and slipped heavier long cotton socks on her feet, fastening them to her eight garters for her. Then, he slipped her heavier leather knee-high toe boots on her.

While their toe boots would be quite warm and water resistant, there was very little surface area of the boot's bottoms touching the ground. The shape of the modified feet prohibited anything more than their toes lying parallel to the ground, that is, flat on the ground. As Andres began slipping Rafaela's boots on her feet, he got a good view of her ankles. When standing, their ankles and feet were stretched tight, pointing downward. Then, their toes bent at ninety-degrees to their pointed ankle as they slipped firmly into place in their boots. Their feet had been broken and reformed so that in this position, the back of their heels were straight above the ends of their toes, there at the sharp bend. The tiny spiked heel that subsequently did touch the ground was immediately behind the back edge of their toes. Thus, while standing on their feet, that is, their toes, their ankles were at their maximum extension. Yet, they could bend their ankles fully upwards, bringing their soles to a ninety-degree angle to the ground. In part, this was what forced them to take such tiny steps. Yet, that was not what Andres was thinking about; rather it was the surface area of the bottom of their toe shoes.

Andres and Rafaela both had gotten schooling from one of the Madiera women. Both had excelled in math, though Andres preferred calculus. He had gotten curious in their physics class when the subject of friction had been introduced and studied. Andres carefully measured the surface area of one of his soldier brother's boots and then compared them to his own toe boots. The results rather surprised him. His boots had one fifth of the surface area of his brother's and yet they originally wore the same size boots. He had learned friction forces were the product of the velocity and the coefficient of friction between the two surfaces. Leather on stone had a large coefficient, while leather on hard packed snow had a low coefficient, making the snow slippery. Yet, that coefficient was proportional to the surface area. He rightly concluded then his coefficient of friction in his toe boots was one fifth of regular boots.

"We have very little traction and slip and slide easily. In the snow, we'll have a very hard time keeping from slipping with every step," he'd announced to Rafaela one day while they were studying.

She had laughed and said, "That's obvious. I knew that from the first time I took one step outside in the winter." Trouble was, he thought, as he recalled their conversation some seven years ago, is we're going out there just as the winter snows are coming. As he slid her last boot securely into place, Rafaela picked up his thought, "Going to be hard on us in the snow, but we will find ways to manage, I'm sure." He grinned, she was always the eternal optimist.

"That's what I love about you." he gave her a kiss before they stiffly traded places and she helped him into his boots, removing his thin knee-high toe boots and thin socks, replacing them with similar heavier socks and his more rugged toe boots, quite similar to hers. He helped her rise and they set to work donning winter apparel. Each wore a heavy fleece lined leather pants, which ended just below the tops of their boots. Tall boots were necessary in the deep snow of the foothills winters, as were the oil soaked leather pants, which would keep the rain and melting snow from reaching their socks. They helped each other into a warm cotton top and then covered that with an oiled leather top. They laid out their heavy winter cloaks and gloves and set to work packing two bags with another complete set of clothing. During all this time, neither said a word about how terribly difficult and physically challenging this expedition would be on them. Their body modifications and fieldwork didn't mix. While both could ride well, the rest of what lay ahead of them neither chose to mention. This mission was too important for petty things like their restrictive modifications. They'd make do somehow.

Andres knew they couldn't be teleported there. It took an entire circle to perform that magic and even then, it would take several teleports to get them all there. That meant the circles would know about their secret mission and that meant Veneradas Ann and Marisol would know and would rightly claim and insist this was their area of specialty. They would be sending their people along, not themselves. No, Andres and Rafaela belonged to the Castle Elite Guards, whose loyalty was to Lord Bolivar, not the tower's venerada. It was imperative the veneradas not know anything about this mission, period. Hence, they'd have to get there and back on horseback, roughing it, as winter was about to begin. Still the criticalness, the vitalness of this mission, the prospect of recovering long lost crystal networks of unimaginable power drove them on.

As they prepared to leave their warm suite, he adjusted the fall of her long hair for her, kissing her gently on her neck. Then, with a saddle bag over one arm and holding onto each other with their other hand, the two began their slow walk out and down to the stables to meet up with his older brother and the men who would accompany them on the long trip. As they stepped outside into the chilly early October morning, they both sensed it would snow later on, probably in the early afternoon. They saw Major Howie adjusting a saddle, along with five other soldiers.

Andres knew his oldest brother well. He was a good fighter and a good judge of his men. His brother would only have chosen his best men for this dangerous trip. Because it took them a long time to cross the cobblestone courtyard, he noticed details ahead. They would be bringing along four packhorses carrying their supplies. Already those were waiting, tied to the long hitching rail. Howie was tightening the cinch on the mare Andres usually rode, though he'd not done all that much riding since his body modification when he turned fourteen. He longed for the saddle many times, but his duties as a *mentales* of the Brom Castle Elite Guards, the special strike force, usually prohibited it, until now that is. "We won't be a liability once we're on horseback," he whispered to Rafaela, who smiled. She was thinking the same thing, picking up some slight annoyance from the men at their impossibly slow walking.

"Ah there you two are. We need to get going soon, going to snow," Major Howie barked gruffly at them. He really didn't want to sound hostile, but his voice did so.

"I know. We can keep up once we're mounted, Major," Andres called out. He was wise enough to allow Howie the benefit of his hard-earned title and the respect of the men in his command. Howie's momentary eye contact told him Howie was thanking him for that bit of respect.

"I hope so," he replied more for his men than Andres and Rafaela. "Going to be a tough, dangerous trip, perhaps impossible for you two, but you know dad's orders. Mount up men." He handed the reins to Andres, but did help Rafaela mount her mare. Then he secured her saddlebag behind her saddle, while she moved her long hair out of the way, vowing to tie it up the first chance she got. They rode out single file right around ten that morning, with Major Howie riding point, followed by his right hand man. Then came the two gifted riders with the other four bringing up the rear, each leading a packhorse. Andres sensed his father's eyes watching them from his office window, but chose not to turn to see or wave. Howie was oblivious to it. Outside the large gates, they passed through the sprawling city. Men and women were going about their daily activities. Some called out their wares, but the riders ignored them, making their slow way through the sometimes crowded streets.

As they passed one particular stone home, a tall man stepped out. "Major Howie. Have a good one," the man called out. Howie smiled and gave him a salute. The man was a little younger than Howie and definitely not in the Elite Guards, but Andres couldn't place him, though he was sure he'd seen him around. With little else to do, he searched his memory and then remembered seeing him several times talking with his father. He was called Tim, if he recalled properly and wondered who he was. His house held no clues either. It was not a shop and had no sign, such as tailor or tinker or money changer. As they passed, he did note whoever he was, he had the gift. Their eyes met for a brief instant. Then Andres moved past the man.

Once free of the city, Major Howie picked up the pace considerably, in effect testing the skills of Andres and Rafaela in particular. He knew Andres probably could keep up, but he wasn't sure of her skill and mastery of riding. She did as well as Andres, and Major Howie soon relaxed his concern about this aspect. While riding, they would not be slowing them down. He begrudgingly gave them that point mentally, though both Andres and Rafaela picked up his unspoken thought.

Shortly after lunch, flakes began to fall. Around them, many brown leaves still clung to the oak trees, though the ground was littered with the leaves of many other types of trees. The thick patches of green, resinous pine trees stood in stark contrast. Ordinarily this would have been a picturesque ride through the rising and falling ridges of these high foothills of the Goza Mountains. However, today the huge significance of their mission overshadowed the late autumn beauty. Already some of the pods had begun closing on some of the groves of the nut trees they passed. Inside the silky pods, the fruits were kept from freezing and often the pods were harvested for the silk and turned into thread and cloth. They covered some thirty miles before making camp.

As Major Howie reined in and issued camping orders in a sheltered glen among a patch of resinous pines covered with a light snow, he turned to the two and spoke directly to them for the first time all day. "Amo Andres, Ama Rafaela, this is a secret mission. We don't dare stay at inns or take the more easily traveled paths through the central part of our kingdom. Wyth Tower might get alerted to what we are doing. So we are going to have to rough it and stay in tents."

He'd used their formal titles, irking Andres somewhat. "Hey big brother, on this trip, kill the Amo-Ama bit. We know this is a secret mission. I take it we'll be skirting the edge of the Goza all the way down, bypassing Wyth west of the city?" Howie nodded. "I thought so. Howie, we trust you to get us there safely. What has us worried is if dad thought of this, then the other Lords probably have too. We could well run into other scavengers from other towers. You get us there as fast as possible. I know we're hobbled up, but that can't be helped now."

"Why? Why, little brother, did you get yourself hobbled up like dad?" Howie finally asked what had bothered him for almost seven years. He saw no reason for it, yet all them had undergone the modifications at one time or another. His father never spoke to him about it; he didn't have the gift and wasn't involved — that was all Lord Bolivar had said to him about it.

"Temper our mighty powers with physical restraint. Well, that's the official reasoning as set forth by our illustrious emperor," Andres explained, realizing Howie had opened up to him a little. "All of us who have the gift and are in positions of power, especially dad and mom — we have to show everyone we accept restraints on our powers. Emperor's orders."

Howie scratched his head, confused. "All this you are all doing so people like me, us here, see you as humbled and restrained and tempered? That's what all that is about? How utterly ridiculous! No offense Andres, Rafaela, but dad's about as unrestrained, untempered man I've ever come across. You've hobbled yourselves for nothing, in my opinion. Well, it's done. I hope you can get by on this trip." He'd dismounted and now he held their horses so they could dismount as well. Both slipped on the snow-covered needles and took an awkward spill. Howie shook his head sadly, leading the three horses over to the hobble line on of his men had just finished stringing up between two pine trees. Already two others were pitching the tents, while another was setting a fire within a circle of stones he'd gathered. Yet another was getting ready to cook their supper in the dim twilight.

After helping each other back on their feet, Andres focused and activated his crystal. The cooking fire burst into roaring flames and several men flashed him a thank you smile. Still, that didn't alleviate the many ill looks Andres and Rafaela received from the men after their fall and subsequent precarious walk over to the campfire, where they carefully sat down out of the men's way. *They think we are a horrible liability to them on this trip*, Andres sent Rafaela.

You can't blame them for that. We are. Yet, if there are still active crystals within the ruins of the towers, they'll get themselves killed trying to recover them. We both know it takes a skilled technician to deal with those protective crystal networks. We'll manage. It's only our egos that were damaged by our spill just now, she sent back, optimistic as always. Andres smiled.

A half hour later, the cook handed out plates and cups to each and Major Howie chose to come and sit beside Andres and Rafaela. "Sorry about being so harsh with you." It was the best he could do for an apology and Andres accepted it.

"You've every right to be bothered about our limitations, Howie. If I were in your boots, I'd feel the same way. This promises to be a highly dangerous mission, especially if other lords have the same idea. If we find them, you know dad doesn't want you or your men to be killed by those ancient protective networks. It takes one of us to disarm them. You get us there and we'll do our part. Besides, Howie, I can't think of anyone I'd feel safer traveling with than you. You were always the best trail rider of all us kids." Howie briefly smiled for the first time.

After a long pause, Howie added, "We've grown apart these last seven years, haven't we?"

"Unfortunately, yes, big brother. All our training and then these body mods — well, let's just say I've been just as busy as you have been. Those Madiera women are incredibly smart. Too bad dad didn't send you to their school like he did me. You might have liked it," Andres commented.

"Ha! All that book learning? No, give me a good sword master and a Hilliard Heights stallion and turn me loose. All these men with us are the best, you know," Howie replied with pride.

"I know, Howie. You and they are the best." Howie smiled again and slapped his brother on his back lightly. "Best turn in soon. We'll be leaving at first light. Long way to go."

That was true. Some five hundred miles to the south lay the old dead-zone around what had been the town and tower of Bedwurth. Another five hundred miles further south lay the dead-zone around Haverhills, town and city. Still about the same distance south of there lay the dead-zone around Oakham. All three towns with their castle and tower had been destroyed by the Valen army as it slowly marched northward, conquering all in its path nearly a century ago. It had been their acid and chemical bombs, which had not only destroyed the structures, but had poisoned the very lands for about ten miles around them. Only now had Nature finally recovered from that devastation. Still, the dead-zone around the Nuclears destroyed Bettingham was still a death trap. The outer warning barrier markers put there by the aliens from the spaceport were still plainly visible. No one dared risk entering that area. Those who did either never came back out or if they did, they died shortly afterwards of a horrible rotting disease.

Howie pushed them hard, making over fifty miles through this rugged terrain each day. This close to the mountains, the jagged ridge lines were hard to cross, impossible by wagons. Even on horseback, they had carefully to pick out a path around some of the crests. Detouring onto the sides of mountains helped some, but each day, more snow came. Slowly the accumulation began to build up. Six days later, even the soldiers were slipping and sliding in the snow when they stopped to camp. At least, Howie and his men took pity on Andres and Rafaela. They simply couldn't stand or walk without help. Strong arms now accompanied their every move while dismounted.

On October 15, 1243, they reached the outskirts of the Bedwurth dead-zone. As they paused at the top of the ridge line above the north edge of the once lush valley, they could see the grey-brown ruins of the city below them, roughly in the center of the valley. Howie's keen eyes also saw scattered movements far below them. "Look there. Motion. We are not alone. Men, stay alert for trouble!" He nudged his horse forward and began the long descent into the dead-zone valley. Six inches of snow covered the valley, but low resinous pines grew here and there, proof that life was returning here at long last.

As the party drew close to the outskirts of the city, they spotted men, women, and children dressed in what could only be described as rags, poking about the ruins of the thousands of homes. "Scavengers," Howie called out. The homes were mere shells, like fractured teeth rising from the snow-covered ground. Some side walls were six feet tall, but most were barely two feet now. The destruction of Bedwurth had been total. As they entered the city, a dozen rag-clothed forms hastily ran off to the south and into patches of low resinous pines, seeking cover.

While Major Howie and his men no longer wore their fancy uniforms, they did carry their weapons. These poor locals wisely ran from the strangers, many carrying bulging sacks. "I bet they are scrounging for anything of value. Probably there are coins to be found," Howie called out to his men. Several chuckled. They rode on into the ghost town.

"My god!" Andres exclaimed. Human skeletons lay everywhere. A skull displaced from the rest of its bones lay in his path and he veered around it.

"They lay where they died," Howie commented grimly. "Look there, probably those were a garrison of soldiers." The bleached bones had rusting swords and daggers around them.

Andres counted twelve sets of remains fairly close together. Howie wisely neck reined his horse around them. In death, he respected his compatriots who had fought to defend Bedwurth from the invading Valen army.

A bit later, they approached the former castle outer walls. Great gaping holes clearly indicated where the powerful *mentales* spells had turned the great stone into mud. What had once been mighty fifteen-foot tall walls were now barely four foot tall misshapen mounds. Suddenly, a quarrel whizzed by his head. Instantly, he reacted. "Drop the pack horses. Charge these bastards!"

His six men dropped the reins of the packhorses, kicked their horses into a canter, and drew their swords, charging through the gaping hole in the crumbling castle walls. As Howie came galloping into what once had been the castle courtyard, six other men were hastily mounting their own horses. By the time that Andres and Rafaela got to the opening, they saw the ambushers galloping off out of a distant hole in the walls on the opposite side. Howie had reined in some distance ahead. He yelled back, "Robbers. Stay alert for more." His men had already begun to fan out, searching for more. They knew what they were doing, Andres observed.

The litter-strewn courtyard was filled with hoof prints and boot prints. The robbers had been systematically searching for anything of value, silver, gold, gems, jewelry. Old rusted weapons and skeletons lay everywhere, protruding above the layer of disturbed snow. Many of the bodies showed clearly the painful death that individual had suffered. Melted bones, fire-blackened bones were quite noticeable even to a casual observer. "My god!" Andres muttered. He felt sick, so did Rafaela.

Soon, Howie pronounced the area clear. "Nasty bunch of robbing bandits. They will not likely be back as long as we're here, but I'll post guards. Come on; let's find that tower."

"That must be the stables there and those the ruins of the manor house," Andres suggested looking at the destroyed remains and trying to visualize what this place once might have looked like before it had been destroyed by Valen's army nearly a century ago.

"Looks like the robbers were searching what's left of the manor house," Howie pointed out. "That would be the most likely place to look for anything of value that wasn't destroyed. In their hasty evacuation, the robbers had left a number of picks and shovels. They had been systematically excavating the manor house ruins. After some searching hindered by the snow cover, Andres finally found what had been their mighty *Círculo de la Torres*. He, Rafaela, and Howie edged their horses closer for a look.

"Well, there's not much chance of finding anything there," Andres commented sadly. "It looks like the whole tower fell in on itself." They were standing beside a pile of rubble and stone blocks nearly ten feet tall. Most of the lower rubble consisted of acid melted stone. "To find anything in there, we'd have to excavate the whole mess and that would take months."

"We don't have months," Howie pointed out the obvious.

"Nope. Besides, what we are looking for are the germanium crystals. Those would certainly have been crushed under the weight of all that stone falling upon them. While there might be some gold or silver buried in there, the crystals would not have survived the total collapse of the tower. We should move on, Howie," Andres suggested. "Do you agree, dear?" he asked Rafaela.

"He's right, Howie. Any crystals that were not destroyed earlier would have been smashed when the tower fell in on itself. No point in wasting time here," she replied.

"Okay, let dad know we're on our way to Haverhills now," Howie ordered. "Men, we're heading south again. Round up the pack horses."

Days later, they reached the northeastern edge of Plateau Grado, where the alien spaceport complex was located. Further south some twenty-five miles lay Exchange City. A well-traveled path led due south to the city. "We best bypass the city. Too many prying eyes there. You two will raise all sorts of eyebrows. After all, one rarely if ever sees your kind out riding like this," Howie attempted to say politely.

"I agree, Howie. Hobbled as we are, we can't go riding

through that city without drawing all manner of undo attention to ourselves," Andres replied, backing his brother's decision.

"Okay, I'll send two men in to lay in more supplies, while we skirt the city to the east. Looks like more snow is coming. Winter is really here now," Howie pointed out the obvious. Large flakes had begun to fall and the winds were starting to pick up some. He didn't have to say the obvious, that a blizzard was likely close at hand.

Although neither of the two *mentales* gifted could control the weather, Andres did send word to his father for a little such aid. The blizzard held off for several days, allowing them to reach Exchange City before it struck. The two who he'd sent into the city for supplies had barely returned, meeting up with them just east and south of the city when the stalled blizzard finally struck.

Although they were within a hundred miles of their next destination, the winds picked up blowing the heavy snow nearly horizontal. In such a whiteout, all travel was impossible in this rugged terrain. They had no choice but to hold up and wait it out in their tents, piling on all the blankets they had to stay warm. No one bothered even to attempt to cook.

A day later, the sun shone brightly, but Andres and Rafaela could not get out of their tent. It was buried. Soon, they heard Howie and another man digging and at last, Howie's frosty breath entered their tent. "Ah, there you are, little brother. Are you two all right?" His face did reflect his worry, though.

"Fine, but cold and starving. Thanks. How bad is it?" Andres asked.

A bit later, his brother holding him upright, Andres looked around. Their many tents had been completely covered, but the soldiers had dug themselves out and were assisting the horses now. "Get some firewood and we'll get us a fire going," he said. Howie nodded and helped Rafaela to her feet.

"You two stay put then." He headed off barking orders for firewood and their cook. An hour later, the nine greedily gulped down the hot stew. Then, they took their time sipping the strong black tea.

"Going to be slower going until we get higher and off this valley slope," Howie notified them.

Although the two tried to walk through the deep snow towards their horses as camp was broken, neither could, falling down easily. Howie carried each in turn and sat them on their horses, much to their embarrassment. Howie just laughed at them.

"Well, we are pretty pathetic, Howie," Andres admitted sheepishly.

"Well, you are restrained and tempered," Howie continued to laugh and his men chuckled along with him, releasing their tensions too.

The 26th of October, they finally reached the dead-zone around what had been Haverhills. Here the snow depth was only a foot, though drifts were considerably higher. Again, they flushed a number of rag-tag scavengers from the edges of the city ruins. "Poor folks just trying to find stuff to stay alive," Howie commented as they uniformly fled across the snowfields as the mounted riders approached.

"Look, riders have been here before us," one of his men pointed out. Howie estimated perhaps a dozen horses had been through here not too long ago. He ordered two men to circle wide and act as lookouts, while he led the rest down into the heart of the city. Like Bedwurth, the outer walls were crumbled, as were the remnant of homes. From the footprints in the snow, the scavengers had been going from place to place digging for treasure. Andres wondered if they really found anything of value. Here and there, bleached bones protruded above the snow pack, a subtle reminder thousands had died here and their remains were just beneath the pure white cover.

This time, luck was with them. They found much of the old *Círculo de la Torres* still standing, though its top stories had collapsed. Howie pushed on the remnants of the main wooden doors and they crumbled into a dust cloud, causing him to endure a fit of coughing. He then held a lantern high and looked inside.

"The wooden floors have fallen and possibly a story or two of the top is missing. There is still a usable but littered stone stairway leading down, but it's a mess down there. Come have a peak, Andres," Howie called out. Then he remembered neither could walk in this deep snow and he proceeded again to carry them to the door, handing them his lantern. "Well, worth checking?" he asked, hopefully.

"It's a good thing you didn't try to enter, Howie. Look down there. One of those scavengers tried it and paid dearly for it. Looks like the tower's protective networks are still operational after all these years," Andres pointed to the recently killed man whose corpse lay on the steps a little ways down.

"That's a good sign, isn't it?" Howie asked, clearly out of his league.

"Yes, big brother, it is. If the defense network is still operational, we could well find what we're after down there in the rubble. The steps begin solid enough, but they are snow covered. About fifteen feet down, a section of the steps has been destroyed. We need to get down there with shovels and sacks."

"Okay, we'll break out the ropes and lower you two down there," Howie replied.

An hour later, six ropes had been lowered into the gaping hole. Four held lanterns. Already a large bag and some shovels had been lowered and were waiting them on the rubble pile below. Slowly, the men began lowering Andres and Rafaela into the tower. At first, they attempted to move down the steps, supported by the ropes. This enabled them to reach the protective network of crystals, a dozen set into the walls. They disarmed four of these small ones, enough so they could continue down. The going was treacherous and soon they merely allowed themselves to be lowered the remainder of the way.

After untying themselves, they began to very carefully explore the ruins. The wooden flooring and support timbers were totally rotten and crumbled when they touched them with their toes. "I sense immense power down here," Rafaela whispered, a little intimidated by some of the skeletons lying scattered here and there, some partially protruding from the rotted wood.

"Me too. Must be some of those power crystals. Start

searching, dear. We could be onto the find of the century," Andres whispered back.

"Find anything?" Howie yelled down to them.

"Not yet, but it is very hopeful. We'll yell when we have something." Howie backed away from the entrance, leaving the two *mentales* gifted to do their work. Methodically, the two began their search.

A half hour later, Rafaela exclaimed, "Andres! Here, look at this one!" She had found a giant nine-inch germanium crystal. It was still glowing blue, meaning it was still active!

"Careful! Don't touch it. Let's get a pod-silk cover over it so we can handle it," Andres said. Moving slowly and carefully, he brought a large pod-silk blanket over to her and she supported him as he carefully knelt down before it. Once on his knees, he covered the crystal and wrapped it up, stuffing it into the large bag. Then, holding onto her hand, he stiffly got back to his feet, toes to be exact. They continued their search.

Time passed and Howie continued to check on them. He was very pleased when Andres yelled up they had indeed found one of the giant crystals. Then, he found another. Again, working together to support each other, Andres got that one into the bag.

Continuing their search, time passed them by. Then she discovered a third crystal and they repeated the process, storing that one with the other two. "Dad was right. Some of the ancient power crystals have survived!" Andres said enthusiastically. "I wonder if there are more?" They continued looking. While they found many smaller networks, some even identifiable as belonging to a comm network, they found no more large ones. They did, however, find the busted shards of several others.

Isolated as they were some thirty feet below ground, they didn't hear the battle taking place above them, not until it was too late. In the middle of the afternoon, Howie's lookouts spotted a number of soldiers coming their way. They took cover and did the best to hide their horses. However, with the foot of snow on the ground, that did little to hide their presence. Before long the column of soldiers rode up to where they were attempting to hide behind some ruins of the old manor house.

Although outnumbered two to one, Howie and his men fought bravely. The sounds of sword upon sword broke the stillness of this graveyard. all the soldiers were handicapped fighting in the deep snow. Worse, as they fought and packed the snow down, their footing became even more treacherous. By the time the skirmish ended, Howie and his men had been slain, but not before they took an equal number of the enemy soldiers with them.

"What's that? Swords? A battle?" Rafaela whispered. Both stopped poking around and listened.

"God, Howie's under attack up there. We have to help him," Andres whispered frantically.

"How? We can't get back up there unless they pull us up. We're trapped down here!" she answered, fear growing in her mind and body.

"Howie's a trained soldier, he can handle himself," Rafaela whispered a bit later, trying to be optimistic and quell her nervous stomach.

A few muffled moans later and all was silent for some time. Neither dared call out. If Howie was alive, he'd contact them. All they could do is wait, hope, and pray. Both felt quite helpless, though they knew realistically they'd be not of much use top side unless they knelt on the ground.

Then a face appeared above them, peering down at them. A strange face. Their hearts sank when he laughed and spoke. He used the Westerlings dialect. "Well, well, what do we have down there? A couple of Midlands rats I see."

They didn't reply, but heard another voice saying, "Ask them what they've found down there." It was a barked order, not a request, which suggested to the two the man above them was just a soldier, most likely from their archenemy, Valen Tower!

Then both felt the touch of another *mentales* mind. They had only a split second to throw up their mental barriers before their enemy attacked their minds with psi powers. Valiantly the two fought back, but quickly, both slumped unconscious to the litter-strewn floor.

They didn't see a number of men climbing down to

them. They didn't see their bodies being hauled up like two potato sacks, along with their bag of three giant crystals. Neither did they see the other completing a thorough search of the tower's remains, finding nothing more. Topside, they didn't see the dead bodies being dragged off to one side, lying in a line on the snow, red streaks seeping across the white ground.

Around suppertime, just as the light was failing, both awoke. "Ah, awake at last. You have been captured by the First Commando Squad of Valen Castle. I am Major Hernandez. Thank you for doing our job for us. The crystals will ensure our future victory over you. What are your names and who do you serve?"

Andres' head was fuzzy. His arms ached at his shoulders and were somehow tied behind him. He was sitting up leaning against what had been the side of the tower. Rafaela was sitting beside him. Something was in his mouth. Metal. A metal ring held his mouth wide open; drool had been dripping down his face and freezing solid below his chin like some icicle. There was an awful taste in his mouth and he came fully alert as he recognized it: *bacal* tea!

They had forced that into him while he was unconscious. That herb totally nullified his psi powers. He was head blind. Normally, the tea was used to assist those with Verge Sickness, but it also rendered captured enemy *mentales* gifted null and void.

Two other *mentales* gifted men, hobbled as he was and holding onto each other to keep their balance on the now exceedingly slippery snow pack, slowly moved into view. "Hernandez, allow us. I am Pino and you are our captives. It seems we underestimated you Midlands rats. Thank you for finding the crystals for us. Now then as you can tell, you have been filled with *bacal* so you cannot harm us. Just so you know, escape is impossible. We tied ropes to your arms behind your back and drew your elbows together back there quite tightly. A metal lock now holds your elbows pinned tightly together. Another metal lock holds your hands together as well and we've got your hands tied tightly directly behind your back so you can't move them from side to side. We've got O-rings in your mouths so we can pour in the *bacal* tea at prescribed times to keep you both head blind. In short, you two are our prisoners."

"Now then I want you both to think of what tower sent you? Where are you from? What lord sent you here? Who is behind this? Come on, think of them," Pino badgered the two over and over. After that didn't work, he then said, "Well, your soldiers there died bravely."

Howie! Andres looked and saw the line of a dozen men, recognizing his brother. Mentally he cursed Pino and these evil men.

"Ah, now we are getting somewhere. Howie, eh? Meant something to you did he? Come on think. What tower sent you? Where are you from? What lord sent you here? Who is behind this? Come on, think of them," he badgered them once more. "Ah, brother perhaps. Yes, brother he was. Come on what's the rest of it?" Both strained to keep all thoughts out of their minds.

"Okay then enough for now. It's suppertime. We'll feed you soon. Then tomorrow, we're on the trail again. Afraid you'll have to tag along with us until we complete our mission."

A while later, a man came by with a bowl of warm liquid soup. Andres hoped he'd remove the O-ring so he would rest his acing jaws, but no. The man tipped him over onto his side and slid the bowl close to his mouth. "There, lap it up like the dog you are!" He laughed and did the same to Rafaela. They were starving, not having eaten since breakfast and they began using their tongues to lap up the warm mashed stew. Sometime later two men came by with the dreaded tea. Andres did his best to protest, but he was wholly immobile. They stuck a funnel into his O-ring and poured the dosage of tea into it. Gagging, he was forced to swallow most of it. Then, they did the same thing to Rafaela. Later, the two men came over to them and laid out a bedroll, placed each on one, and covered them up with a large pile of blankets. One said, "We don't want our prisoners to freeze to death, now do we?" He laughed as he left them.

Their arms and shoulders ached and throbbed

mercilessly, but neither could move their arms in the slightest. It felt like his arms were being pulled from their sockets. His elbows touched each other behind his back. Yet, so tight were their bindings, neither could move any part of their arms, just their fingers, which had long ago gone numb on them. Eventually both fell into an ill sleep, roused roughly in the morning.

At least their captives were kind enough to help them relieve themselves before forcing them to lap up a breakfast and before pouring another large helping of *bacal* tea into their mouths. Then they were lifted up and sat onto a pair of horses. Andres was sharp enough to watch for his precious bag of crystals and was relieved to see it was tied to the back of the horse he was riding. Then the group of twelve Valen survivors headed off southward.

Chapter 6 Captured and the Underground

They rode on all that day, stopping only to relieve themselves and to have lunch, with more of the debilitating tea poured into their mouths. At least the aching and throbbing of his shoulders and arms had vanished, though Andres and Rafaela worried this might not be a good thing. Neither knew then that already their fingers had frozen.

Each day was much like the previous for the two captives. They were roused at dawn, forced to use their tongues to lap up slop called food, drowned in *bacal* tea, then forced to ride until near dark, only to be cast upon the ground once more. After the second day of this, Pino ceased trying to find out who they were and where they came from. Further, Andres began to realize these men were unfamiliar with the land around here. Frequently, they came to an unpassable ridge line and were forced to spend hours finding a way around it.

On the fourth day, another blizzard struck. This time, the two were stuffed into a tent before being heavily covered up, and they managed to keep from freezing. Andres and Rafaela attempted to keep track of the days and an estimate of how far they had come. Soon, both realized they were likely heading for the dead-zone around Oakham!

On the 9th of November, they arrived at that dead-zone, which was buried beneath three feet of snow with drifts as tall as ten feet. It was bitterly cold this high in the foothills. Andres noted unlike the other two dead-zones, there were no footprints. The snow pack was virgin; they were the only ones here. No one in their right mind would be here scavenging. The snow was too deep and would only get deeper as the winter and frigid temperatures arrived full-steam.

He knew Valen was also after these ancient crystals of immense power. Now they had the three he and Rafaela had found. Would they find more here he wondered? As they finally found the remains of Oakham Tower, his heart sank.

Part of the tower still stood, similar to Haverhills. In all likelihood, there would be more of those crystals found and taken to Valen! He was powerless to stop them or free himself. At least he no longer felt his arms and hands. The awful throbbing pains had gone away. They were wholly numb.

Rafaela likewise could no longer feel her arms, but she held out hope now they'd arrived at Oakham. Perhaps their *mentales* gifted would get so involved with their searching they'd forget to give her the next dose of *bacal* tea. Then she could act, she could contact Lord Henry, they could be rescued and the crystals recovered. She hoped so anyway and kept her spirits up and her eyes open for that lone chance.

Andres took the time to gauge accurately the strength of this Valen force. There were three *mentales* among them, apparently their leaders. These three men had also been body modified as he was. Likewise, they were having a terrible time even moving in the deep snow. Nine were mere soldiers, much as his own party had with them. Pino seemed to be their leader. He watched, as the three had to have the others carry them over to the tower, just as his brother had carried them. Once there, they seemed absorbed in a discussion on how to proceed. Meanwhile the nine began to set up camp, packing down the snow and forming shelters by making use of the remnants of the stone walls. This gave them shelter from the whipping winds and drifting snow. All around him, the scene seemed surreal, like something out of a nightmare dream from which he could not awaken.

Sometime later, a few of the men emulated what they'd done up at Haverhills. Lanterns were lowered and then digging equipment. Finally, the three *mentales* gifted were lowered into the ruins of the tower. Any hope they'd forget about the *bacal* tea vanished. As soon as the campfire was crackling, burning the resinous pine logs, their cook prepared that hideous drink. Again, he used his funnel to force it down their throats. The O-rings were working all too well. Evidently, these Valen men knew how to keep enemy *mentales* gifted under total control. His heart sank. For once so did Rafaela's, as she nearly choked on the tea poured into her mouth.

Now sitting with their backs against a stone wall, the

two could see the remains of the tower. Near dusk, the men hauled the three out of the basement of the tower. They were filthy but both noticed neither carried anything out with them. So far, they had not found any crystals, which encouraged the two, if only slightly.

"We will keep digging through the rubble. I can sense there are some there. It's just there is so much rubble in the way," Andres overheard Pino explaining to his men. Shortly, rough hands shoved him onto his side and slid a plate of liquid slop before his mouth. Half-starved, he began lapping it with his tongue. He heard Rafaela doing the same behind him.

The next morning, Pino dropped by to gloat a little. "Well, whoever you are, you will be glad to know we've sensed more of those power crystals down there. With luck, today we will find them and then be on our way back to Valen. Once we get you there, our circles will make you tell all. If you are very lucky, they'll then kill you humanely." He laughed wickedly, motioning for one of his men to come and carry him away.

Well, they can't walk at all either. They are as hobbled as we are, that's something, Rafaela attempted to think of anything positive. So much was negative now. However, her spirits didn't rise at all. She felt cold all over now. Perhaps, she thought, she might freeze to death first.

Late that afternoon, one of the men began hauling up bags. From their conversations, Andres knew they'd found some more of the power crystals and his heart sank even further. His teeth would have chattered if they could have; his body was slowly freezing to death as well. All had been in vain. Their archenemy had all the ancient crystals and was certain to soon use them against the Midlands, probably come spring. All was lost, terribly, horribly so. His brother lay dead. His vital mission, a total, abysmal failure. His tears froze on his cheeks.

Another bag was hauled up, occupying the attention of two of the nine men. Two were stomping their feet trying to stay warm while standing watch over the shell of what had been Oakham Castle. Quite why they did so eluded Andres. They'd seen no one for days now, not since that last blizzard had increased the snow pack to over three feet.

Just then, Andres saw something utterly freakish. He blinked his eyes in utter disbelief. Two great tendrils of the very earth and stone seemed to thrust up out of the deep snow on either side of one of the guards. Then the earth completely engulfed him, muffling his startled cries. The mound of earth then slumped back down, leaving what appeared to be more like a grave. Rafaela sitting to his right made a noise and tried to nudge him. He turned his head and saw a similar mound of earth where the other guard had been stamping his feet. What in the world was going on he wondered.

The two men carried the two bags over to where Andres was lying, setting them down beside his own precious bag with its three crystals. Then they headed to the bonfire to warm their hands before trying to pull their three men up from the basement of the tower. As the two stared at the seven men surrounding the fire, suddenly the fire swelled up, as if someone had poured a mountain of lantern oil on it! Flames engulfed all seven men, setting their heavy winter clothing ablaze! They dropped to the ground and rolled, trying to put the fires out; clouds of steam from the snow rose around them, creating yet another surreal scene from some horrid nightmare. The two stared in total disbelief!

Just then, they saw movement to their left. A second later, they saw four running forms heading to the rolling mass of men. Two had swords drawn. *Chop them! Chop them!* Andres thought, releasing his pent up anger. Head blind as he was, he knew whoever these people were, they couldn't hear him. Swiftly, he got his wish. One by one, killing strokes were delivered until seven smoldering forms remained. The four then dashed on towards the remains of the tower. Andres and Rafaela turned their heads to see, wanting to warn them *mentales* gifted were down there, but were unable to do so.

Then both saw an even more shocking sight. Two of them were women, covered with a heavy cloak much as Andres and Rafaela wore. However, as they reached the tower, their right arms came out from under their cloaks, revealing no hands at all! They saw an enormous blaze seem to flow from one woman's arm, straight into the tower. They heard screams of pain and shock coming from the three men far below ground. Even more shocking, from the other woman's handless arm, something brown seemed to come forth. Then the very ground on which the ruins stood seemed to flow up as if it was water! It settled back raising an enormous cloud of dust in its wake. When the dust cleared, all that remained was a dirt mound. Their three torturers were buried beneath that huge mound! Never had the two seen such a display of raw powers. Who were these four? Were they next? Shivering from the cold, Andres could do nothing about it. He was helpless to save his wife or himself.

At last satisfied the threat had been handled, the four heavily cloaked individuals trudged through the snow over to the two captives, sitting with their backs against a ruined castle wall. Andres tried to make a sound through the O-ring, but it sounded more like a gurgle than anything intelligible. As the four drew closer, one threw his hood back. Recognition came instantly! It was that same man they'd seen watching them ride through the streets of Brom! "Get those gags off of them," he said calmly. He and the other man knelt and began unfastening the leather bindings that held the rings firmly in place.

Free of it at last, Andres tried to speak, but his teeth chattered so badly he could hardly be understood and gave up. Their strong hands lifted them up and all four looked at their arm bindings. "Damn! We've got to get them back fast! Grab the bags of crystals. I'll contact home base," the one he'd recognized ordered.

One of the women said, "What about the horses and gear?"

"We'll send someone after them later. These two won't have a chance if we don't move fast," he answered her. Rafaela saw both men had yellow eyes with brown spots and knew they had the gift. Quite why they were not hobbled, she didn't know. The women had brown and hazel eyes, not *mentales*, yet they'd commanded huge powers. Then she put two and two together. *These women must be from Madiera, the women with elemental powers. My god, they have huge powers!*

The man said, "Relax. We are about to teleport you to safety. You ready?" The other three nodded, bags in hand.

Andres felt the touch of psi powers on his mind and the frozen wasteland vanished. He was standing inside a warm room, probably a basement. A coal furnace was blazing nearby. Strong arms kept him from falling and then carried him over to the heat. Rafaela was right beside him, shivering wildly too.

As warmth returned, he stopped shivering. "Who are you? Thank you for saving us. I am Amo Andres Bolivar, my wife, Ama Rafaela. Where are we?"

"Tim Bellweather, my wife, Petrona. Ben Blackwater, his wife Elana. You are in the Underground at the moment, while we try to save your lives if we can. Okay, they're warm enough. Let's get them unbundled and see how bad it is."

"Don't let go. I don't think I can stand just yet," Andres said nervously. "How bad is what?"

Facing him, Petrona stuck her handless arm beneath his tied arms supporting him, while Tim began removing his mountain of cloaks and clothing. At last, he had all the winter cloaks and wrappings off of him, revealing the metal clamps at his elbows and hands. At his side, the other pair did the same for Rafaela. "My god!" Petrona exclaimed, shocked with what she saw.

"What? What?" Andres cried out, becoming rather sick at his stomach.

"Be brave, Andres, Rafaela. Since you can't see yourself, I will pivot you so you can see the other. You look pretty much the same. Worse, I can't see any easy way to remove these bindings. Damn those Valen soldiers anyway."

As Andres finally saw Rafaela's arms, he gagged. Her fingers were black and frozen solid. Worse, the blackness extended up her arms. Ben carefully cut away her sleeves, exposing the damage, which lightened a little bit as it approached her shoulders. After pivoting both, Rafaela gagged and dry heaved a little, but Ben held her securely.

"Well, there you have it. Grim. Even if we can somehow get these metal clamps off you, your arms are mostly frozen. There is no way to save them. The real question is can we even save you? If we warm them up, the poison will rapidly kill you, so we have to act now and swiftly," Tim explained. "So I ask you now, do you want to live or die?"

"Live, live. Rafaela, we want to live." She agreed.

"Okay, then so be it. You've made your decision. Ben, carry her. I'll get him. To the medical machines fast!" Strong arms picked him up and he was carried into the next room, filled with all sorts of alien machines, none of which he'd ever seen, save the one, the medical machine. It looked an awful lot like the very machine, which had made his body modifications some seven years before.

He sat on the machine, and the machine enclosed him, wrapping him like a blanket. Nearby, Rafaela was also enclosed in the second machine. Both men began working the many menus, while the two women looked over their shoulders.

Shortly, Tim spoke. "Okay, it says you have an eighty-five percent chance of surviving this. You will be unconscious for a time. Any last words in case the worst happens?"

"Rafaela, I love you. Please take the crystals to Lord Henry Bolivar. I'm his son. Don't let them fall into Valen's hands. They'll use them to destroy the Midlands."

"I love you too, Andres," she added. Then both slipped into a quiet, peaceful unconsciousness.

Sometime later, Petrona said, "Well, they survived, Tim, but now what? He's the lord's son. We aren't going to hand over the crystals are we?"

"Never. I checked, love. Lord Bolivar and his whole staff believe Andres is dead along with his brother Major Howie and Rafaela too. For now, we'll leave it that way. Now what? That is the big question. Frankly, I don't know. Let's see how they handle it when they wake up. Meanwhile, we ought to bathe them and get them cleaned up. Bet you wish you had your bots now, love."

She grinned. "That's a thing of the distant past. You'll have to handle their pipe corsets though. I can't." The four undressed the two and bathed them, for both really needed that. Then Tim and Ben got them partially dressed while the two women worked on Rafaela's long hair. They found warm, thick pants for the two and clean, long socks and got them on and then their toe boots. They left their shirts off on purpose, though the two women found a chemise that rather fit Rafaela so her bosom was at least covered, leaving her shoulders bare. All knew the first thing the two had to face was the loss of their arms. It had been a very close call. Tim guessed that another day or two and their lives could not have been saved. They might have made it back to Valen for questioning, but they'd die as soon as their bodies truly warmed up.

Sometime later, both woke up around the same time, thanks to the uniformity of the two medical machines. Both were lying on soft beds beside each other. Rafaela blinked and realized she was alive. She rolled her head from side to side and spotted Andres next to her. He too was struggling to regain consciousness. "Andres! We are alive!" she called out, faintly. He rolled his head towards her and smiled, greatly relieved, but only for a moment.

Almost simultaneously, their joy at being alive changed to one of complete shock. They saw each other had no arms left at all. Then they glanced down at their own shoulders and shrieked involuntarily. At once Tim and Petrona came hastily into the room.

"Well, the good news is we managed to save your lives as you asked. There was a cost, though, as you have seen," Tim said calmly, as their shrieks subsided and shock set in as he'd expected. "You both saw the condition of each other's arms, so deep down you know what had to be done to save your lives. I am going to adjust your bodies a little to keep the shock down, if you don't mind." His crystal began glowing and one by one, he did just that. Their *mentales* gifts had returned. While they were unconscious, the effects of the tea had worn off. Thus, they instantly knew what was happening and began to feel their physical shock die down, their bodies relaxing once more.

"There you go. Let's get you sitting up, shall we?" Tim said calmly.

"Thanks, I was really going into shock there," Andres said softly. "You okay, love?"

"Bit shaky, but okay. We are alive and that's what counts," Rafaela's eternal optimism returned, though a bit shakily. "I am very hungry, pretty weak I think."

Petrona said, "Supper is waiting you. Come on; let's get

you both fed."

The two rose very carefully to their feet. "God, this is truly scary," Rafaela whispered. "We can't catch ourselves if we fall or help each other like we always did."

"Scary is right. Maybe we made the wrong decision," he whispered back.

"No, we are alive. That's what is important right now. It's just scary." She again attempted to sound optimistic, but wondered if maybe he was right after all. Slowly they made their way hesitantly, as the two directed them into another room where the table was set. The rich aroma of roast rabbit made their mouths water. Once seated, Petrona sat beside Rafaela while Elana sat beside Andres, preparing to feed them.

"But you don't have any hands, Petrona. How can you feed us?" Rafaela whispered, thinking there had been a slight mistake in seating.

She laughed, "The guys have made us a whole lot of slip-on extensions. We do most everything for ourselves. See," she slipped her right arm into a metal sleeve. Attached to the other end was a fork. "I admit it is a strange way to eat, but we manage. Open wide."

"I'm ravenous, but that's way too much food for either of us to eat at one time," she explained. Slowly the two ate solid food at long last. Sometime later, they finished up with hot tea.

"Okay, how do you feel now?" Tim asked.

"Full for the first time. That was awful, licking up the slop they fed us. Of course, that was a clever move with the O-rings. They used a funnel and poured the *bacal* tea into us and we had no choice but to drink it. That was clever," Andres admitted.

"Okay then. First, don't try to telepathically communicate to your parents or others. At this point Lord Henry and the others believe you both are dead too. They know your brother Major Howie is dead and they tried for days to contact you. The *bacal* prevented their contact, and they now believe you both died as well."

"Shouldn't we let them know otherwise?" Andres asked, worriedly.

"Let us talk this all through first. You have some tough choices ahead of you, both of you. I have those ancient power crystals stored in a safe place where no one can find them and use them to harm others. I am the son of Emperor Jan and Ben is the son of Empress Amy. We are sworn to continue to help keep peace on Tierra, following in their footsteps so to speak. We are part of a secret group called the Underground. Our job is to prevent the aliens from executing new plots against us all and to prevent further horrors that were seen back in the Dark Ages. We are very grateful for your timely recovery of those ancient crystals. Our mothers destroyed all the active ones, but missed these since they were buried in the dead-zones. Thanks to the both of you, no one will get their hands on them and use them to destroy others. Well done on that!"

"But we were supposed to get them for Brom and Lord Henry," Andres replied.

"We know that. We know all about your mission, almost from the moment Lord Henry gave it to you. You don't think Lord Henry would use them to kill others if you were attacked?"

"Of course he would. That's the whole point of them — a deterrent to keep Valen from attacking us and to ensure we can beat them if they should attack us," Andres answered.

"You just said it. Think of the past. When has the ultimate weapon ever brought peace? Haven't they always eventually end up being used to wipe out entire cities? You just visited three of them. No, he'd use it and many would suffer horribly. There has to be other ways to keep the peace and keep Valen from attacking the Midlands," Tim countered.

Rafaela pointed out, "He's right you know. They thought those would be deterrents, even the air cars, but they got perverted and used in the wars."

Tim continued, "So we have been monitoring your progress."

"How?" Andres asked.

"We have tapped into the alien's geosat system which takes pictures of this general area every few minutes. We zoomed in and saw your party as you made your way down the edge of the Goza Mountains. Alas, we were unable to intervene in time to prevent your capture, primarily because we didn't recognize those soldiers were from Valen. We only have so much time to observe and there is a whole lot of world out there to monitor."

He continued, "We worked out you had been captured and then tried to find ways to rescue you. With them on the move each day, we couldn't get an accurate location to teleport to until they stopped at Oakham. Then we finally were able to act and you saw us in action. Our wives are quite powerful, don't you think?" Tim gazed lovingly at Petrona, who merely smiled.

"I've never seen anything like that. You two are almost the ultimate weapons," Andres exclaimed.

Both women smiled. Ben added, "If Brom does get attacked, there are hundreds of the Madiera descendants with their elemental gifts who will help defend us. So honestly, Andres, Lord Henry doesn't need these crystals to defend Brom, only he doesn't know much at all about the elemental gifts, which we believe are an alternate form of the *mentales* gifts. Anyway, we have Brom covered. No army is going to really threaten them."

"I can see that clearly now. Why haven't you told Lord Henry about this? If he knew, he might not be so worried about building up our defenses," Andres asked.

"He'd just find more ways to 'use' the women for his own purposes. Great power must have physical restraints, isn't that your saying?" Tim countered.

Rafaela wisely asked, "You said something about us having a choice to make?" She gave Andres time to see the wisdom of Tim's statement.

"Ah yes. I know we are rushing you, but here goes. How are you two going to survive now? We've done as you asked and saved your lives, barely. Honestly, that was too darn close for comfort. Anyway, you both have long ago undergone the body modifications and now you've lost your arms," Tim stated the obvious.

Rafaela fought to keep back tears. "So how are we going to live? We are now completely helpless. We always got by nicely by helping each other with everything from walking to dressing. Now we can't do anything."

"Well, that's the point I'm making. Our mothers were once as constrained as you both are, but then they had almost unbelievable psi powers to compensate. Still, they managed fairly well, but they also had domestique helpers most of the time. Our two older sisters took care of them for several years. The bottom line is obviously you two are going to need someone to be with you nearly all the time or at least nearby to help when you need something as simple as going to the bathroom," Tim explained. This was already painfully real to both, had been from the moment they'd regained consciousness.

"We have funds, well dad does. He can hire a couple to look after us at the castle," Andres suggested.

"That is true. That is one of your possible choices. May I offer you an alternative?" Both nodded. "Before I do, let me ask you to look at that choice. Suppose you return to Brom Castle. What kind of a life will you have? Will you ever get to do anything useful, productive? Or will you merely sit around watching others do things?"

Rafaela answered, "Well, the katalyein get by well, but then they avoid the body modifications. Andres, the truthful answer is just as he says. We'll spend our days just sitting around doing nothing productive. We're only twenty-one. I can't take doing nothing for another fifty years! I'll go nuts."

"Then let me offer you an alternative. Here in the Underground, we are always short of trustworthy and able people. We would like to offer you a job with us, where each day you will be doing things to help protect not only Brom, but all Tierra. Of course, we will have someone around to help you with your many physical needs when you require them. Plus, we'll see if there aren't some things we can do to help you become slightly more independent, but that may be a pipe dream. Still your lives would count for something and, I assure you, you wouldn't be bored. If you return to Brom Castle, Rafaela is right. Your useful lives would be over. We both know you'd forever be treated as hopeless cripples. Here with us, we'll kick you in your butts if you adopt that attitude. You are both alive, have gifts, and can help, if you will. In turn, we'll help you. Still, of course, it is your choice to make. It is late. You should sleep on it and give us your decision in the morning. Petrona and Elana will escort you to your bedroom for tonight and help get you tucked in. See you in the morning at breakfast."

"Thanks for everything, all you," Andres replied. Tim and Ben rose and left quickly, and Andres had a hunch they had some important things to handle yet tonight. Meanwhile, Petrona and Elana rose and moved to their sides. Stiffly and very carefully, the two stood up, making very sure of their balance each instant. The two women put an arm on their backs to steady them and off they headed very slowly following Petrona's directions.

After what seemed an eternity of walking, they entered a small room with one large bed. "I'm sorry for the Spartan room; it's our emergency bedroom. Hardly ever gets used. If you decide to stay with us, we'll get you a nice room," Petrona said rather apologetically.

"I'm so tired I could sleep anywhere," Rafaela replied.

She had them both sit on the edge of the bed while she and Elana worked together to get them out of their boots and pants. They used their arms and teeth quite a lot to get the job done, but both Rafaela and Andres were impressed they could even do it. "Oh, you get inventive when you have to," Petrona explained. "In time, I am sure you two will also get inventive. I do hope we don't have to remove those pipe corsets though."

"No, we wear them all the time, except when bathing of course," Rafaela explained, while Elana held her long hair out of the way as Petrona slowly pulled her pants off. They pulled down the covers and again helped the two get into bed, pulling up the covers. "If you need something during the night, just call out. Someone will hear you and come. Want me to leave the lantern on for a night light?" They did.

After the women left them, both wiggled and struggled to their sides, facing each other. Rafaela began passionately kissing him and he reciprocated. "I'll miss your arms around me at night, my love," she whispered.

"And I yours. I do love you so, maybe we can survive

this."

"Silly, we have survived this. Now we have to again figure out how to live. I will, if you are with me," she whispered. He gave her another loving kiss.

The next morning, the two women returned and helped the two out of bed and to the chamber pot. "We have our limitations too," Petrona then stated, as Tim and Ben entered to help get the two dressed.

"It's really hard for them to dress you two, but they can undo your pants," Tim explained. "We've got some shirts for you to wear for today, but you'll need to have some made especially for you as soon as possible. Petrona has breakfast waiting, shall we?" Each man put an arm around a waist, providing much needed support for the two as they made their slow way to the dining room.

Later over tea, Tim asked for their choice. As he expected, they chose to stay with him, joining the Underground. "Okay then first, we need to return you both to your father. Say only the crystals were destroyed when the earth gobbled up the soldiers from Valen. That will satisfy him. You can then tell him you will both be coming to live with us where you can get the proper care you will obviously now be needing. If I know Lord Henry, he will be very sympathetic towards you both and then extremely relieved when you tell him you will be coming to live with us." He went over the story they should tell Lord Henry. Most of it was the truth, only they were to leave out the fact the women cast the spells. As long as they didn't say who cast them, they would not be lying.

After breakfast, the men brought a carriage around to the front of their house. Meanwhile, the two women helped the two make their slow, careful way up the long stairs. "We were in the basement?" asked Rafaela.

"Yes, tiny house up here. Their parents used to live here," Petrona answered.

The two men lifted the pair out of the carriage before the main doors to the manor house in which Lord Henry had his office, that being the western manor house. Their own suite was up on the second floor. Many eyes stared at the two in disbelief. The dead had arisen! With Tim and Ben holding onto them, they led them down the long hall to Lord Henry's office. He came rushing out after an aide reported a miracle had happened. I say rushing, but of course, that is an exaggeration. He, too, moved very slowly, but his eyes were wide with surprise.

"My god! It is you two. Oh my god! What happened to you? Please, bring them into my office at once!" he exclaimed, turned, and made his own slow walk to his soft chair.

After getting the two seated, the men took side chairs, leaving the two sitting before his father. It took them an hour to relate all that had happened. Eyes watered when they told of the death of his older brother. At last, after explaining the crystals were destroyed during their rescue, Lord Henry's face fell. Disappointment lined his face. "So now dad, we are virtually helpless, but Tim has kindly offered to let us live at his place in Brom and see we have someone to look after our needs. Is that okay with you?" Andres asked.

Relief flashed on the man's face, almost as if his son had taken a huge weight off of him. "Absolutely, son. That would be extremely generous of him. I'll see they are given a monthly sum to help pay for your care. I know your mother will want to see you before you go and you'll probably want to get some of your things to take with you. If you like, you can box them up and I'll see they get delivered. Er, perhaps Tim and Ben can box them up for you."

"That's perfect dad. I'd like to see mom too," he replied. As it turned out, the two men left the pair at the manor house that day. Many wanted to see them and they needed time to decide what to bring with them. The men brought a wagon to bring them and their crates the next morning.

After lifting each into the wagon as well as their things, they rolled out of the gates of the castle. "Everyone treated us as if we were hopeless cripples!" Andres said the second it was safe to do so, out of earshot of castle personnel. "I couldn't live like that!"

"Me either. My folks kept crying and telling me my life was over. Well, it isn't! I'm just twenty-one," Rafaela added. "But then, I can see their point."

Tim laughed. "Told you so. Glad you are with us. We

will never treat you that way. Remember, you'll get a swift kick in your butts if you try to play the hopeless cripple around us. Handicapped, yes, in need of assistance with many things, yes. Helpless, never. I hope we don't work you too hard though. There are so few of us and so much is going on," Tim added.

After arriving at their "small house," the two again kept their arms around them as they headed down the concealed stairs to the gigantic basement suites. "We've got plenty of room thanks to the tireless efforts of our mothers and their foresight. You two get suite D. Everything branches off this long hallway. The floors are all smooth and level so that should help you both. This will be your suite." They had a nice bed with a table, chairs, two walk-in closet cabinets for their clothing and a nice commode. A side room offered them a small but comfortable living room where they could relax or entertain company.

Next, he took them to their work station. "In here we have all sorts of alien machines to monitor many different things. This one here allows us to monitor any and all messages the Sector ID minister makes. This one allows you to read any message he types into his computer system. Here is our geosat image viewer, the one we used to track your movements." Ben outlined a dozen other pieces of equipment.

"What we need for you to do is to monitor the Sector ID Minister and any and all communications between him and Valen Castle. You adjust the volume with this knob. Use your teeth, mouth, feet, boobs, whatever to turn it up or down as needed. Same with this one. You need to learn to read Imperium Standard so that you both can monitor what the Sector ID Minister writes. Seldom have we had the luxury of having someone on these machines for long periods of time. Your help in monitoring these will be invaluable."

"Isn't that a comm network?" Rafaela asked, having spotted the telltale crystals on one wall.

"Perceptive woman. Yes, it is. Mom designed it to be a monitor. All messages any tower sends are also received here. We need you to listen in to those as well. This way, we are kept abreast of all the developments we can."

"No one ever knew you are doing this!" she exclaimed,

very much surprised and astonished.

"Naturally," Tim replied coyly. After more discussion, he took them back to their suite. "In a little while, a tailor and a seamstress, who we trust, will come and measure you. Soon, you will have appropriate clothing custom made to fit. Always remember, when you need some assistance, just give a yell. Someone is always around and will come as quickly as they can. Welcome aboard the Underground, Andres and Rafaela," Tim said enthusiastically.

"Ben, can I ask you something about Empress Amy?" Rafaela asked him.

"Sure. Don't know if I can answer it though. Mom was something else."

"Before I got like this, I would have loved to learn to operate all these machines. Now, honestly, Ben, I feel so helpless. We used to use our arms to help keep our balance or catch ourselves when we lost it or help get ourselves back on our feet when we fell. Now I am almost too scared even to walk without someone to catch me. I can probably find a way to use my mouth to turn those two knobs you pointed out and I sure can listen and all that. But how did Empress Amy manage to live like this? Was she totally depended on those domestique helpers?"

Ben sighed. "Like I said, mom was something else. She had an enormous psi power and had telekinesis down to a fine art. She'd sit at the table and eat like the rest of us, levitating and moving the silverware, passing bowls down the line and so on. With the machines, she and Jan would sit there and use their powers to manipulate everything, showing us how to run them. I guess the answer is perhaps you shouldn't think of those two as your role models. Give yourself time to get used to the loss of your arms. Experiment, be willing to try anything. Just don't give up."

"Okay. That's true, it's only been a couple of days," Rafaela attempted to be optimistic once more, though she didn't truly believe what she was saying, not really.

Their wives had entered and overheard this last conversation. Petrona volunteered, "Rafaela, it must really be hard for you and Andres to have arms and hands all your lives and then to suddenly lose them like you did. I bet you never considered anything like this ever happening to you when you got your body modifications."

She cracked a smile, "No, we didn't, not remotely. I mean my tiny twelve-inch waist is all the rage among the women of the castle and tower. I couldn't wait to get it done and to be able to wear toe shoes, nylons, and sexy gowns. Now those very things that I so wanted when I was fourteen are haunting me. I really loved the feel of the clothing and my incredibly curvaceous silhouette. I still do, but now," her voice trailed off.

"So when the dressmaker comes, why not continue to get such fine dresses and things that make you happy? As I understand these things, you are both stuck with the modifications. So why not make the most of them and enjoy them and each other?" Petrona suggested with a wry smile.

"Well, Andres, why not? We are never going to be able to do things the katalyein can do; they are incredibly flexible. We are restricted to bending only at our hips. They use their feet for most everything, and we can't do that either. So why not wear what we want and look the way we want?" she asked.

"Might as well. I love your sexy look, dear." Andres admitted.

"Can I ask you something Petrona?" She nodded and Rafaela asked, "Don't you find it horribly difficult too? Lacking hands."

She laughed. "I never had them to lose. I, we were born this way with thin, cute arms with their small rounded ends. If you never have them, how can you feel bad about losing them? No, we get by similar to the katalyein, but we have a huge advantage; we have our arms to help us. Plus, our men are geniuses at inventing clever clip-on devices to make things easier, like eating. Honestly, we love the way we are. Elana and I don't want hands. Then we'd be just like you. We like the way we are, unique and different. We're us. Just like you two are you two. Make the most of what you've got. That's our motto."

Rafaela laughed. "I haven't got much left now except my curves, so I'm going to make the most of them. You too, Andres, you make the most of your handsome figure." He laughed a little. He knew they were facing big changes in their lives, but he still wanted to help somehow. Tim and Ben were giving him that chance and that meant much to him.

Chapter 7 The Humberhills Twins

The Midlands foothills of the great Goza Mountains consist of great east-west valleys, each between fifty and a hundred miles across, that is, north-south. At either north-south edge, great rocky ridge lines poke their craggy splines skyward. Close to the mountains, many of these splines are impassible, rising to sharp peaks themselves. Locals know the wagon paths, as they have for centuries, though horses can cross in many more places. As one goes down the valleys towards the east, the ridge lines subside. Some two hundred miles east of the Goza Mountains, these ridge lines turn into timber and grass covered ridges, passable nearly anywhere along them.

Cradled up in the rocky zones near the mountains lay a number of small kingdoms, once part of the great Haverhills kingdom, which was essentially destroyed by the relentless march of the Valen Army before Empress Amy Blackwater stopped them towards the end of last century. When that mighty army marched through the hills, as the locals call them, the many land barons, the *Jefe* as they were then known, fled with their families to lower ground, closer to the huge city of Wycombe and relative safety. With the end of the Valen occupation, these rugged foothills men and women moved back to their ancient homelands, reclaiming what was lost.

Most were in desperate straits, having lost much to Valen's plunder. The dead-zone of Haverhills proper divided these small kingdoms for nearly a century. Going south, valley by valley from the dead-zone, lay Wilde Hills, Derby Heights, and Yorkshire Hills. Going north from the dead-zone valley lay Trenthills, Retfordhills, and Humberhills. Here in the spring of 1244, each now had its lord and lady, who owned the valley and leased out the land to tenement farmers, each of whom paid their land lease in whatever they produced. These days, they raised sheep and chickens, trained falcons and eagles, grew a variety of nuts, marketed their pod-silk, raised many varieties of berries, and grew a number of cold weather tubers.

Originally so close to the original explosion of the

alien's spaceport, the psi-dust created a high percentage of *mentales* gifted. Of course, with the Valen invasion, many fled elsewhere or joined Haverhills Tower in their valiant, but losing fight. By 1244, many of these local lords had rebuilt their small fortresses and were beginning to prosper once more. All attended the biannual councils with the emperor and, of late, the Councils of the Lords, where they made their opinions widely known. They also struck mutual defense treaties with the stronger valley lords, who they considered would best protect them, should Valen once again threaten them.

Humberhills Fortress was an old one, built of grey stone mined from the Goza. It lay some thirty miles east of the mountains proper, cradled against the rugged north ridge line of its valley. There, the ridge provided a natural barrier from attacks from the north. The castle was small compared to the great ones in cities like Brom. Nevertheless, it had a sizeable manor house, stables, an eyrie where hawks and owls were raised and trained, giant holding pens for wintering sheep, and a hen house.

Lord Chester Humberhills, forty-five, along with his deceased father, had rebuilt the fortress and manor house, bringing back some of its former glory. He wore his brown hair on the short side, but kept a short rounded beard, outlining his oval face. Lady Lisa was three years younger with blonde hair, with gentle curls, falling to her waist. With her blue eyes, she was always teased as having Wycombe blood. She had borne him three sons, Elden, twenty-one, Evan, nineteen, and after two miscarriages, Eric, fifteen. All had their father's brown hair. Only after these did she finally get her heart's desire, bearing twin daughters, Darcy and Dawn, fourteen.

The *mentales* gift had always been strong in the Humberhills lineage, most assumed due in part to their close proximity to the original explosion. Their gifts manifested itself in an uncanny ability to work with animals, especially falcons and eagles, though the two older boys used theirs with their vast herds of sheep. Eric took after his father and at fifteen was a master of eagles, raising and training them, although he sometimes caught them in the wild. Darcy and

Dawn also took after their father and were masters with the smaller hunters, the falcons. Hardly a summer's day went by without the three spending time flying their many birds. They hated the falls when they would be forced to sell some of their birds at the harvest markets. Still as the saying in the hills went, "You cannot go wrong with a Humberhills bird."

Fifteen years ago, the first crisis struck. Among the hundreds of ruling lords and ladies, emulating the body modifications of the Imperial Court had become *the* thing to do. At the biannual meetings with the emperor and empress and the Council of the Lords that met afterwards, Lord Chester and Lady Lisa continued to see more and more of their peers adopting these new ways. True, Lord Chester often admitted, the many ladies looked extraordinarily attractive in their fancy gowns, small waists, and heels. "Still, how can we do our work if we are all hobbled up like they are, Lisa," Lord Chester protested.

"We may not be able to avoid it, Chester. Look around us. Almost everyone here has done it," Lisa had countered. "We are now on the outside, social outcasts." He could think of no appropriate response to that and wisely said nothing. "Chester, I've been thinking about this. I run the manor."

"Of course you do, Lisa. You are my steward. Without you, the place would not survive one winter. I depend on you, so do the kids," he replied, wondering what this had to do with their political crisis.

"Well, all I do really is keep lists, walk around counting things, and supervising our many workers. Now I've talked with many of the other ladies about how they are managing, Chester. They all say the modifications do take some getting used to, but in the long run, they do not really interfere with the work they do. Most have said their pace of life slows way down. Still, it is not like I am out walking the pastures or mucking out horse stalls. Honestly, Chester, we really should be setting a good example for our people," Lady Lisa argued.

At last Chester gave in as well. He'd talked to many other lords, who grumbled about how awful it had been adapting to such rigid confinements. Two things finally made him change his mind about having it done. First, he learned while on horseback, he would encounter no differences, no impediments. This was crucial for often he had to ride out into the wilds hunting for more birds to capture and train. Second, most of the hills lords were making mutual defense treaties with the powerful tower-castle lords. In his case, with the latest land divisions, Humberhills now was controlled by the very distant Wye Tower, some two thousand miles off to the east. If his lands were invaded and he needed help, Wye would send it, but he knew an army would take months to get to him from Wye.

Hence, like the other hills lords, he negotiated with Lord Wycombe for a mutual defense treaty. While the large city of Wycombe was only six hundred miles to the east-southeast and didn't have any towers, they could send troops far more quickly, should Humberhills be invaded. Lord Wycombe insisted the all his lords undergo the body modifications. Wycombe was almost twice as populous as Wye, and Lord Wycombe was seeking to gain top standing in the court at Wye, naturally.

Thus, Lord Chester and Lady Lisa underwent their modifications fifteen years ago. Immediately thereafter, Lord Wycombe signed Lord Chester's mutual defense pact, giving Chester peace of mind, if not peace of body. True, the first year after that was "murder" to quote Lord Chester, but he and Lisa managed somehow. "Just allow more time, Chester," Lisa constantly reminded him and that became their operating motto.

Lord Chester refused to permit his two eldest sons, Elden and Evan to have this done to them. "Look, I depend upon you both to keep all the tenements in line. You two run our large sheep herds. You are out there daily roaming the rolling hills. You cannot do it hobbled up as I am. One day when you become Lord Humberhills, then you may have it done. Yes before you attend your first council meetings as Lord Humberhills, I will guarantee you both you will have it done by then. Acceptable? Besides if we are attacked, I need your strong arms to fight. I can hardly fight now. Hell, I can hardly stand up!" That convinced the two men to keep quiet about the modifications. Neither had any desire to be all hobbled up as their parents were.

At the fall 1243 meeting, Lord Chester and Lady Lisa had taken their youngest children along with them again. Eric's task was simple: chaperone his twin sisters, Darcy and Dawn. Chester wanted someone who was un-hobbled to watch over his two now of age daughters. "Do I have to?" Eric had pleaded, but he knew it was a lost cause. Look after the twins had become his calling in life, ever since he could walk. Well, he knew why, but didn't dare say so. Mom could barely walk and simply had no way to keep up with the twins, who seemed to want to run everywhere instead of walking. That they were also his mother's darlings didn't help matters.

Over the years Eric began to enjoy the company of his twin sisters, particularly so when their *mentales* gifts had begun to blossom three years ago. The three shared a love of hawks and eagles and were almost always found doing something with the many birds. The last few years had been the best for all three. Not only had their skills with the birds become even better than their father's, he had turned over nearly all the hawk and eagle business to the three of them. Lord Chester only reserved the sale of the birds for himself and that was only in the fall. For three years now, Eric, Darcy, and Dawn had truly enjoyed their art and craft, spending long hours with the birds.

But all three had also been attending the biannual meetings with their parents too. "Eric loves Sally," Darcy had endlessly teased him these past two years. True, Eric had taken a first-love fancy to fifteen year old Sally Retford, who lived in Retford Hills, the valley just south of Humberhills. Occasionally, his eagle training had "accidentally" taken him far across their valley to the southern ridge line which formed the natural boundary between the two small kingdoms. Sally also just happened to be out riding their north ridge line at the same time. Her gift lay in the handling of horses, so she was "on a training exercise" at these times when the two could secretly meet. Just last year, she'd come of age and was permitted to undergo her own body modifications, becoming Lady Sally Retford. She was the youngest of Lord Retford's three daughters. She had a round face with a beak-like nose, which enchanted Eric, reminding him of his beloved eagles.

Because his love was now officially a lady, Eric desperately wanted to become a lord and had been pestering his father all winter about it. Making matters worse for Lord Chester, the twins also wanted to become just like their mother.

"Daddy, all the girls are doing it. Sally says if we get ours done while we are fourteen, then our waists will be the smallest possible, not large like yours and moms are. We are the only teens who haven't, daddy. We look wholly out of place at the meetings," Darcy whined.

"You still ride and train eagles, so we can still do our work too," Dawn added. "We look like freaks at the meetings. Everyone says we can't really be officially ladies until we have it done too. Besides, boys don't even look at girls who don't have tiny waists, do they Eric?" She gave him a look, implying he would be in major, major trouble if he didn't back her up.

"Well, dad," Eric rapidly thought of how to best gain some advantage here, "she does have a point. All the lord and lady heirs we've seen at the council meetings have had it done. She has a valid point. But dad, if I am to continue to chaperone them, I ought to be modified too so I can help them like you help mom." He'd deliberately twisted things around, hoping the mention of chaperoning would make a difference with his father.

It did. That made Chester sit up and take notice. "All right. Eric, if you will get yours at the same time as the twins and if you promise to look after them as always and not let them pester your mother or me for help, then I'll consent." Darcy and Dawn let out squeals, did a girlish dance, and then hugged their father. Both twins nodded and winked at Eric, because they both knew it had been Eric who'd convinced him. Now they owed Eric big time and they knew it.

Lord Chester made the arrangements there in Exchange City at Elegant Fashions Inc, where he and his wife had their modifications done. The three, accompanied by their parents, took the plunge after the fall meetings in 1243. Ever practical still, Lord Chester purchased both an arm-fetter-gown and a normal gown for each daughter along with matching toe shoes.

These, they would wear on formal occasions. He purchased each daughter two pairs of toe boots for everyday use on the ranch. Likewise, he got Eric a fancy formal suit and several pairs of toe boots for regular use. When they returned home, their seamstresses and tailor quickly made the three teens even more appropriate everyday apparel.

The three were initially shocked and terribly worried. Breathing was awful and they could just barely walk. "I hope you two are happy," Eric grumbled. He now went everywhere they did and they, he. By their own agreement with their father, they had to fend for themselves.

"Well, I suppose we are. I had no idea it would be this awful," Dawn sheepishly admitted. "Still, if everyone does it, it can't be that bad. Mom and dad get by. Just don't let go of me," she added fearfully.

"Bet you wish Sally could see you now, well when you wear your fancy suit," Darcy tried to change the subject. The three now wore their everyday clothing. Each wore a pod-silk blouse or shirt, woolen, brown, thick pants which ended just below their knees, and brown toe boots. Each had a light oiled leather cloak thrown over their shoulders, though the twins had their long brown hair nicely resting on top of the cloak as they always had. With Eric between them, an arm around each of their waists, the trio made their slow way out of the house to the eyrie to tend to their bird's needs.

Eric flushed, of course he did, but now there was not much chance of that. He was hip-tied to his sisters. He couldn't walk well without their support, or they, without his. "Well, one day you are going to have to come riding with me so I can sneak away and see her. After all you agreed we'd not be separated, unless you can get by without me." He knew they couldn't and inwardly smiled.

Dawn sighed, "Well, I suppose we will. After all you gave up everything so we could do this."

"Why didn't they tell us it was going to be so hard?" Darcy complained.

"Would that have stopped you?" Eric pointed out. Both twins flushed. It wouldn't have. "Dad did say we'd get used to it in time, but I wish time would hurry up."

Things only got worse for the three. When winter came and the courtyard became snow packed, their toe boots slipped so easily that they took a fall at least twice just going from the manor house to the eyrie. They could not avoid the twice-daily trips; their many birds required care, and they were obligated to fulfill their duties, hobbled or not. Slipping and falling became so common to the three that they soon began paying little attention to it other than the often said, "oops." The three refused to admit they could not care for their birds.

In the middle of the winter, a band of Valen raiders passed by their fortress. Lord Chester's field hands reported them, and he and his two older boys mounted up and rode off to see for themselves. "Are we under attack?" That was the question on everyone's mind in Humberhills. Lord Chester had sent riders out to all the many tenement farmers in his valley warning them of the Valen raiders and to be ready to come to the fortress for defense and safety.

From a low hill, the three watched the band of Valen raiders, who were skirting the edge of his lands staying as close to the Goza Mountains as they could. They did stop and study his fortress further on down the valley, making Lord Chester very nervous. "Well, I count about eighteen. If they attack, we surely can take them out, dad," Elden said confidently.

"Where there are eighteen, there are likely far more. Looks like they are on the move again. We'll tag along and make sure they leave our valley before we head back. Elden, you head to our north rim and keep watch. Perhaps they are scouts for their main army. Let me know if you spot any more of them. We'll trail these from a safe distance," Lord Chester ordered.

By suppertime, it was snowing heavily again, but the entire household was greatly relieved when the three finally returned. The Valen raiders had continued on south and were now leaving their valley. Elden had seen no signs of the rest of the army and had even ridden some distance over into the next northern valley just to be on the safe side. Nevertheless, Lord Chester sent word of the Valen raiders to his neighboring lords and to Lord Wycombe.

During the next few days, the lords to the south of Humberhills reported the Valen raiders had passed through their valleys as well. Still, they found no sign of a major Valen army following behind this small group. Tensions began to ease.

By spring, the three had learned to cope well with their restrictions and looked forward to the spring council meetings, none more so than Eric who would be able to spend some time with Sally. They'd promised to attend the dances together. With an armed escort, the five of them made the carriage trip to Exchange City. The twins were eager to show off their fanciest gowns, having practiced a good deal in their arm-fetter-gowns, following Lisa's advice.

Lord Chester had not forgotten the Valen raiders. While Lisa was enjoying the company and chat of the other ladies, he was hounding Lord Wycombe. "Look, I tell you we all saw the Valen raiders scouting us out last early winter. If they were not planning an attack, why would they send out scouting parties, Lord Wycombe? Answer me that if you can. I tell you an attack on the hills is imminent!"

"Look, Lord Chester. If such an attack does come, and I am not saying it will, then you contact me with the details, and I'll send forces to help you deal with it," Lord Wycombe replied, rather annoyed with the whole idea after all these years, Valen would again threaten the Midlands. What would be gained by starting new wars? In his mind, such an attack was a figment of Lord Chester's imagination. *Well, he is hill-folk, after all, prone to all sorts of wild imaginings.* He totally shrugged off this idea of an invasion from Valen.

"We are so cool!" Darcy whispered to Dawn, as the two walked slowly onto the dance floor. The short meeting was over, something about a regent and a new heir to the throne. The twins didn't pay any attention to that. Instead, their eyes roamed the room looking for other teens like themselves. They were pleased to see their new gowns were the norm. For the first time, they felt like they belonged with all their peers. True, their arms were essentially tied to their sides, leaving only their lower arms free to move, but so were all the other elegantly dressed teens. Their gowns, a light blue and light red, were the height of fashion. The inner fetter skirt tightly followed the flair of their hips and on down their legs, holding the legs tightly together. That tight skirt ended about six inches above their downward-pointed ankles where their black nylons appeared. Their outer skirt had six times the amount of pod-silk material in it, folded many times and hanging straight down from their hips. The center of their outer dress was open, showing off the shapely inner skirt. The outer skirt formed a V-shape across their front sides, and the two sides were about two feet apart at the floor, revealing their black patent toe shoes. The twins had never felt this good, this exciting, this alive in their lives, excepting when they were training their hawks, that is.

Eric in his fancy suit was close at hand, holding onto Sally Retford, who wore a similar gown, a shade redder than Darcy's. As the music began, the twins watched how Sally managed, hoping to gain valuable clues, as they spotted several boys making their own slow way towards themselves. Sally put her lower arms around Eric's tiny waist, and he put his right arm around her waist beneath her long blonde hair, while his left arm rested on her right shoulder. Slowly, the two began to dance, taking the tiniest of steps.

"Lady Darcy, may I have the pleasure of this dance with you?" a tall lad said formally.

"Please, do so," she replied politely, extending her lower arms as Sally had. Winking at Dawn, she tried to follow the boy's lead, just as another lad made a similar offer to Dawn, who eagerly accepted as well. The size of their dance steps were perhaps three inches. Neither partner could gracefully take any larger step. Darcy glanced at the other dancers, noticing all movement was slow, measured, and small in size. She relaxed and began chatting with the lad from the Wilde Hills far south of Humberhills.

"We best move a little closer to Darcy and Dawn, Sally. I'm still their chaperone," he whispered.

Sally giggled. "When will you ever be free of that?" she teased him.

"Maybe soon. Look at all the boys eyeing them. Maybe very soon!" He grinned and Sally giggled again.

Later at refreshments time, Eric held the cup for her to sip. "Thanks. I can't quite get it up to my lips in this gown, but then that's the whole point of it. I get to have you attend to my needs," she coyly teased him, batting her blue eyes at him. Her smile revealed her perfect, white teeth.

"You don't need to wear this gown to get me to pay attention and help you, Sally," he teased back. "So when will you marry me?"

"Just as soon as you don't have to constantly play chaperone to your sisters. We can't even steal a kiss with those two always around, silly. Dad's already agreed we can marry, but I told him we might later this year. Do you suppose Lord Chester will let you marry and stop chaperoning your twin sisters?"

"Somehow, I'll make sure he does. We'll get married at midsummer. How does that sound?"

"I can hardly wait!" Sally whispered back, resting her head on his shoulders, knowing he'd get a good whiff of her lavender-scented hair. In turn, he ran his right hand down her back, following her curvaceous waist, on down over her full hips to the top of her legs. He knew the gentle touch sent waves of pleasure through her body. Both were telepaths and in rapport with each other.

The next day, Lord Chester brought their carriage around to the inn's main doors. Already inn servants had carried Lady Lisa, and the twins down the steps from their suite of rooms on the second floor. They insisted on wearing their arm-fetter-gowns one more day. The fetter skirt made it impossible for them to handle any stairs and the staff at the inns dealt with this aspect constantly. In their toe boots, neither Lord Chester nor Eric could carry them, and Eric waited patiently for the staff to bring the three down. He took his usual position between his sisters, an arm around each, leading them across the barroom floor to the doors, while another staff member escorted Lady Lisa to the door, where Lord Chester waited for them all. Outside, the two men were able to lift the three into the carriage and then Eric climbed in. Lord Chester issued orders to the driver and his armed escort and then joined them.

"Thanks for bringing us dad," Darcy gushed. "That was the very best night of our lives. Did you see all the boys who wanted to dance with us?" she added highly enthused.

"How could I not see," he said gruffly. "Glad you enjoyed it."

"Dear, what's wrong? I can tell when something is bothering you," Lady Lisa asked, growing quite serious. She had been grinning broadly at her darling twins, so grown up.

"Oh it's that damn Lord Wycombe. Look, you know as well as I Valen is planning something — very likely an attack on the hills again."

"Didn't Lord Wycombe and you sign a defense treaty?" she asked. Eric listened closely.

"Well, of course we did. That's just the point. He doesn't think Valen is up to anything at all. I just worked out that, if today we were attacked and I sent word to him and if he responded immediately by sending an army to help up, based on how fast large armies move, he would not get to us for nearly a month! How the blazes are we to hold out that long if Valen hits us with a huge force? Answer me that one," he grumbled.

"You think they will — attack us?" she asked.

"Don't you? I just don't know when, that's all. My guess, if I had to guess, is they might strike us by summer."

"Why then, dad? Sally and I want to get married midsummer," Eric asked.

"That's all arranged, son. I talked with Lord Retford. Why then? Well, armies don't like to travel across country during winter. Valen Castle is far enough from us that it'll take them at least a month to get to us from there. Allow them a month or so to get organized and supplied, and that puts it at midsummer. I doubt they'll move faster than that. It's unlikely they will wait until fall to attack because winter would be just around the corner. Men don't like to fight in the snow, far too dangerous. I can't imagine their whole attack is just to retake Humberhills."

"Dad! That means Sally is in danger too," Eric blurted out.

"And all the hills, for my money, son. My guess is they

intend to retake all the hills, just like they did half a century ago," he declared.

"Enough of such doom and gloom talk. It is a fine day and the girls have just had a marvelous dance, dear. Let's talk about this later and enjoy the day, shall we?" Lisa valiantly steered the dire talk to one more pleasant.

During the spring and early summer, Lord Chester and his men worked on several projects. First and foremost, any and all repairs to their defensive walls were made. Lisa organized the stockpiling of supplies they would need to withstand a siege. He met, via Elden, with many of his tenement farmers, ordering them to come to the fortress both to help defend it and to protect themselves and their families from the attacking army of Valen.

On the lighter side, Lisa and Eric began to clear out a suite of two rooms where the young couple would be staying once they were married. In return, Eric promised to continue helping the twins with their hawks once he and Sally were wed. This pleased Lord Chester, by the way. As midsummer approached, Lord Chester began to send out outriders far to the north of Humberhills. He wanted to have as much warning as possible should the Valen army come marching his way.

Two weeks before the wedding day, Lord Chester came to his twins. "Darcy, Dawn, you are going to have a role to play in this as well. Starting today, I want you to send your hawks out on a spying mission. Send them as far north as you dare. You are looking for a large mass of troops. You are to do this each day from now on." They agreed and left to do as he asked, grabbing Eric on the way.

"Yes, he asked me to do the same with my eagles," Eric said. As usual, he walked between his sisters, an arm around each teen's waist, and they, his.

"It's three hundred feet from the manor door to the eyrie, I measured it," Dawn began chatting. "At three inches per step, do you realize it takes us some twelve hundred steps to get there? No wonder we are so incredibly slow at this and it takes forever!"

"You ought to have thought about that before begging

to get modified," Eric countered.

"Well, we did have fun at the dance," Darcy giggled, leaving Eric wondering why did girls always giggle so? Well, he thought, Sally does too. Must be a girl thing cause mom doesn't.

"At least we have a fun job, once we finally get there," Dawn countered. None could disagree with that. For these three, going into rapport with their eagles and hawks was what made life.

Eric loosened the jesses around Goldie, his magnificent Golden Eagle he'd raised from a hatchling. The great bird scratched his arm with her powerful beak, more than ready to take flight. Sometimes he felt the bird had grown impatient with him. It took him many times longer now to walk her to the open door and set her a flight than it had before his body modifications. Could she sense this, he wondered? She flapped her huge wings and sent dust flying as she headed out of the open door, sweeping gracefully into the blue sky. The orange-red sun was still climbing; it was midmorning. White clouds were moving in from the southwest.

Shortly, the fluttering of Blacky and Spotty shot past him on either side; the twins had released their favorites too. Soon all three stiffly sat down, leaning their backs against the side of the eyrie building, where they could bask in the warm sun. All three had long ago learned to sit down when going into close rapport with their birds. Why? Balance. In their toe boots, they lost their balance when in rapport with the circling, soaring birds. Now the three focused and made the contact that defined their lives, their beingness. They were one with the eagle and hawks.

Just as Eric looked after his twin sisters, so did Goldie keep an eye on possible predators to Blacky and Spotty. Although most of the birds that were to be sold were trained to bring down their prey and bring it back to their handler, who would then give the bird its share of the kill, with these, the three often allowed the birds the freedom to catch their own and eat their kill. Today, the three birds were hungry and the trio allowed them to hunt and kill on their own. In close rapport with their individual bird, they experienced what their bird did, as it ripped savagely into the freshly killed prey. Yes, the three loved the diving sensations from the birds, but were tolerant of this savage feeding emotion. Once full, the two hawks and eagle again took to the sky, flying further northward. Before long, through the bird's eyes, they spotted the two outriders far below.

Twenty miles north, the two hawks turned back, heading for their eyrie home. The more powerful eagle continued on further before turning back as well. When Eric broke his rapport and awkwardly got to his feet, already the twins were holding their favorite hawks, stroking them lovingly with a feather. "See anything?" Dawn asked.

"Nope," Eric replied, holding his arm out for Goldie, while bracing himself. In these boots, he had to use one arm to keep from falling down when the big eagle landed on his arm. Later, after handling the other birds, the three took their usual positions beside each other for the time consuming walk back to the manor house.

The next day, everything changed! Midmorning, the trio again flew their birds of prey, but this time, they spotted what all had been dreading, a large body of soldiers.

Chapter 8 Valen Strikes

Thirty-three year old General Ramiro Valen didn't need any *mentales* gifts to carry out his assignment given to him by Lord Valen himself. Retake Haverhills and then Oakham. Simple enough assignment for a career soldier. Intel gathered from the missing search and recovery team last winter, plus that gained from their allies in the spaceport via satellite images, told him there were no significant armies in these foothills. Merely a bunch of small fortresses, easy pickings, he'd told his majors. Quite why Lord Valen had insisted on each of his three regiments having three of those hobbled, pathetic *mentales* gifted men and women was beyond him, save one small detail. He knew though hobbled, enemy gifted could be a serious threat to subdue.

Yet the enemy *mentales* gifted's inability to move made them vulnerable in the extreme. Well, he'd rationalized, best to avoid undue casualties of my soldiers when taking them out. Quite why Lord Valen wanted the enemy *mentales* captured and sent back to Valen eluded him. A man of orders, he would still carry them out to the letter. He'd promised Lord Valen to wrap up this campaign before the fall council meetings. That had very much pleased his lord, though he didn't know why. Politics. He was not political and could care less about such things.

With three thousand soldiers divided into three regiments, he could easily retake the lands the old Empress Amy Blackwater had stolen from them. He knew his history well. They had already conquered these lands, but she made Valen evacuate them in a god-awful hurry. Now he was poised to retake them.

General Ramiro had a superb plan to avoid detection until his army was poised to strike. Moving three thousand men and supply wagons over the paved road just south of Plateau Grado and Exchange City was tricky, if he did not want to alert all the Midlands lords. If they were alerted, they'd have at least a month to take countermeasures, moving armies of their own to block his. His plan was clever. By night, groups of a dozen plus a supply wagon made the trip over the Goza Mountains, into Exchange City, and then out onto the high foothills. Once there, they'd maintain a low profile until his entire army had joined them. His secret maneuvering has cost him most of the spring, but close to midsummer, he had succeeded. The Midlands lords had no idea he had his whole army in position, ready to make his sweep down the foothills through Haverhills to Oakham, arriving there by the first snowfall.

These first couple of hundred miles offered no real resistance. Isolated ranches and farms dotted these valleys, along with the occasional mine or two, hardly worth bothering with. He didn't, passing these by. Later he'd send a patrol or two to demand allegiance to Valen. No, his first real resistance would be the fortified ranches of Humberhills and Retford Hills. As the days passed and his army drew closer, he called in his three majors to give them their attack orders.

Pointing to his maps, he explained, "Here is the north ridge line that marks the northern boundary of Humberhills. Cleverly, their fortified manor is located some fifty miles from the mountains, due east, right here with its back up against the ridge line. At that location, we cannot assault them from the north. Hence, Major Gregorio will take First Regiment and peel off from us here, just as we enter their valley close to the Goza. He will drive due east and reach the fortifications in two days at most. Major, you have seven days to secure that facility and begin rejoining us."

"While they are driving east, we'll continue on due south, as close to the Goza as possible. In two days when Major Gregorio is launching his attack on Humberhills, Major Poncio will take the Second Regiment and break off from us to go after Retford Hills. Their fortified manor lies ten miles east of the Goza and on their south ridge line. Major Poncio will travel in a direct line to that fortification, arriving there in two days, beginning his assault at that time. Again, I give you a week to secure that facility and head onwards to rejoin us."

"I and Major Faustino and the Third Regiment will continue on into Trent Hills, cutting diagonally southeast to reach their fortified manor located here some sixty miles east of the Goza on the south ridge line of their valley. We will rendezvous and regroup here in the dead-zone of Haverhills, before we strike in a similar manner the remainder of these hill manors. Questions?" There was none.

Eric first spotted them when they were twenty-five miles north of the valley of Humberhills. "It's happening isn't it? We're going to be attacked!" Darcy exclaimed, panicking. They'd just given their father the awful news.

"Eric, keep the twins calm! Elden, Evan, sound the alarms. Alert all our outlying farms. Tell them they have three days to get to the safety of our fortress, no more. They'll be on us by then. My god, it's come at last. Lisa, start making preparations to house those who will be coming. I'm going to contact Lord Wycombe and tell him this terrible news and then contact all the other hill lords," Lord Chester ordered, again cursing the day he agreed to become fashionable, but hobbled. Now he needed swift action and could barely walk. Eventually, in his study, he calmed down, focused, and made contact with Lord Wycombe.

Yes, I tell you we've spotted a huge army from Valen. They will be on us in three days at most.

How do you know those are Valen's army?

Do you know of anyone else who has a huge army just north of us? For god's sake my lord, take action now. Get your mentales gifted on this. Get Wye Tower to observe and send us help. I am requesting you honor our mutual defense contract. Send help now before it's too late. We cannot stand against an army of thousands. No, a month from now will be too late. We need assistance within mere days, I tell you.

"Well, how did it go? Is Lord Wycombe going to send help?" Lisa asked. Her face was pale; she was still in shock from the terrible news.

"The idiot doesn't believe me, but I think I've convinced him to verify the army for himself and request aid from the Circle at Wye. That's our best hope, the circle. Even if the fool sends an army to our aid today, they won't get here for a month. As large as that army is, I don't see how we can hold out that long, but somehow we must. A lot will depend upon how many of our tenement folks arrive to lend a hand."

"Won't some of them flee to the east?" Lisa asked. "I sure would, take everything and flee for my life."

"They are all pledged to come to the defense of our fortification here. It's treason if they don't, and I'll see all those who flee instead of honoring their obligations to me are hanged when this is over." That Lord Chester was angry was an understatement. He knew Lisa was right, many would chose dishonor and flee with their families, heading on down the valley to the east. In all honestly, those in Wye who supposedly oversaw these hills were supposed to be protecting them from just such an attack. Thus far in five years, he'd seen one small patrol of Wye soldiers in the area. Pathetic.

"Dear, what about our girls? They are too young to fight. Can't we send them away to safety?" Lisa asked. She knew better than to ask for safety for her sons, but her twins, she had to save them somehow. If the fortress fell, surely they would be raped and tortured by the victorious soldiers.

"No, they stay and can help with the hawks. When the siege comes, if it looks like we are going to fall, Eric can take them down the escape tunnel to safety. If they flee, so will everyone else. We will face this with honor, Lisa. Honor. Not cowardice and shame, just like my grandfather did."

Lisa didn't add her counter-thought, "Right, and die just like your grandfather did."

The next three days were hectic. Lord Chester had Eric, Darcy, and Dawn flying half of the birds in their eyrie, keeping a close watch on the approaching army. When one third of the army only turned due east heading straight towards them, only then did Lord Chester become optimistic. "A thousand? Well, we can hold them off I do believe! We'll give those Valen soldiers something to think about!"

Two days later, Major Gregorio and his First Regiment finally swarmed around the grey stone fortress, cutting off all escape from that point onward. At this time, Lord Chester summoned Eric and the twins to his balcony, his command post. From here, he could look out over all the fortress grounds, save due north, which was protected by a nearly unclimbable steep ridge. "If all goes badly for us and the fortress is about to fall, Eric, I am ordering you to take charge

126

of the twins here. You are to make for the escape tunnel. I will tell you when that time comes. When I do, you don't question me, just do it. The future of our whole Humberhills line will be in your hands, son. Get them to safety somehow."

"But dad! We can't leave you and mom and our brothers," Eric protested. Elden and Evan had been rushing around the entire fortress for the last three days, organizing those who would be defending them. Hobbled as he was, he felt not only left out, but useless. He wanted to help, but couldn't.

Lord Chester picked up these unspoken thoughts. "Eric, I know how you feel. You and the twins have already done very valuable work for us. Thanks to you, we've had three days to prepare. We're not taken by surprise. I don't want to alarm you unduly, Eric, but think what will happen to Darcy and Dawn here if the Valen soldiers capture them? One word, son."

"Rape?" Eric muttered.

"And probably a whole lot worse. So promise me, son, if and when I should give you the order to flee, you will take your sisters to safety. Protect them with your life, okay?"

"I promise, dad. I will protect them with my life," Eric swore. "But dad, what about Sally? She's in danger too. We saw another third of the army heading to her dad's fortress."

"Son, I know you two were going to be married in a few days. If we survive this, time enough then to worry about marriage. Meantime, you three pack a backpack with spare clothes and some food, whatever you think you want to take with you if you have to flee for your lives."

"Okay dad. Say, if the fortress falls, what about our eagles and hawks?" Darcy asked. Imaging the worst, their poor birds would be in trouble unless someone took care of them.

"Good point, Darcy. When they start their actual assault on us, you three turn all our birds loose, give them their freedom for now. We can always summon them back later if we win out," Lord Chester answered. He knew this would give the three something else to do to help. It obviously had to be done, and he could not spare any able-bodied men or women, for that matter. Besides, handling the birds safely without injuring them required a trained hawk master.

Looking out from his high balcony position, Lord Chester wondered if these hundred men and women, some holding nothing but a hay pitchfork, could possibly hold out against a thousand well-armed soldiers from Valen. Hold, that was the key word. He didn't have to defeat this army, just hold onto his fortress here at Humberhills long enough for Lord Wycombe or Wye Tower to send help. They had to send help. They'd signed all these defense treaties.

Eric! They are coming to attack us too, dad's scouts have seen them! He won't let me come to you, though I begged, Sally sent, causing Eric to momentarily pause in his long walk to the eyrie.

Dad won't let me come to you either. I've got to look after my sisters. I promise you no matter what happens, I will come and get you as soon as I can. Somehow, someway, Sally. I love you and we are going to be married after this battle is over. Remember that, stay alive somehow and I will find you, I promise, Eric sent back. Darcy and Dawn had also halted, since he was holding onto each in their usual way.

"Sally?" Darcy whispered, when Eric's eyes told her he was back in the present.

"Yeh, she can't come here," he said sadly. "But I didn't really expect Lord Retford would let her."

"So what did you tell her?" Darcy probed her brother a little. For her, it was a mixture of girlish curiosity and guilt. She and Dawn knew very well her dad had made Eric responsible for them and not just now when the battle was upon them. Eric had been looking out for them as long as she could remember and thus he'd had no life of his own. Sally offered him a way out but now that looked hopeless as well.

"I promised her after this battle is over, I will come and find her no matter what. So it looks like you both are going to have to come with me to Retford just as soon as we can," Eric put his foot down firmly.

"We will, Eric. We'll help you somehow, we promise, don't we Dawn?"

"Yes, we will. Come on. The birds are getting very nervous. I can't say I blame them at all. So many strange people running about," Dawn added.

Meanwhile Lord Chester argued with Elden. "Look, you know as well as I do longbows can only be used for hunting not as a weapon. That was outlawed by the Blackwater Ultimatum. I won't authorize their use against these enemy soldiers, not unless they use them against us first. We will fight honorably, Elden, whether Valen does so or not. We are Humberhills, not riffraff scum. In the final analysis, son, all a man has that is truly his is his honor. Lose that and you've lost yourself. No, we use forks and pole arms to shove their scaling ladders off our walls. We'll pour boiling oil on those who try to smash our gates, but we will fight with honor, son."

Elden knew his dad was right, but still, somehow he wanted to stay alive, to live. At the moment he could not see how they would be able to withstand this siege. "What about a parley with them? Find out what they want?" he tried a different track.

Lord Chester thought this one over. "Well, son, that we could do. What they want is likely our total surrender. Still, it will help buy us time, time for help to get here. Okay, see if you can set up a parley. I'll head down to the gates in case they will talk. Why did I ever go along with all the other lords and become a damn cripple? I deserve to have my head examined," he grumbled.

"A parley? So that is what the white flag is all about," Major Gregorio said with a sigh. He'd hoped they were ready to surrender. "Okay, I'll go talk to them. That will give us more time to get the ladders built and into position for the assault." He walked up to the gate with six personal guards. If this came to anything, he'd send for his *mentales* soothsayer.

A few minutes later, Major Gregorio told Lord Chester and his son, "Simple. You surrender Humberhills to us and become part of the Valen territories as it was before the Blackwater Ultimatum plus you hand over your three *mentales* gifted children to us. They will be taken to Valen Tower and trained. Do this now and we'll avoid a lot of bloodshed, yours."

"I may be a crippled up lord, but I still have my honor. So do all these people here with me. We will fight to the last man, last woman, last child. Their honorable, brave deaths will be on your conscience for the rest of your miserable life!" Lord Chester said with a good deal more feeling than he really felt at the moment. At least the major saluted him as he turned and walked away from the gates without saying a word.

As he walked slowly back to the manor house, Lord Chester said, "Well, I don't think they will be attacking today. Perhaps tomorrow. They've not got many ladders built yet." Elden nodded, following his father's logic. He was pondering what the major had said. Humberhills would be a territory of Valen. Well, that made sense to him, but why did they want his three younger siblings? Tower trained? They had already undergone some of that in Wye Tower. It had been an expensive trip, but he'd had fun exploring the large capital city during the couple of weeks they'd been there. He shrugged his shoulders. *Some things I will never know.*

Major Gregorio had another reason for accepting the pointless parley. He'd just gotten a closeup look at the grey stone walls and the iron re-enforced wooden gates. He'd made up his mind to make the taking of this first fortress an easy one. He had a blaster concealed on him. Lord Valen's orders were to use it if necessary. Well, it was necessary. The stonework, though ancient, was still quite solid. There were just enough men and women manning the walls to keep his troops at bay for days until attrition wore the defenders down. He had seven days to take this fortress and he'd already wasted one getting the ladders for scaling constructed. Well, that was better than trying to lug them across country by wagons. No, he'd make two holes with his blaster, maybe even shoot Lord Chester as well, he smiled to himself.

At nine the next morning just as the dull orange-red sun had begun its diurnal climb into the partially cloudy sky casting a reddish hue over the land, Major Gregorio brought his hand down sharply. A dozen trumpeters sounded a short fanfare and the first wave of his men carrying their ladders began rushing the walls from three sides. Lord Chester moved pathetically slowly to his balcony position, yelling orders. Likewise, Elden and Evan did similar actions. Elden took charge of those manning the walls, while Evan had those above and around the main gates, the weakest point of their defense.

Eric, Darcy, Dawn. It's time; let all the birds go. Then take your packs and head for the secret tunnel and wait for my signal, Lord Chester send his three youngest their orders.

With nervous excitement of the unknown mixed with fear, the trio took their usual positions, with Eric in between the teens. Slowly they began the long walk to the eyrie. If they had not been hobbled in their toe boots, they'd have gotten there in a minute. It took them a half hour to get there while the battle raged around them. Quickly and efficiently, they began releasing the several dozen eagles and hawks, saving their three pets for last. Fighting back tears, they watched their birds take flight, soaring high into the sky.

Major Gregorio watched as the first wave of ladders reached the walls. As he expected, when his soldiers began to climb them, the defenders used any means at hand to push them over. He smiled. "A little of that is all you get!" He pulled out his alien blaster from its concealed sheath. He took aim at the heavy stone wall, where it met the ground some hundred feet to the east of the main gates. He fired three times, creating a hole sufficiently large enough for his men easily to climb through. He aimed for the wooden gates and fired two more times, both gates splinters, partially disintegrated. Major Gregorio could not resist raising his eyes up to the manor house and its large balcony where Lord Chester stood. "Foolish old man." He fired again and part of the man vanished from sight, the remainder falling down out of sight.

He didn't need to issue orders to charge the two openings. His subordinates did and he watched fifty men rushing through the smashed gates. A second later, many came running back, screaming in pain. Some were engulfed in flames. Evan had reacted and dumped all their boiling oil down on those who charged through the splintered gates. As a finishing touch, he tossed the no longer needed torch down, igniting a lot of the oil. Now he raced down to join his men and women, ordering them to form up a U-shaped line around the oil spill.

Major Gregorio's three *mentales* waited on their wagon currently situated at the rear of the battle lines. They knew with the blaster in his hands, the major would not likely need their immediate assistance. Rather, they waited for their objective to materialize: the three young gifted children of this lord. Their orders were quite clear, capture them alive and unharmed, treat them as prescribed, and send them back to Valen Castle. Further from Lord Valen, they knew the general form that these three children's gifts took, and the fact that here in the Midlands almost none of the *mentales* gifted were masters of the five defense forms from psi attacks or the five attack forms, in which all Valen *mentales* gifted were trained. The kid's gifts were harmless or perhaps useless in battle. Their major risked little if he or his men encountered the three children. No, their work would begin when Major Gregorio captured them alive. The three waited patiently, one woman and two men.

As the major's men poured through the two breeches, his orders were both simple and clear in their minds. Kill everyone except the teens with yellow eyes with brown speckles. Simple and easy to follow. Pitchforks and scythes against trained swordsmen, the battle was lopsided. Eric and the twins were barely twenty feet from the eyrie heading back to the manor house and the secret tunnel in the basement when the first of several explosions rocked the fortress. Far ahead, they saw the gaping hole appear in the stone wall and then the gates splinter. For a second, their hopes rose from the terrible shock when the initial group of Valen soldiers were doused in boiling oil and set aflame. They even cheered Evan, who waved once at them as he dashed down the stairs and began forming up his defense lines.

Eric could feel the twins' shaking bodies through his hands, which he still held around their waists. He didn't need telepathy to know they were scared beyond belief. Worse, they saw their father take a blaster shot. Eric knew he'd never get the order to head to the secret tunnel, but headed there anyway, though obviously they'd never make it in time. The battle was all but over. Never had the three seen such horrors. The three knew these people, some from childhood, and the soldiers were methodically killing them. Even when they attempted to surrender, the Valen solders simply stabbed them with their swords. They watched helplessly as their mother and brothers died, one by one.

All around them soldiers swarmed, but they always gave way and avoided the slow moving trio. Eric was too much in shock to wonder why they were being spared, his sisters, likewise. Finally, complete shock took all three and their feet gave out, they slumped to the ground. They'd gotten halfway across the courtyard towards the manor house and the secret tunnel in its basement. They could go no further and numbly waited for the sword strike that would put them out of this horror beyond belief.

Major Gregorio sat tall on his grey stallion, looking at the carnage around the courtyard. A few of his men were tending his own wounded, but many were now going room by room, slaughtering all who were attempting to hide from them. Slowly he rode over to the three teens, who sat on their knees staring into space, shocked into a complete numbness, approaching death. Major Gregorio barked an order, "Bring the *mentales* now. These are theirs to handle. As soon as you can, men, let's form up outside. Well done one and all!" He neck reined and moved off towards the gate, leaving the three twins still sitting waiting for the swords to fall on them.

Vaguely they were aware of the major riding off, of the many soldiers helping their wounded move out through the destroyed gates, of a wagon with two men and a woman coming into the courtyard, its wheels rolling over their dead friends and defenders, and coming their way. The wagon stopped before the three and the men stepped down carefully and stiffly. Had they been more aware, they'd have seen these three wore pipe corsets and toe boots, just as they did. One of the men helped the woman down. All three stood in front of the trio, studying them for a moment. Eric wanted to say, get it over with, but his mouth didn't work. Had he misplaced it?

"We'll set up back there away from this pile of dead bodies. You two start unloading," the woman barked orders, "I'll move the wagon back there." The wagon and men moved behind them. *Good, they'll do it now from behind so I can't see it coming, that's better,* Eric thought. Time passed, the three still sat in sub-apathy, numb, awaiting the end that continued to be delayed.

Eric heard a voice, "They are in shock. That'll make this all the more easily done. We'll bring them out of it afterwards." Darcy and Dawn felt strong arms lifting them up to their feet, which refused to work properly. Both were dragged a few feet and turned around, and then they were dumped onto a strange seat, which was part of some strange machine.

I have seen something like this before, Darcy's mind slowly began to focus. The men grabbed her arms and stuck them into the machine and she felt the cold of the metal against her hands and fingers. *What is this?* Then it struck her. This was similar to the medical machines, which had performed her body modifications! She mumbled, "But I am not hurt. I don't need to be healed."

The woman said, "Relax, this will only take a few minutes." As she sat there, she slowly began to rise up from sub-apathy, going into heavy grief. Her father was killed right before her eyes, as was her mother and two older brothers, to say nothing of all the others whom she'd known all her life. Grief swamped the teen and Darcy began to bawl uncontrollably. Nearby, Dawn was reacting much the same, as she too had risen back up to grief.

Protect your sisters! His father's voice echoed in his mind from some unseen place. Eric heard them crying. Crying. Slowly, he turned around, while still sitting on the ground. His sisters were sitting on some strange machines and they were crying. Were they being harmed? He saw no one doing anything really. Confused, he stared at the scene, unable think, unable to act.

A voice nearby him — was it speaking to him — "Relax, your turn is next. We'll get you fixed up too." *Fixed up? Am I hurt? I can't feel anything.* Eric continued to sit there numbly. Then, the woman did something and helped Darcy get up, she was still sobbing. Strong arms lifted him up and sat him on the machine's seat, sticking his hands inside it. Cold. He felt the coldness on his hands and fingers. Then, nothing. "Relax," the man's voice said again.

As he did, he too began to rise slowly up from sub-apathy, so close to death itself. Like his sisters, grief overwhelmed him and he cried as uncontrollably as they. Then, the man removed his arms from the machine and strong arms beneath his armpits lifted him up off the seat, dragged him backward, and sat him between Darcy and Dawn. He stared down and could see their arms and his own. His mind reeled, unable to process what his eyes were sending him.

The woman came by and waved something before each of their noses, something that smelled awful, but it brought all three sharply back into the world, conscious once more. Now all three screamed wildly. Their hands were gone. Their lower arms near their wrists now tapered down to about an inch across where their wrists had been, their lower arms were now perfectly shaped cones! Eric screamed.

After a time, all three stopped screaming and now fully aware and alert, the woman addressed the trio. "There, that's done properly. You three will soon be taken to Valen Castle. There, if you swear allegiance to Lord Valen and swear to follow his orders, you will be fitted with alien prosthetic hands, which I'm told will be almost as good as your own used to be. However, each month, those prosthetic hands will have to be recharged. If during that month, you've misbehaved or failed to follow Lord Valen's orders or those to whom you'll report, your hands will not be recharged and will be taken away from you, leaving you completely and utterly helpless in all ways. Do you understand what I am saying?"

"Kill us. I won't do it," Darcy replied, having now risen up to anger.

"We won't do it, kill us now," Dawn added, angrily.

Eric looked at his two cones and shook his head. "You bastards. You ought not have done that to my sisters!" An anger surged through his body the likes of which he'd never felt before. His mind reached out to the only things left to him. He felt the avian contact and felt the birds duplicating how badly the three were injured.

Goldie and six other eagles along with twenty hawks tucked their wings in and dove straight down. Connected as the trio was when it came to their birds, Darcy and Dawn sensed what Eric was doing and slipped into rapport with him and the flock of avian hunters. Their prey — the three *mentales* who'd done this horrific thing to them. At the last instant, the woman looked up to see Goldie mere feet above her head, claws open. Wham! Goldie struck her, closing her powerful claws into the woman's eye sockets. She tried to flail her arms to fend off the attacking bird of prey, but lost her balance and fell hard on the cobblestones, totally blinded, as Goldie's powerful beak began pounding into her sockets to get at her brains. Other eagles struck the two men with similar results followed by the many hawks. In minutes, not only were the three dead, but their faces and bodies unrecognizable, just vaguely human-shaped.

Good Goldie. Thank you. Now it is time for you and the others to be free again. Go now, find a mate and live a free life you were meant to have, Eric sent. He sensed the great bird's reluctance to leave him and he added, *Look, now I have no hands to help you. You must go free now, Goldie.* At last, with a loud cry, Goldie took flight, followed by the many other birds. The three watched their pets fly free, circling higher and higher. While they hated to be parted from them, they knew they could no longer care for them. Life had ended for the three, though death had not yet come per se.

As they sat there on the cold cobblestones, an utter silence greeted them. The soldiers had already left. Faintly, they could hear horses in the far off distance, but nothing else. All around them lay their dead family, friends, and defenders of Humberhills. Only they remained alive, but now utterly helpless. Stunned, the three continued merely to sit there, waiting.

How long they sat there, they couldn't afterwards have said. The sun was past the zenith, indicating mid-afternoon. They saw a man suddenly appear not far from the destroyed gates. He looked around, spotted them, and came slowly walking over towards them. He carried a sword at his waist, his face, stern.

As he drew closer to the trio, he finally spoke. "Damn! Damn! Damn! I am truly sorry we could not have gotten here sooner. Came as fast as we could manage. I think you should see what is about to happen. Can you stand on your own?"

"Aren't you going to kill us now?" Eric asked.

A fleeting smile appeared and vanished, "Hardly. I've come to rescue those we can. Come on, up on our feet. You three do need to see this." He took hold of Eric's conical arm and pulled him up, waiting until he found his balance. He repeated it with the twins. Eric reactively put his arms around their waists as he'd always done, before he realized this was now almost useless. He couldn't help them if they lost their balance.

Darcy sensed this too. "Walk carefully, Eric," she whispered. "I want to see what he wants us to see. I think it is important." The stranger led them to the manor house, though he had to wait patiently for close to fifteen minutes before the three finally got there. He had them direct him to their father's balcony. He went ahead and pulled the dead back into the room, covering them with a tapestry he ripped off the wall before the trio made their slow way into the room.

Out on the balcony, they could see far off into the distance. There was the long line of Valen's First Regiment, heading southwest towards the Goza Mountains at the extreme southern edge of Humberhills. "Watch. My wife and some of her friends are out there now waiting for the army to get into the right position. The name's Ben Blackwater, by the way. Wife's Elana. The three leaned their conical stumps on the railing, giving them much needed support and they waited.

"Ah, there. Look," Ben suddenly exclaimed, pointing excitedly at the line of soldiers, which looked more like ants crawling across the green grasslands.

The three felt the ground tremble and their balcony wave a little and they pressed their arms into the railing even harder. Far out across the grasslands, the saw a brown crack appearing. It grew larger and larger. The soldiers and their horses and wagons began falling into the crack, disappearing from view. The shaking earth continued until the last soldier vanished from sight. Then the sides of the crack swiftly closed, shooting up a tall mound of earth, a long thin line. Ben finally spoke, "Beneath that mound lies the entire Valen First Regiment, buried alive for what they've done here. Come, we need to get down to the gates, they'll be walking back here now."

"Revenge?" Darcy asked.

"Revenge!" Ben replied. "We have no intention of allowing one of the soldiers who entered these hills to survive and return to Valen. They have to learn. They used blasters on you, didn't they?" He had to explain about alien blasters before the three realized that was what had caused the breeches and the death of their father.

Chapter 9 Blackwater Counters

Lord Valen, I've just heard a report from Lord Humberhills that a Valen army is about to attack him. He's begged me to send an army to his aid and to alert Wye Tower also to send assistance. Surely, Lord Valen, this isn't true, is it? Lord Wycombe sent. For many years now, he'd maintained a secret alliance with Lord Valen, and he just could not understand how this could be true. *Perhaps, your soldiers are merely practicing their field maneuvers,* he suggested hopefully.

Lord Valen signaled to his team, hastily scribbling one word, teleport. *Good of you to talk with me first. Can we meet face to face and clear up this slight misunderstanding, Lord Wycombe? I always find chatting with you to be highly motivating. Besides, I wanted to give you some new alien gadgets I've recently acquired. Shall I bring you here, my Lord Wycombe?*

Highly motivating? He'd never thought of himself in those terms. Alien gadgets for him? Now that intrigued him. *Well, yes, yes you may indeed. I knew there just had to be some rational explanation. I am greatly relieved already. When shall we meet?*

Are you free right now? I'd like to get this handled right away. You seem terribly worried about this report from Lord Humberhills. A minute later, Lord Wycombe disappeared from his private study and arrived in Valen Castle, though not where he had expected to arrive. He was in the castle; the stone walls indicated that detail. Rather, it was probably Lord Valen's private study, he assumed. However, instead of standing, he arrived sitting down on a seat of an alien machine. Before he could react, two men clamped arms of the machine over his own arms.

"Ah, welcome to Valen Castle, Lord Wycombe. You do us all a great honor by coming today on such short notice. Don't be alarmed with the machine. It is all part of the alien gadgets I wanted you to have. Relax, only be a few minutes. So have you heard any more from this Lord Humberhills?" Lord Valen asked still maintaining an air of politeness with Lord

Wycombe, who had no idea what was happening inside the machine. Well, he soon would.

"He's reporting about a third of the whole army is flooding around his fortress right now. He continues to demand I honor our mutual defense treaty," Lord Wycombe explained.

"Well, one must always honor one's treaties and obligations. What did you reply, if I may be so presumptuous to ask?"

"I had no choice but to tell him if he was being attacked, then surely I would send an army to his aid. Of course, I've done no such thing, not yet. I have no proof this supposed army is yours, Lord Valen. Hell, it could be any number of other kingdoms wresting for control of the hills," Lord Wycombe replied.

Stalling for time, Lord Valen walked slowly over to his great map of Tierra on one wall. Studying it for a time, he said, "Yes, I see what you are saying, my good Lord Wycombe. It could well be an invading army from Rusden Castle down south, seeking to expand their territory."

"Ah, then it isn't your army, but Lord Rusden's? Why would he want sheep herding lands when he's got all the valuable crops lands of the Midlands?" Lord Wycombe struggled to find a reason for Rusden's attack so far north. Just then the machine ceased and Lord Valen made his slow way over to the seated Lord Wycombe, just as his two men removed Lord Wycombe's hands from the machine. He stared in total disbelief at his lower arms. His hands had been removed at his wrists. His lower arms had been somehow tapered into a cone, barely an inch in diameter at what had been his wrists.

"Ah, perfect, just perfect, Lord Wycombe."

"What have you done to me?" Lord Wycombe screamed, shocked and betrayed. "I've kept all our deals and agreements?"

"I told you I have some alien gadgets for you. Here they come now. These are prosthetic hands for you. They will slip over your nicely sculptured lower arms like so. You press here and a little vacuum pump sucks the air out. You operate them just by thinking they were your own hands. Electrical impulses from your brain are picked up by these gadgets and translated into movements. I see you are already working that out. Excellent. Now I have to caution you, don't try to pick up anything that weighs more than about a pound. It'll pull the hands off of your arms."

"But," Lord Wycombe started to protest. Never before had such a feeling of fear so permeated him. His armpits already stank.

"Yes, to business then. Yes, it is my army that is retaking the hills, which once rightly belonged to us. As we speak, Humberhills is about to fall and Retford Hills will follow soon. As far as these new gadgets go, we will be capturing the younger *mentales* gifted there in the hills. They will have their hands removed exactly as you have, my Lord Wycombe. After they are then brought here to me, if they swear allegiance to me and to follow my orders, then I will give them a pair of these fine alien prosthetic hands, just as I have given to you. However, I got distracted a bit a moment ago. You see, these hands will need recharging periodically. If during that time, I find out you are not obeying my orders to the letter, that you are defying me in any way, then I will withhold the recharging, and you can live without your hands. Same with these new young *mentales* gifted. As long as they obey me and help me with my many projects, I will keep their alien prosthetic hands recharged. If not, they can try to live without hands, if they can. Strong inducement, wouldn't you say?"

"You see, I learned something from Nita Valen, who runs Elegant Fashions Inc. You don't have to torture people to get them to do as you ask. See, I have not harmed a hair on your head, beaten you, cut you with a sword, drugged you — none of those barbaric things. I simply and politely will withhold your next recharge if you do not do as I ask. Without your new alien gadgets here, I don't think you can do much of anything at all, so I am sure you will do as I continue to ask of you."

"But, what? Haven't I been faithful to you?" Lord Wycombe wailed, wondering if there wasn't some way to get this machine to reattach his hands.

"Oh yes, yes, Lord Wycombe, until now, I cannot fault you in the slightest. However, with my army now actually *in* the Midlands and Lord Humberhills demanding the mutual defense treaty be honored — well, even you can see I cannot take any chances. I will have my people return you now. Continue to tell Lord Humberhills and any others who contact you that you are sending help right away. Just do not do so. Further, don't alert Wye Castle either. If Wye contacts you, claim you disbelieve these wild stories. Understood?"

"But I would have done that anyway," Lord Wycombe answered. "You didn't have to maim me like this."

"Of course I did. Surely, you can see the wisdom in it, Lord Wycombe. Now I can sleep at night knowing with utter certainty you will not betray me in any way. However, I would suggest from now on, you wear rather long sleeve shirts to hide the hands, particularly where they join your stumps. Now I have a war to run. My aides here will see you safely home. Enjoy the alien gadgets." He turned and made his slow way out of his study, balancing carefully on his toe boots. Before Lord Wycombe could say anything else, he was teleported back into his own private study, where he quickly vomited on his desk.

"So who are you anyway? Why are you helping us? They, they just killed everyone. They surrendered and they killed them anyway. We couldn't do anything to help them," Eric asked, growing more confused, rubbing his eyes with the ends of his little cones. "Out there? The soldiers? Buried alive? The mound? All dead?"

"I'm Darcy Humberhills, sir," Darcy finally became more aware of her surroundings and politely introduced herself and held out her hand to shake his. When she saw the tapered cones instead of her hands, she lost her tenuous control and broke down, sobbing and leaning her head on Eric's shoulders.

"Dawn, sir. He's Eric. Will you be killing us now too? We're ready. We're helpless now, so please hurry up, sir," Dawn added bravely, also leaning her head on Eric's other shoulder.

"Like I said, I'm here rescuing you three. You've had a shock no one ought to have ever had. I'm Ben Blackwater from up in Brom in the far north. Let's get you out of here and to a place of safety for the time being. What's in your packs?"

"Our things," Dawn answered. "We were supposed to leave by the secret tunnel in the basement, but it all happened so fast that we couldn't get there. Why did we ever want to look fashionable and get like this? Now we are hopeless cripples." She broke down now, crying on Eric's shoulder.

With both sisters sobbing on his shoulders, Eric began to come out of his daze. He remembered his fiancé. "Sally! I have to get to Sally before they do!"

"Calm down, Eric. Who is Sally and where is she?" Ben asked, suspecting the worst.

"Sally Retford, next valley to the south, Retford Hills. We were going to be married in three days. I promised I'd rescue her somehow, now I don't know how, but I have too, sir. I beg you, please help us, help me, rescue Sally before they get to her too," Eric pleaded and begged. He'd never really begged before in his life, but at the moment, he felt completely helpless to do anything at all to save Sally.

"We're going to do our best to get to her in time, Eric. Now, come on you three. Snap out of it. Time is not on your side. Let's get you down to your kitchen and something fortifying in you. I need to know why they are mutilating you," Ben said, nudging them gently. Their feet began to shuffle. It was either walk or fall down. Their toe boots didn't give them many options. A half hour later, Ben began giving each a bit of stout ale, hoping the alcohol would calm them a little.

"Okay Eric, Darcy, Dawn. What did they say when they did this to your hands? Did they say why they were doing it?" Ben hounded them. He'd never seen anything like this being done on people of Tierra before, though his wife and many others from Madiera were born similarly.

Eric finally blurted it out. "We are supposed to be helpless like this and taken to Valen Castle where they were going to give us alien hands of some kind. They said the new hands would be almost as good as ours, but that they needed recharging, whatever that is. If we didn't do what Lord Valen told us to do, they wouldn't recharge our hands and we'd be helpless cripples after that. Why? Why does he want us like this? I don't understand?"

"Neither do I, Eric. Now it is making some slight sense. Like this, you would offer them no resistance while they were transporting you to Valen," Ben theorized.

"I have to pee," Darcy mumbled and began crying again.

"I have to help my wife with some personal things. Let's get you all to the commode," Ben suggested. While he was assisting the three, he made contact, *Tim, we have everything under control here. Army is history. What's the situation there?*

Keeping an eye on them. Another batch is heading straight towards the Retford Hills fortress. Probably they are going to sack it, but I can't tell yet. I don't want to kill them all without knowing their intent first. Besides, we can't do that until you can get Elana and her group here. Petrona and I are going to get into a better position to see what's going on and how to lay the next trap. Anyone alive there? Ben explained about the three survivors. *Take them to our safe house and make sure you also get those medical machines too.*

Roger. On it now. Ben focused once more. *Ah, Andres, get the teleporter ready to go. Two trips. Need to bring back two medical machines and three people. They are in shock and need some helping hands.*

Ben sensed Andres laughing at the pun. Andres and Rafaela had lost their arms last winter when they were kidnaped by the Valen patrol, which was also searching for any of the ancient power crystals. *Okay, home in on you, but don't bring you?*

Right. First, we'll get these three teens back. Have Rafaela see what she can do for them. Sleep might be in order. I'm getting them slightly drunk. Then, we'll get these machines. Elana and her group are walking back to the fortress, but that'll take them some time.

"Kids, we are teleporting you to a safe house. A good friend of ours, Rafaela will be there to help you for now. I suggest you try to get some sleep, if you can." The three nodded and vanished, arriving and falling down on the teleport pad. They had been seated when they left.

"Oops, sorry about that," Andres called out, rising slowly from a bank of machine controls. "I am Andres, my wife, Rafaela. Welcome." The three struggled to get to their feet, but saw no real help from the two strangers, they had no arms at all, but they were *mentales* and wore the same pipe corset and toe boots as they did.

"Where are we? Who are you?" Eric asked, still as confused as ever.

Rafaela smiled, "You are in a safe place in the city of Brom in the far north. I know I won't be of much real help to you three, but I'll try. Come with me and I'll take you to a place where you can rest up until the others get back. We're in the middle of a really big operation here, biggest since Andres and I joined up last year. Not much choice though. We got captured by Valen raiders and they pinned our arms behind our backs and left them that way for a month. Our arms froze and we nearly died, would have if it weren't for Ben and Tim and their wives. Here you go, spare bedroom, unless you ladies don't want to share with him."

"No! Eric, stay with us, we're terrified enough!" Darcy gushed.

"Don't worry, sis. I promised dad I'd always look after you two and I will do just that," Eric said bravely.

"Then, I'll leave you to it. Holler if you need something. Andres and I have lots to do and we don't have the luxury of arms like you three do. Things are so damnably difficult for us," Rafaela said. She turned carefully and made her slow way back to Andres in the control room, where he was using he teeth and lips to reset the controls.

"Medical machines coming, love," he said between adjustments. When all was ready, he used his chin to pull the activation level. The machine hummed slightly and the two medical machines appeared on the teleport platform.

"Come on, dear. We have to find some way to get them out of the way of the next teleport. Can't have Ben materializing inside one of those." Rafaela moved on across the room joining him on the pad, a raised platform about an inch tall. Andres got behind one and leaned into it, trying to push it off the pad. All that happened was his toe boots continually slipped on the floor. He could not get enough traction to overcome the friction of the heavier medical machines. Rafaela moved beside him and leaned into it. Pushing together, their toe boots slipping frequently, they did manage to get it out of the way. Panting for breath, they paused before trying the next one. Again, with their toe boots slipping away, they just barely managed to get this one off the pad.

"That does it, dear," Rafaela said between gasps. "I'm going for the mechanical arms. This is silly." He laughed and agreed. Both were eternally grateful for what Ben and Tim acquired for them several months ago. They'd gotten two of the Madiera women's mechanical arms and loading-unloading arms. Essentially, they pushed their bodies into the contraptions that then fastened around them. Using foot controls, they could maneuver the arms. The loading-unloading version was just a larger, more durable version. With the smaller ones, the two could feed themselves and do various small things. With the larger version, they could manhandle these two medical machines off the teleport pad. She headed off to fetch one.

After Ben watched the two medical machines vanish, he headed into the manor house. Elana and her three friends as well as Tim and Petrona would be hungry by now; it was getting late. An hour later, he loaded the stew pot, tea, and other items into the Valen *mentales* wagon and headed off to meet Elana and her three friends who had been slowly walking back across the rolling grasslands. They hadn't worked out a better plan as yet. Everything hinged around Ben or Tim, teleport-wise. With time on his hands at long last, Ben mulled over the events of the last few days. Had there been an alternative plan that could have saved those three such torture?

Rafaela had been the key. It was she who first worked out what was happening. She and Andres were diligent, hard workers, spending long hours each day studying the geosat images and listening in on the communications between the Rigel-3 aliens at the spaceport and those in Valen Castle. The geosat images were just that, images snapped at periodic intervals, normally a few minutes apart. Still, the resolution was good enough for Rafaela to identify Valen soldiers crossing south of the spaceport on their alien-constructed road and on into Exchange City. When she was later asked about it, she'd said, "My curiosity was roused. Why would so many soldiers want to go to Exchange City?" Each day, she found the soldiers had not stayed in the city, but in fact had moved further south out into uninhabited lands and stopped.

Now keenly interested, she continued to monitor the slow buildup. "Looks like Valen is secretly amassing an army just south of Exchange City, but why?" Rafaela had pointed out to everyone. That had been the start of it all.

Ben and Tim joined in, but even they were unable to discern more of what Valen's plans actually were. Ben sighed, "I suppose we will have to wait and see what they do next. I hate being reactive and not proactive. Lives are going to be impacted because we just don't have enough data in hand to act responsibly." Frustrated, they had to wait.

Then Rafaela spotted the army braking up — her words. A third of the men broke off and headed due eastward towards the Humberhills fortress. All four had a lengthy discussion about what this actually meant. It seemed wrong that an army would only send a third of its forces to attack a fortress. They all ought to have gone to the attack. Perhaps this was not then an attack after all.

"Look, the only way we are going to know for sure is to go there and take a look," Ben finally declared.

"You are right. Petrona and I'll go and see what's up. If they are attacking Humberhills, then we have to find a way to eliminate every last one of them," Tim added.

"We could burn them, but with so many soldiers, it would take hundreds of us Fire kindred," Petrona suggested.

"If they are attacking this fortress, then you want them all dead, right?" Elana asked. When it came to life and death matters, she always erred on the side of making triply sure.

"Yes, if they are attacking, they must be stopped and,

since I can't teleport that many, killing them is the only answer," Ben replied. "Why?"

"Oh, well, it's going to take many of us Earth kindred to kill that many soldiers spread out all around that fortress. It must be rather huge, though it looks tiny on the monitor," she explained.

"Rats, I was afraid you'd say that," Ben said slumping in his chair. "Bright ideas gang?"

"Watch and see what they do next," his wife replied. That settled things for the moment. Tim and Petrona stepped onto the teleport pad and Ben set the controls carefully. Both vanished a moment later, appearing well back of the Valen army regiment that was assaulting Humberhills. It was nighttime, but Tim and Petrona were prepared. Wrapping themselves in heavy blankets, they sat waiting for dawn.

With sunrise, they carefully moved higher onto the north ridge line from where they could see better. Both had a pair of illegally imported Imperium binoculars, but Tim had to help Petrona adjust hers. Then they waited. By midmorning, there were no doubts any longer. Valen was attacking Humberhills. Worse, they had used a blaster to crush holes in the gates and the wall. Ben activated the teleport, bringing the two back to their basement in Brom.

"Damned if they aren't using blasters! The aliens must have struck another deal with Lord Valen, damn them," Tim exploded angrily.

"Hey, Tim, look at what I found this morning," Rafaela called out. Tim stomped over to her monitors. "See there, another part of the army is splitting off going for that dot there. Sorry, I can't point, but you see them?" she asked.

"Yes, yes, I do. So they are going after Retford Hills next. It would make sense that the last third of the army is going on south to Trent Hall. Three battles in just a few days. Clever strategy, especially when you have blasters to wipe out your opponents. We're going to have to teach Lord Valen to play fair," Tim swore angrily, but then calmed down.

"You two go grab some lunch and then head off to keep an eye on the second group at Retford Hills. Elana and I will see what we can do at Humberhills. If I have to, I'll pull in every Earth kindred in Brom," Ben suggested.

A while later, Tim and Petrona left to spy on the group heading towards Retford Hills. Rafaela continued her patient monitoring of the hijacked geosat images. "Look, they are leaving. Battles must be quick things," she called out.

"No, if they had not used the alien blasters, the folks in the fortress may have been able to hold out until help came from other cities, like Wycombe. They are the closest, probably Lord Wycombe has already gotten word and is sending troops. Wait, you say it's over?" Ben finally duplicated what Rafaela had implied. He and Elana took a look at the images appearing on her monitor.

"Hey, if you want them dead, now is a good time. See, they are in a long straight line. Four of us could take them all," Elana pointed to the line with her skinny arm.

"Four of you?" Ben asked incredulously.

"Yes, we station two here and here, on either sides of the line of men. We open up a fissure straight through them like so." Elana moved her thin arm up the tiny fuzzy image of the men leaving Humberhills, heading southwest.

An hour later, with the controls set, Elana and three of her friends stood on the platform, while Ben activated the transporter. Then, he reset the arrival point a small amount and stepped onto the platform himself. Using his mouth and teeth, Andres activated the machine, watching Ben vanish, knowing he'd be appearing just outside the gaping holes in the fortress at Humberhills.

"Yep, four tiny black dots appeared. Elana is where she said she needed to be. I think I see Ben too," Rafaela called out from her monitor. Now the two could only watch and wait.

It was dark when Ben sent word for Andres to activate the teleporter again. Soon, he, Elana, and her three friends appeared. "Elana, you and your friends ought to get some sleep. We'll have two more regiments to handle tomorrow," Ben suggested. "I'll be along as soon as I see what's what and check on the three survivors from the Humberhills massacre."

He found the three now awake sitting on the edge of the bed. As soon as he walked in the room, Eric asked, "Sally? Any word about her?"

"Not yet. Retford Hills hasn't been attacked yet. We'll know more tomorrow, son. You hungry? Come on. I'll show you around a little," Ben offered.

"What is this place? Where are we?" Darcy asked. "What about all our hawks and eagles?"

Ben chuckled, "One question at a time. You are underground, below the basement of our tiny house in the city of Brom way up north. We are called the Underground and we are trying to keep the peace on Tierra, keeping the aliens at bay and now Valen too. Come on. I'll show you more."

A bit later, they entered the large control center where Rafaela was carrying a pot of stew in for them. She held its metal loop between her teeth as she made her slow way over to a back table. Already she'd brought eating utensils, which Elana and Petrona used, figuring the three could make use of them. She also brought the big hollow tubes she and Andres used so they could feed themselves by sucking up the stew. Both hated to have to be fed by others, but they had little choice half of the time.

"How can we eat? We're helpless now," Darcy complained bitterly.

"Like my wife does. Here, slip these onto your arms like so. Now see, you can manage," Ben said. He quickly fastened the others onto Dawn and Eric's arms.

"Hey, it does sort of work. How can you possibly eat, Rafaela?" Darcy asked.

"Sucking it up with these tubes. It's not very — well socially acceptable, but we can at least eat some things this way. You are not helpless. Andres and I are the ones around here with that designation," she made light of her situation.

"You mentioned your bird?" Ben probed a little more.

"Yes, we raise and train eagles and hawks for dad, well we used to," Eric answered before going sullen once more.

"We did the hawks, cause they don't weigh so much," Darcy explained. "We set them all free when the attack started, but when we got harmed by the *mentales* people, our eagles and hawks came to our rescue. But now we are really worried. Blacky, Spotty, and Goldie have never been out in the wild on their own before. What if they come back to the eyrie and we are not there to take care of them?"

"Okay, we can check on them tomorrow then," Ben suggested, and she seemed satisfied for the moment. "So tell me again what those three *mentales* told you about why they were chopping off your hands, please."

Darcy complied. "So, what I don't see is why Valen needs us."

"I'm not sure of that either, but it might have something to do with there being fewer of us with the gifts these days. A friend of mine in the tower here has done a study of this and the number of new *mentales* gifted each year is showing a rapid decline. So maybe that is also happening in Valen and he's trying to steal some of you."

"So Lord Valen was going to give you a pair of Rigel-3 prosthetic hands?" Rafaela asked.

"Yes, and make us work for him. If we didn't he wouldn't recharge them and we'd be helpless again, like we are now," Darcy explained. "But we aren't as helpless as we thought, look, we are eating by ourselves."

"Yes, you are. Very well done for trying," Ben validated her.

Rafaela was off on another line of thought entirely. "Ben, if Lord Valen was planning to abduct a large number of young *mentales* gifted and force them to work for him by removing their hands and substituting the prosthetic hands, then it stands to reason he must have somehow illegally acquired a large supply of these hands, right?"

"Yes, they would be considered contraband technology on Tierra and not allowed by the lease and their own directive," Ben replied. "Why?"

"Well, all those hands would likely be stored in one place. I know I would have them in one spot, if I were in charge of such a project. Maybe we can find that stash of hands and get some for these three?" Rafaela suggested.

"I like your thinking! You are turning out to be one very clever Underground woman, Rafaela," Ben praised her. "If we can find the RFI tag key for prosthetic hands, we might be able to locate them."

"I'll see what I can do tomorrow," Rafaela promised.

Tim reported in the next morning. As expected, the Valen army regiment was assaulting the fortress at Retford Hills. *Damn, they are using blasters too. May they rot in hell!*

Okay, we will stand by until they leave, hopefully in a long line like before. Then, Elana and her friends will strike. If there are any survivors who are mentales and they are treated like Eric and his sisters, see if there is anything you can do to prevent it, but don't take any unnecessary risks, Ben sent.

Eric came yelling from his room, though moving slowly in his toe boots and flailing his arms to keep his balance. Obviously, he was going a bit too fast. "It's Sally! They are attacking Retford Hills. We have to do something, please. She is my fiancé, we have to."

"Calm down Eric. Tim and Petrona are there watching it right now. I am afraid against a thousand soldiers, we can't do much, not until they form up into a single straight line. Then, Elana and her friends will strike. Until then, we can only wait, unless you have another idea."

He didn't and began to cry, heading back to his sisters, who were now slowly coming after him. They put their arms around him and did their best to console him. Ben looked at Andres; he was busy adjusting the teleport machine. Nearby, Rafaela was monitoring the geosat images. By using a wooden stick, she was also typing in something on her keyboard. Well, there was nothing he could do now, so he headed off to see if Elana was getting ready.

It was afternoon before they headed off for action. Retford Hills fell almost as quickly as Humberhills had. Once more the invading army formed up into a single long marching line, heading west towards the Goza Mountains, before turning south once more, probably to join up with the final third of the army which was heading southeast across Trent Hills towards the fortress there. "We will get them both today," Elana declared passionately. "I can't believe these men killed everyone in that town."

Meanwhile, Tim and Petrona kept watch on the fortress from a good distance away. "Barbarians, savages!" Petrona cursed, as she watched the ongoing slaughter. Neither could do anything, though they wanted to rush in and fry some of these men. They resisted the urge, knowing they'd soon be overwhelmed by so many soldiers. No, they waited, though not patiently. As the battle died down, they spotted a wagon with three riders on it moving up and then through what were left of the gates.

"Those are the *mentales* gifted, love. I can sense their minds. I think they have got some captured *mentales* gifted inside to mutilate. I hope it isn't Eric's fiancé."

"We can't get in there right now; there are still too many soldiers in the way. Look, they are coming out now, forming lines like before," Petrona whispered.

"Patience, come on, soldiers leave, leave," Tim whispered, as if his encouragement would somehow hasten their departure. How many were being mutilated just inside the fortress while he waited helplessly outside? After what seemed an eternity, the last soldier came out and moved off several hundred feet. Seeing no further men coming out, Tim finally decided to come out of hiding. He and Petrona made their way carefully over the rough land to the grassy area out in front of the fortress. Now they could see the disintegrated wall and gates. Bodies lay strewn all over, left where they had died, many trampled afterwards. The two moved silently inside, alert for more soldiers. Seeing none, Tim paused a moment, sensing what direction to take.

They were around back of the manor. The two walked past many dead men, women, and children. "My god, they killed babies too!" Petrona whispered, aghast at what she was seeing up close. Around the rear of the manor, they found the wagon. One of the two medical machines was missing and a door into the back of the manor was ajar. The two crept up and listened for voices.

"Leave her on the chair. A little crying will make her more tractable. Come on. Let's get this machine back on the wagon," a male voice said. Tim signed to Petrona and the two backed off, taking cover just around the corner of the stone building. Shortly, two men and a woman came back out of the door, the men struggling with the machine. Tim nodded to Petrona and she acted without hesitation. She focused and summoned a searing wall of fire, placing it on top of all three.

Taken by complete surprise, their hair and clothing burst into flames. Hobbled with their own pipe corsets and toe boots, they vainly tried to extinguish the flames, but only fell to the ground. Their frantic gasping for breath ended swiftly, while the searing flames continued to consume their bodies, turning body fat into flames. Petrona's flames were incredibly hot. Tim nodded to his wife and ducked into the manor house to find their latest victims.

Tim found only a fifteen year old blonde, sitting on a chair, sobbing her heart out. On her lap lay her arms. They were too late to save her. Like Eric and his sisters, her hands were gone, her lower arms tapered into a cone barely an inch across where her wrists used to be. Damn, he thought.

"Hello, miss. Are you Sally?" Tim asked softly. The teen nodded mechanically, but didn't respond. He sensed she had dropped to sub-apathy too. "My wife and I have come to rescue you and take you to your fiancé, Eric. Eric and his twin sisters were the only survivors at Humberhills. Are there any other survivors here?" He had to repeat his question several times before she slowly shook her head no. Petrona came in and shook her head sadly at the condition of Sally.

Tim put his hand on Sally's shoulder and then on Petrona's shoulder. Andres activated the teleport machine. As he looked up, the three appeared on the platform, though Sally fell to the ground at once. She had been sitting and now there was no chair under her, but she made no move to stop her fall. Tim picked her up and carried her to the guest room, where an impatient Eric was waiting.

"Sally! Sally! Oh no, not you too," he exclaimed, frustrated he could only get to his feet before Tim walked across the room and sat her on the edge of the bed. Eric sat down beside her and put his arms around her. Darcy did the same from her other side.

"Look after her for now. Sorry, we could not get to her in time to save her, but those who did this to her are dead, burned alive by Petrona. Back after while," Tim said and hurriedly left.

Tim and Petrona returned and brought back the two

medical machines. Meanwhile, Ben, Elana, and her three friends arrived in their positions some distance ahead of the long column of soldiers. He sat back on the grass, leaving Elana to handle the attack. He was relegated to being their lookout. As before, she placed themselves in pairs some twenty feet apart. They too sat on the grass waiting for the head of the column to get closer. At last, Elana rose and the four focused. As before, the earth shook violently. A huge crack appeared running roughly down the center of the long line of men, horses, and wagons. It widened, dropping screaming men into the abyss. After the last one vanished from sight, the crack closed rapidly. A deafening thunder rolled over the landscape as the two sides met and a mound of earth rose up, the living dead lying beneath it. "Well, two down, one to go," Elana commented dryly.

They joined together and Andres brought them back to their teleport pad. Already Tim and Petrona had taken off after the last third of the army. Using Rafaela's latest geosat images, he'd set the controls for a likely spot and had gone there. "Just waiting for Tim's report," Andres said as Ben and the women appeared before him. An hour later, Tim sent them the good news that they had found them and that they were in a line like the other two. Ben acted quickly and an hour after that, they returned home. The last third of the army was now beneath the earth as well, along with the two medical machines they had with them. Ben saw no way to recover the machines; they were now buried somewhere beneath that long, long mound.

After everyone was back safely and the friends taken home, Rafaela made her discovery known. "Tim, look what I've found. On this monitor, I've found the RFI item number prefix for their prosthetic hands."

He could see that clearly on the screen. "So that's what you were looking for earlier?"

"Right. I found that prefix. Now look at this. I used your RFI locate machine and see there? There are a whole lot of them in one place. That must be where Lord Valen is storing them, don't you think? And how can we get four pairs for our rescued four?"

"Rafaela, you are a genius! Brilliant. Slide over. Let me

see what I can do." He typed away for a short while, and then sat back running his hands over his head. "I think there is a way. He's got hundreds there, so he won't miss eight. Rafaela, here's a trick my mother taught me. You see, the Imperium uses these RFI tags to locate and if need be retrieve an object or person. Say you forgot where you left your keys, you punch in their RFI code and presto, you know where they are. Mind you, I've not actually done this before, but here goes nothing."

He pressed a few buttons and she watched what he did closely. The teleport activated and four boxes appeared. The two left the console and headed there, but Rafaela had only gone a few steps before he reached them. Again, she silently cursed her foolishness in having her feet done. Thankfully, he brought them back to her. "What have we here?" He opened one box and found two pairs of the hands.

"Looks like you got a few more than we need," Rafaela commented. He verified her assumption.

"Yes, we can handle four more people. Spares otherwise. Come on. Let's get these to our guests. I'll walk slow; you deserve much of the credit, Rafaela."

They found Eric and the twins still consoling Sally. She'd stopped sobbing but her eyes were still red. "You four are in luck," Tim said, as he let Rafaela enter first, making her slow way over to them, being extra careful while walking as she always had to now. "Rafaela here found where Lord Valen was keeping the promised hands, the prosthetic hands. We sort of stole them from him. Got you each a pair. The instructions are unfortunately in Imperium Standard, so I will read them to you, but let's get them on you first."

Darcy held out her arms eager to have some way to survive. "They slip on like this, just align them right. You don't want your palms facing outward." All chuckled a little and Sally now began looking at them as well, pulling a bit more out of her intense grief. "Once in place, press here. Hear that noise? It's a vacuum sucking out the air, sealing the hand onto your arm. When you want to take them off, press in the same spot. Now how do they work? It says here you just pretend you are picking up something and the hands translate your body's nerve energies into what they should be doing."

"They are grey, but I can live with that. Look, it opens and closes," Darcy exclaimed. "But I can't feel anything with them."

"Er, right. Sorry about that. It says here they need recharging periodically. Ah, here, to recharge, place in direct sunlight for a day. Well, that seems simple enough," Tim suggested, moving over to handle Dawn next. Then he did Eric and Sally last. Rafaela watched with a huge smile as the four fiddled with their hands, making them do usual actions. "It says, caution. Do not lift more than one pound with them or the hands will come off of your arms."

"Thank you Rafaela, Tim! I can't feel anything with them, but maybe I can at least pick up a fork and dress myself," Darcy said, very pleased.

"Maybe our lives are not totally destroyed," Dawn admitted. That's what Tim so hoped to hear.

"Now then, about your eagles and hawks. Shall we go see if they are at your eyrie and if so, how about bringing them back here?" Tim suggested.

"Can we? We've got traveling cages for them," Darcy gushed, happier than she'd been for days.

"Of course, you are going to have to build another eyrie out back," Tim cautioned them.

Sally finally said something, "Maybe I can still train horses."

"I'm sure that you can, Sally. Come on. Let's go see what we can salvage from your destroyed manors. We ought to see about a burial detail though."

Far below the surface of Tierra, the red hot magma jiggled a little, thrice. A being stirred, *What?* It thought. It waited, listened, but then fell back into its long slumber.

Chapter 10 Valen Reactions

"What do you mean you can't find them?" Lord Paco Valen cried angrily. The veins in his neck throbbed, his face, flush. It had been three days since he'd last had contact with his general and his majors, let alone the *mentales* field agents. By now, he ought to have at least a half dozen new handless *mentales* here at his castle. He had boxes of hands to hand out; he was ready, but where the devil was his army and men?

Amo Hernandez shivered. He'd never seen his liege this angry before. "My Lord, there is nothing. We cannot sense any minds, not even of the three thousand soldiers. We do not understand this at all. Perhaps you could ask the tower circles for aid, just this one time?" He knew he was risking a diatribe by making this suggestion, but he and the other *mentales* working for Lord Valen had no other ideas. The thousands had just vanished. Most peculiarly, they also didn't sense any minds at Humberhills or Retford Hills either. Most confusing.

The verbal assault didn't come. At last, Lord Valen let out a huge sigh. "Perhaps you are right, Amo. I haven't been able to contact them myself. Okay, I will do as you suggest. The tower circles ought to be useful for something. Stick around. I may need you after I get back. Amo Hernandez knew this action on his lord's part was at a great sacrifice not only of face, but also physically. He had a long way to walk in the toe boots. After Lord Valen left him sitting in his office, he smiled. *Serves him right to have to walk too. I had a long walk just to answer his summons I could have answered via telepathy!*

Two hours later, a somber and exhausted Lord Valen made his slow way back into the room and to his chair. Thousands of tiny steps and tricky stairs had taken its toll. Amo Hernandez waited patiently, smiling inwardly. "Well, the Venerada can't find any traces of them either. On my way back here, I've decided to pay Adalina and Emeryk a visit. I've summoned my air car. It's time to call in some of the favors the Sector ID Minister owes me. Care to come along?"

"Wouldn't miss it for a moment, my Lord." To get a chance to be inside the alien headquarters building was a very momentous occasion.

An hour later, the two finally reached the air car and a half hour later, it touched down at the spaceport. The lovely Adalina was there to meet them. She wore her arm-fetter-gown in cherry red satin and shiny black toe shoes that so aroused her husband. "Lord Valen, it is so good to see you again. Amo Hernandez." She waited until the two closed the distance between them, which took several minutes. She opened her lower arms for a hug and Lord Paco obliged, hugging her warmly. Automatically, he put his arm around her waist, steadying the both of them. She did likewise, as best she could with only her lower arm free.

As she led them inside, she chatted, "It has been far too long since you came to visit. I hope you will stay and have supper with us. Do you like my new dress? So evocative, don't you think?" she asked coyly.

Lord Paco grinned, "If I weren't married. . ."

She laughed, "Silly old man, when does that have anything to do with it? That's what fosterlings are for or have you forgotten?"

"I don't want to upset Emeryk; he doesn't approve of wife-sharing," he whispered. "Otherwise we would make a stop in your room first. Yes, I like your new dress. You have excellent taste, Adalina. Your hair is longer too, isn't it?" The two chatted and the long time to get to Emeryk's office passed more quickly.

"Ah, there you are, old friend. Come on in, come on in. I take it that all is well?" Emeryk said rather pleased to have this extremely valuable ally on Tierra in his office. "We meet so infrequently."

"Well, I agree with you on that point. Of course, if you want to share your charming and beautiful wife here, why, I'd be here every day!" Paco replied graciously. This was their long-standing tease. Emeryk looked very pleased.

"Never have I seen such a woman as my dear Adalina! Come, have a seat."

After sitting down, Lord Paco came to the point. "You know that territory recovery program I launched this spring?"

"Ah yes, I do recall it. You were retaking the lands you

lost some time back. In the foothills, right?"

"Yes, precisely. I've come to ask for a little help. You see, we've lost all contact with them some three days ago now."

"What? You have telepathy. Surely?" he asked confused.

"Of course, but we are unable to make any contact of any kind with any we sent on this mission. Three thousand plus."

"Most interesting. How can anyone lose an army? Come, let me fire up our geosat viewer. We'll locate them in no time. One of the many benefits we of the Imperium have — a way to view anything on the ground, as long as there isn't cloud cover, that is. Ah, it's online now. I need to know where to look." Lord Paco directed him to the last known locations, near Humberhills and Retford Hills.

All four stared at the screen as Emeryk scrolled around the area. They could see no signs of the army or the individual regiments. After a half hour, they did spot three large mounds of earth, each nearly a half mile long. When they zoomed in on the Humberhills fortress, they saw a few wagons and carts being loaded with dead bodies, but nothing else.

"How the devil can an entire army vanish without a trace?" Lord Paco asked.

Emeryk scratched his head. "Now that is a very good question! It can't. Well, it could if they were nuked or a massive disintegrator was fired at them, but I can see no signs of that either. There would be enormous patches of scorched earth. They've simply vanished. I see your concern. Perhaps, Lord Valen, there is something going on here that neither you nor I are aware of?"

He added, "Tonight, I will send out two scout ships and see if they can spot a mass of troops anywhere in that region. I suppose they could have lost their way and have marched out of the area by mistake."

Lord Paco discounted that theory. His nine *mentales* gifted would never have allowed such a stupid mistake to have been made. Besides, the last word he had from three of them was they had the three Humberhills *mentales* handled and would have them ready to be transported to Valen Castle in an hour. That had not happened.

"Come, gentlemen. It's time for supper. Will you charming men please accompany your elegant woman here to our private dining room?" Adalina flirted with both men. Emeryk was only too pleased to do so.

While at dinner, Lord Paco received a telepathic message from one of his *mentales* gifted aides. *My Lord, a piece of paper just appeared on our teleport pad. It says: Do not send more armies into the Midlands. They will meet the same fate as the last one has. Sire, it is signed The Underground. What does this mean? Have you located them yet?*

No. Keep this news to yourself until I return.

Adalina noticed his momentary absence from their table chat and knew he'd just received a telepathic message. She read his face and knew it was both important and troublesome. "So, any news, My Lord?" she asked coyly.

"I'm not sure. Emeryk, in your capacity as Sector ID Minister, have you ever heard of a group on Tierra calling themselves the Underground?" Lord Paco asked.

Emeryk scratched his head. "No, I am afraid I haven't. Of course, out there in the galaxy, there are a lot of underground movements, designed to disrupt legal governments. That goes with the territory. But here on Tierra, nothing like that at all. Sorry. Ought I know something about them?" He turned the question around, hoping to gain some additional insights.

"Not at this time, sir. Probably it's a hoax. Valen has lots of enemies."

Emeryk laughed, "Don't we all. Comes with the job. No matter what you do, someone is likely to get their feathers ruffled. My motto is always try to make them ineffective, hobble them somehow." Lord Valen chuckled, as a new brilliant idea appeared in the back of his head.

After the enjoyable dinner, he asked to borrow an electric car to make a trip into Exchange City to visit Elegant Fashions Inc. Around eight that night, he and his Amo parked the car in the underground lot and rode the elevator up to the fourth floor, where Nita was expecting them. After introducing Adalina and Emeryk's daughter and assistant, Dorita, to Amo

Hernandez, she had her assistant entertain the Amo, showing him where he could spend the night. Meanwhile, Nita took Lord Paco into her private meeting room.

"So what is so important that it can't wait until morning, Uncle Paco?" She still preferred to call him uncle. Their blood line was far too confusing to attempt a more direct reference.

"The army is gone, vanished without a trace," he said softly. After her gasp of shock and surprise, he filled in the few details he had.

"So they had three *mentales* teens with their hands removed and ready for the prosthetic hands and then they all vanished? Could we be facing some unknown type of *mentales* gift here?" she asked quite alarmed.

"Yes, they were going to be transported to me for their new hands within an hour of their last message several days ago. Then nothing at all. I visited Emeryk and he used his geosat thing to look for the army. Nothing. We did see three very long and strange mounds of earth — fresh. Nothing else, except some locals trying to bury the many dead in Humberhills and Retford Hills. So I know damn well my army took those two fortifications, but the others are untouched."

"Incredible! What could have happened to them?" she asked.

"One more thing." He quickly told her of the strange message from the Underground, whatever that was. "Probably just someone trying to take advantage of the situation. I've never heard of any such group and neither has Emeryk."

"Well, I'm not surprised with Emeryk. He doesn't know much of anything that goes on on Tierra, only what we feed him."

Lord Paco smiled. "Right. Now I am left with piles of prosthetic hands and no *mentales* gifted to give them to. Well, that's not totally true. I put a pair on Lord Wycombe before all this happened." She smiled, never having liked that lord.

"Emeryk did give me an idea. He said, 'My motto is always try to make them ineffective, hobble them somehow.' Well, my lovely niece you and your grandmother have been doing an admirable job of this, far, far beyond anything anyone else has, though I really hate these toe boots. Still with nearly all the lords, ladies, and *mentales* gifted in power also hobbled, we've made it vastly easier for our soldiers to take them. It looks like my plan did work; it only took one regiment to eliminate the Humberhills fortress."

Nita smiled seductively, waiting to hear more. Since he didn't, she then said, "I am so glad you appreciate all we have done to help our beloved Valen. So how did Lord Wycombe take it?"

"Interesting. I played him well. Now he is my puppet and there is not a darn thing he can do about it. I had such high hopes I could get a number of new *mentales* gifted under my control. You have to admit this prosthetic hands idea of mine is almost as brilliant as Carmen and yours with the toe boots and your fancy dresses."

Nita smiled demurely. "Almost," she said with a note of teasing in her voice.

"Do you suppose there is any way in the world you could somehow make them also desire to have their hands removed and wear the prosthetic hands I have in abundance now?" He came right out with his idea. "The lords, ladies, and especially the *mentales* gifted?"

"I guessed as much. That is a tall order, uncle. The only way possible is to convince them there is some tremendous benefit in so doing it. It is, after all, a huge modification to undergo. We so depend on our hands," Nita pointed out.

"True, but is such a thing even possible?"

"There is. Did you adjust the machine like I suggested — with Lord Wycombe, I mean?" she demurely inquired.

"Well, yes, I made those to all the medical machines. Why? I have often wondered what those changes were for, my charming niece."

"Heightened tactile senses. I programmed the medical machines to jam all the sensory nerve endings from the lower portion of the hand being removed, attaching them into that small conical tip. Your victims ought to have a super sensitivity with their arm tips, which as you ought to know, such sensitivity can be easily misinterpreted as a sexual stimulus. That might be one selling point, heightened sexual pleasures.

No more pain in your hands would be another one. So many of the *mentales* working in the towers get hand burns. This would alleviate such pains. But again, a modification of this magnitude is going to have to be very, very well sold."

"Suggestions?" Lord Valen asked.

"Well, it has to begin at the top. They have to see the key opinion leaders doing it."

"Like yourself?" he asked.

"Yes, I would have to have it done, of course, but you would also need to have it done as well. We'd need another ten more key lord, ladies, or *mentales* gifted done when we first introduce it. I don't think with something of this magnitude I could pull it off myself or even with you too. We need about a dozen key people all bragging it up as the latest in thing to do. Of course, the down side is if we do it to ourselves, we can't undo it. We're stuck with having no hands or rather having prosthetic hands. How far are you willing to go with this? I guess that is the question I have for you," Nita asked.

"Ten more, you say. I can get Lady Wycombe. I think I have a way I can get us those ten leaders."

"So you're serious about this? What's the overall objective here?" she asked. "To get them as close to helpless and ineffective as possible?"

"You would make a superior lord, Nita. Precisely. Always in the past, other *mentales* gifted individuals have been behind our defeats, one way or another. We've had to counter their various counterattacks against us at every turn. As I see it, somehow we need to neutralize them as much as we can. Only then can we hope to take over total control of Tierra and open up our world to all the amazing things the aliens have to offer us. I know for a fact if I control all Tierra, Emeryk will do just that — open us up to all forms of trade. Think of what that means, Nita. All manner of fantastic devices can be ours. Unbelievable technology can lead our people into a brilliant, prosperous future, not this continuous medieval-like, backwards society. I see a bright new future for us all, but first we have to control Tierra. There's not a chance in hell I can get the Midlands or Easterlings to go along with this. They still hate the aliens. So somehow I have to conquer them all. If we can get them even more neutralized, we have a chance."

"Brilliant, uncle, brilliant. Okay, I'm in. I will also work on other ways to lessen their effectiveness. Will we introduce this at the fall council meetings?" she asked.

"I'd like to. Can we be ready by then?"

"I'll be honest with you. I don't want to lose my hands, but I will, if you have your ten additional opinion leaders done and have yours done too. If so, I'll have mine done and make the marketing presentations at the council meetings," Nita explained in no uncertain terms.

"Excellent, Nita. What other things can be done?"

"That depends on just how far you want to go with this. Adalina and I have full computer access, and we've been doing a lot of research into other cultures and their body modification practices. We've seen where Empress Amy Blackwater got her ideas from, the Ataro System of the wasp worshipers. There are all sorts of things that can be done. Let me show you one that has intrigued me some." She rose and activated her computer. Lord Valen rose and moved to her side. Automatically, both put their arms around each other's waists to steady themselves.

"See, in some cultures, women pierce their lips and insert these jeweled plates. Of course, once done, their speech is very difficult to understand. Still we have telepathy, so not a serious problem. I might be able to sell this one. Here's a cult that wires their jaws shut, claiming speech is satanical, whatever that means."

"How do they eat?"

"They've knocked out their front teeth and only eat liquid foods. I don't think this one is sellable though. Now here's another interesting one. This cult actually puts out their own eyes, replacing them with multicolored glass eyes. They claim sight is what leads one into temptations. We certainly can't sell that one."

He laughed, "Well, that one would be helpful. If they can't see — but I see what you mean, un-sellable no matter how you disguise it."

"Now here's a group that sticks all kinds of metal things out of their faces. It's freaky, but useless for our situation. This one here is also a possibility. See, they fasten a series of metal rings around their necks, stacking them on top of each other until the stack of rings is totally tight. Apparently, they cannot then move their necks and it gives them the illusion of having long necks. They claim to have perfect posture as well, but according to the article, they have to turn their bodies to see, since the rings prohibit them from turning their heads. This one has possibilities, but I don't know how sellable it would be."

She went on, showing him some other pages. "This society here pierces their ears, inserting large disks and then hangs huge, heavy ornamental earrings on them, both men and women, as you can see. This one is a possibility, but I don't know how effective it would be for our purposes — an annoyance at most, perhaps."

"Wouldn't women enjoy showing off such jewelry?" he asked.

"Probably. That's its selling point. For men too. Show your wealth, but that flies against being humble for our average citizens," she countered.

"There are others too. I've been thinking a lot about all this since you first came to me with your prosthetic hands plan. You know, we have a golden opportunity to really sell some of these additional modifications. We could claim there is a strange new debilitating illness spreading among the telepaths. For example, it destroys cartilage in necks so you need to wear these neck rings, or just about anything else we want to sell."

"Damn, you are *good*, woman," he complimented her. She smiled, knowing full well she was.

"Another thing, uncle, we could also modify the prosthetic hands and embed in them a timed injection. There are substances, which introduced into one's body, causes blindness. Of course, the downside of that is the aliens would then be blamed, going against what you are trying to achieve."

"I like your ideas. We could claim a plague is spreading, causing *mentales* gifted hands to wither and cause death if not treated. It also weakens necks, so they would need to get the rings attached or die. Of course this will be especially tricky, since there are so many soothsayers about."

"I've thought about that. There is a way. There are drugs out there that can cause these types of symptoms. Of course they're only temporary, but still it could help convince others to hurry up and get it done. But if we went this route, we'd have to be prepared to perform many such operations in a short time. Lots of prosthetic hands and rings," she pointed out.

"Brilliant. Suppose I visited some of these lords. I could slip it into their food, and then when they got ill, I'd come to their rescue with my 'help.'"

"Now who is being devious," she grinned. "I'll get you some soon. I've had it on order for a month now. I kind of figured this might be useful. What about lip plates for the women? Those do look attractive in their own unique way. If I tinker a bit, I can get the lips also super sensitive to touch, dynamite kisses."

He chuckled. "Get me that drug. I'll get it introduced into a lord's food and have the lord begging me to save him."

"Yes, but you will need to be modified first to make it more believable."

He sighed, "You are right. It won't be nearly as believable, if I am not altered the way I'm going to alter them to 'save them' from death. We'll do it to me, when you have the drug. Let me know." They chatted more, but little else was critical.

Two days later, the drugs arrived and that night, Lord Valen came directly to Elegant Fashions Inc, prepared to take the plunge — all for the sake of Tierra's future. "Holy cow! You really did it!" he exclaimed, totally surprised as Nita greeted him at her office door.

"I can't talk very well," she attempted to say, but he didn't really make out what she was saying. *I can't talk very well. You like it? If it doesn't sell, it can be easily undone.* Her lips had been slit and two highly ornamental lip plates inserted, a special design of her own. They had a strong base to them, resting firmly against her upper and lower gums. Plus, four metal dowels were inserted through her gums which helped hold the plates very securely. Each plate was about five inches across, gilded with a few small rubies embedded in them. Similarly, both her ear lobes were slit and held a gilded disk an inch across. Hanging from them were alternating lobes of gold and rubies. The dangles reached all the way down to her shoulders, the last few pairs resting on her shoulders. *You like my new look? Want to see what a truly sexy kiss can be?* She teased him. Nita had already sensed his sharp arousal and didn't need to ask.

"I'm game. My god, Nita, you look so different, so well I don't know what to say. Like it? You bet. Absolutely I would, but first we need to get this all done," Lord Valen replied.

Figures, all work and no play from you guys. This way. Here's enough of the drug to sicken hundreds. All it takes is a few sprinkles mixed in with any food. It begins to take effect within hours of consumption, reaching peak effect a day later. It takes three days to fully vanish, giving you a wide window of opportunity for the victims to really panic. She gave him the large box and led him to her medical machine. He laid out his small box, which held a pair of hands, his new ones, and took a seat. He knew what to do, inserting his hands into the machine. She carefully adjusted the machine, enclosing his lower arms. He felt the two pinpricks and waited. For some reason, he held his breath. Soon, he relaxed, thinking of what he was doing for his beloved world. He, Lord Valen, would be remembered as having made enormous sacrifices to bring Tierra into the modern world!

Nita had to tell him to pull his hands out twice. He was deep in reverie. "Oh. Well, they look like the ones I've made before. I guess you have to help me into my new hands, Nita." She did so, getting them on perfectly. He began to wiggle them. "Sure is strange not to be able to feel anything with them."

Probably takes some getting used to them, I expect. Now then, neck rings?

"Yes, let's go all the way with this. How do we do it?"

Other cultures call them chokers. The rings I had made fasten in the back, see, like this. We keep putting them on until they are fully tight. You'll see. One by one, she began fastening the one-inch tall copper colored rings around his neck. She didn't tell him with his new hands he'd probably not be able to undo their latches himself. The last ring she had to force hard to get it to close. Once locked, she stepped back admiring his look. *Come to my mirror and see how it looks on you. Sexy, if I do say so, My Lord.*

"Oh! I can't move my head at all! Well, that will certainly be debilitating too." Slowly he moved across the room, as she moved in beside him. She adjusted his shoulder length hair.

See, you do look sexy and you have perfect posture, uncle. What do you think?

"Terribly confining, but I suppose I'll get used to it. After all, I am not about to engage in fights myself. That's what I have soldiers for. I can't get over how you look, though." He turned towards her. "How do I kiss you now?"

She was wearing a satin arm-fetter-gown, matching the rubies in her lip plates and earrings. Leaned her head down, Nita raised up her lower arms. They just barely reached. Carefully, she pulled the plates outward until the dowels cleared her gums and then gently removed the plates, sitting them on a table. Her lips were now two loops. *Like this,* she sent. She gave him a kiss on his cheek. He felt the long, warm loops on his skin, electrifying him. His arms encircled her. Soon, they headed to the satin sheets of her bed. Although he didn't know it, she timed it perfectly and sensed his seed impregnating her. She would have his son, but now was not the time to tell him.

The next day while they dined in her room, he worked at learning more how to control his hands. After that, she sent him on his way with the drugs and a large quantity of the rings. Of course, she retained a quantity of both. Now that she proved to herself the powerful physical attraction her new look had on Lord Valen himself, she went ahead with her own plans to introduce them at the next council meetings. That meant she had to have a goodly supply of all them made and sent out to her fifty satellite stores around Tierra.

Two days later, his agent had successfully introduced the drug into the dinner being served to Lord Wycombe and his close associates. Lord Valen took this opportunity to pay an unannounced call on him. "Good evening, Lord Wycombe. I am sorry to come by so late this evening, but I thought I owed you a favor. I took advantage of you with your hands there."

Before he could continue, Lord Wycombe interrupted him, "What happened to you? You've got the alien hands too. And what's with those neck ring things? Please have a seat, tea, ale?"

"Ale, please. Yes, as I was saying, recently, I and my staff have isolated a new strain of virus that's beginning to appear around Tierra. So far, it only affects we *mentales* gifted."

"What does it do? What's it got to do with my hands?" *You cut mine off unwillingly, if you have forgotten.*

"It begins with a red rash on one's hands. There is no known treatment for it. I checked with the aliens, they've never seen it before either. If untreated, not only do your hands wither up, but your neck degenerates until you can't support your own head any longer. Death is inevitable. However, since I suspected you might have contracted the virus, I went ahead and tricked you into having the infected hands removed. Then I watched you — well from a distance. You seem to be perfectly healthy, right? No lingering redness, no weakness in your neck?"

"Er, no, none I'm aware of. Cutting off the hands works?" he asked confused. *Have I completely misunderstood Lord Valen?*

"Yes, that's the only cure we've found to date. Of course, one can risk one's body will be successful in fighting it off. However, if it goes beyond two days' time, not even cutting off the infected hands will save you. I myself got the virus a few days ago. They got to me in time and I am perfectly healthy now. I felt obligated to come and tell you personally that I deliberately lied to you, but only because I didn't know whether or not doing it would be the only thing, which would save your life. I know we did the right thing, so I came to apologize to you personally. If you discover anyone else here in Wycombe who comes down with it, let me know. Send them to me before two days have passed and I'll do my best to fix them up. Right now, we're dealing with those who get ill in Valen.

Before long, I expect the virus will show up in other kingdoms too. Viruses have a way of spreading, you know."

"Well, thank you, Lord Valen. This is quite a surprise. I will keep it in mind, but no one has gotten ill, knock on wood." The two men chatted and after downing his ale, Lord Valen left, knowing he'd soon get a frantic call for help. He was right. Around noon the next day, Lord Wycombe made contact with him, pleading for help. A dozen had gotten ill, only the gifted seemed affected, including his wife and two of his children.

Within a couple of minutes, Lord Valen arrived there. All twelve were sitting around the large table in his Great Hall. All had the infection in their hands, red splotches. Many also complained their necks hurt, but that was merely the power of suggestion. "Oh my. So many of you have gotten this virus!" Lord Valen commented.

"Please, can you help them?" Lord Wycombe pleaded. His wife and two daughters were among those infected. His sons were not; they didn't have the gift, much to his continuing dismay. Sons were his heirs, not daughters. His sons commanded his soldiers and always ate with them.

"Well, has it gone beyond the two day limit?" he asked seriously, knowing it hadn't.

"Oh no. I contacted you the moment we first spotted the symptoms," the nervous Lord Wycombe answered.

"Then, it can be cured. Have you told them the only known cure?" Lord Valen asked.

"Yes, well sort of. Please, why don't you tell them what you told me?"

"As you prefer. We've had an outbreak of this very virus in Valen. The only known cure to this point is to remove your hands and support your necks with these rings. As you can see, the rings hold my head immobile. I've made a humane deal with the aliens for some of their prosthetic hands, since this is a medical emergency. So I can remove the infected hands and give you some like I have given to Lord Wycombe when he came down with it a short while ago. The only other option we know of thus far is to wait and see. Some die, but some manage to fight it off and survive. I think it is fifty-fifty so far, but that might be optimistic, just my guess so far with us in

Valen. It's your choice. This must be done willingly. If you decide to wait and see, I strongly suggest you get your personal affairs in order yet today. This is a virulent virus. You have three days, one way or the other."

Having made his dire pitch, only one aide chose to gamble. "I'll wait and see. Heck, I'm fifty years old already. Hobbled like we are, I don't think I can manage to not even move my head." The other eleven were teleported by their circle over to Valen Castle, one by one.

Lord Valen first operated on the lord's wife and then his two teenaged daughters. When he finished up with them and they were examining their strange new mechanical hands, he added, "Ladies, come to the next council meetings. I believe Nita Valen will be introducing some spectacular new fashions that'll increase your appeal to men." He winked but said no more, though the teens, elegantly dressed in their arm-fetter-gowns, tried to pry it out of him. All that he added in a whisper was, "You will be far sexier than you ever imagined." As he expected, this greatly alleviated the women's fright over this new hideous illness.

After that, he handled five men and three women, who were Lord Wycombe's private *mentales* group, operating as his personal staff outside the circle. Wye Tower had graciously sent them to him to help protect the western portion of their territory. After such success with these, Lord Valen had his spy get to the ten circle members too. Two days later, he performed the operation on all ten. This is too easy, he thought!

Next, he expanded his operation. He alerted Lord Rusden of the virus next, followed by other Midlands lords. During the summer, he was kept very busy doling out his cure. He even had to order far more hands and more of the drug. He followed another suggestion of Nita's, namely to expand in a manner which made it appear to be spreading outward, like a normal flu outbreak might.

A week before the fall council meetings began in Exchange City, he again returned to that city and Elegant Fashions Inc. "Damned awkward not being able to turn my neck. Have to turn my body to see, but I'm managing, Nita.

You look as elegant as ever, perhaps more so."

How's the plan coming along? she asked, knowing why he'd come. Still, if she was going to lose her hands, she was going to make sure he had a very good chance of pulling this off.

"Like handing out honey to a baby. Would you believe I've done over half of Rusden Tower's gifted? all Lord Rusden's extended family and his *mentales* as well. Got the lords of Leedsburough and Woodhill done. He listed off several smaller towns whose lords and ladies had accepted his "cure," along with the few *mentales* they had. My real gem is Wye. Got eighty percent of the tower folk done there, as well as the rulers of Wye and his *mentales* gifted. One hundred five done. Pretty amazing, Nita. Could not have done it without your guidance."

Amazing, My Lord. Simply amazing. Okay, then as we agreed, I am ready to join you. Just make sure it doesn't interfere with my good looks.

He grinned, "Nothing could do that, I'm afraid. Will we also be doing your top managers who run the other storefronts?"

Yes, I've already talked with them. Those who have the gift are terribly worried about this new virus and want to take this preventative measure, but in truth, they are more excited about my new look and modifications. I'm doing them this week, in time for show and tell at the council meetings. Expect many arousals, she teased him, sensing his already. Slowly she rose and made her way over to her medical machine. She had it programmed, not leaving it to chance. Besides, she had no experience with these prosthetic hands. Perhaps he could not work the controls properly. She also had a supply of the rings waiting for him. However, she knew once she did this, she'd be unable to undo the ring's latches, not unless these prosthetic hands were more agile than she suspected they would be.

A half hour later, she looked down at her new conical stumps. *Well, they are pretty, My Lord. Sensitive too. Have you noticed that?*

"Not really, been way too busy. Let me get the hands on

you, Nita." While she began trying to figure out how to operate them, he began putting the rings around her neck.

Make darn sure the clasps are all aligned together and behind my neck.

"Bit tricky with your long hair. These hands can only just barely do the job. Can't exert enough pressure. Ah, there goes one." It took him another half hour of effort to get the rings on, the last one required almost more pressure than he could exert with his hands. Nita now sat up very straight, perfect posture. Combined with the pipe corset waist restriction, she was only able to bend at her hips. She rose and moved slowly over to her mirror, her long earrings bouncing gently on her shoulders.

I do look smashing, don't I? If I should fall, I probably can't get up by myself. Best be extra careful.

"True, very hard getting up out of bed, but doable. With all the *mentales* gifted hobbled up like this, they should prove highly ineffective against our soldiers now. Well done, Nita, well done indeed. Plus, if the women adopt your lip plates too, that will eliminate them from speaking, which will also be of great assistance in overcoming them. So would you like me to stay the night with you? Help you adjust to your new hands?" he asked coyly. He had another entirely different notion in mind.

Would you? How kind. Yes, please. My satin sheets again? Shall I take my plates out now, big boy? That proved very difficult; she'd not figured out how fully to work her new hands yet. Between them, they managed. *Please let me take my hands off. You too. I want to show you what I mean about the tips of the cones.* Lord Valen returned home the next morning with a whole new experience under his belt, promising himself to show it to his wife that very night!

Chapter 11 Fall Councils of 1244

Late September, the hundreds of local lords, ladies, and their advisors and *mentales* gifted staff met with the new regent, though the former emperor and empress were also in attendance along with their staff and domestique helpers. Already Nita was causing quite a stir among the many women, who chatted in whispers waiting for the men to finish their business so they could openly talk with Nita. Her new look was quite different, appealing in a strange way many thought.

Many other eyes were staring at those who now had distinctive grey hands and who also wore the strange copper-colored neck rings. What was going on? Lord Wycombe was recognized by the regent. He'd put in his bid to address the assemblage first.

"My lords, ladies, and fellow gifted, I've asked to be allowed to speak first. Recently, we've discovered a new virulent virus has begun to spread across Tierra. Fortunately, it strikes only those of us who have the *mentales* gift, but it is very deadly. Honestly, I cannot take credit for this discovery, only in helping to combat it. At this time, I call upon Lord Valen to explain further. Lord," he said shifting his body so he could see his benefactor.

"Lord, ladies, I hate to be the bearer of bad news, but Lord Wycombe is right. A virulent virus has been infecting us. Please, don't believe me on this, ask your fellow Midlands lords. Early this spring, the virus began affecting us in Valen. The early symptoms are reddish blotches on your hands. That seems to be the initial point of impact or exposure. From there it rapidly moves up to your neck, usually within two days' time. If you ignore it as many of us in Valen did at first, you have about a fifty-fifty chance of survival by the third day, grim I'm afraid. However, we have found a cure, which so far has been working one hundred percent effectively. If your hands are removed within that two day period, before it highly affects your neck, the virus can be stopped."

"Now we all know how horrible, unthinkable, such an action would be. We use our hands for everything. So I have worked out a humanitarian aid agreement with the aliens on behalf of all us. I have purchased a large number of their top of the line prosthetic hands which you see many of us here wearing today. If anyone becomes infected, we will attempt to cure you and provide you with a set of these expensive hands. No charge. They are a humanitarian gift from the aliens at the spaceport. We've found the virus so weakens ones neck muscles that most can no longer support the weight of their own heads. Nita found a solution to that in the Imperium Archives, these neck rings. While I find it terribly awkward that I can no longer use my neck, at least I am otherwise alive and healthy."

"At first we in Valen thought this was some plot of you Midlands' lords, but soon, I found it had spread to Wycombe, and I treated Lord Wycombe, secretly that is. Actually, I lied to him, not trusting he'd believe me about his virus. Not long after that, many of his own staff became infected and I treated eleven of them. One took the gamble, and I am pleased to announce he survived. I had hoped the virus would die out, but hardly a week later his whole circle on loan from Wye Tower also came down with it."

He and I became very worried about this virus, and we've been plotting its spread since then. Actually, Lord Wycombe has been handling that. I've been swamped handling the many cures. Lord?" He too pivoted slightly, raising his hand to indicate Lord Wycombe should continue.

"Thank you, Lord Valen. Yes, I'm afraid my part pales compared to his. Yes, I've been tracking its spread. I've prepared this chart with dates and locations clearly marked. It's swept down to the Rusden area next, as Lord Rusden can explain further. From there, it's spread out to Leedsburough and as far south as Woodhill. Within the last couple of weeks, it's struck more northerly in Wye, as Lord Wye will tell you shortly. In yellow, I've marked the larger towns now considered in its path and that'll likely be affected next, namely Wyth to the north, Stockton to the northeast, and possibly Southbend to the south and east. If the virus should reach to those areas, Northend, Welsham, and Brom, be on a high alert for it in your areas as well. We don't know yet if it will spread all the way to Adelmira Tower and further into the Easterlings than Southbend."

"Finally, I want to give Lord Valen my highest praise for staying on top of this disaster. To date, he's had to treat over a hundred of us and to his credit, he's not lost one of us. Indeed, removing the infected hands at the first signs of the infection works, though none of us have been willing to gamble on our weak necks, so we wear these supporting rings to be on the safe side. Yes, they can be removed if so desired, but do be extra careful. Oh yes, please do come up to those of us who have had the cure. We'll gladly tell you about it, and how well the replacement hands work. I believe Lord Rusden and some of the others would like to add a few words of their own too. Nita Valen would also like to say a few words to the many women here as well. I believe we've kept our soothsayers very occupied so far this meeting." His attempt at a jest fell on deaf ears. Many were confused, many were worried. Some didn't believe a word of it in spite of thus far not having detected Lord Wycombe was lying.

Both Lord Rusden and the Venerada of Rusden Tower spoke next, describing in detail the symptoms they'd experienced. They spoke of feeling weak in their necks as well and how effective the treatment had been. Both declared they had had no aftereffects and with these new hands, life was continuing fairly normally. Their biggest complaint was they could no longer feel anything with their hands. The Venerada complained this was the worst part.

At last, the women got to hear from Nita, who they were all dying to hear. She looked so different, so elegant and regal, so erect. "I can't talk well like this," she spoke, after the regent introduced her and she moved slowly to the center. She wore her finest red satin arm-fetter-gown, which matched the rubies in her lip plates and earrings. Her long, rich black hair was perfectly brushed and her eye makeup superbly done. Nothing less would do, not for Nita, though she had had to have one of her assistants put on her makeup for her. The alien hands were not working all that well, dismally in fact. After that one sentence, she reverted to using telepathy to the gathering.

I can't talk well enough to be understood, as you've just heard, but we all have telepathy. When I first found out about this horrific, debilitating virus, I knew we women needed a little something extra to raise our own self-esteem. I don't particularly like wearing grey alien hands. I'm not an alien. She paused superbly allowing many to chuckle at her jest.

I spent hours trying to find things, which would do just that. Today, you see the results. My other fifty office managers are also here and you can chat with them as well. First, the lip plates. I've designed them to fit securely to your gums. Plus, to avoid any possibility of slippage, each one had four small dowels which go into small holes in your gums. The process, like all them, is painless. With my rich black hair, I chose to have red rubies embedded in my plates. I do hope you like my color choice. They match my gown, as you can see. At night, you simply take the plates out, leaving you with two dangling lip loops as I call them. Let me show you.

She carefully removed hers and slowly moved from side to side, pivoting in place so all could see. Then she put them back in, a move she spent hours practicing to make it look like it was the easiest thing in the world to do, while in fact it wasn't.

Now why did I show you my lip loops? Because, when you have it done, I've added a lot of extra sensing nerve cells in your lips. Your loops will be highly sensitive to the touch. And when you kiss someone, they will experience a kiss like no other kiss in the universe! Women, you just have to try this! Plus, it is wholly undoable. If you don't like it, your lips can be healed, though I don't know anyone who doesn't just love them, especially after one night in bed.

Next, I designed these incredible earrings. I love the way they lay on my shoulders and touch me as I move around. I made them this long thinking about the many katalyein women of Brom, who have been mostly denied these more elegant fashions. This is something they can share too.

One final detail. I really didn't want to lose my hands either. And when the plague came to me, I decided to help all us who have gotten it. I had Lord Valen make a modification to the medical machines that perform this life-saving cure for us. I learned of this from the aliens. Many uninfected nerve cells from the hand being removed are placed in the very tips of the aesthetic cones. Thus, those of us who have had to undergo this life-saving surgery will discover a terrifically heightened sense of touch at the tips of our arm cones. In bed, you will experience a whole new world of heightened touch. Kind of drives me nuts, she teased the crowd.

Put this all together and I hope I've helped make our awful surgeries far more bearable afterwards. I've done my best for us women primarily. These new ornaments are available at all my Elegant Fashions Inc outlets, beginning today. Thank you. May we all survive this awful virus.

Lord Wycombe rose to add another point. Although he didn't think of it himself, he felt obligated to spread the message. "One last detail. Since the virus attacks ones hands first, having the hands removed before you actually come down with the virus seems to be very effective in preventing your getting it. I mention this because it will soon be winter and travel in the northern territories becomes quite difficult. If you get this virus, you only have *two* days to get to Lord Valen or one of the Elegant Fashions Inc outlets to get the surgery. Beyond that time, you are in the fifty-fifty zone, and I don't want to see any of us here perish from it, not with so easy a cure."

What Nita didn't say was what bothered her the most as she stood perfectly erect, a centerpiece of elegance and beauty at the emperor's council. She wasn't saying how awful it was being unable to feel anything with the hands, how terribly awkward that made using her new hands for anything. She didn't say how many times she'd dropped her tea cups, bent her silverware, and dropped a bite of food on its way to her mouth. The list was endless, including countless droppings of her hairbrush while trying to brush out her hair, and how incredibly difficult it was to subsequently pick it up, unable to bend. She didn't tell them how difficult it was for her to pick up a pencil and draw her new dress designs. Her personal life had become something of a nightmare. She didn't tell them that.

Besieged with questions from the many women present, she did tell them if they got their lip plates, kissing would take on a whole new sensual arena for them, and that they should take the hands off before going to bed and experiment with the tips of their stumps. *One night in bed and you will see what I mean,* she sent over and over. In answer to how could she eat, she sent, *You can take them out to eat, but I just leave them in. Of course, then you can't drink from a cup, so I use a spoon, more lady-like anyway.* To the men that talked with her, she added, *Yes, you men can also have these incredibly sensuous lip plates too; they are not for women only. Yes, if you don't like them, your lips can be repaired good as new.*

The entire emperor's council was spent on these topics, though nothing else of significance was really learned. Only a couple of people recognized eight others who attended the meeting. They stayed completely in the background. Tim had brought Petrona, Andres, Rafaela, and the four rescued teens to the meeting. While Eric, Sally, Darcy, and Dawn wanted to challenge Lord Valen, wanted to scream out to everyone how his army had butchered everyone in their two foothills fortresses, Tim had severely cautioned them beforehand against doing any such thing. "We have no proof Lord Valen did it. It is your word against his. True, someone did this evil act, but we can't prove it was Lord Valen's orders, not yet anyway. All we have are three sets of ashes and three mutilated bodies wholly unrecognizable. I'll take you to the council so we can get a better feel for what he is planning for the future and so you four can see what he looks like. I owe you that much. We'll stay in the background and observe. Kids, there simply has to be more to all this. We must figure out the larger picture." They'd agreed and he'd brought them.

It had worked out. The four had only been to a few emperor council meetings and they'd matured a good deal since last fall's session. Tim was taking a gamble they'd not be recognized. While the four waited for hours to hear any word about the foothills battles, absolutely nothing was said, not even a mention of them. This disturbed Tim even more than it did the four.

With all the talk of the virus and it's only cure

dominating all the men's talk and with the women focusing on the new adornments Nita was introducing, the eight found their minds drifting off of the slaughters and onto these new topics. Tim was wise enough not to take them to the subsequent Council of the Lords, held immediately after the emperor's conference. There, the question of Humberhills and Retford Hills would surely be taken up. Though the four had legitimate claims to be the new rulers of their respective small kingdoms, Tim knew none of them was ready to assume that much responsibility. Besides, they had no others to help them, no army, no domestic staff, nothing. All had been killed. Rather, some of their more distant relatives would step up and try to put the pieces back together. Instead, they would listen in on the meeting, compliments of their hidden microphones and spy equipment.

That evening safe in their underground chambers, Ben and Tim encountered entirely new problems. The women wanted to try out some of the new ornaments Nita wore. "Look, we want to look our very best for you," Rafaela tried to explain. "Like I am, I'm rather ugly, but with those fancy earrings and lip plates, I'll look far more attractive. Besides, she did say kissing was out of this world. I can't do much more than kiss like I am, so I want to at least try it."

"If all the women start wearing them, we'll look totally out of place again," Darcy complained. "I mean we fit in very well today, but that's today's fashions. Next time, I bet all the women will look as gorgeous as Nita and we'll look like old women again."

Petrona added, "Elana and I agree. We want to look as elegant and pretty as we can too. We don't want to embarrass you guys by looking old fashioned when we are out in public."

Ben countered, "But dear you heard Nita. She can't speak with those plates in her lips. She had to use telepathy all the time and you don't have that gift."

"Well they can be taken out when I need to talk," Petrona countered.

Exasperated, Ben added, "You mean one of us will have to do that for you, slowing us all down."

Petrona looked really hurt by his rough reply. She

pouted and added, "What if we try harder to get those alien hands to work?" Twice now, Tim and Ben had tried to get a pair of them on Petrona and Elana. Their arms were quite thin compared to the others, and in order to even get the hands to stay on their lower arms, they had to wrap cloth around them until they did finally fit. However, since these Madiera women never had hands, having been born without them, they had no idea how to send body nerve signals to get them to work. It had been a bitter failure.

"Okay, okay, I'll compromise, Petrona. You can have the new ornaments if you can get the alien hands to work so you can take the plates out when you need to talk," Tim said, knowing he'd barely acted fast enough to prevent Petrona from a big emotional upset. Elana too.

"But what about this virus thing?" Elana asked. It obviously cannot infect us or Andres, Rafaela or the four there. We don't have hands or arms in their case. What about you and Tim, Ben? What are we supposed to do if you both get infected?"

"We're not going to get infected, love," Ben countered.

"Yes, it's all well and good for you to stand there the hero and say that, but what about us? What do we do if you do get it?" Elana continued to make her point. "I can't stand here and watch you or Tim die, not when there is a cure to be had."

"I don't want my hands cut off!" Ben replied.

"Oh, so you think we wanted ours cut off?" Eric entered the fray. "My Sally, she wanted her hands cut off, is that what you are saying? Or Darcy or Dawn? What about Rafaela and Andres? They wanted their arms gone?"

"No! Don't be silly, Eric. Tim and I need our hands."

"Oh, so I and Darcy and Dawn and Sally and the others, we don't need our hands? Rafaela doesn't even need arms? That's what you are saying?" Eric argued, his face getting redder by the minute.

"No, you are misinterpreting things, Eric. Obviously, everyone needs them, but we don't want to also lose ours either," Tim jumped in to help Ben out.

"Fine to say now, but what are we to do if, and I say if, you come down with the virus?" Petrona went back to the original question that she and Elana had been worrying about. "We only have two days to get the cure. Fifty-fifty are poor odds. Do you want us to stand around and see if you die or live? What are we all to do if you die? What happens to the Underground if you both die? It seems to me this needs to be discussed among us all, dear."

Slowly, the two began to see their wives' point of view. "Okay, if we should get this virus, get us to the closest place where we can get the cure." Tim and Ben finally gave in. Ben added, "First, though, I think we need to research this virus more. Something is going on and we just don't know what. One thing is for sure, we have to find out fast."

The next day, they listened in on the Council of the Lords. Already several of the women had gotten the new ornaments and were swarmed by the other women in attendance, besieged with questions. The men discussed the virus and its implications and had even broken precedence by asking Lord Valen and other Westerlings lords to attend. Towards the end, an uncle of Eric and an uncle of Sally stated they were assuming the rulership of Humberhills and Retford Hills, claiming some hideous disaster had befallen both fortresses. They had been attacked, but no one knew by who or where the attackers came from, and that no trace of the attacker had yet been found. Lord Valen did offer a large reward for any information on those attackers. Ben found this a curious twist indeed, but saw his offer was well received among the lords. Somehow, Lord Valen was working his way into the confidence of the Midlands lords.

The next day, Darcy, Dawn, and Sally worked with Petrona and Elana to help them figure out how to get their prosthetic hands to work. Meanwhile, Ben and Tim got an urgent request to visit Lord Henry Bolivar in his Brom Castle office, followed by a similar request from Venerada Marisol to meet with her in Brom Tower. They could not be in two places at the same time, so Tim went to see Lord Henry while Ben went to see Venerada Marisol.

"Ah so good of you to come on such short notice. Sit down, sit down. Tea? Ale?" Lord Henry asked, moving slowly in his toe boots back to his plush chair behind his huge desk.

Tim was fine and Lord Henry explained, "I saw you were at the council meeting, so there is no need to tell you what we are now apparently facing — a deadly crisis of unparalleled proportions, if we are to believe what we've heard. I've asked you here because of your mother. We all had only the greatest respect and admiration for her and Amy. Son, I can't begin to tell you how all this has upset everyone here in the castle. The women are frightened, to put it mildly. I for one seriously doubt this virus does exist, but then I can't prove a darn thing, rather the opposite are all the facts thus far. However, virus or not, I have to take definitive steps, as a ruler must."

"Yes, I understand. Last night, my wife brought it to a head with us as well," Tim replied, putting Lord Henry more at ease.

"Quite right. So what am I to do? There was some discussion of taking preventative measures ahead of time. I can see some merit to that. A few months from now, we'll be under twenty feet of snow as usual. Travel will be difficult at best, though we can use teleports via Brom Tower, I supposed, assuming they don't get sick too. If a lot of us come down with it at one time, like happened at Wye Castle and Tower, well, in the middle of the winter, I don't have to tell you the ramifications of that. Preventative measures begin to look attractive, you see, but only *if* this is truly a real virus and not some diabolical plot against us all."

"I see your point. Here in Brom, between the castle and tower, you have more *mentales* gifted than any other place on Tierra at the moment," Tim pointed out.

"Precisely so, Tim, precisely so. I am afraid if we got an epidemic of this virus here, the small local Elegant Fashions Inc storefront simply could not handle all us in the required two days' time. At least that is the argument many are presenting me."

"So they are suggesting preventative surgery?" Tim asked by way of drawing the logical conclusion the lord hadn't yet said.

"Precisely so. What a quandary I am facing! While I have serious doubts about this whole mess, I can't prove it and

I dare not take a chance. Fifty-fifty? That would mean I'd lose half of my invaluable staff; same with the tower, they'd lose half! Intolerable, simply intolerable."

"You will get no argument from me on that point, my lord. So why have you asked to see me?" Tim asked.

"Son, I know in the past you've been able to supply valuable information for us. Lord knows I have no idea how you could possibly have acquired some of it. I need information if I am to act in good conscience. Here's my idea. At the conference, there was some mention of this 'outbreak' following the known pattern of flu. It was suggested from Lord Wycombe's sketches that Northend and Southbend would likely be the next larger cities to become infected. If so, Brom would be next. At least Welsham and Adelmira are far enough away they have more time to find other cures, perhaps. Could you, with your means, keep track of the spread of this virus, if indeed it is even a virus, and keep me posted? I mean to make a ruling: if those two large cities and tower gets infected, then here in Brom Castle, we'll opt for preventative surgery, since it is only contacted via one's hands. Have none, can't get it."

"Ah, that seems a reasonable way to go for now. I accept your request. We will do our best to track the spread of this epidemic and keep you posted."

"Thank you, Tim. Thank you. I'll see you are aptly rewarded for your services and expenses. I think it would be prudent of me to at least visit our Elegant Fashions Inc and alert them to the possibility of suddenly having all us to handle. My god, son, I've got over two dozen myself and the tower has closer to fifty. Best to be prepared don't you think?"

"Might be wise, my lord." Tim couldn't think of a better response. They chatted further and Tim returned home.

In Brom Tower, Venerada Marisol greeted Ben, "So good to see you again, Ben. How's Elana?"

"We're just fine. I take it you want to talk about this virus thing?" Ben asked, wanting to get to the heart of the visit. He had many things on his mind at the moment.

"Yes, most definitely. Can I ask you frankly what is your opinion on all this? Cutting off one's hands seems terribly barbaric to me. Though I never had them in the first place, most here do, and I have to think about their safety and well-being," Marisol said formally.

"My opinion? I think it is some elaborate hoax, though I can't prove it. Rather the opposite, in fact. Everything seems to lend credence to the fact it is a virulent virus attacking only us telepaths, those with the gifts. I'd like more time to try to study it."

"I see. I rather hold that opinion myself, but then I don't have to fear it, since I apparently can't get it. We have quite a lot of those with the healing gifts here at Brom Tower. I wish some of them could get a look at one or more who have come down with it and see if they cannot use their gifts and cure them."

"In my opinion that would be an ideal approach," Ben replied.

"Thanks. Unfortunately, there has been a good deal of panic among the tower folk. I can understand their fear. What with the gradual reduction of our numbers, this comes along and threatens to cut our numbers in half. Terribly frightening. Yet the supposed cure is awful, but then Lord Valen's deal with the aliens comes at an ideal time. I find that terribly curious, don't you?"

"Yes. Venerada I certainly do. Our lease agreement specifically makes these prosthetic hands illegal contraband. Their own Directive #5 specifically prohibits them. Yet apparently, Lord Valen had been able to get hundreds of pairs imported here. Where were the aliens' compassion after the explosion of their spaceport which so drastically altered our weather and so many perished? A simple gift of food would have saved thousands of lives. No, Venerada, I find this a strange move by the aliens, unless this new leader of theirs has a kinder heart."

Marisol smiled, "He just might have. You know he's married to a Valen woman, Adalina I believe is her name. Perhaps, she's softened his view towards us."

"That would make sense. It is awfully difficult to ignore your wife's pleadings," he jested. Both chuckled.

"So Ben, I am faced with making a huge decision here. Some have suggested taking preventative surgery. They'd rather be alive and slightly inconvenienced than dead. Others are more pragmatic and are asking me to take a wait and see approach, hoping it may never reach Brom Tower. Still others are asking me to prepare for the worst and send everyone off to get cured the instant the virus strikes the first person here. Their assumption is: if one person gets it, the rest are sure to follow. A few even claim it isn't real and to let them take their chances."

"Have you reached a decision, Venerada Marisol?"

She laughed, "You are always to the point, Ben. Yes, though it may not please everyone. I would like to ask you to use the resources you have to research this further. Get us more information on which to base an intelligent decision. However, if the virus does strike either the castle or the tower, I will have no option but to ask each of the *mentales* gifted to get the cure. I cannot order them to do it, though."

"I accept, venerada. There is one thing either you or one of your katalyein could do for us. We've got four teens that have undergone severe emotional trauma and I fear it might affect their *mentales* gifts. Could someone check them out for us?"

"Consider that done. I'll send one around later today. Anything else?"

"Well, I would like permission to visit the Madiera ship and discuss this virus with Alpha. He may be able to give me some insight or some clue I've overlooked."

"I will arrange it. I'll let you know on that one." They chatted a bit longer when a fourteen year old young woman entered. "Ah, Zarita, this is Ben Blackwater. He has four teens for you to work your magic on. Ben, you are responsible for her safety to your place and back again."

A few minutes later her cloak over her shoulders, the two stepped out into the tower's courtyard. "If I had known you would be returning with me, Zarita, I'd have brought a carriage."

"Oh this is just perfect. You see, I get so few chances just to walk into town. See, I look like any other woman on the streets. No one can tell I am really a katalyein, not with my cloak on. It is going to snow today I think. Say, everyone is so worried about this virus. Well not we katalyein, of course, we can't get it, nor can the Madiera women, but then they probably wouldn't get it anyway, they don't have the same kind of *mentales* gifts as we do, you see. Some have been pleading to Venerada Marisol to let them get the preventative surgery. They think with so many of them needing it at the same time, some wouldn't get the cure in two days' time. It's awful to think about, don't you think so?" She finally wound down a little.

"I am pleased to be your escort today and let you see our city. Yes, it is a very troublesome thing, if it is real."

"But it must be, don't you think? They say it is following the usual spread like a flu does. They do have these symptoms. They all reported the same things, red splotches on their hands and all that. What else could it be? Well, I certainly don't know. Rather what interests me more are those fabulous new ornaments that Nita is wearing. You see, we katalyein simply can't afford to wear the pipe corsets. We depend upon being very flexible if we are to be remotely independent of others constantly lending us a hand. And we don't dare wear those elegant toe shoes, though I heard your mother once did. I guess if she could manage it, we could too, but Venerada Marisol has put her foot down on those too. We are limited to wearing the now out of fashion heels and gowns to the parties. But these new ornaments, we could wear them. Those earrings of hers look absolutely stunning, don't you think? And the lip plates — so unusual and dramatic! Everyone notices them! We've been pleading with Marisol to let us get them. Do you know what Nita meant by her kissing statement? We've been trying to figure that one out."

"Honestly, Zarita, I haven't had time to think or ponder that one. This virus thing is far more important at the moment," Ben finally got the chance to talk, but couldn't think of much else to say.

"Well, I understand, Ben. I've been trying to think what would be the best color gems to have in my earrings. I want them to match my hair and eyes, so they have to not clash with black hair, don't you think so?" He didn't get a chance to answer. "Nita has red rubies and those go well, but they are a little too, well I don't know, striking perhaps. Maybe something softer, more gentle like green emeralds. What do you think? But then there are brown gemstones too, which would blend, sort of."

"I think you would look attractive with emeralds or rubies, Zarita." He desperately wanted to change the topic and said, "I've got four teens not much older than yourself that we've rescued. They have undergone intense emotional traumas, having watched soldiers butcher all their families and friends."

"Oh yes. Well, I am looking forward to using my gifts on them. Honestly, Ben, it will be a delightful change from the ordinary cases we've been getting. No offense, but Amy Blackwater's thing where she made everyone experience the horrors of that bomb going off keeps coming up as severe blocks to people's gifts."

"Huh? Everyone from those days is dead now, aren't they? How can they still have that as a block to their gifts?" Ben asked suddenly intrigued.

"Well, it isn't old people we're helping; it's the young ones, teens mostly. Many have it as the major block to their gifts. Isn't that just the strangest thing? We don't have an explanation for it at all. Defies all logic, doesn't it? Yet it continues to be the number one block; we see it over and over. Gets kind of boring for we katalyein. That's why I am so happy to help your four with something different."

A few hours later, she finished up with the four. "Well, you were certainly right. Their trauma was beginning to lock up their gifts. They cried a lot more and the trauma has been released," Zarita reported. "Can I stay a little longer? We want to chat a bit."

For another hour, Ben listened to the four teens discussing the new earrings and lip plates, pros and cons. Darcy, Dawn, and Sally did tell her how difficult wearing the pipe corsets and their toe boots was, and if they had to do it over, they wouldn't have done it, perhaps. All three did admit their desires to be fashionable and fit in probably would have overridden it, and they'd have done it anyway. Sally whispered what she'd discovered about what Nita had hinted at with the heightened sensitivity in the tips of her arm's cones. All four giggled. "Perhaps she meant something like that about the kisses," Sally suggested.

Ben guessed Zarita would probably chat all day with the teens if he let her. Finally, he insisted on walking her back home to the tower. "I don't want Venerada Marisol complaining I've kept you away from the tower too long." She bought that argument and said farewell to her new friends.

The next day Tim and Ben set to work on their Imperium computers, searching for clues to this mysterious illness. They had very little to go on, primarily that it was deadly to telepaths. The three teens spent their time with Petrona and Elana, doing their best to find ways for the two to get their prosthetic hands to operate. The day ended in frustration for the men, but Petrona and Elana finally made some progress; they could wiggle the hands' fingers a little.

Encouraged at last and with an exciting, desired goal in mind, the two continued to work hard on it the following days. At last, the two wives proudly demonstrated they could finally feed themselves using the hands. Ben and Tim did validate them for their efforts and thanked the teens for trying so hard, even though both men knew the women now would be pestering them to get the new ornaments. At last they gave in, hoping Nita's suggestion that their lips could be healed worked if they didn't like them. As Eric escorted the five women to Brom's Elegant Fashions Inc, Tim remained behind, still searching with the computer, while Ben headed off to talk to the robot called Alpha; he'd received permission to visit him.

Ben was led through an underground tunnel by one of the older Madiera women. "This is a very special request. Seldom has an outsider been granted permission to visit our ship and robot saviors."

"I am honored, ma'am." He was led into a control room filled with more computers and monitors than he'd ever seen before. After being introduced to Alpha and Beta, the woman left him in their care. "You look amazingly human," Ben said, admiring the craftsmanship that had gone into its construction.

"Thank you Ben. How may we assist you with this

problem?" Alpha said, flashing a smile, which he thought, must be the appropriate human response.

"It is this supposedly deadly virus which affects only we who have the *mentales* gift, we telepaths, and no one else." He carefully explained all he had heard about the disease and how strange it was and how equally strange the cure was.

Beta said in his monotone, "Computing now."

"Meanwhile," Alpha said, "we have been studying your society for a number of years. Have to, since we are still following our prime directive to see that those in our care flourish and prosper here on this new world we brought them to. To be frank, Ben, we've noticed a most disturbing trend among the *mentales* gifted here on Tierra. More and more we are seeing a trend of self-mutilation, which is symptomatic of a civilization or people on a rapid decline towards their own destruction."

"How so?" Ben asked, this was certainly interesting.

"First, your gifted actively condones promiscuity under the guise of fosterling children. Their insistence on wearing the so called pipe corsets and toe boots or shoes requires heavy modifications to one's physical bodies, modifications that cannot be healed. It is sadistic in nature. Now we've seen the latest round. While women of all generations from our world have worn ear ornaments, none have gone to such an extreme as they are doing here. The new lip plates, while we can admit are quite ornamental jewelry, again they impede speech and eating and apparently provide added sexual stimulus. Again, sadistic in nature."

"From our own vast experience, if nothing is done to alter the course that these gifted is following, soon impotency will begin occurring followed by intense anxiety about their inability to procreate more children, and they will then do all manner of things to try to have more children. Of course, those efforts, while well intended, will only fail. After that, they will merely await what they believe is the inevitable, death."

"Surely it isn't this bad, is it? I know these popular body modifications are unhealthy," Ben replied.

"Sir, look what goes along with this. Are you not seeing more and more viscous and hidden intents behind actions some take? Are the gifted truly ethical doing what amounts to the greatest good for all? I think rather the opposite here. Have you not seen very ingenuous perversions of the truth, perhaps even viscous perversions of the truth? I ask you because we monitored two battles far to the south of here earlier this past summer."

"Er, no, the guilty have covered it up wholly. After that, the guilty man has put all his emphasis on this virus thing," Ben replied, curious these two robots also were aware of the battles at Humberhills and Retford Hills.

"Precisely. Artful lying is at hand. Perfectly predictable. Are not the gifted now feeling highly insecure? This gifted man who doles out his cure, his avowed intent is to save lives, but at what cost? Yes, Beta and I agreed we did make a terrible mistake four and a half centuries ago when we bred hands out of the women under our care. We too have made mistakes. Still, your gifted? Are they now highly active individuals or are they nearly sedentary?"

"Well, constrained as they are, highly sedentary." Ben had to agree with this point.

"You see, it all fits with the patterns of life. Come, let me show you some video images of the world our women originally came from. As you look at their societies over the period of several centuries, pay attention on the slow deterioration and the ultimate end they had." Alpha began playing the sequences he'd shown the women under his care on many occasions in the past. Ben watched fascinated, seeing many parallels to his own world of telepaths. He most certainly did not like the outcome.

When it finished, Beta made a beeping sound. "If I may?"

"Yes, go ahead, Beta," Alpha replied.

"Sir, I have done some extensive analysis on this virus. Frankly, sir, I am mystified. I can't find the virus. While on the surface, the viral spread pattern seems to replicate that of most viruses, when you look more closely, it doesn't. Look here. I've highlighted in red the areas known to have been infected." Ben saw red dots beginning at Valen.

"Look closely. What is missing here?" Beta asked,

192

having decided to test this human's powers of observation. They had such little contact with these humans with the gift that he wanted to study Ben a little.

"Well, there's the spot at Wycombe there, and Rusden down there, Wye up there," Ben pointed out the obvious dots. As he looked at the screen, it dawned on him. "What's missing, Beta, are any reports of anyone getting ill anywhere in between these larger cities. Even small towns have one or two of *mentales* gifted living there. The locals, we call them, folks who use their gifts to live and better themselves, such as raising quality hawks and horses. Those folks should have gotten the virus too."

"Precisely. Yet not one word from them. You best check on that detail, sir. Now I have taken the liberty of firing off one of our tiny probes. I sent it straight through the most infected areas, including a flyover of both this Wycombe city and Rusden. My probe found no virus, most alarming, sir. Look at this display, sir. Found three different strains of flu and four different cold viruses. Your virus is missing."

Ben exclaimed, "Then it is a big hoax, a lie! Just as I thought it must be! Someone is manipulating this making everyone think we are being infected."

"Precisely so, sir," Beta replied in his monotone, in sharp contrast to the emotional outburst of Ben's.

"And what impact does the supposed cure have?" Alpha probed a little. He could not resist the temptation to lead Ben slightly.

"Cutting off one's hands, immobilizing their necks. It is making us virtually helpless individuals!" Ben replied. "I see where you are going with this. Unable to even defend ourselves, we are ripe for an easy destruction. Someone is trying their best to wipe us all out or at least make our effectiveness null and void."

"That would be a logical deduction. Yet, as your people are so fond of saying, where is the proof? Where is the proof there is no virus? How can you prove a thing doesn't exist when all things suggest it does in fact exist?" Alpha asked.

"Quite true, Alpha. I know this virus doesn't exist as a normal virus. Still people do get ill and the cure is working. I have to have facts to counter this. Somehow, I will get them. Can I ask you a question, Alpha?" The robot nodded, once more thankful that his makers had programmed him to do so at will.

"Is there any hope we can reverse this sadistic decline and not end up succumbing?"

"Good question. I do not have enough data to process an answer, sir. The experiential track on the world from which we came says no, but then this is not that world. Perhaps here a way can be found to reverse the slow deterioration and reverse it. I simply have no data."

Ben thanked them and found his way out and down the long tunnel. *Somehow I have to find a way to reverse this succumb path we mentales are following, I simply must.*

That evening Ben intended to discuss all he'd found and seen with his group. Unfortunately, that got delayed. The women were all sporting the new style dangling earrings, which rested several inches over their shoulders and the ornamental lip plates. Petrona and Elana had promised to help Rafaela remove and put hers back in when she needed it.

Don't we just look fabulous? Rafaela sent him. *It is so great to feel them on my shoulders. If I wiggle them, it's almost like my hands touching my shoulders! We look fantastic don't we?*

"Well, I am impressed, ladies. You look really splendid indeed. I like your earrings especially. They add color and sparkle. I'm not so sure about your lip plates, but they are aesthetic, no doubt about that."

Of course, Petrona and Elana can't quite be understood while they are wearing theirs, but we think if we practice enough, we can make ourselves mostly understandable, Sally added. *We all are in love with our new looks, though. You should give Elana a big hug. She's rather worried you disapprove of her and she so wants to please you.*

Ben took the hint and walked over to his wife and whispered, "You look fabulous, you know. Hug." She had already discovered the lip plates hid almost all her facial expressions, so she didn't bother to smile. It wouldn't be visible, but her eyes told him she really appreciated his praise. After admiring and examining each of their slightly different earrings and plates, they all sat down to eat supper.

While those with prosthetic hands with difficulty managed by themselves, Rafaela could no longer use her straw, but Sally had already promised her that she would help feed her from now on so she wasn't left out of the new looks. After all Rafaela would really feel out of place if she was the only woman who didn't have the new ornaments.

After dinner and more praises to Petrona and Elana for being able to use their hands well enough to eat, Ben went over what he'd learned in great detail.

Desperately wanting to tell Tim what was still worrying her, Petrona awkwardly removed her plates so she would not be misunderstood. "So it comes down to this. We can't prove there isn't any virus and neither can we prove there is a virus. I can see a grand plot in all this, but an unproven one. What if someone is somehow intentionally putting the virus into the people? I mean, if someone had put it into those ones who then got infected with it? No matter how they were infected with the virus, the fact remains they have gotten it — all the symptoms. The cure has worked so far. So what are we to do then, if you fellows come down with it? Gamble on your lives? Honey, I'm scared of that! I love you. I don't want to lose you." She had to repeat this several times until he got it.

Tim spoke up, as Petrona worked diligently to get her plates back on, "We are in a pickle barrel on this one, Ben. I say if we should come down with this plague, then we should follow the prescribed and known cure. Have our wives take us to the Elegant Fashions Inc and get cured, either their store here in Brom or perhaps in Exchange City. Can we all agree on this point? If we get it, then you all get us the cure immediately? I'd rather be alive and mutilated than dead."

Ben agreed, much to the relief of Elana. Petrona also finally relaxed as well. While it all might be some great hoax, neither man wanted to take that gamble. If they were wrong and the virus did exist in some form, there was everything to lose. The lives of those around them depended upon them in a large measure.

"I have an idea that is worth exploring, based on what Beta showed me today," Ben then continued the discussion. "Tim and I need to check on the local *mentales* gifted in the small towns and villages between the large cities where the outbreaks have occurred. If it is a virus, some of those ought to have died, at least half, if what we were told is true. Let's try to get a handle on this whole thing."

That evening four men soon discovered a whole new kissing experience. Soft, warm, moist lobes of lips caressed theirs and their cheeks. For the women, the heightened sensitivity of their lip loops sent them into an arousal they'd never felt before. Analytically, Ben thought of what he'd learned today about a decaying society, a frantic anxiety over sex. Though thoroughly pleasureful, he could not help thinking as a group, they were slowly going in the wrong direction.

The next day, they had Andres teleport them down to Rusden Tower, where with some persuasion, they were given the names of several local *mentales* gifted who lived in surrounding villages. Thus, they began their search for more data.

Chapter 12 Caught in the Trap

While traveling from small town to small town down in the kingdom of Rusden searching out the local *mentales* gifted, Ben and Tim received telepathic word the morning of October 12th that the virus had spread further eastward. Most all Southbend was now infected. By the next day, they received word all those who had taken ill, some thirty-four, had been saved. Still, the two men pressed on with their searches. Thus far, not one of the many locals they visited had ever contracted the virus. This far south, it was only fall. The snows had not yet come. Hence they headed on up to Leedsburough, continuing their investigations aided by local information reluctantly relayed to them from Wye Tower via Brom Tower.

"Damn those two meddling fools. What are they trying to do?" Lord Valen exclaimed. He'd received continuing reports from his ever-growing list of contacts in the Midlands, that is, people who had begun once more to trust him. "Why are they checking on all the worthless local *mentales* gifted?" Having no answer, he finally contacted Nita and told her all about what the two men from Brom were doing.

Besides meddling, they must be up to something, he sent.

Of course they are, silly. Can't you see it? They are trying to prove the "virus" is not following the expected paths taken by viruses. That is, it is skipping over all the smaller towns and villages where some mentales reside, she sent back. *While these locals are certainly not worth spending any time on, these two men could well use what they find to argue this is not a virus. You know what that may mean? Others could start looking for a different cause, a direct attack on their cities. They are getting too close to the truth, don't you think?*

Damn, damn, damn those meddling fools!

I know uncle. Stay calm and focused. On the bright side, uncle, we've just installed lip plates in our tenth lord. I think they are going to catch on swiftly with the men. I've heard nothing but fabulous reports from the women who have them, and they are being very convincing with their husbands.

Well, that is surprisingly good news. I didn't anticipate the lords would go for the lip plates. Nita, you are a real treasure.

Of course I am, uncle. I think you would be wise to up your schedule a little and get to Brom Castle and Tower soon. They are the ones I think are instigating the investigations. I rather anticipated this largest concentration of the gifted would be a problem, and I've shipped enough supplies to my office there to handle them. We're ready to handle all them as soon as you work your magic on them.

Okay, I agree. Brom is way too powerful for their own good. I'll make it happen soon. But what about those two meddlers?

Nita thought for a moment and then a devious notion struck her fancy. *Uncle, leave them to me. Here is what I want you to do when your agents are ready to infect Brom Castle and Tower.*

Late October Tim and Ben were approaching a small town where Lilly and Sam Becktold lived. She had healing skills and he had a knack for growing nut trees. *Ben, Lord Henry here. Say I thought you ought to know, I've just had a request from Lord Valen. He wants to come here to Brom Castle to discuss further ideas on how to stop the spread of the virus. I would like you both to be around when he is here. I don't trust him.*

For god's sake, keep him under constant watch and also anyone who comes with him! Ben sent. *We'll wrap this up and be there yet today!*

Petrona awkwardly used her hands to straighten Tim's tie. He had donned his finest suit, fitting for meeting with the two powerful lords later today. "You look handsome," she said slowly and carefully, hoping he'd grasp it. She had her lip plates in.

"I look handsome?" he repeated and she nodded. "Thanks, but you look as lovely and gorgeous as ever, my love. What would I do without you? Don't worry. I'll be careful. We will be watching his every move. I am going to spring our findings on him and see how he reacts," Tim explained.

"Do be careful," she said slowly and carefully, trying hard to make herself understood.

"Careful?" She nodded. "You bet. I'll be watching Ben's back and he, mine. We'll be okay. See you later tonight. Have Andres send us a message if you discover anything on the comm channels." She nodded. In the adjoining room, Ben was having a similar conversation with a worried Elana. The two men walked out, smiled, and headed for the door, donning their cloaks as they left. It was snowing lightly, but already an inch had accumulated from the previous days of light snow, quite normal for this time of year, perhaps a little on the light side.

They walked briskly through the streets, enjoying the fresh air, stimulated by the anticipation of the coming confrontation with Lord Valen. As they approached the castle, the guards were expecting them, and one rushed up to them to lead them inside to the meeting room.

"Ah, good to see you. You are just in time. I'm told he will be arriving shortly. Care to follow me to the teleport pad?" Lord Henry asked. Just then, the door opened and Lady Bolivar entered wearing a green pod-silk arm-fetter-gown. She now wore the new ornaments as well. Her extremely long earrings contained green emeralds as did her golden lip plates, a perfect match with her dress. Perhaps it had been the other way around. Ben suddenly realized it was easier to match cloth to gem than gems to cloth.

How do you like my new look, gentlemen? She sent.

Ben replied politely, "Lady Bolivar, you look ravishingly beautiful."

Why thank you, Ben. Yes, I and Henry are both totally in love with my new appearance. So refined, so elegant, so daring, so attractive, don't you think?

"Why absolutely, Lady Bolivar. All those and more," Ben replied. She moved towards Henry and he, her. Midway across the room, they met. She slipped a lower arm around his small waist and he put an arm around hers, steadying them both. Together, they began their slow walk from this meeting room to the teleport pad. Ben and Tim followed behind them, but noticed he had guards positioned along the way. Lord Valen would have eyes on him every step of the way.

Right on time Lord Valen appeared on the teleport pad, wobbling slightly as he regained his balance on his toe boots. He too wore a finely made suit that contrasted with his copper colored neck rings. *At least he can't be strangled or garroted anymore,* Ben thought.

Why would anyone want to do that to me, Lord Valen sent back. *I heard that by the way.* Ben flushed and redoubled his mental blocks. He was getting sloppy.

After introductions and Lord Valen's extremely complimentary words to Lady Bolivar on her fabulous new appearance, the five made their way slowly back to the meeting room. Ben and Tim both noticed no others came with him. This man was awfully confident, both thought.

Many minutes later, the four men sat down in the formal meeting room. "Thank you for seeing me, Lord Bolivar. I wanted to come here personally. Why? Well, in the Westerlings, we have been fairly isolated from you folks this far north. We don't know much about you, though I have learned a little from some of the other Midlands lords. If I am not mistaken, here in Brom, you have perhaps the largest concentration of those with our gifts."

"Yes, we are so privileged," Lord Henry replied.

"Indeed. Recently I've learned the virus has spread. It struck, as Lord Wycombe anticipated, at Southbend. Some twenty-five Easterlings were struck with the illness. Luckily, all were saved. What a relief."

"Yes, we are aware of that. I think these days whenever an outbreak occurs, every tower gets informed almost at once. Comm networks," Lord Henry answered. He chose his words carefully, revealing nothing.

"That's good to hear. You Midlands folk are on the ball, as we Westerlings like to say. Anyway, after that outbreak, I asked Lord Wycombe to re-evaluate the results and make a better guess as to who may be next on the virus march across our world. As you may recall at the council meeting, he thought it might be Northend. Upon a re-measuring, as he put it, it looks like Brom is closer. I came to give you a personal head's up, so to speak. I don't want to unduly alarm you, but if the virus continues to follow its current path, Brom is next and then Northend and then Adelmira. Who knows beyond that? The Easterlings lands are mostly unknown to us Westerlings."

"Now that is evil news indeed, but not wholly unexpected. Sooner or later it was bound to get here, if it is *indeed* a virus," Lord Henry replied.

"Indeed. I also wanted to double check and make sure you have enough supplies on hand to deal with the potentially coming crisis. I realize it would be a breach of security for you to tell me exactly how many possible victims in dire need of the cure there could be here. So I won't ask you that, My Lord. Let me tell you this, via Miss Nita Valen, I've learned she has sent a dozen of her medical machines to her Brom Office and sent along seventy-five pairs of the alien prosthetic hands. If these quantities are not enough, please let me know and I will see more are sent. Lord knows when or even *if* it will strike here. I hope it does not, but prudence dictates since we at least have a lifesaving cure, we make it available."

"Hum, seventy-five you say?" Lord Henry mused thoughtfully. "Perhaps I might take you up on your offer. Could you possibly send up enough to handle a hundred please? I would be far more comfortable with that amount ready at hand." Ben wondered if Henry was somehow padding his numbers a little, perhaps to confuse Lord Valen.

"Consider it done! I must apologize for our ignorance of your people. They will be here yet today." He focused and sent word to Nita who relayed it to Valen Castle. Later that day, another large pile of boxes arrived on their teleport pad, as promised.

"Now then, you also mentioned something about having more ideas on how to stop the virus from spreading further?" Lord Henry got directly to the reason he had allowed Lord Valen to visit.

"Ah yes. That. We've been doing a little investigation of our own, wholly incomplete, you see, as we have so little contact with you folks here in the Midlands. As I and my staff studied the excellent map of the virus path drawn up by Lord Wycombe and given to us at the council meeting, it struck us that something was missing."

"Do go on," Lord Henry encouraged him.

"Yes, it involves transmittal methods. You see, the average person on Tierra has not the faintest idea of germs and viruses, yet we *mentales* gifted do — much to the dismay of the aliens, I've discovered. They still think we are primitives. Anyway. We began to look seriously at his map. As you know, it struck Valen first and then Wycombe was next. So we asked ourselves how did it get from us to Wycombe? Should it not have also passed through all the other smaller towns and villages along the way? Exchange City, perhaps? Well, of course, there are the foothills in between, sparsely populated. But as you get closer to Wycombe, there are outlying towns from that great city."

He continued, "Of course we don't know if there is any of the gifted living there. So we asked Lord Wycombe about such details. He told us there are always a few locals who have the gifts and who live in such places, even on isolated farms and ranches, I'm told."

"All this leads where?" Lord Henry asked. He already knew what Ben and Tim had found. This seemed dangerously close to the same thing.

"*No* reported cases of illness," Lord Valen pronounced proudly, as if this was highly significant data. He already knew Ben and Tim had discovered this very fact and cleverly brought it up before they could. "Do you see the importance of this small detail?"

"Yes, a virus or disease does not act in such a manner. Ben and Tim here have just returned from an extensive trip through the breadbasket lands of Rusden and have reported similar findings. How is it the virus goes from large city to large city, where we *mentales* gifted reside and operate in large numbers, yet wholly skips over the locals and smaller towns? Answer me that one," Lord Henry jabbed.

"Ah precisely *so*. My compliments. You too are catching on to what we've discovered as well. How *is* this virus being transmitted? That is the *key* question before us. Answer that and we can perhaps find a permanent cure or eliminate it entirely," Lord Valen said with an air of confidence.

Ben spoke up, "We can safely rule out air born virus. It can't skip over vast grounds."

Lord Valen looked at him, pivoting his body slightly with his toe boots. His neck was immobile. "Well done. Exactly my thoughts precisely. Not by air. But then by what other means could it travel?"

No one spoke and Lord Valen then did. "I came here today to toss out another possibility. Suppose for a moment it spreads by hand to hand contact, after all it affects our hands. Suppose that someone came to Valen early this year with the disease. Somehow, by hand contact I and my staff got infected. Then suppose this person left Valen and traveled eastward, perhaps stopping next at Wycombe, then Rusden, and so on. Do you see what I am getting at?" he asked mischievously.

"Hum, so you are suggesting one or more individuals are carrying this disease and are themselves not affected by it, for surely they'd be dead by now, and they are traveling around the Midlands transmitting the virus to us all?" Lord Henry asked for clarification. This was a wild idea, but it held merit, explaining much.

Even Ben began to see this could well be possible. The probe sent by Beta would not have found anything, which it didn't. He asked, "If so, how could such a person or persons be found and discovered?"

"A nail in a haystack, a copper in the muck pile," Lord Valen answered. "Indeed, a daunting task. There is an easy way to test this theory, but perhaps it is already too late for Brom."

"What? Please, Lord Valen, illuminate us," Lord Henry insisted, highly interested. Perhaps Ben and Tim were wholly wrong about everything, including Lord Valen.

"Close the city doors. Let no one inside who does not live here. Let no travelers enter the city or have contact with you or your staff. I know it is a wildly impractical idea, but, if it were truly implemented, then if it were being transmitted by a traveler, then that city would be spared being infected."

"I see your meaning clearly. I will let Welsham and Northend know of this suggestion. It will cause considerable trouble to close a large city, but if it stops the spread, it's worth it. Perhaps we should do the same here in Brom," Lord Henry replied.

"You might try it, but I fear based on Lord Wycombe's time line, it may well be too late for you here. But look, I am alive; I didn't die. I admit these hands are much less than desirable, but I can still function somewhat. I hate this infernal neck support, but I am alive and am suffering no other ill effects from it."

Ben had the sudden thought. *He's very nearly immobile. He isn't capable of any real work or action anymore. Curious. Are we all slowly becoming just that, immobile and incapable of real action?*

The conversation then became rather boring as the two leaders discussed the possible nature of this traveler or travelers. At last it was lunch time. "Please, Lord Valen, stay a little longer and share lunch with us. I'm told that today we have a real treat, dried fish from the sea coast of Alba, from Turda I believe."

"Ah, if you insist. I haven't had fish for quite some time. Yes, I would love to share your lunch," he replied. "I hope it isn't a long walk," he half jested. Both lords grinned, mutually hobbled.

As they walked slowly to the Great Hall, Lord Valen chatted on a more personal line. "My wife has been hounding me to get my lips done too. Nita has told me quite a few lords have done so already. I'd hate to be the only lord without them at the spring council. How about you? Has Lady Bolivar been on you to get it done too?"

Lord Henry laughed, "Well, as a matter of fact, she has. I'll give Nita this; she sure knows how to make something incredibly sexy. Still we need to be able to issue orders."

"I feel the same way, but then she tells me is why we have telepathy. Well I guess she's got a point there. Lady Bolivar certainly looks quite attractive; they do her justice," Lord Valen teased him.

"Keep your alien hands off of her," he teased back. Both men laughed.

I heard that! Lady Bolivar interrupted them. She was standing beside the doors to the Great Hall and had overheard them. Both men laughed even more. Ben couldn't tell if she was smiling or annoyed. The lip places literally removed all key facial expressions, leaving an almost statuesque appearance, emotionless.

Many of his aides and staff were also coming, and most were at least polite to Lord Valen, who seemed completely at ease, confusing Ben and Tim even further. Could he not be involved, they wondered? To be safe, Ben sat between the two lords; Tim, beside Lady Bolivar. They were served a very nicely prepared meal of fish, lentils, rice, and tea laced with honey. The table conversation was polite, but boring for the two men. Lady Bolivar was enjoying playing the hostess, demonstrating the polite way to sip her tea via a spoon. *I think you men ought to have fine lip plates as well. What I can't decide is if you should also have gemstones embedded in them. I think perhaps not. Don't want to upstage us women.* Both men chuckled.

After the meal was finished, they walked Lord Valen back to the teleport pad. He shook their hands, though the three of them felt the prosthetic hands were rather cold and inhuman. A minute later, he vanished. Lord Bolivar then chatted, "He sure did have a great deal of trouble with the silverware. Those hands of his are definitely giving him a lot of trouble, but he kept up a good face. I could tell that. Well, he did give us some ideas. Perhaps we have been barking up the wrong tree. Best get down to business and chat with those in Welsham and Northend. Can't say what their response will be. Can you see yourselves out? Walking is a royal pain in these toe boots." The two nodded and left.

Walking home, they discussed the key ideas of the meeting. That Lord Valen had come up with the very same idea they had — that the smaller towns had been skipped — had surprised them both. "You know, it is almost as if he knew what we were up to," Ben suggested.

"Could well be. We had to get the information on the locals from those lords who have been 'saved' by Lord Valen, directly or indirectly," Tim replied.

"Hi all. We're back. Was interesting," Ben called out to the others, taking the stairs to the basement two at a time. Tim followed normally, heading back to his computer to continue his researches, leaving Ben to tell the others about what they had learned.

Around two that afternoon, Petrona came over to see how Tim was doing. "Tim! Your hands!" she squealed.

He looked up, not quite understanding her, but sensing her alarm. She repeated it and pointed to his hands. Great red splotches covered both his hands! "Good god! Look at them!"

Ben came running into the control room holding his hands in the air. "Look at my hands! God, not you too, Tim?" A shocked Elana came rushing up as well, staring at the men's hands as well. Tim could sense fear coming from Petrona.

Ben! Tom! The virus has struck us! It was Lord Henry and he was panicking.

Get your best healers on it at once. Send word to Elegant Fashions Inc. Tell them to get ready, Ben sent back.

He'd barely had time to relay that to the others when Venerada Marisol reached him. She sounded shaky and somewhat frightened. *Ben, Tim! It's struck our tower folk too! Not everyone has it yet. The katalyein are not affected nor are the Madiera women. We've wakened the third shift circle members. They are taking over now and so far they don't show any symptoms. We are getting all healers on it. Keep you posted.*

Hastily, Ben added her news to the mix. "Keep calm everyone, stay alert. Remember, we are supposed to have two days before it gets critical," Ben attempted to calm his own nerves as well as the others. There were no doubts about the symptoms at all.

How is your neck? Rafaela sent. *It's supposed to impact necks too.*

Both men undid their suit shirts and everyone crowded around looking for signs on their necks. "There, I see one," Petrona attempted to say. Since she was pointing with her hand, the others grasped what she tried to say.

"Hey, we ought to capture an image of these spots!" Tim called out. Quickly, he setup the video system and did just that, creating good images of both their hands and the few spots which were just now starting to appear on their necks.

"There. We got good images. You know, I don't feel sick at all, how strange."

"I don't either. It's not like I feel when I have the flu or a cold. I really feel just fine, well perhaps a little hot. Yes, hot, I am overheating, but that could just be me panicking," Ben added.

Any soreness? Any stiffness? Rafaela wanted to know.

"No, not really. Or maybe I'm beginning to imagine things," Ben tried to jest, but failed completely. For a time they all continued to make as many observations about their conditions as they could. Darcy and Dawn worked hard to jot them all down, struggling to get their hands working as well as they needed them to work to do the writing.

A few hours later, Venerada Marisol made contact again. *Well, this is completely baffling our healers, all them. They cannot find the source of the infection. They claim they've never seen anything like this. Could this perhaps be an alien disease that's somehow gotten to Tierra via the aliens at the spaceport? That's their latest theory. Certainly, there are some foreign particles in our blood streams.*

Damn. I thought for sure some of your expert healers could figure this out, Ben sent back.

I was so hoping that would be the case. Ben, I don't have any other options but to start sending those who have gotten it to get the only known cure, unless you have some other ideas we can try.

Honestly, no. I don't feel sick at all, yet my hands feel like they are burning and they itch. We're out of ideas too. What other choice do we have?

None. Okay. You two get yourselves to the store too. Please don't risk the fifty-fifty option. I'll let Lord Henry know as well. Good luck. We'll have to meet and go over everything with a fine toothbrush when this is over.

Sadly, Ben related what Venerada Marisol had to report back. All were disheartened. "We should get you two to the store soon," Petrona said, but she had to repeat it several times before Tim fully got it. She'd even removed her plates. However, already everyone knew doing that made very little difference. So many of their speech sounds were formed by use of their lips, which now drooped down in two semicircular loops. It didn't matter much whether they had their plates in or out.

"Got you, dear. You can put your fancy plates back in. It really doesn't make all that much of a difference. Just talk slowly and give me a chance to figure it out," Tim said. "Ben, we probably ought to get ourselves to the store too. I think Petrona and Elana want to accompany us, right love?" Petrona nodded, still fumbling with her clumsy prosthetic hands on her plates. Darcy came over as fast as she could and quickly helped her out.

A half hour later, Tim had their carriage hitched and the four headed off to their local branch office of Elegant Fashions Inc. When they arrived, many other carriages were there, and they saw others coming down the street. They headed on inside, where a local woman took their names. She was not gifted and wore gloves, Tim noted, and thus in no danger of contamination, assuming this virus was passed by human contact. She led them to another room where already a dozen men and women were sitting on hastily arranged chairs. All had the red spots, though a few spouses who were not *mentales* didn't.

As they waited, more and more arrived. The two men knew quite a few of them. Some were even children! *God, this is far worse than I ever imagined, they are just kids!* Ben thought.

Several hours passed before the two arrived at the head of the waiting line. Then, the harried young woman came for them. "You and your wives are supposed to follow me now. It's your turns." The four rose and followed after them. "You women go in here and your husbands are to go into that room. Okay. Good luck. So far, we have not lost a patient. So that is the best news I have for you. There are so many of you! It's going to be a long, long day, I'm afraid." The four did as asked.

Hello, I am Annie, the manager of this branch office of Elegant Fashions Inc. You are Tim Bellweather and you are Ben Blackwater? Do I have the right men? she sent. She too had prosthetic hands and wore the latest ornaments, thus she used telepathy to communicate with them.

"Yes, I'm Tim. He's Ben. I bet you have been very busy."

She smiled and sighed, but the smile wasn't visible. *Yes, but then we have been expecting the worst for some time now. We are prepared, but we all so hoped it would not happen this far north. It could be worse, like in January. Okay, I have your orders here and all is in order. If you two will just lie down on those two cots, I'll get started on you. Oh, you will feel no pain and be out for a while. Your wives will be beside you when you recover. Thanks.* They did as asked. She placed something over their faces and all went black. They were indeed out.

The two women waited patiently in the next room. At last Annie entered. *Let's see. Petrona and Elana? Right?* Both nodded. *Okay then. I have your orders here. I must compliment you both. You will love these modifications.*

"Huh? What modifications?" Petrona said, repeating herself several times.

Oh, you are to get your toe shoes and your pipe corsets, along with a terrific collection of our fine gowns. You can choose your colors later on. I think it is a fine thing that your husbands are allowing you both to have the very latest in fashions. I do love your lip plates and earrings. They do you justice. Now we'll have you fixed up in no time.

Both women were confused. Neither Tim nor Ben had mentioned they could get these done to themselves. Both had felt rather out of place when surrounded by all the elegantly dressed women, but then they also saw how difficult it was for Darcy, Dawn, and Sally. Both were baffled and tried to ask about it, but they were unable to make their protests clear. Part of them wanted to get this done so they would be as sexy, as fashionable as the others. Part of them rebelled against it. Had Tim and Ben secretly arranged this? If so, they dare not upset them by refusing it. Confused, the two laid down as asked, looking at each other with wonder in their eyes. Then they too went unconscious.

Petrona and Elana awoke sometime later. All was quiet, but neither could breathe. Gasping they tried to sit up and found they were now wearing a pipe corset which heavily restricted their breathing and their ability to bend. They struggled and sat up, and then noticed their feet. Their ankles pointed straight down now, and they could no longer put their feet flat on the floor, just their toes. A young assistant walked in with a paper and pad.

"Hi there. All went very well. You each now have the prized fourteen-inch waist. Of course, if you had this done when you were say fourteen, you'd be able to have a twelve inch waist. Anyway, I've come to ask you what colors you want for your dresses. You each have six already paid for. With your red hair and your brown hair, let's see what will bring out the very best in you and not clash with your fancy lip plates and earrings? Usually, women get this done first and the ornaments second. No matter, we will have you both elegantly dressed in time for you to sit beside your husband until they awake. Oh yes, they are recovering and should be just fine. We have gotten to them in time and they are wholly out of danger. You can relax on that account."

Petrona had red rubies in her plates and earrings, so her first dress choice was a matching red pod-silk gown. The assistant insisted she also take an arm-fetter-gown in the same color. Meanwhile, Elana had emeralds and chose a matching green satin gown. Likewise, the assistant insisted she have a matching arm-fetter-gown in the same color as well. Next, she helped the two women don their thin, black nylons. They needed help with the garters, because they only just barely had control of their hands. After putting a white slip on each, the assistant helped them into the gowns of their first choice. Annie had told her not to let them start out wearing the arm-fetter-gowns because they would likely be having trouble walking and would be having to help their husbands soon as well. This, however, she did not tell the two women. Finally, she gave each a pair of black patent toe shoes, explaining some warmer toe boots would be part of the rest of their outfits, since winter was upon them.

"Now you have to practice walking." Two frightened, gasping women rose carefully to their feet, really their toes. At least because they had already had lots of experience with the other women, they knew what to expect. Still when the shoes were on their feet, it was a different story. "Yes, that's the best way. Hold onto each other. I'll leave you two to practice walking around this room while I go gather up all your other prepaid purchases. Your husbands have spent quite a lot of silver on you two. I can see why. You both look positively stunning!" Both women were quite pleased, not realizing that's why the assistant had said what she'd said. The assistant was well-practiced on such matters.

Like the other women back at home, they were now only able to take about a two to three inch step, minuscule compared to what they were used to taking. Plus, they found just standing in one spot terribly challenging, so little of their feet were actually on the floor, just their toes.

Later, they were led into another room. Each held onto the other as they followed after the assistant. There they saw their husbands, each lying on a recovery cot. Lanterns were on; it was quite dark outside. They stared at them in total disbelief! True, their hands were gone. Their strong, muscular arms gradually tapered down to two tiny cones, barely an inch across where their wrists had been. This they were expecting. Both men had the familiar copper colored rings around their necks, making their heads immobile, but again, they'd expected this, as the virus had infected their necks as well.

Rather the rest was what shocked them. Both now wore a similar pipe corset and their feet were also altered like their own had been. Even more surprising, they too sported lip plates about the same size as theirs, only theirs had no gems in them. They moved slowly over to their bedsides and sat stiffly beside them. "I don't understand. Maybe they wanted us all to look the same?" Petrona said, repeating it several times until Elana grasped it.

They also saw their new prosthetic hands sitting near the prone men. Both were still unconscious, their breathing shallow as it would always be now, but steady and relaxed. All they could do was wait and wonder about why their husbands had not told them about having all these modifications done.

It was late when the two men finally roused. Annie had been slavishly following the instructions given to her about these four. Nita had given her the *very* specific orders, which she now carried in her hands as she made her slow way into the room, having timed their waking precisely. She had much experience with this aspect of the surgeries. Annie had handled forty people today and had another thirty-five scheduled for the morning, leaving the whole afternoon available for more who might show up in desperate need.

Ah, you are waking. Everything went absolutely perfectly, Ben, Tim. There, there, easy does it. Take shallow breaths; don't fight it. Your corsets won't permit it. See if you can sit up on your own. I know it's difficult, but you'll soon get used to it. Everyone gasps when they first wake. We've done a superb job on your feet and lips too. Your half dozen new outfits are ready so let's get you up and dressed, shall we?

"What's happened to our lips. Damn! I can't talk right!" Ben gushed and gasped. *We didn't want our lips done! What's with the corsets and feet? That's not what was infected!* Both men struggled mightily to get to a sitting position, gasping when they finally made it. Their eyes looked down at the gold plates and then at their feet which they could only see by raising their feet. They sat perfectly erect, unable to move anything from their head to their hips. Both were panicking and gasping.

Calm down, men. Relax. Everything went just perfect. I've done a superb job with both of you, though I wish you would have had these other things done and your wives too on some other day when we were not so swamped with all the other emergencies. Still I did a perfect job on you both. But I am exhausted and need to get home. Have to be back at it early in the morning, because there are still thirty some to go. So please calm down. We've done everything you have asked us to specifically to do for you and for your wives. All their new gowns and footwear are packed and ready to go, as are your six new outfits, except the one that I'll be helping you into shortly. We certainly do appreciate the rather large amount of silver you've spent here today and look forward to serving you in the future with all your fine outfits.

Wait! Wait! What orders? We only came here to get cured of the infection. Not all this other stuff! Ben fairly screamed at her. Reactively her arms went up towards her ears.

These orders. Here, I have a copy for you to take with you, along with a lengthy list of guidelines to assist you during your periods of adjustments. She held the pages out before him. He raised his hands to get them and saw only the conical stumps.

Annie recovered and held them so he and Tim could read them. *See, there are your signatures on the bottom lines, and here, on your wives. Now let's get you dressed shall we?*

There must be some mistake, Annie. We didn't order these modifications, not ever.

Hey, I'm exhausted. The best thing to do is to contact Miss Nita Valen at our main office in Exchange City tomorrow and get it all sorted out. I just follow the orders you signed. Now, let's get your new hands on you shall we? Petrona, can you take charge of these papers, please? She took them and held onto them tightly.

Annie quickly showed them how to put on the hands, but they already knew, except not on themselves, which was a whole new experience. *Do you gentlemen want to wear black nylons like your wives do or would you prefer thin stockings? Oh heck, it is too late for all this. I'll see you have a half dozen of each. Let's get you dressed and on your way home, please, gentlemen. I've done forty operations today and face nearly that many tomorrow!*

Ben and Tom shut up and concentrated on controlling their gasping breathing. She slipped a pair of the nylons on Ben's legs, but like all who had prosthetic hands, she had a most difficult time with the garters. He could tell she was quite exhausted.

As she started in on Tim, he sent, *Thank you for helping so many of us today, Annie.* She smiled, but it was invisible of course. Next, she brought out a pair of tapered dress shirts that fit their slimmed constricted torsos tightly. Again, fastening the buttons was quite challenging for her, and Elana lent her fumbling hands with Ben's shirt. Annie appreciated her help and nodded to her.

She helped them into their tweed, pod-silk trousers, again designed to fit their unusual shapes snugly. After struggling to get their belts shut, she and the two women took a look at the men's new appearance. *You two have a fine, handsome pair here,* Annie sent to Petrona and Elana, complimenting the men. She helped them into their matching suit jackets. Finally, she slipped their new toe boots onto their feet. *Okay, dressed. Some time ago, I instructed my assistants to take all your many new purchases out to your carriage. So let's get you up. Ordinarily we would take time to get you used to walking, but it's **way** late. Ladies, if you will put your arms around your husband's waist, let's get them over to the mirrors there by the door on our way out. Gentlemen, trust me, you both look just fabulous; your wives will be extremely pleased, I am sure.*

Both men wobbled wildly as they stood up on their toes, and their wives did only slightly better, having practiced some. Slowly and carefully, they followed after Annie who led them out of the recovery room. Pausing at the mirror, the men got a good look at themselves and their wives. Now they finally realized fully what had been done to them. Both men were shocked. They did look like all the others who had undergone these body modifications, but they were anything but pleased. They continued their slow, stumbling steps towards the exit doors.

Nearly fifteen minutes passed before they reached the doors. Annie had their cloaks already brought here, hanging on pegs. To speed things along, Annie helped each of the four into theirs and held the doors open for them, as they stepped out into the cold night air. Snow was falling; footing was treacherously slippery for the five. *Damn, snow already. Watch your steps. It is very tricky walking in these boots and shoes,* Annie sent them.

The four barely moved, taking minuscule steps towards their carriage. Annie, Ben noted, was moving just as slowly and carefully as they were, towards her lone horse buggy, the only other one there. He recalled the huge number that had been there when they first arrived and wondered how long they had been out.

You really ought to have planned ahead and had a driver waiting for you. Okay, you four get yourselves in among all the packages. I'll get someone to come here right away and drive you home. Men, you ought to have planned this better, honestly.

Thank you, Annie. Like I said, there is some huge mistake here; we didn't order any of this, except to be cured of the virus, Tim sent back. By the time the four finally got themselves into the carriage, a man came running up, his breath frosty.

"You be needing a driver tonight?" he asked.

Yes please. Tim told him their address, and the four rummaged among their old clothes for their coin pouches. They struggled with controlling their hands, but finally managed to grasp some coins to pay this kind soul. When they finally pulled into their home, Tim asked, *Sir, I'll give you ten silvers if you will carry all these packages inside for us and take care of the horse. Our small stable is around back.*

"Well, thank you sirs! I'll carry you folks in for ten silvers," he exclaimed with a hearty laugh. Tim hoped that would not be necessary. The man did help each one safely down and assisted them, one by one, up the short snow covered walk to their front door, before he began bringing in the many packages, depositing them on the front room floor. A bit later, he returned, having handled their horse. Tim gave him the coins and thanked him again.

All four headed for the stairs that led to the basement. At least one of the others here had long ago lit the lanterns so they were able to see. They took the stairs very, very slowly and carefully. As they neared the bottom, Eric heard them and came slowly to greet them. The second he saw the four, he let out a yell. "Everyone, they are back. What the devil happened to you? My god! I didn't know you wanted all this done!"

We didn't. There has been a huge mistake somewhere. God help us now, Ben sent. *We're starving. What time is it anyway?* When they reached the sub-basement floor which was perfectly smooth stone, their walking became as easy as it would ever be, which was not good. all the others arrived and stared at the four. Then they began helping them out of their cloaks, staring even more after that. Finally, Eric took charge.

"Okay, food. Darcy, Dawn, you heat up what's left of

supper. Let's get them into the eating room where they can sit down. It takes quite a lot of getting used to those boots and shoes to stand still or even walk, we know!" he said feeling rather important now. Suddenly, he was in a position to help out those who had saved him and his new wife and sisters. He felt a big surge of self-pride.

We kept it warm for you, Darcy sent. *Didn't expect it would be this long before you got back. It's nearly midnight. We were getting a little scared.* She and Dawn headed off slowly to fetch the food, tea, and utensils. Slowly, the four headed down the hall to the communal dining room they used far more frequently than the real one of the house above ground.

What's that you're holding? asked Eric, noticing Petrona's right hand was tightly crushing some papers.

"Our orders," Petrona said shakily, finally releasing them into his hands.

"Your orders?" he asked by way of making sure he understood her. She nodded, but continued watching her every move, trying not to fall down or pull Tim down too. She never dreamed walking like this was so terribly difficult.

At last they sat down, but the two men sat perfectly erect, unable to move their torso from their heads to their hips. Darcy and Dawn came in with their arms full and set four places. Neither Tim nor Ben could work their hands well enough to manipulate the silverware, and Eric and Darcy automatically began to feed them, pleased they could return the help they'd received. Still stunned by the sheer magnitude of their modifications, both men ate in silence. Besides they all knew speaking with lip plates was nearly impossible for any reasonable conversation. They needed time to absorb what had happened. Fortunately, the others allowed them to be silent and didn't pester them with questions yet.

As Darcy finally began spooning tea into Ben's mouth, Ben finally opened up a broad telepathic link to all them. *We've been had, sabotaged, hoodwinked or something. Annie — she's the one in charge at the store — she had these orders apparently signed by us, ordering her to perform all these modifications on us and our wives. Further, apparently those orders also included a whole lot of dresses and suits for the four of us, costing plenty, all paid for in advance. Please can someone lay out those orders so we can see them; we can't even bend anymore.*

Many eyes stared at the neatly done orders, coming directly from Nita Valen in Exchange City. Ben quickly noted everything that was on the order had been done. Well, he didn't yet know if all the clothing items matched. The total cost was nearly five hundred silvers. Further, their own signatures were across the bottom of the orders!

Those look like our own signatures, Ben! Tim sent, growing more and more furious with this mess.

Elana, Petrona, we need to know exactly what the women said to you about all this. Rather than trying to make you tell them to us, can we just touch your minds and see your memories, please?

Both women nodded and felt the gentle touch of their husbands, as both went into rapport with them. To be honest, both women cherished these highly special times when they did this with them, usually at night in bed. Ben sent, *Elana, Petrona, it's not your fault. You were just as confused about all this as we. I can see how you were purposely made to think we wanted you to get these modifications. Someone has gone to great lengths to do this to us. Who and why? That, we are definitely going to find out!* Both women suddenly relaxed, very visibly. They had been scared that somehow they should have done something right at the start to prevent all this from happening, that it was all their fault somehow.

Someone has deliberately set us up to take us out of action, Tim sent. *No one messes with Tim Bellweather!*

God, I am really tired for some reason. I think we should all get some sleep and try to sort this all out in the morning. Darcy, Dawn, please handle making breakfast for us all; we obviously can't do it now. Eric, you are on house security duty, Ben sent. *God help us all now.*

The four usually slept in their bedroom on the main floor of their home. Rather than disturb the sleeping arrangements of the others, Ben and Tim braved the stairs once more. With their wives going up side by side with them, they found going up was far easier than going down. Further, their wives' necks were free, and they could look around and down easily, guiding them as they strode up the stairs awkwardly but perfectly erect.

Getting undressed turned out to be a huge hassle as the men struggled to get their prosthetic hands to do the simple actions. Their wives were a bit better at it and the four helped each other until they at least got their outer clothes off along with their shoes and boots. Twice, Ben put too much force and pulled a hand off his arm, much to his annoyance. As they stood on their toes still wearing their nylons and corsets, the latter of which was to be worn at all times or so the documentation stated, they realized they probably couldn't undo the many garters. *We'll sleep like this,* Ben sent.

"We should remove our hands and lip plates," Petrona said a few times, pointing with her hands to both until Tim duplicated her. They did so, but the women had to help the men remove theirs. Carefully, they also removed their hands and finally got into bed, the men having an awful time doing so, unable to bend above their hips.

Elana whispered, "I'm sorry this happened to you, my love." She kissed him; her lip loops touching his cheeks. He returned hers and quickly discovered how incredible this greatly heightened sensitivity of their lips was. Elana then did to him what she had him do to her. As her tongue slid over his lip loops, his arousal was instant, only confirming what he had already concluded.

Remembering what he'd heard from Alpha, he realized Nita had played her role well. Their society of telepaths really was sinking into an almost frantic craving for sexuality. Well, it certainly *was* pleasurable. As he drifted into a deep sleep greatly needed by his body after so much surgery, he wondered if now there was any way at all to reverse this awful decline the telepaths of Tierra were undergoing. Part of him wanted to continue with Elana, but part of him also knew the overall direction was towards further succumbing, and they didn't have much further to fall.

Chapter 13 Discoveries

When Ben awoke the next morning with Elana lying partially on him, their lip loops entangled with each other, he knew he could not possibly get up without totally waking her. As his tongue touched her loops, the electric charge roused them both and she responded. A bit later Elana got up and helped him into a sitting position. For a moment the two sat there, the tips of their cone stubs lightly touching each other, sending intense pleasure through their bodies. Elana obviously was enjoying this most intimate contact, but both needed to use the commode and get dressed. Already they smelled breakfast cooking and knew they would be a long time getting dressed.

Ben discovered he could not easily get his own hands on and Elana quickly realized that. She couldn't get her own on either; her arms needed a wrapping bandage to enlarge her stump to fit the larger prosthetic hands. Hence, she struggled to get his on. Once done he began focusing on making his work or at least do what he wanted. Eventually between the two, he was able to get hers on her arms. They looked at each other and broke into a laugh. This much effort and they only had their hands on!

An hour of wiggling, fumbling, and struggling to make the unfeeling hands do what they wanted, both were finally dressed. They rose and headed down stairs to the Underground, just as Tim and Petrona came out of their room. Both couples had arms around the other and took the stairs down very slowly and carefully. The women quickly realized the men were having a much more difficult time of it. By daylight, they saw the problem: the men couldn't bend their necks in the slightest, whereas they could.

Once more, the men needed help with eating, but continued to work on controlling their hands. "You will get the hang of it in time," Eric volunteered. "So what's on our agenda today?"

We need to get as much of this undone as we can, Ben sent.

We need to find out who was behind having this done

to us and why, Tim sent simultaneously. *Divide and conquer, eh?*

Half of the team went with Ben, the other half with Tim, determined to follow up both paths. Following Ben's guidance, Elana, Eric, Darcy, and Dawn, worked on getting one of their medical machines up and running. This proved to be an enormous challenge. Constantly Ben and several others kept pulling their own hands off by exerting more than a pound of force on them. At last around noon, they had it ready for operations, pathetic Ben thought very depressed. That should have taken him a couple of minutes. Worse, they had all broken down in fits of laughter as they attempted to push the machine away from the wall so they could fully open it up. Their toe shoes and boots kept sliding on the smooth stone floor, while the machine just sat there. There simply was so little traction from their small amount of soles.

One by one, Ben had each person lie down on the machine. Then he activated the menus, and it diagnosed the person, specifically detailing what could be repaired. Darcy watched what he did carefully, and finally got to practice it on Ben who went last. Elana and Eric had to help him back up and onto his feet. Then all went around to the display to see the results.

As expected, it reported he had had two ribs removed on either side and those could not be replaced as well as his hands. That was a no-brainer. The machine found no reason he needed to continue to wear the pipe corset, medically that is. In fact, none of them had any real reason to continue wearing them. As expected, their feet could be partially restored, but they would need to wear heels, which were about six inches tall. That Ben also knew from past analyses. Their lips could also be mended, which was both good news and bad. He rather enjoyed their heightened sensitivity, Elana certainly did. Rather what shocked them was that as far as the machine could tell, there was no reason to be wearing the terribly confining neck rings.

As they finished up, Venerada Marisol checked in with Ben. *Status report, Ben. Are you and Tim okay?* He sent that they were and she continued. *That's good to hear. The last of our ill have been cured this morning. So far this afternoon, no new cases have been found. Though we all found it strange the third shift circle members came down with it during the night, right after they all had a late night snack on some of our left over fish we all had for lunch the other day. It has been a nightmare here. So many were affected, it's awful.*

Wait a second. You had dried fish too?

Yes, why?

We all had dried fish for lunch there at the castle. Not long after that, we all got sick. You had fish too and got sick. Then later the late night circle ate some and got sick. Marisol, quarantine what's left of that fish! Have Lord Bolivar do the same thing. I think we got the infection from the fish. Have it checked out if you can.

Will do! This could be the breakthrough we've desperately needed!

Ben then sent a quick synopsis of their conversation to everyone and his group headed off to join Tim's group.

Andres said rather excitedly, "Boy is Tim ever good! I've learned a good deal already! He's hacked into Nita's Elegant Fashions Inc computer. Look what he's found! Oh, he says I am to do the talking. Okay. He found the original orders that were given to Nita. It appears she's not the guilty party — we think so far at least. Here they are. Notice the signatures are truly ours but they are a photocopy, whatever that is, of your original signatures on these documents here. Someone has accessed these files and copied and pasted, whatever that means, the signatures onto these orders. Someone has definitely set you four up! Now comes the hard part, finding out who did it."

Well, Tim, we goofed by being out in the open above ground, when we should be where we are supposed to be, the Underground, Ben sent to all. *We exposed ourselves and someone discovered us doing something that is seriously threatening whatever they are doing or planning and had to nullify us as a force. They've certainly done just that.*

"Well, almost no one saw you coming to the rescue of Humberhills and Retford Hills," Andres pointed out. "You've had only a tiny amount of contact with Lord Bolivar and

Venerada Marisol. As far as I can tell, the only time you both were 'above ground' and actively doing something has been your recent scouring of the smaller towns of the central Midlands, checking on the local *mentales*. Of course, you found nothing, but that too is important to the spreading of the virus theories."

"He's got a point, Ben," Eric added. "That really is the only above ground exposure you both have recently had. Ergo, whoever did this to you is somehow connected to the virus and epidemic. Perhaps, you both got too close to something and just didn't know it. Like a viper, if you get too close, even if you don't see it, the viper can feel threatened and can strike." He put his argument in terms of animals he knew well. They discussed this further and everyone had basically the same conclusion. The two had been singled out to be stopped in their search for clues about the viral infection.

Just as the supper hour approached, a distant monitor began flashing, a signal that some search had ended in success. However, everyone was some fifteen feet away when they saw it begin to flash. One by one, they attempted to get up and take a look, but Ben and Tim were terribly slow, compared to their usual instant reactions. Tim started laughing wildly, causing everyone else to stop and look at him, confused. They could see nothing that was humorous or funny.

It's our new high speed reactions we now have when something important occurs. Look at my new super speedy reaction, Tim sent to all, still laughing at himself. Between sixty and seventy tiny steps later, the group gathered around the monitor holding on to each other to steady themselves, leaving Tim to rigidly sit down and operate the keyboard, pointer, and swipe screen.

Ah ha! Bingo! Ta da! Magic fingers has done it again! Oops, no more fingers. Anyway, gang, I found our virus! Tim fairly yelled telepathically to everyone. *It is not a virus at all! It is a simple drug, which reacts to above normal levels of the enzymes produced by pituitary glands. Oh, those are glands in our heads, which give us our elevated psi powers. So this drug is only going to affect us, not the head blind — no offense Petrona, Elana, you've just got different psi powers*

222

than we do. Sometimes I think I am a genius. See, all these days I was running a galaxy-wide search involving the key words of virus-death-telepaths. Since I found nothing and after trying other variations, when I got the red splotches, in desperation I uploaded an image of my hand and searched on red splotches-hands-neck-pituitary gland. Here it is, ameodiaxic chloride, whatever the hell that is. Look, it is a dust like compound found only on planet Abelard-6. One minute please, the Underground is at work, sort of, my substitute fingers barely work. Make that five minutes, crap. This is debilitating, but I am going to get you, whoever you are!

Even though everyone was hungry, none moved; all continued holding onto each other to keep from wobbling too badly and watched Tim, as he used one finger typing methods now, instead of his usual flying fingers approach. After setting up his search, which took him five minutes versus his usual ten seconds, he pressed the Enter key.

"Now we wait," Eric explained. He'd already learned pressing that key meant Tim had sent off his request for something.

While we are waiting, look what I also found out. I have been cursing these pathetic prosthetic hands since they were put on me. So I did a little checking. Look at this. Tim switched to a secondary pair of pages, tiled side by side for easy comparison. *Sorry, gang, the text is in IS, er, Imperium Standard. On the left are the prosthetic hands we've all got, the cheapest possible model that is nerve-activated. On the right, is the best model available, costing ten times more per hand. I'll sum it up. The better hands can lift up to five pounds before slipping off our stumps. As slippage occurs, the inner vacuum pump increases suction until the maximum load is reached. According to the specifications, these more expensive hands are over twenty-five times more sensitive to our nerve signals. Ta da. We were given the worst possible hands; they work just barely well enough for us to do menial things, such as lift a fork, but only with a lot of effort and concentration our part.*

"So can we get some of these better hands?" Eric asked

what everyone was thinking.

Give me time. I'll get them here, Tim promised. A tiny ray of hope sparked among the group.

Just then, his monitor flashed once more and automatically switched to the results of his search. All eyes stared at it, but again it was in IS. Tim translated. *Ah ha. Just as I thought. A large amount of this drug was shipped to Tierra. It arrived earlier this year. It was ordered by — oh this is too good to be true! Ordered by Nita Valen and delivered to Elegant Fashions Inc, but a shipment reroute at the spaceport sent it to Valen Castle. Further, guess who purchased the hundreds of hands? Nita Valen! So Nita is our culprit. She is the one who set us four up. Damn that woman anyway! Oh, she should never have messed with Timothy Bellweather! Okay lady, let us see your credit account.*

While the others discussed the impact of this enormous news, Tim slowly typed away. He added, *Oh yes. Almost forgot about that drug. It is harmless, causing only those red spots, which go away on their own in three days. Clever bastards, I'll give them that. Okay, I'm in. She had over ten million credits. She's unbelievably wealthy. Okay, lady, it is time to pay the Tim. What say as a first action, you purchase all us a fine pair of hands? There, I've just ordered five hundred pairs of the most expensive hands.*

He then doodled with the shipping orders. *They will arrive here in one large crate marked "baby formula." It will be delivered to Elegant Fashions Inc and from there to here. One month, ladies and gentlemen and we'll have better hands to work with. Crap, that still leaves her with seven million credits. Okay. Mom showed me how to do this once, and I have always wanted to do it myself. Here comes the credits evaporation. Woo hoo. Oh, this will be a good one.*

He explained as he pressed the Enter key again. *My program just removed seven million credits from her account, leaving her one credit in it. The credits all go into a single account on Proxima Prime, which, if she is any good at all, she can discover herself. However, once there, that sum is then broken down into small credit transfers to thousands of accounts all over the galaxy, giving the appearance of your money simply evaporating into thin air. From those small accounts, a timed transfer goes to other accounts. Eventually, it all ends up back here in our Tierra account that our moms setup years ago. So Nita is paying us all back for what she and Lord Valen have been doing. Never mess with Timothy Bellweather! I'm starving.*

"Can I learn to do all that too?" Eric asked, amazed at what had just been discovered and done in the last few minutes.

Certainly, but it takes a lot of training and study, Tim replied.

The women headed off to work together to make their supper, a chore Tim and Ben had been doing, though Petrona and Elana usually helped.

As the men sat around discussing these incredible discoveries, Ben pointed out, *Look, they really have taken us out of action. I can't even protect us at all now. See.* He tried to draw his short sword from its scabbard. All that happened was his hand was pulled off his arm. Since he was unable to bend, Eric moved over, retrieved it, and put his hand back on for him. *I'd laugh if it wasn't so serious. Lord Valen really has taken us out of the game. We can't move except at a snail's pace, can't defend ourselves physically, let alone perform well, turning our whole bodies just to see to one side or the other. He's screwed us up good. Worse, he's done this to nearly all the lords and circle members, the ones that would be the first to oppose him.*

"So what do you suppose Lord Valen is trying to do?" Andres asked.

Let's review what we do know, Ben sent to all, including the women working in the kitchen. *Last year, he sent a small band to see if he could recover some ancient power crystals from the three dead-zones Valen created when they destroyed those three towers and cities. Andres and Rafaela beat them to the crystals but paid dearly for it. Still, we stopped them from getting those crystals.*

Now early this year, we know he sent an army of around three thousands soldiers to retake at least Humberhills and Retford Hills, lands he once had conquered years ago when he destroyed Haverhills Tower. We also know he needs more mentales gifted, so badly he devised a scheme to capture all the younger ones at those two fortresses. With your hands removed, there would have been little you could have done to keep from being taken back to Valen and turned into his puppet mentales gifted. Again, we intervened and totally thwarted that whole plan.

He can't retake former lands, can't get the ancient power crystals, can't kidnap and torture new mentales gifted into his control. What is he to do now? Tonight, we know a partial answer to that. He gets Nita to order that drug dust and a mountain of cheap prosthetic hands. Although I haven't yet checked, she probably ordered quite a lot of the medical machines too. While we have no proof yet, I can speculate he sent an agent into an area to specifically put the drug into the lord's and gifted's food. Then he fabricates this story about a deadly virus and offers the frightened lords a cure, cut off hands, substitute nearly useless prosthetic hands, and wear the neck rings, making it almost impossible to do anything physical at all. Nita adds her touches making the stumps hypersensitive, stimulating sexual urges and also does that with her lip plates. Man, are those ever something else. Anyway with the plates in, we can't speak and be easily understood, adding one more hurdle for us to overcome. But their hypersensitive nature will make us all want to keep them. I can see why too. The sex is just incredible. So what we are left with is just why is he doing this and what will be his next move?

Tim filled in the silence that followed. *Okay, since we are not sick, can someone please get these awful neck rings off me?*

"After dinner, we'll try," Eric replied. "Supper is ready. I'll help them. You two see if you can get to the table. Andres, watch them. I know you can't do much to help them, call out if you need help." He slowly rose, catching his balance, and began his slow walk to the kitchen to help. Even carrying in the pots was problematical, since most weighed more than a pound. They got around this somewhat by picking the pots up and holding them such that the weight pulled the hands down harder onto their stumps. Clumsy, but it worked.

Over dinner, Ben sent, *Okay gang. Some of these modifications can be undone or at least remedied a little. First, the most critical thing to do is to get these neck rings off of us. Before we tackle the other things we can do, we should think this through. Lord Valen and Nita obviously wanted us hobbled and out of the way. If we undo everything we can undo, that will give them a big tip off that we have the medical machines to do so and blow our cover, somewhat. If nothing else, it will call their attention to us even further! They could even send an assassin here, and I can't even pick up my sword to defend us without pulling my hand off. We can't fight them with our stumps. So as I see it, we need to retain some of the more obvious restrictions so we don't call their attention back onto us.*

"So what are you suggesting?" Eric asked.

Neck rings go. We can safely remove the pipe corsets. While our waists will still be small and our muscles there weak, we'll gain back our flexibility and ease of breathing. Of course, our clothes will have to be altered a little as our waists expand some. There's nothing we can do about our hands, except wait for the better versions to arrive. Maybe they will work better. I know the women love their earrings, so there is no point in losing them. We need to appear to others that we are still immobilized, so I suggest we somehow learn to get by with these toe boots and shoes. Besides, all that can be done for our feet really is to straighten them enough so we could then wear those fancy high heels our women used to wear before the toe shoes. Men never wore them, so we guys would stick out badly if we did wear them.

I think maybe we should keep these lip plates too. Between them and the toe boots, at a casual glance, we will appear to be wholly helpless just like they left us, save for the neck rings. What do you all think?

Darcy sent, *He has a point about the heels we used to wear. Dawn and I used to wear them at parties. The heels are so high walking in them is almost as bad as these toe shoes, not quite though, we could take larger steps. They were just as treacherous in the snow, though. So I think he is right. If any spy is watching us, the toe boots are instantly visible.*

So are the lip plates, added Dawn, *very noticeable at the briefest glance. But how can we alter our dresses? It is all I can do to hold a fork and spoon.*

Ben replied to all, *We'll have to get a trusted dressmaker to come by. Okay, then if everyone is in agreement, we'll see what we can do to make our lives more comfortable and bearable. However starting now, since we are all going to continue to wear the lip plates, for Petrona and Elana's sake, we should all speak aloud and learn to understand what we are saying. In time I think we can, but others outside our group probably won't be able to catch what we are saying. That may one day prove useful for us.*

"Okay," Ben added vocally and slowly, "we forgot our horse. Eric when you and the twins take care of your birds, could you please feed and water her?"

Although Tim and Ben had always done most of the cooking and all the dishwashing afterwards, now it became a group effort. "Damn, dropped another one. We can't feel a darn thing with these hands. I can't tell if I am gripping the plate tight enough or not, until it falls out of my hand," Tim complained.

"I don't think will be any better with the fancier hands you found us," Petrona replied, unhopefully. "At least now I am able to sort of help too. Of course we're never going to be able to feel with them. I can't imagine what you all are going through with that aspect. I've never had them in the first place, but with these, I am able to do more things, and I really like that feeling, my love."

"Welcome to the club, Tim," Darcy teased him, after dropping one of her own. "We've been fighting this too, you know."

"And you've been doing an admirable job of it. I guess I am still pissed off about the whole thing."

After the dishes were finally done, the two men laid down on the medical machines so the others could see if they could get their neck rings off. While they could see how they were fastened, they did not have the strength or dexterity with their hands to undo them. It took the combined efforts of all them to finally get one ring off. It was again late at night when the last ring was finally off the men, much to their great relief.

The next morning, Venerada Marisol contacted Tim and Ben. *Sorry for not getting back to you sooner. It's been just crazy around here. Many of those upon whom we depended for their hands are, well you know. I have good news and bad news. Good first. You were right about your hunch that it was the fish. Our chemists Madiera women discovered a chemical compound that is foreign to Tierra in it, and have proved it caused a harmless red rash on hands and necks of us. There is no virus. Hands do not have to be amputated! Nor do they need to wear those awful neck rings. We're in the process of getting rid of the rings on everyone, but it's a slow process. Lord Bolivar has been informed, and he believes this is some monstrous plot of Lord Valen's.*

The bad news is that two days ago, it struck the remaining towers, including Adelmira. Naturally, they all followed the prescribed cure. My god, Ben, Tim, almost all our mentales gifted are now crippled up! It's awful. Combined with our dwindling numbers and falling birth rate, I foresee a very serious crisis looming. Perhaps we can discuss this later on, after you've had time to get adjusted?

Ben decided to tell her only a little of what they found. *Good news you've found the cause. I will tell you a little of what we found out, but never reveal you heard it from us. It was Nita Valen who imported that compound and had it shipped to Valen Castle. Don't ask how Tim figured that one out, but we have proof of that. The two of them are behind this catastrophe. Give it some thought. We need to figure out why they are doing this to us all and what their next move might be.* She agreed, but was not too surprised to hear who was behind it.

After their usual struggle to get dressed, Ben decided to get help with their clothing alterations. In the past, they had purchased their usual clothing from Mary's Stitches, a shop a block away. He contacted her telepathically, since he knew in the snow he'd never be able to reach her store on foot. *Hi Mary, Ben Blackwater from up the block. Say, we'd like to hire you to make a lot of alterations to our clothes. Are you up for a lot of business soon?*

She was and promised to drop by in two hours. "I'd best clean off the snow so she doesn't have to tramp in it," Petrona said, when she heard the good news. She and Tim headed outside, where a couple more inches had accumulated. She focused and a wall of flames appeared over their cobblestone drive and walkway. A cloud of steam rose and soon dry cobblestones appeared. She smiled; this was a good use of her special skills.

By the time Mary arrived, sewing basket in hand, the group had managed to get their pipe corsets off. "Wow, look at my lower torso!" Ben exclaimed. His once well-muscled abdomen was concave and anything but muscular. All felt rather weak and knew they'd have to start exercising regularly for some time.

Mary was an older woman, and when she saw the magnitude of what was needed, she laughed heartily. "You will be keeping me busy for a month! But, yes, I can do it. Since you don't want those corsets any longer, I would suggest wearing simple garter belts to hold up your socks or nylons. I believe there is enough seam material in these shirts and dresses so they can be readily altered. Let me get everyone's current measurements and identify which clothes belong to which." She was all business and efficient. Each person decided on one outfit to be altered for them first and then put them into some canvas bags. Mary's husband would drop by later on to pick them up.

During the next few weeks, they practiced their speech to each other, and with some effort were able to understand the strange sounds that were made without the use of their lips. The four also spent long hours walking around, getting more accustomed to their toe shoes and boots. Additionally, the two men spent time learning to control their hands better. Andres and Rafaela found life without their corsets infinitely better and began to use their feet more while sitting at their stations, monitoring the alien communications network.

When Lord Valen returned to Valen Castle after dining with those at Brom Castle, he smiled and made contact with

Nita. *It is done. I saw them all eating the drugged fish. Your people should find themselves swamped with men and women demanding to have their hands cut off.* Both laughed. *However, it is as I suspected. Some are starting to figure out what's going on. You were right; we need to knock this Ben and Tim out of the game. They are vassals of Lord Bolivar, but I can't have them meddling any further. So put your plan into play. I'm pushing up the timetable. Brom might figure this out soon, so I don't want to risk a good thing. The remaining towers and castles are going to be drugged within the next couple of days, just in case.*

A couple of days later, a frantic Nita contacted Lord Valen. *I've been robbed! Someone has broken into my Imperium store account and stolen it all, millions of credits. Gone, vanished without a trace! I'm broke! Someone is on to us! I just know it! What are we going to do?*

Damn. all it? Okay, don't panic. The other towers and castles are being infected as we speak. After today, it won't matter. We'll have immobilized and made helpless most all the powerful lords and tower gifted. Hell, they can't even draw a sword now, let alone move or dodge an attack. We have them set up.

She sent back, *When will you attack?*

It's winter again. In the spring, I'll begin amassing the armies and send them into the Midlands. It should be an easy conquest. But it can be even easier if you can convince more of the lords to also get those lip plates of yours. Then they can't easily issue orders. I'll send you some gold to help out. You just get more of the men to go for the ornaments, Nita.

I will. I'll make a big push for that during the winter. Thanks for the gold. She did just that, sending word to all her branch managers they were to begin visiting all those who they'd fitted with new hands and get them to also get their lips done, but earrings were optional. For the next few weeks, their reports came in and were highly encouraging. The wives who already had them were actually doing most of the sales pitches to their husbands. The utter sensuousness of their lips when they had their plates out drove them mad with sexual desires, almost to a craving pitch. Between their wives and the pitch of the sales managers, many men began to get their lip plates. Three weeks into the program, she tallied them up and was surprised to see that over seventy-five men now had them to go along with almost two hundred women. She fired off bonuses to those sales managers who had gotten the most men to get their lips done.

It was early winter in Brom when Annie Wiola Waters was contacted by her boss, Nita Valen, and got her orders to visit the men and convince them to get their lips done. The promise of a bonus helped convince her to try. Already the snow was accumulating and travel was difficult, more than precarious for her in her toe boots. Still she made the attempt and, for the first week, she was able to get a dozen men to do it. The second week, only ten. Then came the shock of her life. Lord Bolivar ordered her out of the castle and never to come back or he'd have her killed.

Why? She sent, shocked with waves of panic sweeping across her rigidly held stomach.

We know Nita and Lord Valen drugged our food causing those harmless red spots. It has all been a diabolical hoax. We've lost our hands for no reason at all. Now get the hell out of my castle! You watch your back. You have made hundreds of enemies by cutting off their hands!

She staggered back to her small buggy, slipping in the snow twice. Back at her office, she contacted Nita to tell her what had happened.

Oh just ignore the old coot. Just keep on trying to get more men to get their lips done. Nita wouldn't say more.

Annie sat in her office as the sun went down, glued to her chair, petrified. Nita had not denied it! She'd expected to hear a furious denial, but hearing nothing at all was maddening. Finally, she headed off to Sam's Pub, where she went to dine each evening. Her life was unraveling faster than she could watch the pieces flying apart! The hitching rail was filled with other horses and a few buggies, and she had to park almost a half block away. She carefully stepped onto the snow packed ground and felt her toe boots slipping in several directions at once. She was barely able to hold onto the side of the buggy to keep from falling. Moving extremely slowly and placing each tiny step carefully, she finally made the boardwalk and now faced nearly a half block of slippery, snow-covered wood to traverse. She almost gave it up, but her stomach was growling. She had not eaten since breakfast and now it was dark.

Miss, can I give you an arm and you give me one too? A voice appeared in her mind. Cautiously, she turned her head to see a tall young man moving as precariously as she just behind her. He too wore lip plates, but his golden plates lacked the rubies hers had. He was dressed much like a soldier, but his oiled cloak covered his uniform, and she couldn't tell much from the bottoms of his pants, save that he too wore toe boots like she was wearing. Company in misery, she thought.

Please, sir. I am going to the pub to eat. I can barely stand up.

Me too. This is hideous. Let's help support each other, he sent, continuing to move very carefully an inch at a time towards her. As he finally drew close, she had a sting of panic. She recalled performing the hand operation on him weeks ago when the big outbreak came. Was he going to kill her? She saw him reaching out with his grey alien prosthetic hand. He had no weapon, and it dawned on her that he couldn't even lift a sword without pulling off his hand. She allowed him to slip his around her tiny waist, and she then slid hers around his, noticing his tiny waist as well. Cousins in misery, she thought. With each supporting the other, they continued their inch steps and finally entered the packed pub. It was far later than she usually came. Her table was filled with four men playing cards. She looked around. There was only one table vacant, back in the far corner where the lighting was not so good.

Over there, please, she sent. Together, now taking two inch steps, they headed for the empty table, though several men turned to stare at them briefly. At each look, Annie feared they might be an assassin after her. Herb, the barman, noticed her and the solider with her, and made an exaggerated arm motion, indicating the sole remaining table. At long last, they made the table, and he pulled out the chair for her, pleasing her slightly. Then both struggled with their hands trying to undo the cloak clasps. She sighed; everything was now so hard for her. She draped her cloak over the third empty chair and he did the same. After tossing her long black hair back, she stiffly sat down, very erect as her pipe corset dictated. She noticed he also made a similar stiff motion as he sat down across from her.

Soon Herb brought her usual order and asked the soldier for his. She made no move until Herb left to bring the soldier his meal. Both were having roast rabbit, taters, nut bread, and ale. Tonight she felt like getting good and drunk. She sighed and began trying to make her hands pick up the napkin and spread it out over her dress. That took a good five minutes to accomplish, as she finally pushed it into place. Unable to feel anything with these hands made even the simplest actions difficult to accomplish. Now came the even more embarrassing part. She had to use the silverware and feed herself without making a complete mess by dropping them. Having to negotiate the five-inch pair of lip plates made it all the more challenging, as if she needed more of a challenge. She missed the fork, knocking it askew and had to try for it a second time, embarrassing her further.

"That's all right, Annie, isn't it? I can't even work them as good as you are. Name's Sam, you did me a couple weeks back, but I don't expect you'd remember me though. There were so many of us in dire need," he said. By now, Annie could at least understand barely what someone who wore the lip plates was saying.

"Yes, Annie. Annie Wells. It's horrible really. It is all I can to do use them to eat, just barely. My whole life is ruined utterly," she replied. Grief long suppressed came unwanted to the surface. She fought to keep from breaking down completely, though her eyes did water.

She finally got the fork between her fingers just as Herb came running up with a steaming plate for Sam, setting it before him, and then setting two mugs and a large pitcher of ale in front of the two. He nodded, turned, and hurried off, yelling, "Coming, coming."

"Please don't laugh at me. I am worse at this than you," Sam said and made his first attempts to grasp his fork. Again, unable to feel anything, he misjudged and knocked both the fork and spoon several inches to the left. "Damn! Er, sorry ma'am." He tried again, after sliding them back into place. On his third try, he got the fork gripped and attempted to get his first bite between the plates and into his mouth. His missed and the bit of rabbit fell back onto his plate. "This is almost impossible, isn't it? We are hopeless cripples now, aren't we? My whole life is ruined. I should have just died. But now, I know it was all an evil, wicked hoax. There never was any damn virus. Just some alien drug thing that made our hands red. My life is ruined for nothing at all!"

"You are alive," Annie said, unable to think of anything else to say.

"Lot of good that does me. I was a Corporal in the Elite Castle Guards. Good swordsman. They said I had the makings of a major one day. Hell, now I can't even draw my sword. Pulls the hands off. Can't walk much at all. I fall down all the time in the snow. Can't speak well enough to be understood. I've just been fired from my job. 'You can't be a soldier now. Can you draw your sword and fight our sword master? No, that's why.' That's what they said to me today. I know they are right, really, but all my life I just wanted to be a good soldier and protect people, you know? First, they came along and said, since I had the gift, I had to look the part. Ordered me to get this accursed pipe corset and my feet done. Told me I was transferred to the cavalry unit. Well, I can ride all right and could fight from the saddle well enough. Now this, no hands. Now all my goals are gone, wiped out in an instant and for what? Absolutely nothing. What the hell am I supposed to do now, Annie?"

Tears streamed down her cheeks and dripped into the corners of her mouth where the lip plates protruded. "I don't know," she whispered.

"Say, you didn't know about this all being a hoax, did you?" he asked looking her directly in her eyes, causing her to cry now.

"No, no, I had no idea. I thought I was saving all you from certain death. My life's ruined too. I am so sorry, Sam." She wailed softly. "If you came to kill me, just do it."

"I'm sorry. I didn't mean to upset you, Annie. I never did think you knew this was all a big lie. Please stop crying. Hell, I don't dare wipe your eyes for you. With these unfeeling hands, I'd probably poke your eyes out. Damn, damn, I'm not good for anything at all now. I'm a walking deadman."

"No, you are alive still." She stopped crying and struggled to continue to eat. She had to; she was feeling rather weak now and regretted not taking a lunch break. She'd been too upset by Lord Bolivar to attempt to go back outdoors.

"Lot of good that does me. I can't go back to my folks; they disowned me when I went off to join the Elite Guards back when I was eighteen. I'm twenty-two now and a totally helpless cripple, thrown out on the street with only a few silvers in my pocket, though with these hands, I can't even get to them. Going to have to ask the barman to dig them out to pay for this meal. I've no place to stay. I probably have enough silvers to stay here one night, and then I get to sleep on the streets and go begging. What else is there ahead for me except a life of begging? Well maybe I could find someone who could use my *mentales* gifts, if they would even consider hiring me. Doubt that though, who would want to hire a hopeless cripple? No one. I own the clothes I'm wearing, that's it."

"Didn't they pay you in the guards?" she asked.

"Yeh, but. Well, okay, I lived high and mighty, spent all my wages on food, drink, and having a good time. Now I'd give anything to change that. Snow over the cliff, as they say. So probably this time tomorrow, I'll lie frozen in some alley. Be my luck they won't even find me until spring thaw comes." He shut up and fumbled his way into his meal. His stomach's desire to be fed finally won.

Annie had struggled with her food while he was talking and now was pretty much done. With the tight waist, she never did eat much at one time, but she felt full. She felt like talking now. "I'm Annie Wells, a fosterling. Though I don't know who my real parents were, I kind of suspect Wiola and Waters blood lines, given my gifts. You and I are the same age. All my life as I was growing up I wanted to heal people and design elegant clothing. I was going to be a Great Healer when I was ten, but I was going to be a renowned fashion designer when I was twelve. I got my big break when I was fourteen, though now I can see this is where my life started going downhill to the pits where I am now at."

"Back then, my fosterling parents were poor, and I knew at fourteen I had no chance of achieving any of my dreams, though I was healing friends and neighbors from time to time. But that only fueled my dreams. Then, Nita Valen of Elegant Fashions Inc came to Brom to set up a storefront here. So I ran away from my fosterling parents and went to see her to beg her for some minuscule job in her new office. There were dozens of women interviewing for jobs and I just knew I'd not get a chance."

"She interviewed me towards the end. She found out my gifts are in the healing category and that I really wanted to design dresses. She said since I was fourteen and a fosterling I would be perfect. She said she seldom saw a young woman as pretty as me and that I would soon grow into a woman as elegant as she. It all went to my head. Whatever Nita is, she is a seller. She told me I would be trained as her new office manager, but only if I got my body modified to meet the latest in fashion. Back then, it was just these tight pipe corsets, you see. Not so bad all by themselves. She said I'd be a stellar example of womanhood with a tiny twelve inch waist."

"I threw my all into the job of a lifetime. Then, a few years back, she introduced these toe shoes and insisted I always wear them. Getting around after that was horrid, almost impossible in the winters. I can't tell you how many times I lost my footing and fell. I hate going out in the wintertime now. But still, I wore elegant makeup and the exotic gowns, and everyone looked to me as their model of elegance and perfection. Then the gowns got more and more difficult to manage. The ones in vogue now, the arm-fetter-gowns, those make walking very difficult. We can't do stairs at all in them and our upper arms are pinned to our sides. Let me tell you, life became hellish for me because I was always supposed to wear that kind and look elegant and smile and entice other women to wear them. Hellish. But I did it," she admitted.

"Early last spring, Nita told us a horrible virus was

spreading across the world. The only known cure was to remove the infected person's hands! Worse, it only affected us *mentales* gifted, and we were sure to get it. The disease was always fatal, she claimed. Well, I was shocked and frightened, but she calmed me down. She told me she was taking preventative measures and had gotten the aliens to donate some of their prosthetic hands to those of us who would be losing ours. She said I had to get it done soon and get trained on how to run the medical machines so I could save all those in Brom who got sick. She teleported here along with all the machines and hands, and I saw she had already gotten hers done. She assured me with these stupid hands here, we could do everything we could do with our own hands. Stupid me, I believed her. She did me, and when I woke up, I also had the new style earrings and these lip plates. She claimed she forgot to mention those."

"At least she drilled me over and over until I could run the machines that would save everyone's lives. She told me the Lord and Venerada would be singing my praises forever for having saved them and their family members and friends from a certain death. It all went to my head, Sam. It really did. After she left, the reality of it hit me heavy. I can only just barely make these hands work. I lost all ability to put on my makeup. Like you, I keep pulling them off my arms every so often. So much of what I handle is heavier than a pound, you see."

"Most people can't even understand our speech any longer, and I have to continually use telepathy until I'm utterly drained of all my psi energies each night. I gave her all I had and then some, working long hours just to continue to produce what I had been doing before I lost my hands. I have no friends, no social life, no one at all. I can't cook at home anymore and have been eating here every night since I lost them."

"Then, she tells me to go around and visit all those men I saved and plead with them to get their lips done too. Well, I did try. I got some to do it, against my better judgment. It's winter. I won't tell you how many times I've fallen in these toe boots. Then today, Lord Bolivar tells me it's all been one big lie — that Lord Valen and Nita executed this hideous, sadistic hoax on all us — that there is no virus — that I cut off all those people's hands for no valid reason at all, turning them all into helpless cripples! He ordered me out of his castle and never to return or he would have me executed. He told me to watch my back, cause assassins will surely be coming after me. My life is more than ruined now. I asked Nita about it, and she didn't deny it, so I know Bolivar was telling me the truth. While I have saved my pay, I live in a one-room boarding house. I've no friends to go to for help. I can't go back to the fosterling parents; they won't have me. I can't go to work anymore; that's one big lie. Now I am terrified someone will be stabbing me in my back every time I go outside. Maybe that's best. I am a complete and utter fool and totally helpless too. Worse, I haven't hands to work my healing skills. I'm useless. Maybe I should just stand out on the street and wait for someone to stab me. I can't do anything else."

"Damn, Annie, I had no idea. Don't we make a fine pair?" Sam said consolingly. "We need a drink! Shit, my hand just fell off trying to lift the pitcher to pour our mugs! I'd laugh if it wasn't so pathetic." He struggled to get his hand back on to his arm.

Annie waved her arm and caught Herb's attention. He came rushing up. "Please, Herb, can you pour our mugs for us? Our hands keep coming off; it's too heavy for us."

"Sorry, Miss Annie. I ought to have known better. There you two go." He hastily did so and raced off to handle another request.

"Hell, Sam, we can't even drink our ale. We have to spoon it in like a couple of infants," Annie sighed morosely.

"What are these lip plates good for anyway?"

"They look pretty and call attention to ourselves. Supposed to be the latest in fashion, but now I think they are to make us more unable. Still, Nita says they are to make kissing extremely sensual and drive us all mad with desire. Well, I don't know about that part."

"Me either. Spoon up, Annie," Sam made a feeble attempt at humor.

A bit later, both laughed. "We will be all night on just one mug. How the hell can we even get drunk, as pathetically slow as we are, and spilling every other spoon-full onto our plates?" Annie asked.

It was quite late when they finally finished their ale. They hadn't noticed but most all had already gone. "Well, I guess it is time for me to go find some alleyway to sleep in, Annie."

"Say, Sam, I really don't want to be alone right now. I'm so scared. Please come home with me and sleep. I know my place is very small, but it is at least warm."

"You sure you want a hopeless mess like me coming home with you?"

"Yes, you can protect me. Bat the assassins with your stumps. So will I," she jested. Both laughed. They rose very carefully and spent another ten minutes fumbling with the clasps of their cloaks trying to get their unfeeling fingers to work to fasten them. Then arms around each other, they made their slow way out. They were the last ones out, and Herb was already cleaning up.

They took another half hour to get safely to her buggy, slipping quite a few times on the slick snow. Another inch had fallen with more on the way. Her horse was now white. Both were very relieved finally to be sitting in the buggy. She drove them to her boarding house, where a servant took the reins. "Late night, Miss Annie," the lad said. "Don't worry. I'll take good care of her."

Slowly and carefully, the two got out and made their way inside. Her room was the first one on the right, a short distance. Inside, she was thankful the landlord had already lit two of her lanterns for her so she didn't have to fumble to get one lit. Another half hour passed before the two finally got themselves undressed. Both sat on the edge of her bed with satin sheets, a gift from Nita some time ago. Both still wore their pipe corsets, since those were only removed when bathing and now they would probably never take them off since neither could possibly get them back on by themselves. She smiled a little.

"You are wearing the black nylons like I wear."

"Well, you did tell me women would find them sexier. I never had the chance to find out. I can't take them off anyway.

Can't get the fingers to work the garters."

Annie laughed. "Same here. I sleep in mine and when they tear, I used to have one of my helpers in the office change them for me. Okay, let's get these plates out. One thing is for sure, you can't sleep with the plates in, not easily." After another intense round of struggling, they had theirs out and then slipped off their hands, leaving them in a good place to be able to get them back on in the morning. Awkwardly, they both fell into the bed.

Curious, they wanted to see what the kissing was all about. As soon as they did, they understood. Once one ran their tongue over the other's loops, passions literally exploded. A while later, two exhausted bodies lay there. "My god!" Sam whispered.

"No kidding! That was beyond belief, Sam. If I wasn't so tired, I'd go for it again. Kiss me in the morning *please!*"

They were awakened in the morning by the other lodgers stumbling into the dining room. Since she was always so slow after her hands had been removed, she was always the last to get there for breakfast. That was a good thing, since almost no one saw how clumsy she was trying to eat. As the two struggled to get their plates back in and dressed, a small card fell out of Sam's sharply tailored pod-silk shirt. He couldn't bend over to pick it up. Annie squatted down and fumbled with her hands before getting a grip on it. He helped steady her and pulled her back up. "What's this?" she asked. "Fell out of your pocket."

"Oh in all the nastiness and confusion about being fired yesterday, someone stuck that in there telling me to go see them about a possible job. Hell, I can hardly get dressed. What kind of a job could I possibly do like this?" Sam replied.

"Don't know. I'm out of a job too, Sam. Come on, landlord won't leave breakfast out all morning."

An hour later with breakfast done, the two donned their cloaks, and the landlord's young son brought her buggy around for them. He also helped steady them as they got in. Six inches of new snow covered everything, turning the world white, save for the grey-black smoke curling into the sky which was blue and clear, at least for a few hours. By afternoon, it would be snowing again.

They arrived at the address on the card and stared. The cobblestones leading to the front door were entirely free of snow, totally dry, while snow lay everywhere else. "Well, finally we get a little break, Annie." He helped her down and arm in arm, they headed to the door, most grateful for having secure footing.

They knocked and received a telepathic message. *Hang on. Takes us forever to get to the door.* At long last, Ben opened the door. Sam said, "I was given this card, but it is in my pocket and with these hands, I can't get it out. Anyway, the card said you might have a job we could do? We both need a job, sir." *Crap. I forgot. Can you understand what I was saying?*

"Sure, we've all been practicing. Come on in. Say, aren't you Annie of Elegant Fashions Inc? You did us a while back."

"I am truly sorry. I didn't know it was a lie and hoax. It is okay if you want to kill me. Please make it quick," Annie said with a sigh, resigned to finally meet her end.

"Why would I want to kill you? Don't be silly. Come on in. Let's hear your stories. Tea perhaps? Damned hard to drink it now. Have to use spoons," Ben replied. A couple hours later, Ben led the two down the long stairs to introduce the two newest members of the Underground to the others.

"Here is the rest of the gang. We are going through the new supply of prosthetic hands we just got in. Thousand times better than the ones you both have. Come on. Let's find you two some new hands, hands which work vastly better. Still they won't replace our hands, but they are much better. You'll see." Later that day, the new hands began to be handed out to many others in Brom, compliments of the Underground.

"Excuse me, sir, but what exactly are our jobs going to be?" Sam asked.

"Well you are a trained soldier. Your job will be to provide guidance and advice on matters that deal with soldiers and armies, Sam. I'm certain that is coming down the line. We just don't yet when and where Lord Valen will make his first move. None of us have that kind of background, so your guidance will be valuable," Ben explained talking as clearly as he could so they could understand him.

"Annie, you're going to be our resident healer, though I hope we don't need it. Besides, you know a little about operating the medical machines. They can do perhaps a thousand more things than the crippled ones Nita gave you. We've got the real deals here. It will be best if you both move your things in here. Annie, it's obvious for now you need to, shall we say, just 'disappear.' Someone is likely to want to take their frustrations out on you. We know you thought you were saving lives, but not everyone is going to believe that."

"What about my things?" she asked.

"What you see is what you get with me. I don't have anything else, not even clothes," Sam added. "I can help Annie fetch her things."

"First, we have to get you both fixed up a little, get some of these new hands on you. Believe me, these new ones are a great improvement. We've decided for now to keep our lip plates and toe boots. That way, if we are spotted by some of Lord Valen's spies, they will report we are all still hobbled and helpless. Without the pipe corsets, you will find life a whole lot easier to manage. In truth, we can't do much about our feet, except fix them a little so we could wear the kind of heels you women used to wear before these toe shoes became the rage. We'll explain more later; let's get you both fixed up and then get Annie's things," Ben explained.

Part III Entering a New Era

Chapter 14 A Force for Change

"So who can we trust?" Venerada Marisol asked. She had cleverly dropped by the Underground for a consultation. Already she had begun doling out all the replacement prosthetic hands and the accolades were coming in from all sides. They made quite a difference to those who received them. Now she and Ben were trying to work out the four huge problems facing all Tierra.

Word had spread throughout the Midlands and the Easterlings of the treacherous and wicked virus hoax so well played on most all the more powerful *mentales*, who were either kingdom leaders or worked in the towers. Lord Valen's name had become synonymous with the devil, though Nita Valen's was a close second. While these many lords called for wars and retribution against Valen and the Westerlings, these men were effectively powerless physically to do anything about it.

The first problem Ben, Tim, and Marisol foresaw was that Lord Valen was not finished. Why cripple all the *mentales* and tower folk? The only logical answer was to remove them from action, meaning he planned further armed invasions of at least the Midlands. Tim and his group continued to monitor daily the geosat images, looking for the buildup of armies within the Westerlings. Once found, they would track their paths. After that point, these planners had not worked out what could be done.

The second problem, which concerned Marisol the most, was the wholesale deterioration of the *mentales* gifted as a whole. They were definitely heading towards death as a group of people and as individuals. Once they were proud, powerful people, using their gifts to help all others survive the climatic upheaval several centuries ago. Hindsight is a good teacher — no mistakes. As time went by, they had dropped down into antagonistic ways and then even lower towards hate and anger. With all the wide implementation of, first, the very sexy outfits for the women primarily, and, later, of the so called body modifications which had all manner of sexual

245

twists in them, that is, the heightened sensitivity of their lip loops and the tips of their arm cones, they had, as a group, dropped even further down the scale of life with their almost frantic sexual drives, ignoring the routinely accepted practice of married couples having extramarital affairs and whose children were called fosterlings. Already with the unbelievable betrayal of Lord Valen which left most all them very nearly helpless, some had begun to drop down another rung into the grief zone. Below that lay apathy and death.

Venerada Marisol and the Underground desperately wanted to find a way to reverse this dwindling spiral and bring the *mentales* gifted back upwards towards a renewal of life and vigor. As yet, they had no idea how that might be accomplished. There were no historical precedents to follow. The only possible clues lay in a study of what Ben and his group had done with the four foothills teens they'd rescued, Andres and Rafaela, and now Annie and Sam. These eight, Ben had pointed out, were found in deep grief or in apathy, waiting for the assassin to come or to freeze in an alleyway. All eight, here in December, were rising back into life slowly but surely.

The third problem was each year there were fewer and fewer new *mentales* gifted babies being born. Per the charts Marisol now had, the drop in the total number of telepaths on Tierra was going downward at a very rapid rate. In fact, if you extended the curve, in perhaps a century they would be extinct as a group. Frightening. How could this be avoided was the key question. Again, they had as yet no solution. Marisol knew only too well what would happens if they continued to inner breed among themselves in a closed group. At least at this point in time, most all other lords knew this as well. Besides, they'd just done this intentionally with the emperor and empress, breeding weaklings and morons, if the children lived at all.

The fourth problem, Ben and Tim had not known existed as a problem until this very meeting. Marisol had just asked, "So who can we trust?"

Ben's only safe answer was, "Us, Marisol. I vouch for us, but I simply can't say that about anyone else with total certainty. Why?"

"Well, then there is a fourth problem I want to share with you. Frankly, this one is only known to us katalyein. We've uncovered this one only because of our special gifts. Let me explain this in simple terms. Some of the gifted have mental blocks, which wholly or partially block their inherent gifts. In the worst cases, they appear head blind, although we can sense they have powerful psi potentials locked away. They have the yellow eyes, for example. Our gift is to help them confront the mental blocks and thus free their locked psi powers. You with me so far?"

All nodded. She continued. "Now as everyone knows from history, back in the Age of the Towers, Valen began invading and destroying the existing towers, one by one. It was an age of the giant crystal networks, of unbelievable powers and unimaginable weapons of such lethal destruction that whole areas became what we know as the dead-zones. At the end of that age, your mother, Amy Blackwater, with her incredible psi powers forced every adult with the gift to fully experience in great magnitude the terror, horror, pain, and suffering of all those who died, when Valen dropped the Nuclear on Bettingham City and Tower. Still with me?" They were.

"Okay, as you might imagine, that was an enormous psi trauma, and, for years after that, we katalyein were kept busy helping others who had their gifts blocked by that experience. Now here we are a century or so later and guess what the most common mental barrier to psi powers we are continuing to have to help the gifted face?"

Ben replied, "Sorry, I have no idea, Marisol."

She smiled. "That same traumatic incident of the Nuclear destroying Bettingham." She paused letting them attempt to grasp the significance of this.

Ben frowned, "But none of those people could still be alive, unless they used the alien rejuvenation machine."

"I wholly agree, Ben. We are removing this from children who are five years old, from those suffering from Verge Sickness as they reach puberty, and even in some young adults," Marisol replied and paused again.

Ben frowned. "But they were not living back then. How

could they be suffering an emotional trauma block from something which happened long before they were even born?"

Again, Marisol merely smiled. "Can I say something?" Annie asked rather meekly. She was very new to the group and hesitant to speak up. She didn't even know if she was really allowed to ask questions of Venerada Marisol.

"Sure, Annie." Marisol replied, putting her more at ease.

"The question is how could a five year old have suffered a trauma which happened a hundred years ago? The only possible answer is the five year old was alive and around a hundred years ago."

"Astute observation, Annie. You are precisely right. What does that mean?" Marisol asked and then answered, "We katalyein believe this means we or some part of we have lived before, have had bodies just like those we do now have, and have experienced that trauma when Amy allowed it to happen. What lived before? It cannot be these bodies; obviously they die and turn to dust. Our minds perhaps? Or are we all really spiritual beings who have a mind? I think it is the latter, that we are spiritual beings who have a mind and occupy a physical body. The being via its mind records the experiences of a lifetime, and, when the body perishes, it moves on and acquires a new baby body, starting life over. Only it isn't always as clean as that, in the case of these recorded mental traumas, which block their subsequent psi powers in that new body. That is the theory we katalyein now have."

"So the fourth problem is if we are spiritual beings, how can we learn more about our own selves and our own powers? Can we learn to remember our past lives? We find speculation in this arena extremely fascinating. Now couple this with the fact that we know for certain that there are several spiritual beings residing on Tierra who do not have physical bodies as we know them: Lysandra, the Goddess of Life and of Death, and Wystan, the men's God of War. We suspect there are three others, but have almost no proof of their existence. These two we are quite certain do exist and do interact with us on very rare occasions. Women in dire need have called upon Lysandra to help them. Of course, she always seems to demand a huge sacrifice from the supplicant, if she grants her assistance to that woman. So how do we proceed in such an investigation of our own natures?"

"Er, is it permissible for me to speak too?" Sam asked.

"Of course, Sam. Go ahead," Ben said kindly.

"I think you will find there is yet a fifth problem, one which may be more important than some of the others. I don't know about these spiritual being things. I am a trained soldier. I have been in Lord Bolivar's Elite Guards for four years now and I have been seeing some subtle changes occurring and they are escalating," Sam said.

"We soldiers look up to and follow orders from and obey strong leaders. I was promoted to a corporal because I became very good with my short sword and learned to lead my squad of men. Of course, now I can't even draw my short sword from its scabbard without pulling my silly hand off my stump. It is the same all the way up the line. The Elite Guards will obey and follow our general because we know he is a great swordsman and is physically strong and knows strategy and will be right there in the battle leading us directly. What's happened to me is but a microcosm of what's going on in the entire Elite Guards."

"First, I was ordered to get body modified due to the fact I was gifted. Once I wore the pipe corset and these toe boots, I could bare even walk. I lost the respect of my squad as their leader immediately and got transferred to the cavalry unit. I could at least ride a horse and swing my sword from the saddle. Then, I lost my hands, ignoring the whole lip plates thing. I can't even draw a sword now, let alone swing it or even use it. I certainly can't fight and can barely walk. Shortly after that, I was fired from the guards for being physically unable to fulfill any of my duties as a soldier."

"So what I am saying is there is a fifth problem. At some point, the soldiers are no longer going to follow Lord Bolivar. Other high ranking men of Brom, who are not gifted, are sooner or later are no longer going to obey him either. In fact, they will likely push him out of office, preferring someone who is physically fit to run the territory. I've no idea who will be making such a move though. I don't know those kinds of men and women, being a mere soldier."

"Sam, brilliant. You are right. We do have a fifth problem facing us!" Ben declared, praising him. He smiled, but it was invisible.

Marisol spoke up again, "Well said, Sam. I've added it to our list. Once again, I ask you, who can we trust? We need much more help in solving these five major problems or situations. Right now, the entire tower structure is in flux, so many are having monumental problems adjusting to the loss of their hands. Many have gone ahead and gotten lip plates and are indulging their sorrows in sex. I can't say I blame them. My circles are in disarray, right when we need them most, compliments of Lord Valen."

Elana spoke up, "You can count on many of we Madiera women to help. If they march to war in lines like they did this spring, we can get rid of them, if someone can get us into position to do so, like before. With Tim's monitoring setup, we will have plenty of advance warning and could stop them. That might help solve the first problem of Valen's attacking the Midlands when we are in so much disarray."

"I was hoping you'd suggest this, Elana. I will accept this as a potentially solved problem, as long as we continue to implement that successful action," Marisol agreed.

Ben spoke up, "I could speak with Lord Bolivar and see if I can work out a solution to the fifth problem. He and his group are now getting my new hands. Give him a few days to fully appreciate them and he'll likely listen to what I have to say."

They talked longer, but had no real ideas of possible solutions for the other three problems. Still, all felt they'd accomplished a lot, two problems looked solvable.

Two days later, Ben was escorted into Lord Henry's private chambers. Sam had tagged along to help him negotiate the deep snow. Neither could walk alone without constantly slipping and falling down, though twice, both slipped and pulled the other down with them. Once inside the castle grounds, Sam waited with their carriage, too embarrassed even to visit his old friends who might be around. It took Ben nearly a half hour of tiny steps to walk that distance, but he made it and wasn't panting for breath for a change.

"Ah, Ben, I must say these are just fabulous," Lord Bolivar said as Ben moved slowly into the well-heated room. The thirty-two year old man waved his new hands in the air. "I can actually pick up my own fork fairly well now. Amazing. I guess I ought not ask you how you could have possibly come by these and in such quantities?" *Oh, I forgot in my enthusiasm. Could you even understand what I was saying?*

"Absolutely. We've been practicing speaking and grasping what was said. These lip plates make it a challenge. Are you able to understand me?" He was. Ben said, "Okay, you best not ask me how I got them, my lord. Let's just say I have my ways."

The lord chuckled. "I like you, son."

"Sir, I've actually come to talk to you about something that's very serious indeed. First, we all know probably in the spring Valen is going to launch armies to attempt to retake all the Midlands again."

"Yes, that is what all us lords fear. We are so damnably hobbled now, may Lord Valen rot in hell. I can't even pull my sword let alone fight with it. Hell, I can't walk much without Isabella's arms around me."

"Yes, my lord. That's why I've come. I felt I owed you a warning." He began to explain what Sam had told them about the *mentales* gifted, who had been in his Elite Guards. "Have you considered your own fate? If war comes and we are all positive it will come, will your army follow you, if you can't draw a sword or fight or walk? Will your own other nobles or *Jefe* here in Brom continue to back you, when you have no hands and can't walk much? My lord, I fear sooner or later you are going to face a coup of one kind or another."

Lord Bolivar laughed, a wholly unexpected reaction, putting Ben ill at ease. "Son, don't you think I know that? I've had to fire nearly all my top men in my Elite Guards and several in the small army of Brom. I'm holding on now mostly because it's the middle of winter and hardly anyone travels in this weather. So, have you also come to me with an answer?" he asked cleverly.

"Indeed, my lord, I have. What if you and your other

mentales gifted staff resigned and appointed capable non-*mentales* men and women to fill these positions? What if you then formed up an Elite *Mentales* Protection Group, headed by yourself and the others who wish to help defend Brom? You would still have some power and still be able to help defend Brom, plus you would be picking your own heir."

"Son, I've been thinking long and hard about this. In many ways, it would be ideal for such a new lord to have the rest of the winter to get organized and ready for what must inevitably come with spring, but I had not thought of that idea of a protection group. I like that. I would still hold some power. Most all we lords are in this same messy situation, thanks to the traitorous Lord Valen. I had hoped to rule Brom until I was an old man, but now I am mostly a helpless man, doing much better, thanks to your new hands here. I think you are probably right. I should arrange for a change in rulership while I am still able to do so with my own choices."

The two chatted further and then Ben left, declining the offer to stay for lunch. Poor Sam was probably freezing out in the carriage. A half hour later, Ben finally reached the carriage and found him shivering. "Home Sam," Ben teased him.

"Did we succeed?"

"I think so. We ought to hear something soon."

A week later, all Brom began talking about the new rulers. Henry had passed the throne on to his head blind brother, who became Lord Phillip Brom. He was thirty-five and his wife Rita, a year younger. Neither had ever had any of the body modifications, but she did begin wearing the arm-fetter-gowns with her tall high heels, a compromise gesture for their Easterlings allies. At least everyone hoped the Easterlings would join in the coming battles. As Ben had suggested, Lord Phillip immediately announced the formation of the Elite *Mentales* Protection Squad, led by Henry. Many other changes in rulership followed. One of the principle duties of the new squad was to use their telepathic gifts to join Lord Phillip with the other Midlands lords.

During the winter, similar changes began to occur in most of the other key territories. The severely crippled lords took the hint from Henry and appointed their own heirs, before civil unrest or political coups brought them down. Ben and Marisol were very pleased problem five was actually wholly solved. If war came in the spring, Lord Valen would not be facing hobbled, crippled leaders. Of course, they were all new to the job and would make mistakes. The instantaneous communication the telepathic rulers had was now gone, unfortunately. On the other hand, in the years to follow the Council of the Lords took on a more significant role, for the leaders now had much to discuss when they met, not already having sorted them out via telepathy.

By spring, Venerada Marisol had her circles reorganized and back in operation for the most part. The new hands helped stem the terrible bouts of depression that had struck so many of her gifted. Elana had also been busy rounding up others of her Earth Kindred who were willing to volunteer to help stop Lord Valen's armies. Not all were willing to cause so many deaths, but she gathered twenty who were ready to help protect their new home world and Brom. Andres acted as coordinator between Brom Tower and the Underground. All knew it was only a matter of time before Lord Valen would strike.

Strategically, he had only two real points of entry into the Midlands: across the paved road south of the spaceport into Exchange City in the central part of the Midlands and around the southern coastal patch of land where the Goza Mountains ended. Originally a century ago, they had first attacked from down south, sweeping north to wipe out Oakham Tower. The tall mountains offered no other options for moving large armies from the west into the Midlands. These two routes, Tim, Andres, and Rafaela watched daily, taking shifts.

In April, they began to see large concentrations of forces building up, one in each of the two areas. At once, Tim sent out the alert to Venerada Marisol, who then had it relayed to all the other lords. She and the Underground hoped and prayed they could stop the armies before they did too much damage and before the other kingdoms would have to field their own armies to fight back. Marisol didn't tell others why she greatly feared this latter possibility. If the opposing armies met on the field of battle, surely that would be enough to awaken the sleeping Wystan.

In May, it began. An army of some three thousand poured over the paved road south of the spaceport, while a second army of an equal number swarmed around the southern coast. When the northern army cleared Exchange City, they formed long lines and headed straight for the largest city closest to them, Wycombe. As the southern army cleared the Goza and reached the southern lands of Rusden, they too formed into long lines, heading directly for Rusden.

Twenty-five miles southeast of Exchange City, a dozen Earth kindred led by Tim and Elana waited patiently for the lines to come into range. Andres and Sam had calculated their path perfectly. Then they struck much as they had a year ago. Several long mounds of fresh earth marked the graves of the men who were buried alive when the giant cracks in the earth suddenly closed over them. Far below in the soothing magma, Wystan awoke. *Battle cries! Death! Fighting!* He shot up to the surface and looked for the bloody battle. He saw nothing at all, only several long mounds of fresh earth. Puzzled and chilled by the cold morning of the foothills, he sank back into the warmth of the magma. He was confused.

Two days later, the Earth kindred attacked the southern army with similar results. Five minutes after they started, the women were safely teleported back to Brom. Again, Wystan was roused by the pain and death of valiant soldiers, and he shot up over the battlefield, ready to enjoy another good battle. Again, he was totally disappointed. No battle, no armies, only long mounds of fresh earth could be seen. Sadly and most confused, he slipped back into the warmth of the magma.

"What do you mean my northern army has disappeared? How can this be?" screamed Lord Valen to his aides and venerada. Shaking with fear, many made their reports. At last, the venerada took Lord Valen into her tower and joined him in one of her circles. He saw the huge ruts in the ground where his army had passed and was able to follow them to a half dozen long mounds of fresh earth. There were no signs of any enemy army, nothing to indicate where his men had gone. They'd just vanished.

After his long slow walk back to his own office, he found a message had arrived on his teleport pad. "Do not continue your invasion of the Midlands or your southern army will vanish. The Underground." Fuming with anger, he summoned his air car and headed to the spaceport. After some discussion with the Sector ID Minister, Emeryk brought up the geosat images. Together accompanied by his wife and Nita, they watched the jerky images taken minutes apart. There was his mighty army moving out across the grasslands of the high foothills. Then in one image, they saw giant cracks in the earth opening up. The next image showed men, wagons, and horses falling into the crack. In the next image, they saw only the mounds of fresh earth.

"How can this be, minister? Have you been selling secret weapons to the Midlands lords behind my back?" Lord Valen accused the minister, who turned white as a sheet.

"Absolutely not! I am as mystified by this as you are. Never have I seen anything like this. It is as though there was an earthquake, which opened up a hole beneath them and swallowed them up. I will speak with my geologists and see if there are known fault lines there." He summoned his Minister of Geology who came running. No, there were no active fault lines anywhere on Tierra.

Lord Valen thanked Emeryk and left. At this point, Nita began to become very frightened. All her many Elegant Fashions Inc stores had dismal sales since last November, hardly any shoppers had come. Now this, the mighty conquering army had completely vanished! all her years of hard work were evaporating. Worse, she was terribly helpless herself. The prosthetic hands were pitiful substitutes for her own. With lip plates and all the other modifications she'd undergone, she could barely function. Wearing makeup had gone by the boards after she lost her hands. She was more miserable than she ever admitted to anyone. Plus, she was totally broke and had no idea who had stolen her hard-earned fortune.

Once she returned to her office, she summoned her fourteen year old daughter Inez, who had already undergone all the same modifications that she had. Inez, though, still had the enthusiasm of youth propelling her over her miserable physical limitations. "Inez, I am retiring. I am due to give birth in a few months. So I am giving the whole business to you as of today. I'm going home to Valen and have my son and rest up. All this has been entirely too exhausting for me."

Inez was ecstatic and hugged her mother with her lower arms. "Thank you mom. Let me know when the baby comes. I can come and help you with him." They chatted a bit longer and Nita left her all her passwords. Quietly, she packed a dozen outfits, sent for a helper to get them to the ground level and loaded into her own air car. She made her slow way down and struggled to get herself into the car, her arm-fetter-skirt made that extremely challenging for her. At last, she took off, but she didn't go to Valen. Rather she headed as far away as she could get, landing at Benito, Trujillo, several thousand miles west of Valen on the western coast of the Westerlings. There, she was unknown, and she used the last of her money to purchase a new simple home for herself; selling the air car provided her with enough to live on for a time.

When the second army of Lord Valen's vanished without a trace, a nasty political coup occurred. A cousin of his, head blind Pedro Valen marched his large squad of men into Lord Valen's office. "You are hereby deposed!" Pedro swung his sword and severed Lord Valen's head from his body. Quite a few others perished that day. The tower stayed out of the coup and remained intact but now had a new lord.

Via the venerada and a circle on the third day, Lord Pedro Valen spoke into the minds of the key new lords of the Midlands. "I am the new ruler of Valen and the Westerlings, Lord Pedro Valen. I've killed Lord Paco Valen, who has betrayed us all. From this day forward, Valen and the Westerlings will stay on our side of the Goza Mountains and never set foot on your side. There will be no war between us. I will not attend your Council of the Lords or that of the pathetic emperor either. If you do not bother us, we will not bother you. Good day."

He also met with Sector ID Minister Emeryk and re-established relations between them. Now Emeryk had a new reason for the alliance. He's seen something terribly awesome in power, something that had no explanation of any kind. At night, he sent some of his field agents to one of the mound to take some samples. Sure enough, they found the bodies of the soldiers beneath the soil. Now he wanted to learn all he could. How could this have happened? In the back of his mind, he suspected the answers might not be found in the Westerlings, but he had no contacts elsewhere at all. Well, he'd have to work on that. His interest was pricked. One way or another, he would find the answer.

Inez Valen was shocked to learn of Valen's complete defeat against no armies at all. Further, to her complete dismay, Elegant Fashions Inc was broke. All her fancy ornaments and body modifications were suddenly no longer wanted by anyone. Yet, her body had them all, and she was extremely vulnerable and almost helpless herself. She steeled herself and began to have her staff observe the new ladies who took office. She saw at once the new market was for the older high heels and the elegant gowns. At least the arm-fetter-gowns were still popular. Slowly, she began a new marketing campaign and within a few years, the business was again making a good profit. She, however, seldom went out in public, except those times when others who were modified as she was were there. Inez kept a low profile to the world at large. She had little choice. She could barely walk, barely be understood, and needed help as her prosthetic hands were pathetic. Try as she might, for a long time, she could not locate her mother. In short, for quite some time, Inez was perfectly miserable.

Venerada Marisol met in early June with the Underground. Thus far, two of their huge problems had been solved. Three more remained. Though they talked long, still no solutions were found. However, they refused to give up. If they did, they all knew the days of the *mentales* gifted on Tierra were quite numbered.

Chapter 15 Seeking Help

After the June 1245 meeting with Venerada Marisol proved fruitless, Ben strolled out to their formal gardens in the back of their home. It had been originally created by their fathers and two of the Earth kindred whom their mothers had let stay with them. Over the years, Ben had occasionally hired gardeners to come in and fix things up a bit. He wasn't a gardener, not remotely, and not as his modified body now was. His wife and the women of the Underground did love it out here, and he made his slow way to the seats by the central fountain. It was warming up; June was here; the sky, blue, though he knew by late afternoon, it would likely rain.

Three seemingly insurmountable problems remained. He had no solutions for either of the three. Quietly, Elana made her slow way out to him and sat down beside her husband. She sensed his moodiness, but remained quiet. What should they do about the plunging birth rates of *mentales* gifted babies? What should they do about the slow decline of the overall emotional tones of the *mentales*, which were now approaching a fall into the grief band, with apathy and death close at hand? What, if anything, could or should be done about the startling discovery they were spiritual beings and were apparently living life after life?

The armless Andres and Rafaela walked carefully out to join them. They had decided to get rid of lip plates and also had their feet repaired as much as possible. It had been a tough decision for Andres, for now he had no choice but to wear the old style women's back patent six-inch spiked heels that were returning into vogue. He found it embarrassing to be forced to wear them, but it made walking many times safer and easier for Rafaela and himself. Their heels clicked on the cobblestone path as they came up to the couple and sat on the next bench. Neither said anything. They too were somber. All that could have been said had already been said at the meeting. No one had any real solutions or possible solutions to these grave problems facing them.

Ben sighed and decided to try one other wildly remote

possibility. There were at least two active gods around. Wystan, he hoped, was sleeping or at least not paying any real attention to Tierra, but Lysandra always seemed to be somehow aware of Tierra and its women who were in need. Well, women were in need, he thought. *It can't hurt to try her,* he resolved. *How does one contact a goddess? Must be by telepathy I suppose. After all, apparently she doesn't have a body, as we know them. Okay, here goes nothing.* He focused and emptied his mind and then expanded his awareness around himself, sensing the others close by.

Goddess Lysandra. I need your help, not for myself, but for many women of Tierra who are suffering and will suffer more unless I can find solutions to three problems. Birth rates for those of us with the mentales gifts are falling off rapidly. We know there has been a huge emotional slump downwards towards apathy and death, with a heavy emphasis right now on emotional escapes through a powerful emphasis on sexual acts simply for pleasure not procreation. We've figured out we are spiritual beings occupying and using these physical bodies. Yet, when our bodies die, we seem to get into a new baby body and start in all over again. Yet, if we are all so emotionally low now, in our next lifetimes we may well drop even lower, until those of us with these gifts that can help all others here on Tierra vanish entirely. I've done all I could to prevent another huge round of wars and have brought some political stability back into the kingdoms. But I am at a loss on how I can alter the sinking birth rates, how I can turn the dismal slump in overall emotional tone around, getting women and men going upwards towards happier, more cheerful lives, and how I can do anything about all us being spiritual beings, apparently immortal, to help us understand our true natures and become better women and men? If you are even listening to me, Goddess Lysandra, please help me or give me some guidance. Perhaps there aren't any answers. So even if you aren't listening to me, know I am not going to give up trying to help our women and men. There has to be a way to solve these problems.

A yellow glow appeared out in front of the four right in

the middle of the small fountain. It took shape and Ben saw what appeared to be a young woman in thin, shimmering robes standing before him. He heard her speak in his mind, just like any other telepathic contact he'd had.

Well, this is a first. I've never appeared or spoken to a man before. Yet, I am doing so only because I am fully aware of what you have done for all women of the Midlands. Thanks to your efforts, Wystan still sleeps. He was roused, and I fully expected he would once again wreak havoc over Tierra and women would bear the burden, but he didn't solely because of the way you handled it. Thus, I will speak with you.

If I help some woman, I demand a sacrifice of her, but it is always something she can give, if she is truly willing and truly wants my help. So I ask you, are you willing to make whatever sacrifice I ask of you for my aide, Ben Blackwater?

Anything, Goddess Lysandra, if it will help me help the suffering women and men, he replied without hesitation. Somewhere in the back of his mind, he wondered if he ought to have asked what that might be before agreeing.

So be it. Sacrifice is being taken now. From now on, you must go forth as a woman of Tierra and learn what it truly means to be a woman. You shall be called Benjamina. Know this, Elana is already bearing your son. You are now bearing her daughter. You must bear three more children from men of your choosing. I am also giving you earrings similar to those of your wife, but adding to them to remind you and mark you as having been touched by me.

As for your first question, you already know why the rates are declining. The katalyein have told you why, only you have not grasped it. You have also in your travels in the breadbasket seen the solution to the birthrate problem, though once again, you have not realized what you've seen. Two of your friends have already shown you a partial answer to the second one, though a permanent solution lies in the remaining one. As for the third problem. Indeed this one is the greatest and most important one of all. For centuries, that secret has been lost. Only now have you and the katalyein rediscovered it. Work closely with the katalyein, observe, and conclude. Then create what is wholly absent on

Tierra, a science of the mind and spirit. Perhaps then one day you and I will meet as equals.

The yellow form slowly vanished from sight and Ben felt his body changing. He felt weird, as he later described it to the others of the Underground. His pants seemed horribly tight around his waist and hips; his shirt literally burst open at the top of his chest. Something was pulling down on his head. His ears felt as though they were being pulled off his head. The last flicker of that gentle yellow vanished.

"My god! That, that was Lysandra! Wasn't it?" exclaimed Elana.

"Who else could it have been? We've been visited by the Goddess Lysandra herself!" Rafaela called out.

"Unbelievable! Did you all just see her? I actually saw the goddess!" Andres exclaimed, shocked utterly. "I heard her speaking too. Ben, did you?"

He turned towards Ben, and, mechanically, the other two did so too. Elana was about to tell him the goddess told her she was pregnant with their son. She'd suspected for the last few days she might be pregnant, but now the goddess confirmed it. Instead, she gasped, bringing both of her prosthetic hands up against her mouth.

Ben looked down to see why he felt so many unexpected pressures. His body had been changed into that of a woman with the enormous breasts similar to those Elana and the Madiera women all had. His hips had filled out significantly, nearly bursting his pants. His hair had grown, though sitting he had no idea how much. And he felt very weird. "My god, I am now a woman!" he said and didn't recognize his own voice which had changed from his normal baritone into that of a soprano! "Oh my god, she meant it!" he added. Sheepishly, he said, "I am supposed to be Benjamina now."

"What did you do? What's going on? I thought only women could talk to Lysandra?" Rafaela asked, very confused. "I've heard she always demands a bad sacrifice for her help. Ben, you shouldn't have done this!"

"What happened, Ben? Is this really you?" Elana asked.

"I don't believe my eyes," Andres blinked, unable to rub them, which he desperately tried to do with his missing arms.

Ben or rather Benjamina explained, "Well, I just called upon her for help with our three huge problems, and she answered me! She told me I was the first man she'd ever talked to and only because of what we all did to prevent the wars and political upheavals. Wystan nearly woke up again, but we kept him sleeping. So she agreed to talk to me."

"What did she say? Why are you a woman now?" Rafaela asked.

"She said from now on, I must go forth as a woman of Tierra and learn what it truly means to be a woman. I'm supposed to be called Benjamina. I suppose that's because I was called Benjamin. She told me Elana is already bearing our son. Are you, my love?"

"Well, I heard her say that much. I kind of thought I might be pregnant. Our son! That's what I always wanted to do, bear our son," Elana answered.

"That's the best news ever, Elana!" Benjamina replied enthusiastically. He went on, "And she said I am now bearing Elana's daughter. Does that mean I'm pregnant too?"

"I heard that too, but didn't understand what she meant, Ben, er Benjamina. Our daughter? Thank you. I did want a daughter too," Elana said.

"What is really weird is she also said I must bear three more children from men of my choosing. Well I guess there is time enough to worry about that later on. I feel so strange right now," Benjamina added.

"Well, she certainly demanded a huge sacrifice from you, Ben or Benjamina! A giant one," Andres added. "Say, you do have mighty impressing earrings!" Hers were similar to the other women's. Namely an inch circular plate in her lobes supported the usual gold and gemstones dangles, draping several inches down onto her shoulders. However, unlike the others, each earring had three such long sets of dangles, the center one held pure yellow stones, Lysandra's colors.

"Did she tell you the answers to our insoluble problems?" Rafaela asked.

"Sort of. Kind of roundabout. Her words are rather burned into my mind. She said, 'As for your first question, you already know why the rates are declining; the katalyein have told you why, only you have not grasped it. You have also in your travels in the breadbasket seen the solution to the birthrate problem, though once again, you have not realized what you've seen. Two of your friends have already shown you a partial answer to the second one, though a permanent solution lies in the remaining one. As for the third problem. Indeed, this one is the greatest and most important one of all. For centuries, that secret has been lost. Only now have you and the katalyein rediscovered it. Work closely with the katalyein, observe, and conclude. Then create what is wholly absent on Tierra, a science of the mind and spirit. Perhaps then one day you and I will meet as equals.' So gang, that's what she said. I got to get out of these pants! They are cutting me in half!"

"Come on. Let's get you inside and out of these clothes," Rafaela suggested standing up.

"Crap! Elana, I'm sorry. I didn't think about you and us. I mean. . ." Benjamina suddenly realized Elana no longer had a husband! That through no choice of her own, she was married to another woman!

Elana laughed. "As long as you are still you, the person I love, it's all right. You forget us Madiera women are used to being married to other women. Besides, we will have two children of our own. If we want more, we can ask Alpha for help, the way Madiera women have children. Come on, up you go."

She rose and her thick brown hair fell nearly to the floor. "Oh! So long! No wonder my head felt as if it was being pulled down. Man, I have to get these pants loosened!" She struggled and finally got them opened up and the belt loosened up.

Once back in their underground chambers, the others gathered around, gasping and demanding to know what on Tierra had happened to him! Again, he had to explain and recite what he'd been told, paying particular attention to the "solutions" she'd given him. To be on the safe side, Tim recorded it for later reference. That Andres, Rafaela, and Elana also saw the Goddess Lysandra added credence to what he claimed happened. Further Elana told them what little she'd heard the goddess say. Immediately, several congratulated her on her pregnancy.

"Okay, you ladies get our new lady fixed up. We guys are going to pour over the answers the Lysandra gave him, er her," Tim ordered. "Ben, you do mostly look like yourself. Dig the boobs!" he teased her. Petrona, who also had soccer ball sized breasts, gave him a little shove. Both laughed.

A bit later, as the women began helping him or her out of his clothes, she felt extremely embarrassed. "What?" Elana asked, seeing her red face as she was about to pull off his underpants.

"What if?" he whispered. "Can you turn your backs please?" she asked the group of now giggling women. They complied. He pulled them off and stared over his bosom. "It's okay. It's really gone." Now they all giggled wildly.

"Of course, silly. Women don't have one," Elana could not resist teasing her even more. She added, "I'm glad your breasts are as large as mine and Petrona's. We are used to them being big. It makes it easier for me. And I do like your new hair. Okay, now we have to get her dressed somehow. You are going to need a whole new wardrobe, dear."

An hour later, with her hair brushed out and being held in the back with one of Rafaela's bluebird clasps and wearing parts of several of different women's apparel, Benjamina and the women headed back to show her off to the men. "Wow, you are a knock out," Tim exclaimed as she walked into the room, embarrassing Ben even further.

"Hey, this is not easy! I feel so weird right now. So let's forget me and focus on the hints she gave me," Benjamina attempted to force a total change of topic.

Tim replied, "Okay, okay. We've think we have a handle on the second one. How to start to undo the awful drop in emotional tones we've suffered? She said two of your friends have already shown you a partial answer to the second one. So your friends must be us here. No offense, but you don't have many others outside of the Underground. So two of us must come from me, Petrona, Elana, Andres, Rafaela, Darcy, Dawn, Eric, Sally, Annie, and Sam. We just haven't figured out which two she meant."

Benjamina looked around at all her friends, one after the other. Then it struck her. "It's Andres and Rafaela! You are showing the way to back out of the serious drop in emotional tones, at least partially! I get it! Well done, Andes, Rafaela!" Everyone stared at Benjamina in total disbelief.

She laughed. "Look, they've set the example, and none of the rest of us had the guts to follow! First, they got rid of the lip plates. We haven't. Why? Because we just love the incredible sex we're having from the super-sensitivity of our lip loops. I won't deny it. Elana and I have had unbelievable orgasms as a result. Pleasure beyond imagination, so we just didn't get our lips healed up. They had the guts to do it. Look at them now, they are happy and doing much better. They also got their feet healed as much as possible and are now walking vastly better and more swiftly, though they will admit it is still slow. Six to eight inch steps sure beat our two or three. They've gotten as much of their body modifications undone as is possible. We need to do it also. Plus, we need to get all the others who've been modified to get theirs undone as much as possible."

"Shit! Just when we thought we were going to always have super-sex," Tim complained, half-heartedly. Everyone laughed nervously, this revelation hit too close to home. "Okay, okay, everyone to the medical machines."

Several hours later, everyone had had their turn in the healing machine. Their debilitating yet sensual lip loops were gone. If one looked very closely, a thin, tiny line could be seen where their lips had been slit. Everyone's feet were partially healed and the group spent considerable time digging out the women's old high heels and finding ones that now fit. Benjamina insisted tomorrow they all visit Elegant Fashions Inc in Brom and see about getting better ones and tall boots as well.

"Well, Benjamina, I will admit it," Tim said after they had finished up, "I do feel far better than before, though like Andres, I am somewhat embarrassed to be wearing women's stilettos now. Guess I'll have to get used to it. Walking is certainly a whole lot easier than those awful toe boots!"

"How about some supper, guys?" Rafaela asked. They

divided up again. The women headed to the kitchen, while the men headed back to the monitor to continue to unravel the other clues.

"Elana, I got to go pee. How do I do it?" Benjamina whispered. She giggled and led him to the commode and helped her figure it out. "It's so different," she whispered when she finished.

"Did ya figure it out?" Annie teased him when the two returned. "She did say you have to *learn* to be a woman."

"No, she said learn what it *means* to be a woman," Benjamina corrected her. All laughed.

After supper, the whole group was in high spirits. They all felt far more alive than they had in many months, and they began to tackle the first problem. Tim read aloud the hints Lysandra had given Ben. "You already know why the rates are declining; the katalyein have told you why, only you have not grasped it. You have also in your travels in the breadbasket seen the solution to the birthrate problem, though once again, you have not realized what you've seen."

He then asked, "Okay Benjamina, what have the katalyein told you?"

"I don't know. Let's see. Marisol did point out there have been many close kin breeding. With the katalyein, that line was recovered by breeding brothers, sisters, and cousins. Oh, I see what Lysandra meant! Look. Let's take Brom here as an example. Nearly all the marriages are between families that are related, though often distantly. No one at Brom ever marries someone from Rusden. No one at Wye marries someone from Leedsburough. Get it? Each tower pretty much continues century after century to breed among their own."

Tim interrupted, growing more animated as the solution began forming in his mind, "You are right! I see it now. Wye Tower *mentales* gifted usually marry others in their city, as do all the towers. Hence there really are no new outside blood lines coming into the mix!"

"Yes, and that ties into what we saw on our many small town visits in the breadbasket areas down by Rusden. There are a whole lot of other *mentales* gifted people living their lives far beyond the key towers and the kingdom rulers with their *mentales* folk. We need to get more marriage partners from outside Brom, either from other towers or from the smaller towns and villages. That will bring new blood lines and hopefully increase the number of babies born with the gift," Benjamina explained. "Now we have to sell this to the powers that be and let them figure out how to do it. Amazing, the answer was right before my eyes only I didn't see it. Lysandra was right!"

Tim chuckled, "Dear, if you had seen it, then you wouldn't have had to become a woman to see it." Benjamina laughed.

She then said, "As for the third one, I will have to work closely with the katalyein, observe, and conclude, creating a science of the mind and spirit. That one, it looks to me like I will have to work on that one myself. I'll leave you all to deal with trying to get all the modifications undone. Tomorrow, we can visit Venerada Marisol and tell her the solution to the second one and let her figure out how to implement it. Oops, first we need to get me some proper clothes and shoes and boots for everyone."

Annie volunteered, "Hey, there is a whole back storeroom at Elegant Fashions Inc full of the obsolete heels and boots we used to sell. That should not be a problem."

That night as Benjamina and Elana got ready for bed, a whole new set of experiences began for her. "What do I do with my hair, dear?" Elana giggled and then helped her figure out how to brush it out nicely.

"I love how long it is, just pull it over your left shoulder so you don't lay on it or so I don't. I want to snuggle on your right as I always have." The two removed their hands and got into bed. "Now I am going to show you what it means to be a woman, well some of it anyway," Elana teased her and then moved her stump over Benjamina's breasts. She learned rapidly.

As they dressed in the morning, Benjamina again had a bout of nervousness. "Love, you got to help me when we go to Elegant Fashions. What colors do I choose? What dresses? I don't know anything about these things. I always just let you get what you wanted."

Again, Elana giggled. "Don't worry, love. I will. Look, women want to look their best for their husband or wife in this case. We'll figure it all out. I think I'd love to see you in a light red, perhaps, maybe a sky blue. We'll make you look sexy, so don't worry."

Late afternoon, the group finally returned home, laden with many packages. All had acquired two pair of stiletto heeled boots and two pairs of pumps. Although these had the usual six-inch heels, they were of exceptionally high quality. More importantly, all could walk well in them, a vast difference from the awful toe shoes and boots. Benjamina now had many different outfits, including four satin gowns of various styles, but predominately light red and sky blue. Only one was the arm-fetter-gown style, just in case she went somewhere where this style was required. She also had everyday apparel, pod-silk blouses, cotton blouses, wool sweaters, warm pants in the usual style where the hems were at her knees where her knee-high boots ended, suitable for winter weather. She also had several nightgowns, all manner of underwear, some of which she really didn't know their purpose, and of course, garter belts and nylons, as well as tall, warm stockings for winter wear.

The following day Benjamina planned to visit Venerada Marisol. "Okay, love, what should I wear to meet with her? What's the accepted dress?" Elana smiled and proceeded to lay out her sky blue satin gown and black patent heels. After exchanging a passionate kiss, she helped her get dressed and helped her with her long hair.

"Remember, don't sit on it. Pull it over one of your shoulders before you sit," Elana cautioned her. "Okay, you look gorgeous, my love. Don't be surprised if many of the men there give you stares or even whistles as you pass by. Let's get going. I can't wait to see the expression on Marisol's face when she sees you!"

They took Annie's buggy. It was smaller and easier for Elana to drive. Benjamina wanted to drive, but was talked out of it. "Look, you have enough to manage just now. Let me. I can handle it with these new hands of ours. We'd both be in trouble with those old hands."

As they entered the tower complex, many men and women were outside enjoying the early summer day before it clouded and rained later in the afternoon. Flowers were blooming, filling the air with various scents. "My god! All the men are looking at us!" Benjamina whispered. They had just parked their buggy and climbed down, preparing to head to the main door of the manor house.

"Of course, dear. We look good and men respond. Try not to pay them any attention," she whispered back. Heels clicking on the cobblestones, the two women walked to the ornate double doors. There a guard wearing his green Elite Guards uniform asked their names and then opened the doors for them, watching them as they entered.

Benjamina whispered, "My god, I've aroused that guard!" Elana giggled.

"Oh. Hello Elana. I was expecting Ben. And who is this young woman? I don't believe we've met," Venerada Marisol said pleasantly, though a bit surprised, wondering where Ben was. She wore an embroidered cotton dress of the type she could put on herself along with flats she could slip off so she could use her feet when needed.

"Hi Venerada. I'd like you to meet the new Ben, Benjamina. She's really Ben. Lysandra's doing."

Marisol's jaw dropped. Her eyes opened wide. "Ben? Just wearing women's gowns? Lysandra? The goddess? What?"

Benjamina laughed. "That was worth the surprise, Venerada Marisol. Yes, I'm Ben, well Benjamina now. Yes, Goddess Lysandra changed my body into that of a woman, a pregnant one too. You'd better sit down."

Marisol gasped and did as he asked. She'd never had quite a shock before. The two walked over to chairs and Benjamina fiddled with her hair to get it over her left shoulder before sitting down. "Long story, Marisol. I had to get the three solutions or answers we desperately need. This is the price I am to pay." She began to tell her the entire story, which was not too long. Then she explained the first two solutions in detail. "Already, we've seen a resurgence of life in the other Underground members, a striking change. All are far more cheerful now. So that is part of the solution. We know from Annie that the medical machines of Elegant Fashions Inc have had most all their healing functions disabled. This means the Underground really have the only machines which can be used to undo these things, except for the one you have here."

"Tim has suggested you convince your people here to get their modifications undone, and he'll see you get another two medical machines and the training needed to run them. That way you can work on three people at one time. After you get everyone here fixed up, you can work out how to handle the other towers and all the others. Tim suggests that, if you don't want all them coming here to get it done by your people, he could take the two machines around the Midlands and help the others. Your call."

"This is going to be a challenge. So many are going nuts with the sexual stimulation of their lip loops. Still I will get it done. It's for their own good, even if they can't see it," Marisol replied.

He then discussed at length the breeding problem. She instantly saw his solution would indeed work. "So your greatest challenge will be to work out a way to get the young ones to meet these others in the outlying areas, fall in love, and marry. I leave that mess to you, but that is the solution to our dwindling numbers. We have to cease marrying *mentales* gifted within the local city."

She agreed and promised to get her staff working on this one. "So what about our discovery that we are spiritual beings? That one interests me more," Marisol asked.

Benjamina quoted what Lysandra had said. Then she said, "I will have to work closely with your katalyein, observe, and conclude, and somehow create us a science of the mind and spirit. That's the main reason for my visit today. How am I going to do this with your women?"

Marisol asked, "Elana, she is really a she, right?"

Elana laughed. "Every inch so, much to her dismay. Nothing male about her now, but that's fine with me."

"Okay, I had to ask to protect my katalyein. Males going into close rapport with them while they are working totally distracts them, you see. Well, you don't yet, but you'll see. I shall introduce you to them and explain what you are trying to do. I won't tell them that you were Ben or about Lysandra — that could confuse them too much. In fact, let's keep this detail between us for now. You can just be a close friend of Elana's. That will make you totally acceptable around here."

"That's fine with me. Honestly, I get so embarrassed trying to explain all this to others."

Marisol grinned, "Well, Benjamina, you will sure turn men's heads around here. You are a gorgeous looking woman, but if you are pregnant — oh, you really are!" she exclaimed, just sensing it. "Congratulations to the both of you. Where was I? Oh, if you are pregnant, once it shows a lot, the men will not pay so much attention to you. Until then, try not to flirt with the men."

She laughed, "I don't know how to flirt yet. If I do it, it's by accident. Just let me know, please."

A bit later, the door opened again and her twelve fellow katalyein women walked into her office. All were dressed similarly to Marisol, easy clothing for them to manage by themselves. They ranged in age from their late fifties down to fourteen. There were a few more who were younger, but they were not yet allowed to work their magic. She introduced the two. "Ladies, this is Elana's dear, close friend Benjamina. She is going to work with you and study what is happening with those who you are helping. Benjamina hopes to find a way to help us develop our spiritual natures and hopes to create our first true science of the mind and spirit. I want you to give her your full support. The main question now is how do we best implement this?"

"She can stay with us, if she wants," a woman about her own age volunteered. "We can talk a lot about what we know. I'm Adriana, by the way. That way whenever we get someone here who needs our help, she'll be right here, and we won't have to wait until Benjamina gets here."

Benjamina felt ill at ease. She barely knew how to dress herself, what with all the unfamiliar garments. "Give me a week to get my things together. You are probably right, that would be the best way, if that's okay with Venerada Marisol."

She smiled, "Yes, that's probably a wise decision,

Benjamina." She was referring to the week delay so Benjamina could get more used to her new body and its needs. They chatted a bit more, and the katalyein left. The two did as well, returning home as the sprinkles began.

"Okay, we have a week to get you grooved into acting like a woman would," Elana stated. "We have some work to do." Both chuckled.

Chapter 16 Formation

The last week of June 1245, Benjamina officially moved into Brom Manor. She still felt very self-conscious about herself. She was used to being in charge and carrying her things. Right away, a soldier came to carry her bags to her new room, only adding to her discomfort. He said, "It's rare someone is actually going to stay with one of our katalyein." She had been assigned to stay in Adriana's room with her and to accompany her wherever she went.

"I didn't know that," Benjamina said, wondering if that was the appropriate thing to say.

"No matter. It will be nice to have another beautiful, young woman around the manor," he added, giving her a wink.

Damn, this is harder than I imagined. What do I do? "Thanks." Just then, Adriana came bounding down the hall to her rescue.

"Hi Benjamina. We're all set and ready for you. James has your bags. Just put them on the bed, please." Adriana moved up to her and pressed her body into Benjamina's and raised a leg around her back, giving her the special katalyein hug. Her surprise enthusiasm and greeting further embarrassed Benjamina.

"I'm really glad to be here. I hope I'm not putting you to any trouble, Adriana."

"Oh no, none at all. You can help me at night with my hair and I can do yours. First thing, we have to get you unpacked. You can use the top drawers. I can't easily reach them and there's nothing in them. Come on. I'll help."

Benjamina began to think this maybe wasn't such a good idea after all, rooming with Adriana. "Oh, you do have good taste in dresses, Benjamina. I wear nylons like yours too, when we have our dances. Of course, someone has to help me with them. Maybe you could, if your hands work well enough. Here's your dress." She had the sky blue one held between her head and neck and was handing it to her, impressing Benjamina.

"Oh yes, we're not as helpless as people often think. We

273

just have different ways, but I admit, we need help with things others don't. Such is life. Well, I admit I will never find anyone who will love me. That's life. Come on. I'll show you around."

That night as the two headed into Adriana's bedroom suite for the night, Benjamina's nervousness returned. "I always like to sleep in the buff in the summers. It's warm. Come on; get yourself undressed, unless you need some help with something." Adriana leaned on her bed and began wiggling. Soon she had her dress over her head and shook it off, leaving her long black hair rather disheveled. She picked it up and sat down on her bed. Using her feet and toes, she folded it neatly. Tucking it between her head and neck, she got up and put it on her dresser, bringing her hairbrush back with her by holding it between her teeth. Meanwhile, Benjamina focused on making her hands work well enough to get out of her dress. "Boy, you sure are slow, but I can see why. It must be really hard making those hands work right. Everyone says these new ones are so much better than the old ones, but I can see they still have a lot of trouble. People get so frustrated at times. There, now you're done." Benjamina picked up her things and emulated Adriana, folding them and laying them out on the second dresser ready for her in the morning. She turned and saw the naked young woman about her own age sitting on the edge of her bed, hairbrush at her side, her hair still a mess.

Benjamina could not resist looking, but she also saw Adriana staring at her huge chest, double the size of Adriana's well-endowed bust. "Pardon me, but I always wanted to see what they looked like, you know, the Madiera women. Yours are so big. Come sit by me and do my hair please."

She complied, fumbling her way through the process all the while hoping Adriana would not sense her embarrassment. Then Adriana did hers. "Incredible, Adriana. I didn't think you would be able to do mine."

"Oh sure, lots of things most people don't think we can do. Put your hands over there and let's snuggle and get some sleep." As Benjamina complied, returning to the bed, she added, "You know, they are rather attractive — nicely shaped."

"Oh, thanks. That's something at least."

"Toss your hair like this, see, bend, and toss. I got mine on my left side so I don't sleep on it." Benjamina bent and moved her head, but used her arms to get all hers out of the way. She crawled into bed beside Adriana, who insisted on snuggling up to her. A bit later, she whispered, "You really like women not men, don't you? I can tell but I won't say anything." Benjamina was glad the lanterns were very low.

The next day much to Benjamina's relief, Adriana had someone arrive who needed her help. A thirteen year old girl was having a mild case of Verge Sickness; a blockage kept her ill for several days, and her parents had finally brought her to the tower. "I don't know how I do what I do, I just do it. I guess is what you are here to find out," Adriana said.

"Right. I'm going into deep rapport with you and then I'll just observe," Benjamina explained. Focusing, she easily slid into the whole consciousness that was Adriana.

"Okay, Ellie, put your hands on my shoulders, and no matter what happens, don't let go." The feverish teen did as asked. Benjamina saw a large dark mass sitting on the girl's forehead. Then it began to swirl and an image appeared. Like a moving picture, an entire incident slowly presented itself both to Adriana and to Ellie who was reliving it. She was actually looking at a traumatic incident, which had happed nearly a century ago — the destruction of Bettingham city and tower by the Nuclear. Benjamina watched fascinated. The images were quite real; colors, vivid; the sounds were clear and very loud; the emotions unbelievably heavy; and the pain, overwhelming. Still both Adriana and Ellie continued to re-experience them over and over. Each time through the whole incident, the unconsciousness, the pain, and the heavy emotions lightened until at last, all was stripped off. The black mass was gone. Ellie's fever broke at once. "Okay, all done, Ellie; you did very well indeed."

Later after Ellie had left, Benjamina began a lengthy discussion with Adriana about what she'd seen. "Yes, it is always like that. In the black or grey masses lie some kind of incident, always traumatic, emotionally or painful. Sometimes in the lighter ones, the person's wife, husband, or child died. They always run like that, a continuous stream of images, just as if it was happening again for us to watch. Usually the person has to go through it several times before they see and hear and feel all it. It's like it is in layers, and the heaviest pain and unconsciousness is always at the very bottom, re-experienced or seen last by the person."

After answering several more direct questions, Adriana said, "Benjamina, you have some of them too, black masses. When you were in rapport with me, I could not help but see them. If you want, we could get rid of them. That way you could see how the patient sees what I do."

"I do? My gifts aren't blocked, not that I know of," she replied, biting her lip a little. *I've got blocks? How can that be?* "Okay, let's. This should be interesting." The two sat down across from each other and Benjamina put her arms on Adriana's shoulders and closed her eyes.

She saw herself getting her feet done. There was Annie struggling mightily with her prosthetic hands, working the machine. Then his feet were removed from the machine, looking horribly distorted, as they had been. She wondered how this could be a blockage? Certainly she'd felt no pain. Annie had said she'd only feel pin pricks which she had. Adriana had the whole moving picture show beginning again. Ouch! Benjamina felt a sharp pain in one foot and then the other. The next time, the pains were acute; she flinched hardly able to bear that overwhelming pain in both her feet. Again and again, the images rolled by until at last, she felt nothing at all.

Hey, there's another one. You are doing super, Adriana sent. Now Benjamina was getting her lips done. The first time through, she felt nothing but saw Annie working the controls. After more times through the short film strip like series, she again felt the awful pain of her lips being slit. Then that pain too seemed to be erased. Another mass opened up; Adriana merely found the next one and handled it. Benjamina saw her waist being modified, a simple thing on the first run through it. After that, the pain was almost unbearable as the machine cut out his ribs! It was all she could do to keep her arms on Adriana's shoulders. After more times through, the pain and deep unconsciousness vanished completely. Then she saw her hands being removed and the aesthetic conical forms being made. A few more times later and she re-experienced incredible pains in both wrists, but after a few more passes, that too vanished.

"Okay, we're done, Benjamina. You can take your arms down now."

Benjamina opened her eyes and blinked, "My god! The room seems brighter! I feel really happy, relaxed, really good, and alive. Thanks!"

Adriana giggled. "That's always a good sign. I saw *them* all too. I won't *say* anything. Does Marisol know? It *was* Lysandra, wasn't it? She did this to you?"

Benjamina flushed crimson. "Er, well yes. To all three. I guess my secret is out with you. Marisol knows all about it. She is allowing me to study all this because that was Lysandra's wishes. It is probably best if you don't tell anyone about me. No one will really understand."

Adriana giggled. "Probably not. I won't tell. Lysandra once helped one of us katalyein, you know. Say, you can help me a little. I've this boyfriend, and I can't tell if he really loves me or not, but then I just know I will never find someone who will love me. I like him, but when we get close, I always get a headache." Benjamina found herself explaining men's views and actions to the young woman, something with which she was intimately familiar. However, now Benjamina had some concrete facts that were starting to align, shedding some light on the entire situation.

"Look, Adriana. I did not know I had somehow recorded all that pain and unconsciousness. I knew Annie had put a rag over my face and I was smelling something. After that, I awoke with my body modified and all healed up. I felt no pain. Yet, if you cut off someone's hands, the body hurts terribly. The anesthetic simply made me wholly unaware of it."

"Yes, it knocks you out, just like all the other traumatic things that happens to those who I have to help," she replied. "Oh my! This means we katalyein now have to do this to nearly everyone in the tower and the castle! They've all got this huge amount of buried pain and unconsciousness from their body modifications!"

"Adriana, we are on to something huge here! Right now, I can recall all what happened to me during those operations. Before you used your gift on me, I couldn't. They were simply not there. I could recall everything up to smelling that rag over my face and then waking up with Elana with me, but there was that huge gap, filled with all kinds of pains, terrible pains. We need to find someone who broken an arm or a leg and who has not had one of you work your magic on them. Come on; we've got to talk to Marisol about this!"

A couple hours later, a young soldier who'd broken his arm during sword practice last year was now sitting in the chair. First, Benjamina had him recount all he remembered about the fall and accident. "Well I was doing a practice session. I stumbled and fell. I probably hit something wrong. Next thing I know, I'm in the infirmary, and my arm is being healed by a healer. It's fine, really it is. I just don't move fast enough anymore."

Next, Adriana had him place his hands on her shoulders, and she worked her magic on him with Benjamina in full rapport with her. As the images were re-viewed several times, the heavy pain of the break appeared, and he really did jerk and flinch from it. A few more times through the series and Benjamina heard the sword master saying, "He just wasn't moving fast enough." After that, the incident was gone. "You know, Adriana, I recall now the master was saying I wasn't fast enough. Well, I wasn't then, but I sure am now. I bet I am faster now than I was then. Interesting. Thanks." He left and both looked at each other, knowing they'd made a monumental discovery this day.

"Blockages of *mentales* gifts are one thing, but this is an entirely different thing, Adriana. People have other mental blockages, which adversely affect their lives. Incredible," Benjamina exclaimed.

"Isn't this really interesting? Now what do we do? There are only a few of us katalyein in the whole world. Until now, we have not been all that busy. Thankfully, there are not too many of the gifted who come to us to get their debilitating blockages removed. Now we are going to be so incredibly busy trying to do everyone here who got body modified, I don't see

278

how we can keep up with this, let alone all the hundreds of others in the other towers and cities who got modified too. Maybe that will make up for me not being able to find someone who will love me," Adriana explained.

"Come on. I need to write some of these things down while they are fresh." Adriana had a low writing table in her room and Benjamina tried to pick up a piece of paper with her unfeeling hands. She ended up crinkling it before she got it. Again, when she went for the pencil, she slightly misjudged and her unfeeling fingers bumped it instead, knocking it onto the floor. "Damn these hands anyway. I can't feel anything with them, Adriana. I keep misjudging unless I put my full attention on what I'm trying to do with them." She bent down, grasped the pencil between the sides of the fingers, and forced the hand to squeeze its fingers together around the pencil. Lifting it up, she took it in her other hand so she could reposition it in her writing hand. It slipped and fell on the floor again. Benjamina growled.

Adriana grinned, "Here, let me. I'm good at writing. She sat down before her desk, slipping off her flats. Her feet took the paper and laid it on the desk, and then she swivelled on her butt and picked up the pencil. Using her other foot, she pushed herself back. Adjusting the pencil between her toes, she announced, "Okay, I'm ready."

"Thanks, heart-felt thanks," Benjamina replied with a sigh. "Okay then."

"Assumption One: we record everything that occurs in our lives in a sort of moving series of mental images which contain everything we perceive, including sight, sound, emotions, smells, pains, and so on, storing them as memories."

"Assumption Two: these memories are ordinarily available for us to recall, such as eating our breakfast this morning."

"Assumption Three: when the event contains sufficient trauma, such as pain or severe emotional loss or upset, the perceptions being received are too much for a person to face analytically and somehow the person goes unconscious."

"Assumption Four: even though unconscious and no

longer analytically aware of what is occurring during the receipt of this traumatic incident, it is still being received and stored as complete memories, but they are no longer available as normal memories are to the person. Often, they are visible to the katalyein as black or grey masses about the person."

"Assumption Five: the person who has one of these traumatic incidents cannot see its content on their own, since they were unable to withstand viewing it when it was happening to them in the first place, i.e., they went unconscious."

"Assumption Six: the katalyein with their gift touches these masses with their mental psi energies and, in doing so, makes the images with all the perceptions that were recorded visible to the person as well as the katalyein."

"Assumption Seven: the katalyein has the person re-experience what happened to him or her during the incident, going through it many times."

"Assumption Eight: upon sufficient re-experiences, the trauma, that is, the emotional charge, the pain, the unconsciousness discharges, and the trauma appears to be erased."

"Assumption Nine: when done, the incident with all its perceptions now is available as normal memories to the person, and the damage of that mental block is also erased."

"Assumption Ten: these traumatic incidents do not necessarily have to only block a person's *mentales* gifts."

"Assumption Eleven: the katalyein plus the person is required to erase the blockage or the trauma. The katalyein alone or the person alone cannot erase the blockage or the trauma."

"Assumption Twelve: the words spoken around the injured person appear to have a serious adverse effect on the person later on in his or her life."

"Assumption Thirteen: a non-katalyein cannot see the person's masses or blockages or their traumatic incidents, these black or grey masses. Thus, they do not even know they are there."

"Query: can a way be found for a non-katalyein to get a person with one of these unseen traumatic incidents to run and erase in a similar manner as the katalyein do it? The katalyein cause it to be run by touching the mass with their special mental psi energies. After that, they simply have the person re-experience it over and over, a process that could be done via word commands by a non-katalyein. Is it possible for a non-katalyein to be able to get the person to that initial starting point via word commands? If this can be done, then a non-katalyein could be trained to help many others undo traumatic events they have experienced which do not seem to be affecting their *mentales* gifts, per se."

"There, Adriana, what do you think of those?"

"Incredible, Benjamina! That sure does sum it up very concisely. Can I add another one? Sometimes, there are a series of related traumas, like yours with your body modifications," she suggested.

"Assumption Fourteen: separate traumatic incidents which have similar content tend to group themselves together somewhat like links in a chain. The most recent one of these appears to be the one that is handled first, while the earliest one does not appear and get handled until the very last."

"How does that one sound? It's on shaky ground so far. We need to study that one more."

Adriana answered, "Yes, that says what we katalyein have seen several times. We should show these to Marisol."

"Hey, each one of these assumptions must be thoroughly studied to see if they are truly accurate. I can see I've got an awful lot of research to do now!"

Later in Marisol's office, she read them over. "Ben, Benjamina rather, this is incredible! Brilliantly stated! You are a genius! If these hold up, you are well on your way to helping every woman and man on Tierra! Okay, I know, lots more study is needed. I am assigning Adriana to be your personal assistant in the research. Wherever you go, she goes to help you in any way you need. All I ask is you take responsibility for her safety and well-being. She is, after all, dependent on others. While we try to be as independent as we can, lacking arms is a horrible barrier to many things in life. Will you accept such a heavy responsibility, Ben, er Benjamina?"

"Absolutely. I will guard and protect her with my life,

Marisol."

"Okay, then. She's assigned to you until further notice. Adriana, wherever she goes, you go. This is absolutely mind blowing in scope, revolutionary. Meanwhile, I am going to see that the other katalyein proceed with handling of our tower members who had some body modifications. We'll see if we can't get those traumas erased. Hell, Ben, er Benjamina, we didn't even know they were there!"

"I am very honored to help and will do all that she asks, Marisol. Really I will. After all I am never going to really find someone who will love me, so this gives me something important to do with my life," Adriana replied.

After other chatting, the two women headed back to Adriana's room. Benjamina was thinking all the way back there. *Damn. She keeps saying the she'll never find someone who will love her. I'm rather tired of hearing that line. True, it is probably really hard for her to get out much and meet young men her age, but it's annoying to hear it so often. Wait a second! You don't suppose she has some traumatic incident behind this do you? I wonder how I could get at it?* "Say, Adriana, didn't you say you had a boyfriend who was interested in you and who you liked?"

"Well, yes, Tom Hanks. He's a horse trainer from up by Hilliard Heights, to the north of us. He comes down here several times each year bringing batches of well-trained horses and reindeer to us. Maybe he likes me, but every time we get close to each other, like at the dances, I get these awful headaches and have to go lie down. So really, I am never going to find someone who will really love me, Benjamina, not really. What do we do next on this project?"

She used her foot to slide the slat over and then pushed her way into her room, Benjamina followed her in, sliding the slat back into place with her foot. *I have no idea where or what this traumatic incident is, only those words. I wonder what would happen if she said those words over and over? Would that bring the incident into view? I wonder. Worth a try.*

"Adriana, let's try some experiment on you. Have a seat. I want you to close your eyes and repeat 'I am never going to really find someone who will love me.' Okay?"

"Sure, but I don't have any traumas, not really. Okay. I am never going to really find someone who will love me. I am never going to really find someone who will love me. I am never going to really find someone who will love me. Ouch! My head hurts so."

"Okay. What are you seeing?"

"Oh! I see a room. Some woman has just given birth to a katalyein baby. I see a midwife woman there holding the baby. I think that's my nana."

"Very good. Now move on through it and re-experience what happened, telling me about it as you do it."

"My head is hurting. I hear a voice saying she is never going to really find someone who will love her. Then, nana lays the baby by her mother and it is starting to suck. That's all."

"Okay, go back to the beginning and go through it once more."

"Ouch! Oh! I'm the baby! It's me. Oh, mom is saying that to nana. Nana is holding me up so mom can see me and mom gets all upset. She's crying. She's just like me. Oh no, nana. She is never going to really find someone who will love her. Nana wipes me off and lays me beside mom, and I am sucking on her breast and relaxing. That's all. My head hurts badly."

Benjamina had her go over it several more times, but nothing else new presented itself. "Okay, let's go back to the beginning again."

"Wait! I think it starts earlier! It's all dark and warm. Comfy and cozy, sort of. I'm relaxed."

"Good. Now move on through it and tell me what is happening."

"Oh! Pressure. I am being born. Oh my head. It feels like it is being crushed or something. Lights. Seems really bright to me now. Cold. I am freezing all a sudden. Nana is wiping me off, but my head still hurts and I am freezing. She holds me up so mom can see me and mom gets really upset. She's crying. She's just like me. She is never going to really find someone who will love her. Nana wraps me up and lays me beside mom and I start suckling. Oh my god! That's mom's idea that I'd never find someone to love, not mine. I've found someone. Oh! No wonder every time I get close to him I get a headache! If I am me and am loving someone, like I did mom, my head hurts. It doesn't hurt if I think I will never find someone who will love me. That's ridiculous!" She started laughing really hard, ending the therapy session. Benjamina grinned and watched the young woman laugh. Here was a trauma, which had been adversely ruining Adriana's life, but it wasn't interfering with her *mentales* gifts.

A half hour later, Adriana had finally calmed down. Benjamina said with a wry smile, "Well, Adriana, we have just proved Assumption Twelve: the words spoken around the injured person appear to have a serious adverse effect on the person later on in his or her life."

"No kidding! And we have found an answer to the Query too! You just did it to me and you are not a katalyein, not remotely!"

"Say, get your pencil ready. We need to add another one."

"Assumption Fourteen: an aberrated phrase that person uses, if repeated enough times, brings the underlying traumatic incident into view, where it can be run and erased. The phrase is then no longer affects the person."

"Assumption Fifteen: if the traumatic incident you are handling does not vanish and erase, then see if it has an earlier beginning in time. If not, see if there is an earlier trauma incident similar to the one you are handling now."

They chatted at length over their discovery. That night when they retired for the night, Adriana said, "I know you are married to Elana and I don't want to have you do something you don't want to do, so you don't have to if you don't want to."

"What are you talking about, Adriana?"

"Well, it is awfully hard for us katalyein to pleasure ourselves, *really* hard. I really would love to have you pleasure me. I miss it badly. Please, would you do this for me?"

Benjamina smiled and did as asked. Later, a satisfied Adriana asked, "Can I ask you a question about men?" She agreed. "Do men like it when we position ourselves like this?

We are really flexible and I've heard from some others that they do." She lifted one leg up and put in behind her head, then the other. "Like this?" Benjamina answered her question by pleasuring her again. "Thank you very much. I so want to please Tom if we get married. I don't want to be wholly ignorant of such things and how they are done. I've got no one else I really can talk to about such things, except you. It means the world to me. I so want Tom to love me, cause I do love him. He's so handsome, strong, and smart. You'll see. He'll be here tomorrow for the midsummer's dance. Maybe Elana can come and you both can dance too."

Benjamina began to realize Adriana was also teaching her more about what it meant to be a woman. She grinned silently to herself. Lysandra was terribly devious in her methods, but the breakthrough was quite real.

Elana wore her bright red satin gown to the dance and Benjamina wore her sky blue gown. As they met and hugged and shared a passionate kiss, Benjamina whispered, "You wore the gown I always loved to see you wearing."

"Of course. I still want to please you, silly, even if you are a woman now. I see you are doing the same thing."

Benjamina laughed, "I know. I wore this one because I know it's your favorite color. Adriana taught me that. Women do want to please their partners. I'm sorry as a man I frequently didn't pay much attention to that."

"You are learning, dear. Amazing." She gave her another loving kiss. "So how is it going? I miss you."

Benjamina then began explaining all they'd discovered. "I would have come home sooner, but I wanted to see if what we did does make major changes in Adriana's life. Her love is here. He's dancing with her. Let's see if her headache comes back. Keep an eye on the two."

They spotted the two young lovers stealing passionate kisses several times. Unlike all their previous encounters, Adriana didn't get a headache, and they were together all night long. When the dance was done, the couple came over so Benjamina could meet Tom Hanks. "He's asked me to marry him and I've said yes! But of course I have to get Marisol's permission too, and I told him we'd have to wait until our research is done." Adriana was more cheerful than Benjamina had ever seen her before.

A day later Marisol and Benjamina agreed. Adriana would spend the rest of the summer helping Benjamina. When Tom returned with the fall herd, the young couple would be married. They'd spend their winters in Brom Tower and their summers up in Hilliard Heights, where he had to train his horses. If Benjamina still needed her assistance, she'd be available during the lengthy winters that ran from October through late April.

With the agreement made, Adriana and Benjamina packed their bags and returned to the Underground, where they would begin further studies, proving or disproving the assumptions, but working their therapy sessions on the many Underground members.

Chapter 17 Expansion

"Welcome back, Ben. Missed you around here," Tim said as Benjamina and Adriana walked into the underground base. "Status report: the medical machines have to be operated by me. No one else reads IS, unfortunately, and the menu system is far too complex. Annie gave it a try, but no go. Her machines from Nita simply had one button to push for each of the different modifications. So I've been spending my afternoons in the castle running them. Been doing about ten people a day now. How many have we got done, dear?"

Looking up, Petrona replied, "Sixty-six."

"Okay, how many got modified around here?"

Annie had that number; she'd preformed them all. "One hundred ninety-five."

"That means then we ought to be done with the Brom area by late August," Tim concluded. "So what about all the hundreds of others who got modified? How are we going to get to them? We can't make them travel to Brom. My god, they are only barely able to live."

Benjamina bit her lip. "We have to speed this up, Tim. As much as I hate to interrupt what I'm doing, I don't think we can spend years getting around to everyone. Honestly, we know how much better our lives are without those modifications. We are getting by with these new hands, and these heels are not that bad, comparatively speaking. Okay, let's get the word out to the other towers and castles. We will arrange for the towers to teleport their victims here to Brom Castle, and we'll run two machines at one time. If we can do, say thirty each afternoon, then that will speed things along and leave me mornings and evenings to carry on with the research project. That way by the end of August, we should have undone all that can be undone here in the Midlands and the Easterlings."

"Meantime gather around; you have to hear what Adriana and I have discovered. This is even more important," Benjamina said.

She had Adriana read off their list of assumptions.

When she finished, she added, "These really do seem to work! I had this trauma at birth unknown to me and it was destroying my life. Benjamina discovered these supposedly painless body modifications are anything but painless. This stuff is incredible. Wait until you see for yourselves."

"Adriana is going to sleep with Elana and me. As soon as we get our things unpacked, Tim, you and I will go to the castle and see if we can't get things moving a whole lot faster. Meanwhile, Adriana will start in with our research on one of you. Rafaela, you'll be her first test subject. Tonight, I'll work with Elana. If Adriana gets done with her, she can do Andres next," Benjamina suggested.

After the two left for the castle, Adriana sat down across from Rafaela. Eric alone remained at the monitors watching over the geosat images and listening for alien communications. "But I swear, I didn't feel anything when they did my lips, Adriana," Rafaela declared as she sat down opposite here. "Besides, I don't have any arms to touch you with. How can this even work? I thought the person had to touch you for you to use your gift."

"I am not going to use my gift on you, Rafaela. I'm going to use what Benjamina and I discovered. Now close your eyes. I want you to go back to the first moment when you got your lips done." After a couple of times through it, the images became very real for her along with the sights and smells in the room. More importantly, she felt again the sharp, intense pain in her lips as they were sliced. After more runs through it, Rafaela brightened up.

"My god! That was really real! God, did that ever hurt! I was unconscious, but my body still felt all that pain! Wow!" Now everyone was suddenly keenly interested.

"Very good, Rafaela. Now can you locate the beginning point when you lost your arms?"

She did and began to re-experience those awful days once more. "My arms ache, shoulders mostly. So cold. Can't move them." She continued, but mostly it was an intense grief she experienced, grief over having failed to get the ancient power crystals they'd discovered back to Brom, and grief over the ever-growing fear her arms and hands were freezing, and that she'd soon die. "I really don't want to live." She related how she ended up near the end. "Then, I am in the medical machine. I don't feel anything as they are removed. That's all."

A few more times through it and she began to feel the intense, acute pains in her shoulders when her arms were amputated. She gagged as she had done back then, when she first saw what had become of her arms. Black and frozen fingers and hands were ghastly to see and, "I knew right then I was lucky to be alive, but also I was now a hopeless cripple. I still am, really, though everyone here tries to say otherwise."

All the rest of the afternoon, Rafaela continued to go through and re-experience that long incident. Each time through it, more details continued to appear. As suppertime approached, she suddenly brightened up, "Oh! When I got here, I decided life was now too scary to live! Really, it was. With the pipe corset and toe boots and no arms to help me, even standing up was frightening to me! Well, I guess I can change my opinion of life now."

After supper, Adriana continued with Rafaela, pointing her to the time when she got her waist and feet done. This one went far smoother. When she finally re-experienced the real pain of having her ribs cut out and her foot bones broken and reformed, she did shriek. A few more times through it and she was laughing about the whole thing. My god, Adriana, that was more than incredible! It was so real, like I was right there witnessing it all happening again! I never knew any of the intense pain was even there!" The others noted her eyes were sparkling; her complexion was vastly improved, as well the mere fact she was far more cheerful than any had ever seen her be. Andres was most impressed with his wife.

Andres got his turn the next day, and it took nearly the entire day for Adriana to get him finished up with these same basic traumas. He and Rafaela had endured them together for the most part. He too was noticeably brighter, cheerful, and looked much healthier than before.

Adriana then said, "Okay you two. We need to spend some hours together, and let me show you how we katalyein do things." Both heartily agreed to try anything she suggested. While it took several months, both Rafaela and Andres learned to do far more things for themselves, thanks to Adriana's constant nudging. Even more importantly, both realized they needed to learn how to do this new therapy. Not only was it intensely valuable and rewarding, it was something they really could do. Delivering the therapy had nothing to do with arms and hands.

Hence, the next day, Benjamina began to teach the two how to do it. He'd already finished helping Elana with the modifications she'd undergone, much impressing her. She too sat in, wanting to learn how to do it as well. After that, Benjamina and Adriana sat back, overseeing the three who were working on Tim, Darcy, and Dawn. Although highly impressed with the results, Tim was not interested in learning how to do it on others, but the twins were. By mid-August, everyone in the Underground had been fully handled on these quite obvious trauma incidents. All were doing very noticeably better in life, happier and more alive.

"Now comes the research part," Benjamina explained to everyone, save Tim who was off with his monitoring. "We all knew those traumas were there; we all had been body modified. In this next phase of research, we are going after other unknown trauma which may be impacting your lives. We have at least one clue, thanks to Adriana. Birth. We all have that in common, but there could well be all sorts of other things, like broken arms, legs, cuts, losses, who knows."

"We need to prove conclusively each one of these assumptions is valid and also work out just how we do this therapy, that is, what commands we should use, how to find the hidden traumas, and so on," Benjamina explained. "We've got our work cut out for us."

"Complicating matters," Adriana pointed out, "is the simple fact that right now, we have the ability to wipe out the traumas we know all our women and men have undergone with the many body modification operations. Ought we not at least start to deal with those, so they can get a better hold on life and do better? You all know how much better you are after getting those traumas erased. Right now, we have the ability to get all the others this same relief and gains. Shouldn't we at least start helping them while we continue the research?"

Tim spoke up, "I hate to say it, Ben, but she has a point. all the modified folks are having a hard struggle with just living day to day. Undoing the modifications has been huge help, but getting rid of those unseen traumas has made me feel tons better, more alive, happier, more willing to do more in life. To me anyway, this seems to help or finish off fulfilling the problem of increasing their overall emotional tones upwards from the pits to which they have sunk."

Benjamina sighed. She longed to get on with the research and development, but she could see their point. It was a good one. "Okay, I concede the issue. Tim, you and I will continue on our undoing modifications process in the afternoons. Annie, as much as you want to help give therapy sessions, right now here in Brom, it would be far too risky for you to reappear right in front of the very people who wrongly blame you for having cut off their arms. If this works out and we start giving therapy sessions to others from other towers and castles, then you can help with those. Meantime, you and Sam will be my test subjects for further experimentations."

"We'll form up a Therapy Team. Eric, Darcy, Dawn, Sally, Rafaela, Andres, you six will be the main therapy givers. Adriana will be your boss, watching over the sessions, helping you if you run into problems and such. Elana and Petrona will be in charge of scheduling the people and keeping accurate records of those who we have helped. From what we have seen, most will be handled in two days at most, though some may be done in one long day. Make sure each one has had enough sleep and food in them so they don't get distracted by hunger or sleep. This is pretty heavy stuff we're doing. I'll arrange for rooms and meals at the tower with Marisol. I'm sure she will be more than willing to provide that for us. With luck, we ought to be able to help at least a dozen to eighteen each week."

"Wow, this will be a least a three month project to get to everyone," Petrona pointed out, rapidly doing the math, which she was very good at. "We should have the Brom area done by mid-December, if we get cracking."

Elana laughed, "By then, Benjamina and I will be too pregnant to do much else." Benjamina smiled lovingly at her.

Already she had a slight bulge, though it didn't show very much unless one knew what he was looking for. They expected to deliver in mid-March, if all went well.

"Hey, at least by the fall council meetings, our people from Brom can spread the word about the tremendous benefits of getting modifications undone and the therapy sessions," Eric pointed out.

Sector ID Minister Emeryk and his Valen wife, Adalina, took the news of the coup in Valen Castle in stride. "My dear, coups are commonplace in the galaxy. Suck up to the new leaders and move on. I know he was your relation, but he's history now. This new guy, Lord Pedro Valen, is now the man in charge. We make the best of it. He's coming to visit me tonight, so we need to give him a warm reception."

"Yes, my love. I will look my best and play the gracious hostess," Adalina promised, keeping back her tears for her own private time.

"That's the spirit. Do you need help getting back to our quarters?"

"No, I'll manage," she replied, turned slowly, and began her long way back to their large suite. In her toe shoes, she could just barely walk. The arm-fetter-gown prevented her from taking too large a step, but it also prevented her from using the stairs. Well, she used the elevators anyway and here at the spaceport so that wasn't a problem for her. The pipe corset gave her an incredible shape. Everywhere she walked, all eyes followed her, much to the admiration of Emeryk, who puffed up in pride when he spotted them doing just that. She also had the new lip plates and had worked hard to make herself understandable. Her long dangling earrings also caught the attention of many of the women around the port. However, she was miserable. She could just barely move and talk, but she thanked her lucky signs for not having her hands removed. Lord Valen had told her not to do that. The Sector ID Minister would find that intolerable and ask too many questions about this fictitious virus.

Now, *all* their plans were nullified, and he was dead. Worse, a head blink cousin ruled in his place. For years, she had been spying for Lord Valen, passing on valuable information to him. Should she do the same for the man who murdered him? She was loathed to do so and promised herself not to do that. *I'll remain quiet about having ever done that. Maybe he doesn't even know about it.*

The only bright spot in her life was now bedtime, when she took her lip plates out. Her hypersensitive lip loops drove her mad with lust. Emeryk knew just how to use them to his advantage. As she rose each morning, she longed for the night once more.

Emeryk pulled up his new listing of potential spies. With Adalina having gone from his office, he felt safe in looking these over. He was determined to figure out what diabolical weapon had completely wiped out two entire armies, six thousand men. This, the Imperium simply had to know about, somehow, someway. His son, Antoni, was married and off somewhere in Valen. He wouldn't do. His daughter, Dorita, was likewise married and expecting again. He couldn't use his own children. Besides, the mission was far too dangerous to risk his and Adalina's children on — no, he needed someone else to infiltrate the Midlands. He scanned the list again.

His eyes lighted on the grandson of an ex-spacer, Pedro del Marco. He was a second generation half breed, the child of the child of one of Exchange City's many prostitutes and a spacer who had long ago left Ashford-5. The man was perfect, having no real loyalty to either side. He sent for Pedro.

Later that day, the tall thin man was escorted into his office. His skin had a slight grey hue, but he easily looked like a native. He was twenty-two and fit, Emeryk noted. He was an excellent judge of men, had to be since he was the Sector ID Minister. "Sit down, Pedro. I have a proposition for you. You've probably heard the rumors that two entire armies of Lord Valen were totally wiped out a few weeks ago just as they entered the Midlands."

"Aye, heard lots of those rumors. I saw one army pass through Exchange City. What of it?" he asked gruffly, wondering why the most powerful alien man had sent for him.

"Someone, something, some incredibly powerful new

weapon did this. Let me show you what is left of those two armies and where they perished." Emeryk brought up his image viewer and showed Pedro the mounds. He played back the geosat time-lapse images of what had happened. "See there. We think those might be the people responsible. See, now they just vanished."

"I want you to travel around those foothills and other places. Find out who did this to the armies and how they did it. If you succeed, I will put twenty thousand credits into your account. If you accept this mission, I'll put a thousand credits in there now for your expenses."

Pedro grinned; this was his lucky day. Twenty thousand credits would buy him almost anything he desired! *Play it cool, man.* In a dry tone, he said, "Might be very dangerous."

"Okay, forty thousand credits and three thousand in expense money," Emeryk bargained.

"Twenty thousand now, whether or not I find the answers you are looking for. If I do, then I get the rest," Pedro countered. *How the hell am I supposed to find this information anyway? I want something for my troubles.*

To his surprise, Emeryk said, "Deal!" He typed a few entries on his computer. "There, your account has twenty-three thousand credits in it. How soon will you be leaving?"

Pedro grinned. "Tomorrow. Soon enough?" It was. He left a wealthy man, whether or not he ever discovered this Intel. Further, he now carried an Imperium Navigator and a Communicator as well. He felt important as he rode his horse out of Exchange City, leading a packhorse behind him, leading southeast.

Following the army trail was so easy he could have done it blindfolded. The passage of so many men, horses, and wagons over the thin soil of the high foothills was unmistakable even after a few weeks. He stopped and examined the mounds in detail and even scouted the surrounding countryside for any possible clues. He found absolutely nothing. Something of immense power had buried the entire army and left no signs. This he found amazing.

All summer he rode through the foothills, stopping at every small hamlet or village, asking them what they might have seen or heard. Nothing. Nothing at all. In mid-August, while in Wycombe, he picked up some rumors that a group called the Underground might have played a role in it, but no one knew anything about them or where they were located. This much he relayed to Emeryk, who felt finally they were getting somewhere.

Chapter 18 Finding Help

As the time for the fall council meetings approached, Inez Valen, just turned fifteen. Misery seemed for follow her. It took all her energy to manage to walk in her toe boots, but she worked at it. She knew she would have to look and walk as an elegant woman, if she ever hoped to get the company back on its feet. She fell countless times. Her waist felt like it was being cut in half. If only she could have had another two inches! A twelve inch waist was torture to endure. With her arms glued to her sides in her arm-fetter-skirt, her neck rings made getting back onto her feet nearly impossible, requiring a huge effort to finally get back up. Her long, heavy earrings pulled hard on her ear lobes, and the lip plates made talking and eating most difficult and challenging. Yet these things could have been endured by the young teen, except for her prosthetic hands, which only just barely worked. Lacking any feeling in them, she constantly banged into what she was trying to pick up. Things continually slipped from her feeble grasp. In her arm-fetter-skirt, pipe corset, neck rings, and toe boots, retrieving something from the floor was nightmare itself. *This is a living hell*, she thought to herself dozens of times each day.

As the summer came, the bright spot lay in the sudden huge demand for the old style, six-inch heels and boots. Here she was lucky; her stores had large supplies of them, unsold and stored in backrooms, after the toe shoes and boots craze struck. Also she was happy about their sales of dresses. While there were still some arm-fetter-gowns being sold, most were regular gowns, again of the styles, which had been popular before the sales fetter gown styles took off. Because of these sales, Elegant Fashions Inc continued to make money, and by the end of summer, she was more than solvent.

Yet Inez had always dreamed of designing her own gowns. Valiantly during the early summer, she tried her best. It took her a half hour with her poorly working prosthetic hands to finally get her drawing pencil properly positioned in her fingers, assuming she didn't drop it, which happened more often than not. As she finally was attempting to draw one line, usually the pencil slipped out of her unfeeling fingers. She gave up entirely attempting to use the charcoal sticks. Her fingers just snapped them in half once she finally managed to pick one up.

She rose early on the morning of the conference at the Imperial Court. Why? It took her ages to get herself dressed and fed. Unable to bend except at her hips, dressing took her hours to accomplish. It would have been shorter too, if she still had her hands and not these insensitive prosthetic ones, which barely worked. Hours after she'd risen, she looked at herself in her full-length mirror, making sure she looked absolutely perfect in her bright red satin arm-fetter-gown. After all her, mother never missed a council meeting. Rather, it was prime selling time; she'd had drilled into her head. Well, just now, she needed all the sales she could get. "I look perfect at last," she told her image.

She took a deep breath, rather a shallow one actually, and began turning, ready to face the hideously long and treacherous walk from her office on the fourth floor, down the one block to the Imperial Castle, and from there into the huge throne room. She estimated she had to walk close to eight hundred feet, maybe more. That meant taking over five thousand tiny steps. With each one, she had to use extreme care to keep her balance, all the while being seen to be walking with grace, as if this were nothing at all. She began her hour-long walk to the meeting, hoping she would not get there too late.

Once outside the Imperium Admin building, the winds were a little on the strong side today, blowing her nicely brushed hair about, often flying in front of her face. With her upper arms pinned at her side in her gown's sleeves and unable to bend at all, she mostly had to stop and wait until the wind blew it out of her face before taking another tiny step.

She finally entered the Imperial Castle, but the meeting had already begun. Hundreds of steps later, she entered at the back of the packed room and stood looking about. She recognized only a few people! A whole new set of lord and ladies were present! Worse, all were head blind! As she looked at the women, she saw they were wearing a mix of the old style gowns and the arm-gowns out of deference to the empress. The women wore the old style heels as well.

Finally, she saw a few *mentales* gifted, who she recognized, though none seemed to remember her. Well, that was likely; she'd only been fourteen at the last council and had not really been introduced by her mother, who guarded her daughter. Now she was shocked. The only woman in the room wearing toe shoes was herself. The only woman who wore the lip plates was herself. All wore the old style heels; even the *mentales* gifted men wore the women's old style heels! No one had neck rings on excepting herself! She took a tiny relief in that many women still had the extremely long and dangling earrings as she wore. As she looked even closer, she also realized none now wore the pipe corsets either, excepting herself. Inez stood there utterly shocked. What had happened? Her whole world was turned upside down!

As she stood there petrified, a *mentales* gifted woman, who she vaguely recognized as having come from Wycombe, walked up to her. "Oh dear child! You haven't gotten your modifications undone yet? Why your mother should be ashamed of herself! Everyone has now. If you continue to wear all those things, life is simply unbearable, you poor dear child! Most everything can be undone, excepting our feet. We all have to wear these old style heels we used to wear, even the men. Still life is so much easier now. Oh dear! Your hands! Why haven't you gotten the new replacement hands like mine? These work ever so much better than those awful ones we were given. Haven't you heard about all these things?"

Inez finally found her voice. "No my lady. I've been out of touch. Where do you get the hands? Where do you get these things undone? Surely not at the Elegant Fashions Inc."

"Oh certainly not there! They have no idea how to undo what they did to us. No, the kind folks in Brom Castle are handling it for us. They handed out the replacement hands months ago to everyone. I guess they somehow missed you. After that, they began taking eighteen of us at a time, using our circles or theirs to teleport us to Brom Castle, where very kind woman and man operated special machines that undid the changes, at least as much as is possible for us. It was all done free of charge. My dear, you simply *must* get yourself to Brom Castle and get *out* of all these things and get the new hands. Trust me, life will be ever so much better for you once you do."

"Thank you, my lady. I will do it as soon as I can." Inez thanked her. Still stunned and petrified, Inez turned and headed back out of the doors, thankful no one had recognized her!

She found herself facing the wind, which blew her long black hair out behind her. However, the added air resistance made walking even more difficult. Plus now, she was going slightly downhill, vastly more treacherous in her toe shoes. Several times, she very nearly lost her balance, wobbling like mad to keep from taking a spill on the street. She noticed many other people going about their business, but they all stopped to stare at her. She felt like some hideous freak!

An hour later, she finally entered her office, home at last. Her feet throbbed; she longed to get off them; her hair, a wind-blown mess, which with her pathetic hands, would take her hours to brush out. She did neither. She stood and bawled, crying her heart out! Ruined utterly. She fell, but managed to keep from smashing her lip plates into the floor. There she lay, sobbing uncontrollably.

Hours later, with a great effort, she at last got to her feet and walked to her bedroom to change her dress, if only to free her arms. Then she headed to her small kitchen to make some tea. A half hour later, she sat down with her spoon and teacup. After ten tries, she got the spoon between her fingers. After three spills, she finally got a teaspoon of the tea into her mouth. She cried again as she realized none of the others now faced this awful nightmare, only she! She was the last tortured woman in the world.

"Somehow I have to get to Brom Castle. It's more than a thousand miles north of here! How am I going to get there? I can't ask the Imperial Circle to teleport me, the circle has been abandoned now; the emperor doesn't need them any longer. He's a mere puppet of the lords. I can't ask Valen Tower; they all hate me and mom. Maybe I can get a carriage to take me there. Wait, that would take weeks of traveling! I can't get in or out of a carriage on my own, and we'd waste hours while I get dressed each day. I am doomed." She broke down crying again.

Mid-afternoon one of her head blind assistants came in. "Miss Inez, Miss Inez?"

Quickly Inez pulled herself together. "Yes, Mary, what is it? I am in the kitchen." Shortly the nicely dressed middle-aged woman walked in.

"Oh here you are. Yes, well, a young man, who says he is from up around the Brom area, has brought in a wagon load of pod silk and wants to sell it to us. I know we are tight on funds, so I thought it best if you inspect the goods and see if you want to pay him for his load."

"Yes, I should. Please assist me in getting down to the wagon." *Brom! The magic word. I wonder if he is returning there? Maybe I could pay him to take me there!*

Walking with a steadying arm around her made all the difference. She made far better time this way, although it was still pathetically slow going. At last, they stepped into the basement, where she saw a wagon loaded with pod-silk. A tall lad stood near it smoking a pipe, quite bored. He wore trail-worn, heavy pants and the usual tall boots. His shirt was white cotton and a bit dirty. He definitely needs a bath, she thought as they moved slowly towards him. As he spotted Mary, he quickly tapped out his pipe and stood front and center before his wagon, ready to make his sales pitch.

"This is my boss, Inez," Mary said. "She does all the buying, son." She purposely always refrained from mentioning her last name. Valen was now akin to a cuss word and synonymous with the devil.

"Hello Inez. Wow! You look," he paused as his eyes moved from her face down to her feet and back, "er, well different. Haven't you gotten fixed up like all the others have? I guess not, obvious. Duh me. I'm sorry. I've come from up by Brom with a year's worth of pod-silk. I have heard you pay top silver for it and to be honest, ma'am, I do need the silver."

"Well, let's see the silk, shall we?" Inez replied slowly, making sure he understood her. *At least he isn't head blind. It could be worse I suppose. He looks like a country fellow.* With

Mary's arm still supporting her, she moved slowly over to the wagon. With her upper arms still held tightly to her sides, she couldn't possibly reach up and into its bed to sample it. Thankfully, with her free hand, Mary began bringing up random samples for Inez to see. Mary was thorough and examined samples from various locations.

"Okay. Say, I didn't get your name," Inez suddenly realized.

"Peter Franks, but you can call me Pete, everyone does. Forgetful Pete, that's my nickname, because I keep forgetting things. All the time. Have you ever done that — forget things? Anyway, what do you think of the load?"

"How does a hundred silver sound for the load?" Inez replied. The load was at least average quality and worth at least that much.

"Deal!" he replied cheering up considerably. He offered her his hand to shake to seal the purchase. She raised her prosthetic right hand and he looked rather embarrassed. He touched it gently and hesitantly, as if he might somehow break it.

"Unhitch your wagon and come on up to the fourth floor. We'll get your silver ready. Tomorrow, the wagon will be unloaded and ready for you to pick up."

"Thank you ma'am," he replied and set to work unhitching his two horses.

"Have you a place to stay tonight?" Inez stopped and slowly turned around to face him again.

"Well, not exactly, ma'am."

"Okay then, you can stable your horses in one of those stalls. I've a guest room where you can stay the night. The inns are pretty full; it's council time," Inez explained.

"Thank you, ma'am!" the lad replied very much relieved. She guessed he had probably planned to sleep in some alleyway. She again had to take a few steps to turn back to see where she needed to go, inwardly again cursing the neck rings which held her head immobile.

She and Mary had just set foot inside her fourth floor office, when Pete came out of the elevator. Inez cringed. Was she really this slow? He'd taken care of his team and got here while all she'd been able to do was get this far. She was torn between wanting Mary to help her walk to her private quarters and to go count his silver for him, showing him to their guest room. She decided the latter would be least embarrassing. "Mary, please take Pete to the money room and get him his silver, and then show him to our guest room."

"You sure you can make it to your room?" she whispered, a little concerned about her boss. Inez said she was and felt her security blanket, Mary's strong arm, abandoning her. For a moment she wanted to call out to Mary and cancel what she had just said, but didn't. *Even if he is a country bumpkin, I must look elegant for him.* She continued her slow walk, taking much smaller steps, being exceedingly careful of each one.

She had covered half the distance to her quarters, when Mary returned, having paid the lad and shown him the guest suite. "Didn't think you'd be there yet," the observant Mary said softly, slipping her hand around her boss' waist, being careful not to catch any of her lush black hair. Though horribly disheveled from the wind earlier, it still fell to her calves, one of the few things of which she was any longer proud.

Once she was finally seated on her couch, she said, "Will you ask Pete to come here for a minute? I want to ask him something." She agreed and a couple minutes later a cleaned up Pete joined her. "Thanks, Mary. That will be all for now. You've been a big help as always." Again she said it slowly and made sure Mary understood her.

Alone with this stranger, Inez decided to risk everything on him. "Pete, I need to get to Brom Castle so I can get myself fixed up. Are you returning to that area tomorrow?"

"Sure am, Miss Inez. Why? I can see why you would want to get fixed up. I don't see how you can stand all this," he said sincerely.

"I can't stand it. Pete, can you take me to Brom Castle? I will pay you well if you do." There, she'd asked it. For all she knew, he would rape her endlessly, maybe kidnap her, and take her home with him as some kind of sex doll. She was helpless to prevent it, but she was now desperate to get to Brom Castle someway.

"Sure I can take you, Inez, but I've only got a open wagon. I camp out each night. It's fall now and a whole lot cheaper that way. My wagon isn't fit for you. You are like a queen or something."

"I don't care about that. If it is good enough to get me to Brom Castle, that's all I care about, but you'll have to give me a lot of help. I'll pay you for it, because I can do almost nothing on my own. Please, Pete, take me to Brom Castle."

"Anything you say, Miss Inez. We'll need extra food and a lot of blankets. Your clothes are not any good for the trail."

"I will try to wear something better. How long will it take us to get there?"

"About a month, I suppose. I kind of forgot how long it took to get here. I do that a lot, forget things, but I told you that already, didn't I? I hope you don't mind company on the way. I came with a band of a dozen of the Sisterhood fighters who were bringing a load of leather and furs here. Paid them extra to allow me to tag along with them, and they would protect me if trouble came. Of course no one ever messes with the Sisterhood fighters."

"No, that would be great to be traveling in their safety. That's good news, Pete. Good thinking on your part. Would a thousand silvers be enough for you to take me there and help me with everything?" she asked.

"A thousand silver? That's way too much, Miss Inez!" His eyes nearly popped out of his head.

"No, it is reasonable, Pete. You are going to have to help me with everything. You'll see."

"Okay then. In the morning, I'll go get the extra supplies and make sure I know when the Sisterhood women are going to leave. Then I'll come back and let you know." He walked back to his suite, skipping every few steps and repeating, "A thousand silvers! Whoopee!" She smiled, but it was invisible, of course.

Two excruciating hours later, she finally was undressed. Inez knew nearly all her clothes would be wholly inappropriate for the trip. Hence she began searching through all her drawers, looking for anything that might be partly reasonable. Looking was also challenging. Besides just getting into

303

position before the drawer, she then had to bend carefully at her knees without losing her balance, until she'd lowered her rigid body enough so her eyes could look into the drawer. Next while in this precarious position, she had to get her fingers on the knobs and pull the drawer out, all without falling over and without pulling her hands off. Both she did five times, landing hard on her butt.

Two hours later and long after full dark, she finally had laid out three old style dresses, one blouse and one pair of pants that still fit her. A quarter of an hour later, she reached her bed and had her brush beside her as she sat down at last on its edge. She proceeded to do her hair, following her nightly ritual, knowing another two hours would pass before she could lie down to sleep. Dozens of times, the brush slipped out of her unfeeling hands, causing her to go through very awkward and precarious motions to retrieve it from the floor. Even retrieving it took several tries before she successfully picked it up. To say her life was frustrating would be a gross understatement. Wholly miserable, but maybe in Brom Castle, she could beg for relief from this hideous torture which never seemed to end.

When Mary found out about her plans in the morning, she tried everything she could to talk her boss out of this wild, crazy idea. In the end, she failed. Inez was adamant about it. "Until I get back, if I ever do, the store is yours to run." That appeased Mary, who then prepared the large bag of silver for Pete.

"Now help me get into the blouse and pants, if they will still fit me well enough. If they don't, there are three gowns there that will." The pants didn't fit, nor did the blouse, which she'd not worn since she was ten. Mary got her dressed in one of the old style, red satin gowns and packed the other two along with her hairbrush and other smaller personal items into a large bag for her. Then she fixed the two a light breakfast and watched as Inez struggled mightily to actually eat it with her crude hands. She didn't offer to help, knowing Inez didn't want help with that unless she asked. She'd gotten chewed out before when she tried to feed her.

Pete came by around noon. "Hi Miss Inez, Miss Mary.

Sisterhood will be leaving in an hour. I have enough food and supplies for us, but we have to hurry up. They won't wait for us."

After hugging Mary, Inez had Pete put his arm around her waist, and they began walking. After a few steps, Pete said, "I'm sorry, Miss Inez. At this rate they will leave without us. May I carry you to the wagon?"

"I think that is best if you can lift me." Inez felt humiliated as he lifted her up and began carrying her swiftly across her office and towards the elevator. She was once the height of fashion; everyone looked to her and Nita as *the* elegant fashion models. Now she was hardly more than a sack of potatoes. Still she swallowed her pride. She was ready to endure anything to get to Brom Castle.

He sat her up on the driver's seat. The rear was now filled with blankets, camping supplies, and a lot of food and cooking gear. Well constrained as she was to perfect posture, sitting up front would be best, she thought. Pete hopped up beside her, and the wagon began rolling out of the underground parking area. The noon sun struck her face, warming her cheeks. The fresh air felt good, what little she could breathe in. Before long, three other wagons pulled in around theirs, along with a half-dozen women riders.

"Ama, are you sure you want to travel all the way to Brom Castle in this wagon?" one of the Sisterhood women asked her, as she drew up beside her. Inez had to use her feet to turn her body enough to see the woman fighter.

"Yes, I am sure. I will make it somehow with Pete's help," Inez said slowly and bravely.

"But we are camping out under the stars and rain. That's no way for an elegant woman like yourself to have to travel. Besides, it might snow on us."

"I have to get to Brom Castle."

"Okay then. I hope you know what you are doing. Once we leave town, there's no turning back. If Pete here treats you badly, you just holler out, and we'll jump all over him. Pete, you treat the Ama here with respect or I'll slit your throat myself!"

Pete gulped and his voice croaked a little. "I won't

mistreat her, Ellen."

"You better not. Okay, we've tallied too long. Let's get this show on the road." Ellen kicked her horse and took the point position.

Inez adjusted her long hair, draping it across her left shoulder down across her body and over her right side. It fell to her feet while sitting, and this way the wind would not blow it around too badly. Ordinary people were on the streets, many hawking wares. Children scampered about playing what looked like tag to her. Everyone seemed so happy to her, but then she was anything but that. Sitting erect with perfect posture like some golden doll, Inez was miserable. She focused her mind on the hope Brom Castle might bring her. Then the last stone house of Exchange City passed by, and the wagon rolled out onto a simple well-traveled, dirt track. Craggy stones thrust themselves upward, as if some giant underground hand had cleaned house. Resinous pines dug their gnarled roots into any available crevice, threatening to crack the stones even more. A deer darted across their path just in front of Ellen. Inez felt a surge of panic; she'd never been out of Exchange City before!

"So what's it like out here in the wilds? I've never been out of the city before?" she asked, having used her toes to turn her body slightly to the left so her eyes could just barely see Peter Franks.

"You're teasing me, right?"

"No, honestly I haven't." Pete turned and looked at her in disbelief. How could anyone have lived their whole life in Exchange City?

"Well, it's beautiful and deadly. I like the trees, flowers, grasses. Plants are what interest me the most. Did you know that one there," he pointed to a rather ugly weed off to the side of the track, "makes the best yellow dye? Like a canary bird. With those over there, why you can make a gorgeous, rich brown. I like the smell of the outdoors. Of course, there are always bandits around, plus you have to be alert for bears, wolves, and those giant cats, but they don't tend to bother us humans much. The cats prefer our horses. Then of course, you always have to pay attention to the weather, but not so much in the summer. Winters are deadly, you see, because you can easily get caught out in the open in a blizzard and freeze to death and not be found until the spring thaw. It is fall now, so we might get some snow, more than likely as we get closer to Brom. We just have to be alert for flash flooding, if we get a whole lot of rain. Probably won't this time of year, it's fall. Now it will get chilly at night, mind you, and probably snow some, so I brought you plenty of blankets, but it won't be like lying in your fancy beds you have at the store."

"I see. So Pete, where do you live? Have you got a mother?" she asked, then realized this was a silly question. Everyone had a mother. Well she didn't; hers had more or less abandoned her. She had given her the entire Elegant Fashions Inc, but had not told her it was bankrupt.

"Folks have a nut tree farm south of Brom. We harvest the pods too, making use of all the land provides. Mom, dad, three older brothers and an older sister and two younger sisters. Oldest brother is married and they have a baby. Everyone helps around the farm, but honestly, Inez, I got really bored there. I wanted to see more of the world. I like people but we don't see hardly any on our farm. I do get to go into Brom, especially for the dances. I look forward to them, so many people — girls all dressed up looking really pretty." He flushed, "Er, no offense Miss Inez." She smiled but it was invisible.

He rambled on, "Dad knows I am not really happy working the nut farm. That's why he let me bring this year's load of pod-silk to Exchange City. 'See the world son, then you'll be back, you'll see.' Well, the more I've seen, the less I want to go back there. To be honest, Miss Inez, there is so much of the world out here to see. But then, there are also so many bandits too and I am not much of a fighter. That's why I jumped at the chance to travel with the Sisterhood women. Now they know how to fight, and they have trail sense, which of course I don't. They've been showing me the ropes on the trip down here. Between you and me, I think they all have been badly mistreated by men at one time or other in their lives. Still they haven't taken it out on me. I think everyone ought to just be happy and enjoy life and others."

"I'm supposed to be a nut tree farmer, but honestly Miss Inez, I hate it. I want to do something more for people. After seeing all the girls looking so pretty in their fancy gowns and the guys looking smart in their suits, I kind of want to maybe be a tailor or something, but I can't. I would have to become an apprentice somewhere, and I haven't got the money for that. Well, maybe I do now, after I get you to Brom Castle. Have to see. I think it would be rewarding to make clothes make people feel really good about themselves, don't you think Miss Inez?"

"Yes, I do or did."

"So where's your parents? I bet you were a really pretty girl before you got all modified up there like you are now." Pete suddenly realized his gaff; his face turned red as a beet. "I don't mean to say you aren't pretty like you are, Miss Inez. I've heard your look is supposed to be the latest fashion." His embarrassment grew, and he didn't wait for her reply. "Can you tell me why all the lords and ladies had their hands cut off and got those strange looking alien hands? I'm just a farm lad, really, and we never knew why they all did that." He relaxed a little; at least maybe he'd learn the reason. His whole family had spent many evenings pondering this mystery. They had seen all the fancy lords and ladies looking much like Inez did at the spring dance, but then they were also talking about a war that was coming.

She decided to try to explain it all. "I always wanted to be a teen fashion model, you know, help show all us young girls how we can look our very best. Mom said I was very pretty, and I did everything she told me to do." A tear formed and she tried to wipe it with her hand, but her unfeeling hand bumped her eye rather hard in doing so, caused more tears. "It's all so crazy. Last spring, I was the teen fashion model. I looked like I do now, only I was wearing the latest arm-fetter-gowns then. Everyone looked at me as if I were the young goddess of fashion. I loved all the attention I got. Everyone was trying to look just like me. Now today, I haven't changed at all, but everyone has suddenly gone back to the older fashion styles, everyone but me. I feel totally out of place. Now they look at me as if I was some kind of freak. Even you think I am an ugly freak."

"No, Miss Inez, I didn't say that. You are still very pretty underneath all that stuff."

She didn't believe him, but continued her admissions, "I don't have a dad. I don't know who he was; mom never told me. She said it was none of my business and that he wasn't important. The last few years, mom kept inventing all these new fashions. Most were in keeping with what the empress wanted. She's an Easterlings bound woman, you see. The empress said we Midlands women needed to compromise, so mom invented the fetter-gowns first and then the really popular arm-fetter-gowns, like the one I was wearing when I met you. Last spring, every lady who was anything was wearing them, just like me."

"As far as the hands go, there was supposed to be this really awful virus that struck we *mentales* gifted. It infected our hands and necks. If left untreated, we would die in three days! That's why they had to cut off our hands so we either wouldn't get it, as in my case, or to save someone's life if they got it. Mom went to huge expense to get the machines from the aliens to do this for everyone, and then she spent a fortune getting us these alien hands so we wouldn't be completely helpless. Still, she and I, we continued to do our very best to look our best and to help all women and men look their best too. Even this spring, every teen still looked at me as their role model, copying all my fancy gowns. Now this fall, somehow that is all gone. Everyone looks at me as if I was a freak, and they've all gone back to the old style things. I don't know what happened or why I am now a freak. What did I do wrong? I did my very best to look my best at all times. I never complained. I always kept a smile on my face, well until these lip plates. You can't see me smile now though. I can hardly be understood either. For the life of me, I can't figure out what I did that was so terribly wrong, but I must have."

"Then this summer mom took off and left me. Well, I can understand; she was pregnant and going to have another baby. I think she wanted to have it in some quiet place, but I can't find her now. She won't answer my telepathic attempts at communication. No one knows where she's gone. What have I done to mom that she so disowns me? I am really lost, Pete, and scared and wholly on my own. Pete, I am so utterly helpless like this. Mom, she always helped me with everything, and now I'm on my own, I can't do it. These hands are next to useless. I can't feel anything. I can hardly pick up a fork, let alone a pencil to draw out new dress designs for everyone. I can't walk much at all; you've seen that. I can't move my head, can't bend. It takes me hours to get dressed or undressed. This is a living torture, Pete, and I can't take it any longer. That's why I have to get to Brom. I heard they can get me out of this somehow. If they can't, then I don't want to live anymore."

"Oh Miss Inez, don't say that! I think you are still very pretty, even if you can't get out of all this stuff. You just need someone to help look after you. How about your boyfriend? I bet you have a lot of boys there in Exchange City who would love to help you with things. Probably lots of girlfriends too. If they can't fix you up there in Brom, you should go back and let your boyfriends and girlfriends help you some."

Inez giggled. "I don't have any, Pete. No girlfriends, no boyfriends. It's just been mom and me, and, of course, those who work in our store. I never go out of the store much at all, only once or twice. Mostly I would get out when we both went to the councils at the Imperial Castle. I've got no one to help me, Pete. I spend half of my day just getting dressed, undressed, my hair brushed, and so on. I am totally pathetic, I know. So if they can't help me in Brom, then I just don't want to live anymore."

"Oh Miss Inez. Don't say that! Look, if they can't help you in Brom, then I'll look after you, only you'll have to tell me what to do. I think you are the prettiest girl I've ever seen, so I'd be honored to help you."

"Thank you, Pete. You're going to have to do just that until we get to Brom. By then, I'm sure you'll change your mind about me. I'm so totally helpless and useless it's not even funny."

"We'll see, Miss Inez. Aren't the fall colors just beautiful here? I sure do love what the plant world does for us all. Incredible, isn't it?" He decided to try to get her attention onto the world around them. He had no idea what else he could say or do for her.

Inez looked about her at the fall foliage for the first time and really saw them. Her attention slowly moved off her own nightmare physical self to the greater world around her. She'd never been out among the world before, only looking at the distant trees from the windows in her office building. Inez was impressed. She started asking questions. "Pete, what kind of tree is that orange one over there? That yellow one? Why is that one red and that one orange?" Pete happily chatted about his favorite things, the plant world.

Later a light drizzle began to fall, and Pete put an oiled cloak over Inez, covering her head with its hood. "So that's why they are oiled!" Inez watched as the water beaded off her cloak.

"Yes, the oil repels the water, mostly, so you stay relatively dry. It'll likely be freezing by nightfall. Might have some light snow, but it won't stick. Too warm for that yet. It's only September, you see. She didn't, but took his word for it.

Near dark, Ellen pulled them into a secluded glen for the night. Pete pulled his wagon a little apart from the Sisterhood wagons, explaining, "They prefer men to stay well away from them. Remember, men have done bad things to them." Pete then lifted her down from the wagon, and now Inez confronted trying to walk over rough, uneven ground. She panicked utterly, wobbling like a slow spinning top about to fall, but Pete was there with his arms.

Gasping for air, she said, "Don't let go of me. I can't walk by myself." He helped her sit down, her back against a pine.

"You sit there while I make camp." He began to move stones to make a fire pit.

Ellen walked over to him. Inez noticed she was wearing a man's outfit, except for her heavy cotton blouse and vest. Nothing could hide women's huge bosoms. She too wore an oiled cloak over her. "Pete, I suppose you would like to share our meals again?"

"Er, yes, Ellen. I've brought along a whole lot of supplies to donate and help out, please." He seemed rather propitiative, Inez thought.

"I figured. Men!" she said, looking at Inez with a rather disgusted look. "Men sure don't know how to cook. I think all men would starve to death if we women didn't cook for them. Perhaps that would not be a bad thing, eh?" she teased, but Inez couldn't tell if she meant it or was joking. "Bertha?" she called out. A plump woman came over, picking her way carefully across the rocky ground. "Pete and the Ama here will be sharing our meals. He claims he brought food. Go see what he has and take what you think might be edible."

She laughed roundly and walked to the wagon with Pete scampering ahead of her. "Here you go. I tried to get a goodly amount this time, Miss Bertha."

"Lands sakes, Ellen, the lad really did this time! Sisters, we are in for some real trail food this trip back! Thanks son," Bertha replied, pulling out several large sacks. "Mind if we take these?"

"Not at all. You know how to cook, not me," Pete grinned. She handed some to Ellen, who finally smiled, looking impressed as well.

"My cooking is awful," he explained.

"I cook very well, that is, I used to before I lost my hands. Now it takes me an hour to peel a potato, so I don't have them anymore. I usually spend about two hours fixing supper. It is almost impossible for me to manage it," Inez admitted.

"I can see why. That's why you need me to help you, Miss Inez. Don't worry. Pete will always be here to help out." He headed off to build a campfire. The Sisterhood women already had theirs blazing. After that, Pete got their beds laid out beneath their wagon and his two horses handled, before one of the Sisterhood women brought over two plates of steaming food. Pete sat down beside Inez and took both plates. "Thanks, smells delicious." The woman finally flashed the briefest of smiles and walked back.

Inez felt another rush of panic. How could she hold the plate without spilling it? Could she even manage to use the fork without dropping it in the dirt and pine needles? "Okay Miss Inez. I'll feed you. These plates are tricky to balance. I've never done this before, but it can't be too hard. Open up. Gosh, it is tricky getting between your two plates." Inez wanted to cry again. She felt not only helpless but almost like a baby being fed by its mother. Still, her hunger drove her to eat and she did. "Say, this is good. See, I did the right thing by letting Bertha cook for us," he whispered. She finally was able to whisper a thank you to Pete without crying.

Later the same woman brought them two mugs of steaming strong black tea, laced with honey and took their empty plates back with her. Again Inez felt a surge of panic, swallowing hard, she whispered, "I can't drink without a spoon." He sat the cups down and found one in the wagon.

"Sorry, Miss Inez. I didn't think about that. Here we go." As they sat back and sipped or spooned their tea, the light drizzle changed to sleet. Now comes the impossible things, Inez thought, how am I going to manage sleeping out here?

Pete helped her over to their wagon, his arms holding her tightly as she wobbled along, not even able to see her feet, but rather feeling her way along with two-inch steps. Soon she realized Pete was not going to let her fall no matter how badly she lost her balance, and Inez relaxed a little. At the wagon, she now had to face how she could get beneath it. With Pete holding her, she bent her knees and lowered herself down. "I can't bend, Pete," she said panicking again.

"Relax, Miss Inez. I see the problem. I'm going to lift you down and under." He lifted her up, but she lay flat as a board across his arms. She pulled up her hair armful by armful until she had it all on her chest. Then, he knelt down and laid her on the bedroll. He crawled in beside her and began covering them up with a large number of blankets. "There you go, snug as a bug in a rug, as my mother always told me. If you get cold, let me know. Got more blankets."

"Thank you Pete."

"Best we sort of snuggle up to keep each other warm," he suggested, and she did just that, getting as close as she could.

In the morning, once Pete had her up, two of the Sisterhood women came over to help her use their latrine for which she was extremely grateful. Then Pete fed her breakfast and lifted her up onto the wagon once more. They broke camp as the orange-red sun rose, melting the light dusting of snow. Before long the day began to warm up and the brilliant fall colors again dominated the scenery.

Slowly a week passed. Pete and Inez continued chatting the long hours away, sharing more and more of their lives with each other. She finally relaxed completely. She was almost totally unable to do anything except sit and talk with him, but now she was comfortable with his constant assistance with nearly everything, though the women insisted on helping her with her personal needs, for which she was continually grateful. Inez found she cared for this young man, who could be really handsome, she thought, if he cleaned up and put on one of her company's elegant suits. As they rolled slowly along, Inez looked at Pete and realized she was falling in love with the teen. Pete, for his part, greatly admired this young woman. She had an enormous spirit, he'd concluded, enduring all this without a complaint. Did she like him, he wondered? Ought he make the first move and kiss her? If so, how did he kiss her with those huge lip plates? She picked up his thoughts and blushed.

That evening while they were snuggling beneath the wagon as a light snow began to blanket their campsite, Inez took the initiative. She wiggled a bunch, got to her side, and pressed her lips against his cheek. "That's the best I can do without taking the plates out," she whispered, thankful the dark prevented him from seeing her blush. He returned her kiss, feeling for her cheeks and using that to guide him. She felt electrified as his lips touched hers, and wished she could take her plates out and kiss him properly, but that was out. It would take her clumsy hands at least a half hour or more in a lighted room to accomplish that, wholly impossible in the dark with the unfeeling hands. Against the odds, the two had fallen in love with each other.

"No matter whether or not you can get fixed up in Brom, I will always be here to take care of you," he whispered. She knew he meant it, and she also knew how desperately she wanted that security!

Late the next day, they approached the ruins at Bettingham. Suddenly Ellen raised her hand, calling an unexpected halt. Her five guards moved up and rapidly dismounted, drawing their swords, forming a V defense line. "What's happening?" Inez whispered. Pete pulled back on his reins stopping the wagon. Behind him, the other Sisterhood wagons did the same, and several also jumped out, taking up defensive positions along side of the wagons.

Just then, a dozen riders moved out of the nearby rocks and pines, swords drawn. "Damn, Sisterhood wagons!" their leader called out moving closer to the women and looking at the two on the first wagon behind them.

"We are not looking for a fight, but we will give you one if you press us," Ellen said quite gutturally. She whipped her horse around, drawing within striking distance of the leader. The men were ruff, their clothing dirty, yielding the obvious conclusion they were bandits looking for prey, easy prey.

Pete looked very anxious. Inez could just see him from the corner of her eyes. Once more, panic swelled up within her stomach; she fought to catch her breath, as the bandit leader stared at her. *Why is he looking at me like that?*

"Hey, I recognize that one," the bandit leader called out very loudly. "She's the traitor's daughter! Traitor Nita Valen's daughter! What the *hell* do you Sisterhood women think you are doing by bringing the traitor's daughter up *here*! Nita's got a *huge* price on her head!" His voice had gone up almost an octave, as he screamed out this tirade of hate and utter disgust.

"What?" yelled Ellen at Inez, almost as loudly. She pointed her sword at Inez, "You — are you that bitch of a traitor Nita's daughter? Don't lie to me, woman!"

Inez's panic swamped her. She wanted to nod, but couldn't. All that she could do was say softly, "Yes, but. . ." She got cut off.

"Damn you bitch! Pete, did you know she was that filthy bitch's daughter? Out with it!" Ellen demanded angrily. Blood vessels in her neck swelled and throbbed.

"No, ma'am, she is just a teen," Pete stood up for Inez. "She didn't hurt anybody."

"Damn!" Ellen swore again, but sheathed her sword. As she did so, her fellow Sisterhood fighters followed suit, giving the bandit leader an unmistakable signal these women didn't know her identity, would not continue to allow her to travel with them, and most importantly, didn't care what the bandit leader would be doing next to the most hated woman in the Midlands' daughter. Silently Ellen flashed a hand signal and her women mounted up or climbed back onto their wagons. Without a word, Ellen led the Sisterhood party on down the track, leaving the lone wagon still parked there as the dozen bandits moved in around them.

"Your bitch of a mother cut off the hands of hundreds and hundreds of our best men, women, and children. We'll hold you and make her come out of hiding and accept her just punishment. If not, we'll torture you instead. Bring them, men," he called out.

The steadily growing waves of panic crescendoed. Inez simply couldn't breathe. Just as she passed out, she saw Pete trying to defend them with his sword. As her eyes closed, she saw him go down beside her, wounded or dead, she didn't know. All went dark.

She came to sitting on a crude chair in a rough-hewn, one room, log cabin. A fire was crackling in the hearth. She raised her hands to rub her face and panic again struck her. Her alien prosthetic hands were gone; she was staring at her conical stubs. She gasped as her lungs met the unyielding steel of her pipe corset, once again restricting her desperate attempt to breathe. Using her feet, she turned a little to her left. There was a crude bed of sorts, and Pete was lying there. Even from this distance, she could see he was bleeding from a wound on his left shoulder. Someone had put a crude bandage on it, but blood soaked it fully. He was unconscious.

The door opened and a flurry of falling snow came inside, along with a blast of cold air and the bandit leader. Stomping the snow off his boots, he walked over to her. "Well, daughter's bitch, you are now our bitch, our play toy. You damn well better hope and pray your traitorous mother comes to rescue you. If not, you will be our play toy for the rest of your life." He laughed wickedly. "Now then, fire's going. You go cook us our supper."

"But my hands?"

"Oh, I forgot to tell you, I put them in the fire. You don't need hands, not really. Why that's what your mother decided — none of the *mentales* gifted really needs hands. She cut them all off. Did that to my sister, may she rest in peace. So you don't need hands either. Cook our meal, bitch. If not, my men will rape you until you are raw. Hell, we might even do that anyway if it snows too much." He laughed loudly.

"You are now our housekeeper. If you don't do your duties as our housekeeper, then we'll make some more body modifications on you of our own, starting with your eyes. If you don't do your housework around here, then you obviously don't need your eyes anymore. Get the idea woman? Now get your ass up and make us some supper. Oh, your driver over there don't look so good. You might want to change his bandages. Then again, you might just let him die; he's just a country lad anyway. I'll be back later to get the supper. If you want to keep your eyes, you'll have it ready for me when I get back." He turned and left; a blast of cold air again struck her.

Sobbing, Inez got carefully to her feet. Pete's life was now more important than her own, which was soon to end horribly. *Mary was right. I should never have come on such a foolish trip!* She sighed. *But then, I wouldn't have met Pete. I have to try to save him, nothing else matters now.* She used her feet to turn herself in the right direction and began taking her two-inch steps over to the bed where he lay on his back. *I used to be able to heal with my hands!* She looked down at her stumps; those days were long gone now. She carefully bent her knees until she could touch him. Gently with her right stump, she touched his neck above the wound. *Sword wound. Deep cut.* Slowly her gifts started to return to her. She knew what the wound was, and furthermore she knew if she did nothing, he would die from it, albeit slowly. Instinctively her crystal activated. *I have to try something.* She focused and began to perceive the sliced artery and veins. Without thinking, she began slowly to mend the artery's walls, pulling nearby particles and putting them into place. With the artery repaired, she turned her psi skills onto the veins, which she was able to repair more quickly. *There, he won't die at least.* Ordinarily, she would next cleanse the wound and then heal the flesh. However, the bandit's words came back to her again. Reluctantly she rose carefully. If she survived longer, she'd come back and finish healing him.

Slowly and carefully, Inez shuffled over to the crude cooking area next to the fire that was crackling still. She looked into it and saw the weird bits of metal and wires that had been her prosthetic hands. He hadn't lied to her about them, so she reasoned he probably wasn't lying about blinding her if she didn't do as asked. Inez looked at the table, a rough-hewn series of boards held against the outer wall by a support. On it, she saw some of the food supplies Pete had brought along which Bertha hadn't yet used, along with one large pot. She moved over and looked into the pot. It was filled with water. At least he'd done that much for her. She had no idea where the source of water was here. So far, she'd not seen any pipes or wells. About the only thing she could think of making was a stew.

Using her stumps, she began fiddling with the sacks, finding dried beans, lentils, a few potatoes, and dried meat. Fumbling with her stumps, she worked to get the bags open and some of each out and then into the pot. She ignored those that slipped out of her stumps and fell to the floor. Finally, she had enough bits in the pot and began to figure out a way to get it over to the fireplace. She turned on her feet and studied the fireplace. She was in luck. There was an iron cooking hook on a swivel. She moved over to it and pushed it outward into the room, then went back to the pot. She stuck her arms through the metal loop. Cradling it between her elbows, she tried to lift it. It took all her strength to do so and with sliding steps, she moved it slowly over to the metal arm. Bending carefully at her knees, she got it onto the arm. Then her knees gave out and she fell awkwardly onto the floor. After a lengthy struggle, she used a foot to push the arm and pot into the fireplace where it could slowly simmer. Another fifteen minutes passed as she fought to get back onto her feet. Her mind was numb.

Panting and gasping for air, she just stood there for a time. Then she remembered Pete and made her way back to his bedside. *If nothing else, I am going to get him healed up before they blind me or hurt me worse!* She sat back down,

318

focused, and began to work again. All her healing skills came back to her, and for the first time in years, she felt self-pride. An hour later, exhausted and drained, she again rose and made her way back to the lone chair, collapsing on it. She drifted off into an ill sleep. Inez had used up all her psi energies and now desperately needed to eat calories. If not, her own body would start in digesting itself! This, she ignored, too exhausted to move again. Let come what was inevitable. She'd die, knowing she'd saved Peter Franks, the only man who had ever loved her as she was. *Better this way. He won't have a helpless cripple to take care of now.*

A blast of cold air roused her. The leader had returned. What time was it? She had no idea, but it was dark outside. Must be night. The fire was down. He said nothing but walked over to the pot and sniffed it. He rummaged around and filled a plate, found a spoon. He sat them on the crude table, before turning to Inez.

"Well traitorous bitch. I see you've made our dinner. I'll take it to the men now. There's your portion. Eat it if you are hungry or don't. See if I care. Get some sleep. You'll need it for your house chores in the morning. Night toy dolly. Unless you want us to rape you first before you sleep."

"Please, no," she whimpered. Her voice sounded so distant. He merely laughed, picked up the pot, and left. Another blast of chilly air struck her face, but she no longer cared. A lamp-blackened lantern provided dim light at best. For a time, she just continued to sit there. Finally, she decided to at least try to eat something somehow and took fifteen minutes to push her chair over to the table. If she didn't have her lip plates and could have bent her neck, she could have eaten dog style. There was the food she desperately needed, but she had no way to get it into her mouth. She fiddled with her stumps but couldn't pick up the spoon. In desperation, an idea came to her. She carefully got down on her knees. Her lip plates were level with the plate now. Carefully, she used her arms to tip the plate a little. The broth and bits slipped out and onto her plates. While much flowed off either side of the lower plate, some got into her mouth and she greedily began chewing and swallowing. When the plate was empty, she'd eaten about half of it, while the rest was on the floor in front of her knees. She rose carefully, and then pushed her chair back to where it had been and collapsed into it again. Sitting perfectly erect, she drifted into sleep once more, only this time, her body was rapidly devouring the needed calories.

Night turned into day. A cold blast woke her. "Morning toy dolly. Time to get at the housework. Oh my, such a messy floor we have here. Well, first thing I want you to do is to sweep the floor. Clean up that awful mess over there by the table and all this dirt on the floor. I'll come back around noon, and it had better be cleaned up or I'll take out your eyes as your first new modification. The men decided that after your eyes go, we'll take your tongue next. That way you can't back talk us none. Now get your lazy ass up and get this place cleaned up, toy dolly." He re-laid the fire and warmth again began to fill the room. That done, he turned and left again. From the corners of her eyes, she saw a white world. It was day, probably morning, but it had snowed a good deal.

Now left alone again, she rose mechanically. Turning in tiny, slow steps, she looked around the room for a vacuum sweeper, the kind Nita had imported from the Imperium. Finding none, she looked all around a second time. Completing her second circular in-place turn, she spotted a broom. That must be what he'd intended for her to use. She made her way over to it. Holding it between her arms, she tried valiantly to sweep, but it was useless and the broom fell from her grasp. As she bent over at her hips to look at it, she realized she was powerless to lift it back up. She was doomed. Inez made her way back to the chair and sat down. She'd wait for noon to come and be blinded. Maybe she'd die shortly after that.

Sometime later, Pete moaned a little. *Damn! I can't leave him alone with these evil men! They'll kill him as soon as they finish me off. God damn them anyway. I have to stop them somehow!* A moment later, she said aloud, "Duh! Inez, you are a complete fool! Use your gifts like you were taught, you idiot!" When she'd reached puberty, Inez had been trained at Valen Tower. She'd not made any use of it since then. Rather, she spent her days being the teen fashion model for

Elegant Fashions Inc. All her training came back to her in a flash. She steeled herself and waited for noon now, vengeance in her mind.

Pete moaned several more times, but she stayed put. As long as she was seated, she didn't have to worry about falling over. This was her most stable position, other than lying on her back in bed. She waited. Again, a cold blast of air announced his arrival, along with foot stomping. "Snowing pretty good. Ah, hell. So you don't want to do the housework. You are too good to stoop to doing ordinary chores, eh? A fine young woman like you doesn't want to get her hands dirty sweeping the floor. Oh, you don't have any hands. Well, that traitor of a mother of yours doesn't think you need them, did she? That's okay, you can still be our play toy, toy dolly." He walked over to her and stood in front of her. He ran his grubby fingers along the underside of her chin. Well then, you are only good for being a play toy for my men and me. You won't need your eyes to do that, now will you?"

Inez focused and let loose a powerful Mind Blast. Then she did it again and again. The leader shrieked, his hands grasping his head, as if it were about to explode. Slowly, his arms fell away and he slumped to the floor. Blood oozed out of his eyes, nose, and ears. He was dead. "One down, eleven to go," she whispered, more than satisfied. She waited.

After a time, Peter moaned again. He seemed to be coming around. So far, no other men had come into the cabin. Inez decided to gamble and check on how Pete was doing. She rose and pushed her chair back some. Carefully, she made her way to the bed and sat stiffly down on its edge again. Gently, she rubbed his forehead with her stump. "Pete, wake up if you can, please." He moaned and slowly opened his eyes.

Suddenly fear shot through him. "It's okay for now, Pete. We're safe for the moment. Can you sit up?" she asked. He did and looked around and then at the bloody bandage on his shoulder. "You can take their crude bandage off now. I've got you healed. The sword cut your artery and veins, so you would have died from their poor attempts at healing. We're in some cabin somewhere. I killed the leader fellow, over there," she pointed with her other arm.

"I feel really weak. Where are all the other bandits?" he asked softly.

"I don't know. I only saw that one there since yesterday. He kept coming by to give me orders and things to do."

"What happened anyway?" Pete asked, slowly rousing alert. Tearfully, Inez explained all that had happened to her, and what she'd done.

"You fainted and I tried to fight them off, but I lost. That's all I remember too. Let's see if I can stand." He was able to get to his feet. The first thing he did was open the door and look outside. "Hey, there's our horses and wagon, covered in snow though. Looks like our stuff is still there. Where the devil are we? Out in the middle of nowhere. I don't see any of the other bandits around." He closed the door. "I best make us something to eat before I faint as well."

Sometime later and after feeding the both of them, Pete felt much better. His strength began to return. He went outside and brought in some more of their things, including their winter cloaks. He'd also fed the horses, which were very hungry as well. "Looks like we are in some cabin up in the foothills. About six inches of snow cover the ground. We have to get out of here before the other bandits come back. Trouble is, I don't know which way to go. Guess I'll have to use some of my gifts this time." He bundled them both up well for the cold ride. As he was about to carry her outside, he whispered, "I love you! I would be dead if it wasn't for you, my dear."

"I love you to, Pete. I swore if I was going to die, then I was going to make sure you lived somehow." She gently touched her lips to his. He smiled and carried her out to the waiting wagon. After stowing their gear, he climbed up and focused. "Ah, that way." Slowly the wagon began moving through the snow-covered foothills. Inez finally began to relax a little.

After the cabin had long since vanished from sight and no one seemed to be riding after them, Inez asked, "Where are we going?"

"I sense a village in this direction, kind of small. If we can get there, we'll be all right. Well maybe. Is your last name really Valen? That seems to be a nasty word around here."

"Unfortunately, it is, but I didn't have anything to do with all this. Mom did. Well, I guess I had the roll of being the teen fashion model, trying to get all the other teens our age to look like I do now — only with those alien hands. Pete, without them, I'm totally helpless now. I can't do anything at all."

"Ha, that's not true, my pretty woman. You healed my death wound. You saved both of our lives back there. I'd say that was quite a lot. At least to me it was huge, but I know what you mean. Say, I have an idea. Marry me. That way, your last name isn't Valen anymore. Maybe that will keep the dogs off us. What do you say to that?"

"Pete, I love you. Yes, I'll marry you as soon as we can. Are you sure about this? I might be stuck like I am. When we get to Brom, they might refuse to help fix me, and then I'll be like this forever. I won't lie to them. I'm a horrible burden to put on you. I hate myself for doing this to you, but I need you and love you too."

"Prettiest burden I ever had, Miss Inez. If they refuse to fix you up, then we'll just make a home for us someplace else where no one knows you. We'll manage somehow; I know we will. You are the prettiest woman I've ever seen."

"Like this? Lip plates and all?"

He laughed. "Well, even those are sort of pretty too. Maybe someone will have a spare set of those alien hands we can buy for you." He leaned over and gently kissed her lips. "Gosh, your lips are really cold. We have a new problem, I think. Those metal lip plates are as cold as the air. If we are not careful, your lips are going to freeze. I never thought of that. Okay, I'm going to cover your head to keep you warm."

Late that night, they rolled into Bushy Hollow, a village of some three thousand. There was one inn. Inez remained in the wagon covered up, her lips staying warm, while Pete went inside to see about getting a room. He returned with a big grin on his face. Uncovering her, he said, "This will be perfect. Our room is on the main floor and we don't have to walk through the whole bar area; there's a private side entrance. He'll bring our hot supper to us in our room. Plus, my love, they have an old Church of God priest here, who will marry us tonight. He sent a boy off to fetch him. So come on; let's get inside." He lifted her down and carried her to the side door, before setting her down carefully. Then with his arm around her, they walked slowly down the long hall to their room.

They had barely gotten inside when the old priest arrived. Pete realized just how slow she was with her walking, but rightly had allowed her to get to the room on her own feet. "Are you the lad who sent for me? You are the young couple who wish to marry?" he said, mildly surprised.

"Yes. Please, sir. We want to marry now, if you can. I know we don't have any fancy clothes and all, but we really want to marry each other," Pete answered, his voice fully of youthful excitement.

"Miss, is it your wish to marry this young man?" he asked Inez.

"Very much so," she answered very slowly, making sure the priest could understand her.

"Well, this is a bit unusual. I've brought my Holy Book. We can begin then." He was taken aback by her lack of hands, but continued with the short ceremony. "I know pronounce you man and wife, Peter and Inez Franks. You may kiss your lovely bride now, son." He did just that, though the priest watched how he did it. He'd never seen such lip ornaments or such earrings before. Pete gave him two silvers, and he left them.

"There, Mrs. Franks, you are safe. I'll go take care of our wagon and bring us in some clean clothes. The landlord will be bringing hot water for us soon, I hope. The tub is over there. Will you be all right until I get back?"

"Yes, my love. Hurry." She grinned and beamed, though her smile was invisible as always.

A half hour later, Pete undressed her down to her pipe corset, which they wisely decided to leave alone. He'd never seen one before and she knew she'd be in trouble if he couldn't properly get it back on her. "You are the loveliest woman under the sun," he told her as he began washing her off with the warm waters.

"Really? As modified as I am?" she asked.

"Sure my love. Say, can those lip things come out? There's dried food stuff on them I ought to wash off."

Carefully, he followed her instructions and removed them, her lip loops now hanging down free from their tension. He washed them off, but she suggested they leave them out for the night. While she was working on drying herself off using her arms, he bathed himself fully. When a man brought their food tray, quickly he had to wrap a towel around himself.

After they ate their fill, Inez whispered, "Let's go to bed now, my love. Now I can really kiss you properly, but slip into rapport with me as we do it, please." Standing beside him on her toes with his arms around her balancing her, she kissed him. Both felt the huge sensations coming from her warm loops. Later, with Inez lying on her back, her long hair laid over her, the two consummated their marriage. Passions ignited in this young pair that night, a night both would never forget.

In the morning, Pete managed to get the neck rings off her. "My god, Pete, this is so much better. I can move my head now! Thank you, dearest, thank you." He then got her dressed in a fresh gown, and, after a breakfast, they headed out on the road once more. "We're going to stay at inns from now on, if we can. It is way too cold for you to sleep out. Me too, for that matter." Inez loved to hear that news, being able to sleep in the warm bed with Pete was only one of her reasons, but a big one.

Pete wanted to stop at his family's farm and show them his beautiful wife, but Inez pleaded with him to wait. "I don't want them to see me looking like some freak, unless Brom people won't help me." He agreed.

On the first of November, they rolled into Brom. Shortly after that, they entered Brom Castle. "We've come to get my wife fixed up, if you can," Pete explained to the gatehouse guard.

"You'll have to come back this afternoon, son. The folks who do this are here in the afternoons only. If I can take your name, I can let them know to be expecting you, son."

"Inez Franks, sir," Pete replied. "Is there an inn nearby where we can stay?" He received directions and the two headed there. After getting a room, they sat down to wait the two hours.

Inez worried, "What if they won't fix me up, Pete? You

are going to be burdened with caring for me all the time. What if they want to arrest me or something? I'm scared. I can't do anything for myself, but at least I have my head free."

"I married the most beautiful woman in the world. I don't care if you have to be this way forever. I love you and that's all that matters to me. I don't know what we'll do, if they want to arrest you, though," his face fell. Now he began to worry too. "Sorry, I keep forgetting things."

"I didn't know they put a price on mom. Maybe this is a bad idea, Pete. Maybe I should stay like I am forever, as punishment for having convinced so many teens to look like me. I probably can since I am so much better with those awful rings off me. If I only had my hands," she suggested.

"I suppose we could just ask them for some new hands for you," Pete suggested. They decided was what they would do. Both greatly feared she'd be arrested or worse.

Around one, they arrived again only to find there were quite a lot of others there as well. As they waited their turn in line, Pete put his arm around her and made certain she would not fall. Ahead of them, a woman with very long brown hair, wearing an old style, sky blue, pod-silk dress with the old style, black patent heels and some strange colored hands was apparently in charge.

When their turn came, Pete spoke up. "We would like to get a new pair of hands for my wife here. A bandit stole hers and burned them and she is helpless without them."

Her eyebrows rose. "Hello there. My name is Benjamina. I thought we'd gotten everyone fixed up, but it looks like we missed you. Your name, miss?"

"Inez. Inez Franks." They watched as the woman struggled a bit to pick up the pencil and wrote down her name. She asked for her maiden name as well. Inez hesitated. Should she tell this woman the truth? She too had obviously lost her hands, she might hold a grudge too. Inez sighed, for better or for worse, she'd be honest. "Inez Valen," she said softly so no one else could overhear them.

Benjamina looked up at her. "Nita's daughter?" Fighting back tears, Inez nodded. At least she could nod now, if nothing else.

"Let's not mention that name around here, Inez. Too many hold valid grudges. I know you had no real role in all this."

"But I did. I was the teen fashion role model. Many teens emulated the way I looked. I'm guilty."

Benjamina smiled. "Yes as a role model, you influenced many young teens, but that's all you did. Come with me. Let's get you fixed up."

"Can Pete come with me? I can't walk much without him supporting me."

"Sure, it's this way." Benjamina led her into the room, where they still had their two medical machines. "Okay, Inez. We can completely repair your lips. As you can see, mine are as good as new. The pipe corset can safely be removed, but you will need to do plenty of back exercises to strengthen up your lower muscles. As far as your feet go, they cannot be completely repaired. You will have to wear heels as tall as mine. We're having everyone wear the older style heels until something else comes along. Oh yes. I'll get you a new set of hands. Honestly, those hands your mother supplied everyone with were just awful, the cheapest possible ones. We're giving everyone these like mine. They make a huge difference, but still, we can't feel anything, and they are damnably awkward. Best we can do; lost hands are just that, lost. I assume you wanted all these things fixed."

Inez looked at Pete. "Is that all right with you, love?" He nodded.

About an hour later, Inez had her original lips back, and her feet were repaired as much as was possible. She sported a new set of hands, whose skin color nearly matched her own. She now wore similar black patent heels to those of Benjamina. Plus, she could breathe deeply, no longer held in the steel grip of the pipe corset.

"Now then, let's also get rid of the unseen trauma that went with these many body modifications, shall we?" Benjamina suggested. She had to explain further, before Inez agreed. It was suppertime before Inez finally erased most of the surgical trauma. "Now you both return here tomorrow so I can finish you up, okay?" They agreed.

The next day, Benjamina finished her and then decided to experiment a little on Pete, who'd been waiting patiently with Inez the whole time, unwilling to let her out of his sight. "Pete, let's see if we can do something about all this forgetting you seem to have. I want you to say 'I keep forgetting things.' Over and over, please."

Pete did so, "I keep forgetting things." After saying it the tenth time, he complained his head hurt so. He saw a childhood image and Benjamina began to run this one on him. After a few re-experiences of it, the whole trauma came into view. He was three years old when his mother left the top off their root cellar. He'd fallen down into it, hurting his head badly. His frantic mother kept saying, "I keep forgetting things. It's my fault. I just keep forgetting things."

Pete laughed, "That's so funny. If I am me, then I have a splitting headache, but if I am her, then I am always forgetting things. How silly of me. I don't forget things after all. Mom did." Benjamina ended the session.

"I feel so incredibly alive," Inez declared. "Can I do something to help you with this?"

Benjamina explained they were in the process of trying to give this therapy of theirs to everyone who had undergone the awful body modifications. She said, "Well, perhaps you can, Inez. You have an Elegant Fashions Inc store in most all the larger cities and towns. How about making some space in them where others can come and get their therapy done there?" Benjamina suggested. "Also, keep on making elegant new dresses. I love this one here."

"Oh I will, I will. Just as soon as I get back to Exchange City, I'll get all the stores to do just that! But first I have to meet Pete's family."

"Okay. When you are ready to go back, let me know telepathically, and I'll arrange a teleport transfer. You don't want to travel that distance now; it's the start of winter up here. No one dares travel much until March or April comes. Just let me know, and I'll get you both safely to your office there."

"How can we ever thank you enough?"

"Be happy and help others and help us all continue to

look elegant for our significant others," Benjamina replied and she meant it. She wanted to look good for Elana's sake. "One little thing, Inez, Peter. I would not tell your parents her last name. While they might not realize she is Nita's daughter, the name Valen is synonymous with the devil around here. Oh, here, you'll need these too." She handed Pete a pair of the high heeled boots everyone wore when they were outdoors in the deep snow.

On their way back to their room at the inn, Inez giggled, "Pete, she's given me back my whole life! Now you can learn to make fine clothes for men after all."

He grinned, "I was hoping you'd say that, love. Now you look even more ravishing! I've never seen you so happy before."

"I haven't been, silly. Kiss me!"

Vic Broquard

Chapter 19 The Unforgiven

Paco Valen, whose plot almost succeeded, lay decapitated on the floor of his private study. His cousin, the head blind Pedro Valen, stood over him, blood dripping from his sword. "It's done." He turned to the shocked Lady Adora, whose prosthetic hands barely reached her mouth. "I'll give you until tomorrow to get you and your kin out of Valen Castle or you will meet the same fate. Get all your kind out of here now." He turned and marched smartly out of the room. *Easiest damn assassination ever! Pathetic man couldn't even defend himself. Serves him right. Those freaks got ten thousand of our finest young soldiers killed and for what? Nada. Now we'll do it my way!*

He meant the twenty-one others of Lord Paco's group, twenty-two counting his wife, who Paco had body modified to help convince the Midlands and Easterlings lords and ladies there was a life threatening virus running rampant among the telepathic community. Lord Paco had to take some other lords and ladies with him to the emperor's council meetings, along with some advisors and their families. A good show had to be made to be convincing. Hence, he had chosen them well, and they had willingly agreed to the massive body modifications, once he outlined his plan for the total conquest of Tierra and the subsequent union with the aliens and their Imperium. All were farsighted men and women, though their children were not.

Lady Adora finally screamed and screamed. Soon, others arrived, albeit at their incredibly slow, careful pace. When Paco's brother, Roberto finally arrived, Adora had calmed down enough to tell them what had happened and that they had until tomorrow to vacate the castle. "I'll kill him!" seventeen year old Pino Valen swore, Paco and Adora's eldest son.

"We were that close to total success," wailed Roberto, "that close!"

"What do we do? Where do we go, dad?" asked Ana, Roberto's fourteen year old daughter, his eldest.

"I'll kill him myself if you don't get him first," declared

330

Roberto's son, fifteen year old Chico.

Of course, none of these was at all likely to succeed. All were fully modified as were the now dead Paco and his grieving widow Adora.

His advisor Amado de la Parte, forty, argued for calm, "Relax everyone. Rational thought, please. Now is not the time for angry outbursts. We must not abandon Paco's visions, his dreams. We must survive to fight another day. There are things we must make sure leave with us. If we act swiftly, we can get out safely, and with what we will need for the future."

Donato de Portales, his second advisor and forty-three, added, "Boys, assist your fiancés; you normal kids, help your parents. Pack your things. Roberto, Amado, Fons, let's talk in private first." Fons Valen was Paco's forty-five year old cousin and Lord of Arabella, the largest city on their southern seacoast and once the capital of the old kingdom of Almendia. The four modified men made their slow way over to the side of the room where they could not be overheard.

"We need a place where we can all live as an extended family. We must stick together. Think of how we look. Together, we stand a chance of surviving this mess," Donato whispered. "We should get as far away from Valen as we can. We have to avoid snow. None of us can walk in the snow. Ideas?"

"I've got a retirement hacienda down in Villa del Rey we could use. It's large enough for us all and the climate is always balmy," suggested Lord Fons. "Delfina and I had planned to retire there one day, just not like we are and not this soon."

"Okay, Villa del Ray sounds perfect. Let's get some of our staff to get these damnable neck rings off of us pronto. No more need for them. Pipe corsets can go too," Donato added.

"Absolutely, but the women might not want to give up their tiny waists," Fons suggested. The men chuckled; just the thought of getting out of these massive restraints was welcomed.

Advisor Amado spoke up, "So what were you suggesting we take with us?"

"All of the medical machines and the supply of hands and lip plates. Hell, take the neck rings, all the toe shoes, toe boots, and pipe corsets too. We may find others sympathetic to our cause," he said snidely. They broke into pairs, each supporting the other, as they walked out of the private study.

Within a few hours, the twenty-two were finally free of their neck rings. all the men also had their pipe corsets removed. However, as Fons speculated, the women and teens didn't want to have theirs removed. Their staff then began packing their many clothes and personal things, filling dozens of crates, ready for shipping. Meanwhile, the four men had trusted members of their staff pack up the six medical machines and all the other items Lord Valen had stored here, on the chance Paco needed more volunteers to help maintain their cover story of a massive virus outbreak. That done, they sent a messenger to the new Lord Pedro Valen they would all be leaving in the morning as ordered.

"Spread the word, we leave tonight," Amado advised, "in case Pedro has other plans for us." He would not put it past Pedro to have them all executed in the morning, as they gathered to leave the castle! Ten wagons were fully loaded and five carriages awaited the twenty-two, who made their slow way towards the carriages. These included the widow Adora Valen, thirty-seven, and her children: Paco, seventeen, Imelda, sixteen, Lucinda, fifteen, and Rafael, thirteen, but he had not undergone body modifications because of his age. Lord Roberto and his wife Natalia were both thirty-three. Their children were Chico, fifteen, Ana, fourteen, and Fidela, thirteen, who was also not modified. Lord Fons, forty-five, and his wife Delfina, forty-three, brought their children: Hermina, twenty, Andres, eighteen, and Gracia, sixteen. Both Andres and Gracia were also not body modified. Fons wanted heirs who were not as helpless as he was. Advisor Amado, forty, and his wife, Consuela, also forty, brought their children: Benita, eighteen, Estavan, sixteen, and Donica, fourteen. Advisor Donato, forty-three, and his wife, Adelita, forty, brought their children: Raul, twenty, Renato, eighteen, and Anita, fourteen, but she was also unmodified, having only recently come of age. Most of the children were already engaged, a lot of planned marriages between these five families.

Considering how terrible their physical conditions were,

the four men decided for morale's sake, those who were betrothed ought to ride together in the same carriage. Hence, one carriage held Pino and Benita, along with Estevan and Imelda, and Chico and Lucinda. Another carriage held Ruperto and Ana, Renato and Donica, and Raul and Hermina. All twelve children were fully modified, less the neck rings, and the men, less their pipe corsets, all which made their mutilations slightly more tolerable.

Another carriage carried Adora Valen and her young son Rafael, who had hands to help his mother with what she might need. Roberto and Natalia rode with her, and their young daughter Fidela came with them to help both her parents. Another carriage carried Amado and Consuela, along with Donata and Adelita and their youngest daughter Anita, who was to help them with their needs. The final carriage carried Fons and Delfina. Their two youngest were in prime condition and chose to ride their horses, leading the caravan of carriages and wagons. Andres and Gracia were well trained as fighters, and both felt the enormous pressure of being the only ones left who were able to fight. "I hope we don't run into too much trouble, Andres," Gracia whispered. "We have a load of really helpless people to protect. Damn, I can understand why they all did this to themselves, but hell, Andres, now what are they going to do? How will they even live? Dad's hands keep falling off."

"Sis, I surely don't know. Maybe things will improve at the hacienda. God, I hope so for their sake. Have you got one of the six blasters that Roberto stole?" Andres asked. While Pedro had been confiscating such things, Paco had a hidden cache. Roberto had raided it, finding six of them. Gracia said she had. "Come on; we best get this show going," Andres replied, nudging his horse forward. It was full dark when the long line pulled out of Castle Valen. It was late spring, 1245. Once clear of the castle, Gracia dropped back and brought up the rear, constantly looking back over her shoulder making sure no one was following them.

Andres, we can't stop at inns in the villages. They'll be recognized at once.

In know sis. There's a lot of hatred for Paco right now

in the villages as well. Too many of their young men are gone. Way too risky, even with the mentales gifts. Someone could easily slip poison into their stews. Maybe we could go into the villages and bring back pots of stew or something. I suppose we could cook out on the road, but we'd have to get the food and pots.

Just then, their father butted into their conversation. *Kids, you are right. Too much hatred. Don't worry so. I've been planning for something like this happening. Always have contingency plans. Remember that. Since we are not being followed, I want you to veer off the main track and go due west until you hit the Alcantara River. We should make it by morning, if you can keep up a good pace.*

Why? I thought we were heading to Villa del Rey on the coast, Gracia sent.

We are, only not by the way you thought. We'd never make it in these carriages overland. No food and way, way too risky stopping at the inns right now, especially with no armed escorts. I've had this planned for some time now, though I really didn't think old Paco would get assassinated by his brother, well not this soon. At the river, we'll find a number of grain barges waiting for us. If we are in luck, we'll simply have disappeared sometime after dawn.

Dad, you are a genius! Andres replied, greatly relieved.

Contingency plans. I won't forget that one dad, Gracia added.

Shortly before dawn, they spotted a large number of grain barges tied up on the shore. Manned by Fons' men, they were safe at last. The carriages were loaded onto two barges, the wagons split between another three. The passengers were helped onto a sixth. Here, crude beds had been setup along with a large supply of food in the rear galley. While the accommodations were crude, they were safe. A canvas roof kept out all prying eyes. As the sun rose, two cooks served up a hot breakfast.

The hobbled found the going tough, though. Each had to be helped to walk from the bed to the table's bench. The rolling barge made walking on their own almost impossible, especially for the women, who still insisted on wearing their pipe corsets. That they had food and were safe was all that really concerned them right now. At last, Lady Adora let her grief flow freely, comforted by her closest friends.

Early June, the barges pulled up along the shore just north of Villa del Rey. The crew unloaded the wagons, carriages, and horses. At the same time, those who were unmodified, helped the others get to shore. As slow as they were, all the cargo was unloaded and waiting for them to get aboard by the time the last one was finally ashore. The convoy rode into the laid-back port town in the early morning hours, before the streets became fully alive, also helping to hide their arrival from prying eyes.

The hacienda was quite large and sat on a hill overlooking the ocean below to the south and part of the town to the west. Along the northern outer wall of the rectangular complex sat a row of domestic suites, each with two small bedrooms, a living room, bath, a dining room, and a kitchen with attached pantry. The north wall had ten of these suites, with another two along the east and west walls. The other half of the east and west walls had six much smaller servants quarters and a laundry room. The long southern wall housed gaming rooms, studies, and two huge living rooms that could also serve as dance halls and Great Halls for important, large scale meetings. Behind the north wall lay a long stable and hay and grain loft. All the wagons and carriages were easily housed here.

The roofs were all the typical Westerlings red overlaying tiles. More importantly, the entire central area was a beautiful formal gardens with a pond at either end. Awnings covered the first eight feet out from the suits, providing protection from the rains and allowing one to walk all around the complex without getting wet. There were numerous entrances with ornate iron gates that could be locked and barricaded if need be.

More importantly for these crippled folks, Fons had hired a man servant for each male and a woman servant for each female in the whole party, including the five who were not modified. These were in addition to the maids, gardeners, cooks, and various other support staff. Eugenio and Esmerelda del Mira were the chief stewards of the staff, who numbered some fifty.

This had partly appeased their children's bitter complaints while they were on the barges. "Dad, how can we even live like this? We can't walk without help and our prosthetic hands are almost useless," Hermina complained to Fons.

"You will all be glad to know once we reach the hacienda, each of you will have your own personal servant to attend to your needs at all times," Fons replied, with an invisible smile. That had alleviated some of their concerns.

"But dad, we look like freaks. Even if we try to go into the town, everyone will think we are ghastly freaks," Hermina complained bitterly.

"I think you are beautiful," her fiancé Raul interjected.

"First thing we do once we get there and all get a bath is to get those of you, who are ready, married," Fons told the children wanted they most wanted to hear, making a dozen of their children very happy.

"But dad," Hermina continued, "we will still be freaks!"

"Ah, so I suggest we then begin to make our lip plates, your delightful earrings, and our toe shoes and boots the latest fashion statement. That's why we've brought along the machines and supplies. In time, I am sure we can get some of the locals there to want to look like we do. Give it time and you'll be the height of fashion again, dear Hermina. However, there is nothing we can do about these pathetic alien hands of ours. Chins up; we will make do somehow and get by. All of you, we must plan for the future. Already Pedro has made his first terrible blunder. He didn't follow us or kill us. Now, he doesn't know where we are at and likely doesn't care. We rebuild, gain new allies and support. One day, we will return to Castle Valen in triumph!"

He went on, "Paco, may his soul rest in peace, made one terribly blunder. He underestimated the Midlands and their *mentales* skills. While we may never know how they murdered three entire armies, we will not again underestimate them. His grand plan very nearly worked. Do you realize thanks in part to all *your* sacrifices, we disabled nearly all the Midlands' *mentales* gifted in their castles and towers? That alone is a remarkable feat, not soon forgotten. In future days, your sacrifices for the good of all Valen will be remembered and praises sung about your valor. You, all you, are Valen's true heroes. Never forget that."

"Once we get settled in, we are going to take our next step in rebuilding. We have twenty-six highly gifted *mentales* here. We are going to form our own *Círculo de la Torres*! It will be called the Renegade Tower! We will act in secrecy, spying and learning all we can." That brought cheers to the group. He'd given the hopeless cripples a new goal, one they could achieve and likely excel in accomplishing.

The children had much to discuss to pass the many days of traveling with nothing to do but sit. Money was no object for these five families. For years, they had been skimming funds off the top of the yearly tithes sent to Lord Valen, with his consent, of course. All five had very large sums at their disposal. This had allowed Fons Valen to purchase this huge hacienda two years ago.

Until recently, a small caretaker staff had kept it maintained for just such a situation. He'd hired Eugenio and Esmerelda del Mira to watch over it and hired a minimalist staff to keep it ready for his family's occasional visits, which had not yet happened. He'd given them carte blanche to hire whomever they desired, as long as the place was well maintained and ready for occupancy on short notice. When they were all safely on the barges, Fons had telepathically contacted the two and outlined the new requirements. They had complied and done additional hiring, retaining their original maintenance staff.

The stewards had purchased uniforms for their employees. The personal servants wore suits and gowns, as fashionable men and women of the nobility wore, all purchased from their local Elegant Fashions Inc outlet in Villa del Rey. This way, their personal servants would be intimately familiar with the needs of those they would be dressing and assisting. The maids all wore simple black day dresses; the gardeners wore brown pants and shirts, and so on. Knowing the precise moment of their arrival via telepathic contact from

Fons, the two had their staff lined up in the courtyard gardens. In one line, the suited men and gowned women stood await to be assigned their charges. The stewards had chosen them based on the age of their proposed charges, older men and women for the adults and younger teens for the children.

Indeed Eugenio and Esmerelda del Mira knew their craft very well. None would be disappointed in their choices of personal assistants, as they were to become called. The two had fully explained the handicaps their charges faced so they knew what was expected of them. No surprises were anticipated, though their lip plates did shock more than one.

The carriages stopped inside the huge stables and the able assisted the many down. While all were long in need of a good bath and clean clothes, the moment they walked into the huge formal gardens with their ponds and many shrubs and flowers, the mood changed to one of excitement. "This place is really great, dad!" Hermina exclaimed, as she took her tiny, careful steps into the gardens for the first time. She and Raul had an arm around each other, supporting themselves. "Beautiful, dad, just beautiful."

Slowly the large group made their way over to the southern side of the gardens where the lines of servants waited for them. "Ah, Señor Valen," Eugenio exclaimed, as Fons and Delfina appeared, leading the way for the others. "Welcome to Hacienda Valen. All is in readiness. Your staff awaits you. These are the personal assistants as you requested."

The assistants gaped at the body modified men, women, and teens. None had seen such wild ornaments, such magnificent earrings, or such strange toe boots, let alone the alien grey prosthetic hands. For the next half hour, some confusion reined, as the personal assistants were assigned to each member. When the children got their assigned assistants, they also were given their suite assignments. Fons took the liberty of allowing the soon to be married couples to have their own suites, pleasing them immensely. One by one, the six young couples were led by their new assistants to their new suites.

With the children handled, Eugenio then took Fons and the other adults on down to where the other staff stood waiting patiently in their new uniforms to greet their new masters. One by one, Eugenio introduced the men, while Esmerelda introduced the women to the five sets of adults, along with Andres and Gracia. (Rafael continued to escort his mother, Adora.) At the very end of the line, they all stopped and stared in complete disbelief at the older woman and her two teen-aged daughters, nicely dressed in the black maid's uniforms.

"My god! Esmeralda?" Fons protested what he saw standing there, presumably as hired maids! The older woman definitely had no arms at all, no trace; her blouse had no sleeves. The two teen aged daughters also had no arms and were standing on a single leg!

All of the men and women of the Westerlings had black hair and black eyes. The men wore theirs cut short, while the women seldom, if ever, cut theirs. Westerlings hair was always thick and lush, and, with the women, quite long. These three were no exception, their hair fell to the backs of their calves, thick, lush, and perfectly straight.

Esmeralda introduced them. "Señor Fons, this is Dorita dela Handro." The woman was rather pudgy and short. She was thirty-eight with an oval face and thick lips with bushy eyebrows, echoed in her daughters. What also surprised him was the simple fact that all three had yellow eyes with brown speckles. *Mentales* gifted. "Her husband is a fisherman, and she and her daughters here are most desperate for income. In spite of their appearance, señor, I assure you they are hard workers and are up to their assigned maid duties. This is Alicia and Juana."

Alicia was eighteen and her large bust was fully developed now. She stood on her single, centrally positioned leg, and was almost as tall as Fons had been before his feet had been modified. Alicia was thin and stood almost six feet. Her face had high cheekbones and an oval shaped nose. Fons thought if she were whole, she would be quite a beauty. Juana stood on her single centrally positioned leg, two inches shorter than her sister. Her face was round more like her father's. Both teens had the thick lips of their mother, which were shaped into a perpetual smile, even if they were not intending to smile. All three's eyes were bright and alert.

"But how, Esmerelda," Fons attempted to ask how these three could possibly perform any duties whatsoever. Instead, he changed thoughts mid-sentence. These were obviously gifted. "For give my ignorance, Amas, I assume you've all been tower trained?"

"What's that?" asked Alicia. Of the three, she was the most forward. "We don't know what you mean by that, señor. We know there is some tower thing way north in Valen by the Goza Mountains. How come all you have such strange colored hands and walk on your toes and have those strange lip things? We've never seen such things here in Villa del Rey."

Fons looked at the three more closely and saw that none had their special germanium crystals, given to all young *mentales* gifted when they reached puberty. Evidently, these three were not remotely trained. Alicia read his mind and spoke up again. "We hop well."

"Well, I don't see how you could get around otherwise. So you've never been trained. Interesting. Oh, these lip plates are or were the latest in fashion in the courts of Valen and primarily in the Emperor's court and the Midlands. The toe shoes and boots too. A bad virus struck most all the *mentales* gifted of the Midlands and we here too. To save our lives, our infected hands were removed. Fortunately, the aliens provided us with some of their mechanical prosthetic hands so we are not wholly helpless, just mostly."

"I see. How strange. Well, we are not helpless, señor. We have been doing all the maid work around here for the last two years. Just ask Esmerelda. Please señor, we really need this job. Papa doesn't make enough to keep our home going. He's a fisherman and is gone at sea for long times," Alicia added, pleading for their jobs.

"We should discuss this. Esmerelda, arrange for a tea in my new office," Fons decided. "Delfina, why don't you and the other ladies go to our new suites and get cleaned up. We men will be along later. Eugenio, see that all our personal crates are brought in and sorted out. The ones marked special all go into one lockable room for now. Gentlemen, I believe the new office is down this way somewhere."

"Allow us to show you, Señor Fons," Alicia insisted. The

women were led off by their new personal assistants, who were eager to get started on the right foot, so to speak. Roberto, Amado, and Donato followed slowly after Fons, who followed behind the three. Alicia and Juana began hopping along on their foot, their long black hair bobbing up and down, as did their enormous breasts. Dorita walked normally. Andres and Gracia, quite curious about these three women, followed behind. Esmeralda dashed off to fetch the tea.

"Oh, you are so slow!" Alicia commented, as she stopped hopping forward and did a hopping turn to look back at the men, moving at a snail's pace.

"Yes, Alicia, we are that. I must say you hop swiftly. Perhaps, Andres and Gracia would go on ahead with you three and get the room ready for us," he suggested. *What the devil is going on with these three,* he sent to all five. Andres and Gracia moved ahead of the four men in their toe boots.

"Lead on, Alicia," Andres said. "How fast do you go anyway?"

Alicia giggled. "Quite fast, but we can't run, if that's what you are thinking." She and her sister began hopping along at a much quicker pace. The two teens had to walk very briskly to keep up with them.

"Oh stop showing off you two," Dorita said in an exasperated, but motherly, manner. The two teens giggled and slowed down some.

When they got to the door, Andres guessed he'd have to open it for them. He was surprised, the knob turned on its own, and the door opened. Alicia and Juana hopped on inside. *Telekinesis?* he sent to the others.

Inside, Alicia and Juana didn't know where they should sit and so waited against the wall, along with Dorita. "Wow, that's impressive, Alicia," Andres commented, genuinely surprised.

Alicia giggled. "I know. You and Gracia thought we couldn't do anything at all. Everyone does — think that at first. We are freaks; we know that, but we work very hard and do our work very well. Esmeralda says that is true." She again pleaded for their jobs.

"I am beginning to see how you do that. So where do

you live at, nearby?" Andres asked, becoming fascinated with this strange young woman his own age.

"We live way down close to the docks. Dad has a fisherman's home there. We used to go swimming every day on the white sandy beach, until two years ago when Esmeralda offered us the maid's work here. We need the money, but we still find time to swim. Do you like to swim, Señor Andres?"

"Er, I don't know how, sorry. I've lived in the foothills all my life. Is it hard to do?" he answered. Gracia started chatting with Juana, while waiting on the slow moving men. Esmeralda soon entered carrying a tray. She placed the nine teacups nicely around the table and poured the tea. "You three and I ought to sit on this side, leave our employers to sit on those there," Esmeralda suggested.

"Do you need assistance with your chair, Alicia?" Andres asked.

"Huh? Is it broken?" she asked a little confused. "Oh, I see what you mean. We manage just fine." Andres realized she'd just looked into his mind and seen what he'd meant, sliding her chair out for her and then adjusting it as she sat down. This rather startled him. Alicia and Juana's chairs seemed to move out for them on their own. The two hopped in front of them and then carefully sat down, with the chairs sliding up on their own. The four men saw this as they finally arrived and moved into the room.

Andres asked, "Alicia, will you need one of us to help you with your tea?" Gracia hastily asked Juana the same thing, figuring Esmeralda could help Dorita with hers.

"Why? Is there something wrong with my tea?" Alicia asked again a little confused. She probed Andres' mind again and laughed. "No, we don't need arms to drink our tea." But she added, "Thank you for offering. Everyone thinks because we are freaks we can't do anything, but we can or Esmeralda would not have hired us." The men had finally seated themselves and awkwardly got a hold of their cups and then struggled with their spoons to take a sip. Andres watched from the corner of his eyes to see how Alicia could possibly manage this feat. Her cup rose up to her lips and she sipped like everyone else. So did Juana and Dorita.

"Esmeralda, an explanation is in order here, please," Fons finally said.

"I've known Dorita here since childhood. She and I used to play together. I was her bridesmaid when she married Geraldo dela Handro, a fisherman. She had her arms back then. I think it's best if she tells you about it all," Esmeralda suggested. "Go ahead, Dorita, you can trust these men."

"Well, if you say it is okay, then I will. all it, Esmeralda?" Dorita asked hesitantly. Esmeralda nodded sternly.

"Geraldo is a deep sea fisherman. He goes out in his big boat long distances and catches larger fish. We were married a year, when one day he returned with the most unusual fish, the diablo rojo, he called it. I cooked it and never have we tasted such a delicious, mouth-watering fish. It started after that. I felt funny. My arms began going numb. We thought maybe the fish was poisonous, but Geraldo, he felt just fine. My arms began to wither and soon I couldn't use them at all. We visited all the doctors, but they had no cures that worked. One day I arose and found them lying on my bed. They'd fallen off, much like a snake sheds its skin or the lizard loses its tail!"

"I was terrified, but my mind started doing strange things. Geraldo said my eyes turned yellow. It's true, they are no longer black like they used to be. I heard thoughts, everyone's thoughts. Until I figured out how to block them, I thought I was going mad. Then, things just started moving of their own accord. I mean, I needed my shoes, and they slid across the floor to my feet. Soon, I realized I was thinking what I wanted done and it happened. Geraldo said I should practice making things happen and so I did. Now I move everything I want to just by thinking it so, like my tea cup here."

"Then, I got pregnant with Alicia. We were so happy finally to have our children, but when Alicia was born, we were both terrified. She had no arms like me and only the one leg! After much crying, Geraldo noticed Alicia also had yellow eyes and told me to be hopeful. We tried again and a year later Juana was born. She too was just like Alicia, but she had one leg too. When they grew older, they began moving things like I did. In time, we saw they were able to move far heavier things than I could. Alicia once even moved Geraldo's boat onto the shore so he could clean its hull! I also discovered I can make others think what I want them to think and I always know what they are thinking too. So can the girls, only more so with them."

"Geraldo keeps on bringing back more of that diablo rojo fish and we keep on eating it. I think maybe we are getting stronger by doing so. The girls, they love to swim and hop to the beach all the time. Then, one day, I see them at one place and in the next instant they are somewhere else. I don't know how to explain this. Our home is a long way from here, down the hill by the beach and docks. It is way too hard for them to hop uphill and takes way too long. I get pooped from the long walk here too. They hop once outside our door and then they are here at the door."

Alicia broke in, "Mom, we call it jumping to differentiate it from the hopping that we do. We can jump most anywhere. It is very fast and easy for us. I don't think Juana and I could hop all the way here from our house, so we jump. Once, we jumped out of the town to pick some wild flowers, but mama told us never to do that again — that it was too far for us to go, so we didn't do that again."

"Simply incredible!" Fons exclaimed, now fully realizing what was going on here.

"Señor Fons, can we ask you something that has bothered us since we first met all you today?" Alicia asked.

"Why sure you may, Alicia," he replied, wondering what silly thing was troubling them. They seemed so innocent and ignorant of just what impressive *mentales* gifts they actually had.

"Why do all you, except the little children and Andres and Gracia, have those nasty black clouds over your heads? Are they important? They seem to us to contain lots of pain."

"What black masses?" Fons asked.

"Oh that one," Alicia touched one with her mind. At once, Fons began to re-experience having his hands removed by the medical machine! Fortunately, for everyone, Roberto saw instantly what was happening!

"Keep on doing what you are doing, Alicia, until that

thing is gone from Fons, please!" he ordered.

A while later, Fons exclaimed, "That was incredible! I thought there was no pain in having our hands removed. The pain was almost too much to bear but it's gone now. Alicia, thank you. Can you get rid of the others that I have?"

"Oh sure." An hour later, Fons was free from the trauma of the many surgeries he'd endured, and he felt vastly more powerful and happier, though he was just as physically restrained as always with his lips, feet, and prosthetic hands.

"Esmeralda, how much are you paying them? I want their salaries quintupled! Alicia, Juana, Dorita, I will pay you whatever you like to move in here with us. You will have your very own master suite, the same size as mine!" Fons exclaimed.

"But what about poor Geraldo when he returns and does not find us at home?" Dorita complained.

"We will leave someone there waiting for him and bring him here. He can stay here too, when he is not out fishing. I want to hire him to get us more of those diablo rojo fishes!" They could not believe their incredible good fortune. All four men watched as Alicia and Juana jumped home to start packing their things. One second they were about to take another hop, but mid-hop, they simply vanished.

Fons had Esmeralda send along a wagon and some men to help bring the three women's things back with them. Finally alone, Fons said, "My god, do you realize what we have here? Our own katalyein and powerful teleporters to say nothing of their telekinesis skills! They are untrained and doing all this without the power boost of the germanium crystals! Think how powerful they will be with a little training and their own crystals! Our luck has just changed enormously for the better!"

He added, "Andres, we need to see what Alicia's and Juana's children might possess. Unless you are totally opposed, I want you to start courting Alicia. It could well be your children with her may become the most powerful *mentales* gifted on the planet!"

"Dad, she's only got one leg," he protested a little. "Well, at least she's otherwise attractive. I'll see," he finally consented.

"Thank you son. A Renegade Tower with our own katalyein and teleport specialists — this is way too good to be true," Fons replied.

"Maybe our exile isn't an exile at all," Roberto added with a wry smile.

Far out in the ocean south of Villa del Rey, the God called Calder had awakened, though none yet knew this fact, save Lysandra. She began to wonder what Calder was planning to do now he was fully awake. *I'd rather have his interference than Wystan's any century.*

The End.

Other Books by Vic Broquard

Without Warning (fantasy)

The Trident Series: (fantasy)
> Volume 1 The Trident and the Book
> Volume 3 The Trident and the Scepter
> Volume3 The Trident and the Resurrection

The Adventures of Elizabeth Stanton Series: (science fiction)
> Volume 1 The Evolution of the Path
> Volume 2 The Great Messiah
> Volume 3 Of Kings and Queens and Troubadours
> Volume 4 Chaos in the Aftermath
> Volume 5 Power Plays
> Volume 6 Age of Exploration
> Volume 7 Abducted
> Volume 8 The Emperor and Empress
> Volume 9 A Job Worth Doing
> Volume 10 Degradation
> Volume 11 The Second Crusade
> Volume 12 When Worlds Collide
> Volume 13 Dark Ages

The Lindsey Barron Series: (fantasy)
> Volume 1 The Rod of the Apocalypse
> Volume 2 The Board of Governors
> Volume 3 The Crown of Moses
> Volume 4 Dominus for President
> Volume 5 The National Health Care Program
> Volume 6 States Justice
> Volume 7 Cross and Double-cross

Zoran Chronicles Series: (fantasy)
> Volume 1 A Dragon in Our Town
> Volume 2 Dragons, Power, Courts, and War

Planet of the Orange-red Sun Series: (science fiction)
    Volume 1 When Kingdoms Fall
    Volume 2 Dark Ages
    Volume 3 Age of the Towers
    Volume 4 Difficillis Exitus
    Volume 5 Age of the Lords
    Volume 6 The Renegade Tower
    Volume 7 Rebellions
    Volume 8 The Aliens Return
    Volume 9 Power Struggles
    Volume 10 Guilds, Genetics, and Gods
    Volume 11 Magi, Witches, Swords, and Superstitions
    Volume 12 The Voyage of the Eagle's Seed
    Volume 13 Justifications
    Volume 14 Responsibilities

The Return of the Wizards: Twelve Companions – The Making of Wizards (fantasy)

www.ingramcontent.com/pod-product-compliance
Lightning Source LLC
Chambersburg PA
CBHW072118250626
47159CB00007B/2489

* 9 7 8 1 9 4 1 4 1 5 2 2 1 *